Praise for Laura Scott and her novels

"The fast-paced action and Scott's well-utilized secondary characters will keep readers actively engaged."

—*RT Book Reviews* on *Twin Peril*

"Readers will enjoy…these characters and following their fascinating story."

—*RT Book Reviews* on *Undercover Cowboy*

"The dialogue is well-written and the characters are solidly crafted in Scott's Christmas tale."

—*RT Book Reviews* on *Her Mistletoe Protector*

"A good mystery with intelligent characters and a nice building of suspense."

—*RT Book Reviews* on *Lawman-in-Charge*

LAURA SCOTT

Twin Peril

&

Undercover Cowboy

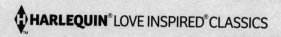

HARLEQUIN® LOVE INSPIRED® CLASSICS

LOVE INSPIRED BOOKS

Recycling programs for this product may not exist in your area.

ISBN-13: 978-0-373-20875-3

Twin Peril & Undercover Cowboy

This edition published by arrangement with Love Inspired Books.

www.Harlequin.com

Printed in U.S.A.

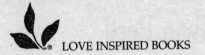

CONTENTS

Laura Scott is a nurse by day and an author by night. She has always loved romance and read faith-based books by Grace Livingston Hill in her teenage years. She's thrilled to have published over twelve books for Love Inspired Suspense. She has two adult children and lives in Milwaukee, Wisconsin, with her husband of thirty years. Please visit Laura at laurascottbooks.com, as she loves to hear from her readers.

Books by Laura Scott

Love Inspired Suspense

Callahan Confidential

Shielding His Christmas Witness
The Only Witness
Christmas Amnesia
Shattered Lullaby

Classified K-9 Unit

Sheriff

SWAT: Top Cops

Wrongly Accused
Down to the Wire
Under the Lawman's Protection
Forgotten Memories
Holiday on the Run
Mirror Image

Visit the Author Profile page
at Harlequin.com for more titles.

TWIN PERIL

All the prophets testify about Him, that everyone who believes in Him receives forgiveness of sins through His name.

—*Acts* 10:43

This book is dedicated to Pam Hopkins,
with deep appreciation for your ongoing support.

ONE

Mallory Roth awoke with a start, her heart thundering against her ribs in terror.

Had she imagined the noise?

The interior of her uncle Henry's cabin was shrouded with darkness. It was nestled in the woods in central Wisconsin with the back porch overlooking the town of Crystal Lake. The trees blocked any light from the moon, and in the darkness, she strained to listen.

Just when she figured she had let her imagination run wild, she heard it again—a low creak of the wooden floorboards from the main living area.

Her pulse surged into triple digits. There was no time to waste. Anthony Caruso had found her.

She sucked in a quick breath and swung her legs over the edge of the bed, rolling into an upright position. She knew only too well that whoever was out there intended to silence her forever. As quietly as possible, she dragged a sweatshirt over her head and jammed her feet into running shoes. She picked up the thick stick from where she'd left it propped in the corner next to her bed, tightly grasping the only weapon she possessed.

Another muffled sound came from the other room.

Closer. She imagined the intruder stealthily making his way toward the bedroom.

For half a second, she considered waiting for him behind the door so she could hit the back of his head. But then her self-defense training kicked in. Running away from an attack, if at all possible, was better than staying to fight. Weapons were all too often used against the victim.

She'd been lucky to escape the last man Caruso had sent after her with nothing more serious than a cut on her arm.

Looping her purse over her head so that it lay across her chest, leaving her arms free, she crossed the room and slid the window frame upward. She winced when the window gave a small groan. She'd already removed the screen in case she needed to use this window as her escape route. She quickly threw her leg over the threshold, stick in hand as she ducked through the opening.

The door to her bedroom burst open, and she turned in time to catch a glimpse of a tall man in black with a matching ski mask covering his face. She ran.

Dressed in dark clothing, she blended into the trees as she pulled up the hood of her sweatshirt to cover her blond hair. She ducked under low-hanging branches, making her way through the woods toward the highway. Trees and thick brush lined the highway on both sides, and her closest neighbor was located just a half mile south of the cabin.

She had to stay hidden long enough to get to the Andersons.

She could hear Caruso's thug swiping at branches and hitting trees as he followed behind her. Stark fear coated her throat.

The brush in the woods became less dense, and she could just barely make out the road. The guy behind her was closing in, and she pushed herself to go faster. But the moment she broke free of the woods, strong arms reached out to grab her. The shock of finding someone there waiting for her caused her to drop her weapon.

She'd run straight into a trap!

She tried to scream but the man clamped his hand over her mouth. "Don't," he whispered. "I'm a cop. If you want to stay alive, Mallory, come with me."

A cop? Or a partner to the guy in the black ski mask? Or both? She didn't know who to trust. The sound of the ski-masked thug crashing through the woods behind her helped make up her mind. She barely had time to pick up the stick from the ground before the cop dragged her down the road toward the car he'd parked along the side of the highway. She also noticed a large black truck parked across the street.

Pop! Pop!

"Keep your head down!" the cop yelled, yanking open the passenger-side door and shoving her inside. More popping sounds peppered the air as he ducked and ran around to the driver's side.

She barely had time to strap on her seat belt before her rescuer cranked the engine and floored the gas. He peeled away, her heart lodging in her throat as they careened down the highway.

Gripping the handrail with white-knuckled fingers, Mallory tried to find her voice as the cop drove through the night like a madman, taking the sharp curves in the highway at breakneck speed. She glanced over her shoulder to see the headlights dropping farther behind.

The cop changed directions as often as possible in order to lose the truck.

She should have been reassured by his ability to evade the man behind them but she wasn't. Her teeth chattered and her body began to shake. She recognized the aftereffects of shock from the last time she'd narrowly escaped Caruso's thug.

She closed her mind against the memory of the bloody room in her twin sister's town house as she struggled to breathe.

The guy in the ski mask wasn't the same guy as before. He was tall and broad-shouldered compared to the shorter, stockier guy she'd taken down in Alyssa's town house just a few days ago. When her rescuer slowed his breakneck speed, she glanced back, relieved to see there were no longer any headlights following them.

"Who are you?" she finally asked. "How did you find me?"

He didn't take his eyes off the road as he tossed a small leather case in her lap. She opened it and was slightly reassured when she saw the shiny metal glint of his badge. At least it looked real enough.

"My name is Jonah Stewart and I'm a detective with the Milwaukee Police Department." There was a long pause, before he added, "Your sister, Alyssa, sent me to find you."

Jonah didn't slow down until he was a good fifteen miles outside of town. And even then, he maintained a decent clip, pushing the posted speed limit, carefully watching the rearview mirror to make sure the guy in the black truck hadn't found them. When he was reasonably sure they were safe, he unclenched his fingers from their death grip on the steering wheel.

That had been way too close. If he'd arrived a minute later, he might have lost Mallory for good. When he'd gotten to the cabin just after midnight, he'd noticed the black truck and grown suspicious. Just as he started making his way down the driveway toward the cabin, he'd heard someone running through the woods. It only took a minute to rule out a four-legged animal—he'd heard the distinct sound of two people. He'd braced for the worst and been immensely relieved when Mallory had raced out of the woods first, apparently unharmed, just in the nick of time.

"Did you get a good look at him?" he asked in a gruff tone.

"No." She slowly shook her head. "His face was covered by a ski mask. But why were you waiting on the road for me after midnight? You claim Alyssa sent you, but I know her and she would have come to meet me herself."

"Alyssa did send me. How else do you think I knew about the cabin? She also told me your uncle Henry is really your mother's cousin, and he hadn't been up here in a long time because he recently had a stroke." He hoped the additional information would reassure her that he was on the right side of the law.

"Yes," she admitted. "That's true."

"I found the place a few minutes before you came out of the woods." He sent a silent prayer of thanks, knowing God had been watching out for the both of them. "Alyssa didn't come herself because we didn't even know for sure you were here."

Mallory's scowl deepened. "What do you mean she

didn't know? I left a message on her cell phone. I told her to come to the place she least expected to find me. As kids, we had to stay at the cabin for two weeks in the summer while our parents took an Alaskan cruise. Alyssa loved it, but I hated every minute. Do you realize I spent the last few days in a place with no indoor plumbing?"

For the first time in a long while, he was tempted to smile. He could well imagine how a cabin on a lake with an outhouse was not Mallory's idea of fun.

"Alyssa lost her cell phone and must not have picked up her messages. And the other reason she didn't come is she tore the ligaments and tendons in her ankle pretty bad. I convinced her that she'd only slow us down and she agreed I could protect you better by myself. She's scheduled for surgery later this week."

That news made Mallory sit up in her seat. "Surgery? What happened to her?"

"It's a long story." He continued to drive, deciding he wasn't stopping anywhere for a long time—maybe not even until daylight. "Several days ago Alyssa fell and hit her head. When she woke up, she had amnesia. Alyssa's boyfriend, Gage, thought she was you. They asked for my help because someone was trying to kill them. Don't worry, they're safe now. And once Alyssa's memory started to return, we realized you were missing and in possible danger. That's when we began searching for you." He glanced at her expectantly.

"Are you sure they're all right?"

"I promise they're fine," Jonah assured her.

"Then what happened to her ankle?" Mallory asked.

Was she really worried about her sister? Or was she simply asking more questions to put off telling him the truth? He wanted to believe the former, but his instincts warned him not to trust her too easily. He'd been burned by an apparent victim before.

"According to Gage, they had to climb out of a warehouse window and drop down to the ground, about ten feet. She landed hard on her ankle. Frankly, we were both surprised she hadn't broken it." He turned his attention back to the road, slowing down since they were approaching a small town.

"Are we stopping here?" Mallory asked.

"No."

"Why not?" she demanded. "How do I know I can really trust you? Let me out. I want to talk to Alyssa."

He stifled a heavy sigh. "Be reasonable. It's one o'clock in the morning."

"Reasonable?" Her voice rose a few decibels and he tried not to wince. "A man in a ski mask broke into my uncle's cabin to kill me. And suddenly you're conveniently waiting for me when I run out of the woods? Don't you dare accuse me of being unreasonable."

He held up his hand in surrender. Good thing the rental car didn't need gas—he didn't doubt that Mallory would bolt the first chance she was given. He'd already saved her from the guy in the ski mask, so why was she so uptight?

"If you want to call your sister, go ahead. But the only number I have is Gage's cell." He tossed his phone into her lap.

She picked it up and grimaced. "Gage doesn't exactly like me," she said as she scrolled through the contact list. "How do you know him?"

"Gage and I went to high school together. Both he and Alyssa have been worried sick about you," Jonah added. He had been worried, too, mostly because he believed Mallory was the key to solving the case. Just a little over a week ago he and Gage had uncovered a money-laundering scheme that involved a man named Hugh Jefferson. Jonah had also been betrayed by a cop who'd tried to kill him. Soon he'd discovered that Jefferson had been searching for Mallory, who'd disappeared.

Now that he'd found Mallory, he wanted to know exactly why she'd been hiding at the cabin. And why Jefferson had wanted to find her. All along they'd suspected there was a man higher up the chain of command, the one truly in charge of the money-laundering scheme. He was convinced Mallory knew the identity of that man, or at least someone working for him. Why else would Jefferson want to know where she was?

Mallory held the phone up to her ear. After several rings, the call went into voice mail. There was the faintest tremble in her voice as she spoke. "Gage? It's Mallory. Will you please have Alyssa call this number as soon as you can? Thanks."

She ended the call but kept a tight hold on the phone, as if waiting for her sister's return call. In the darkness, he was able to see the glitter of tears in her eyes. His gut clenched and he tightened his grip on the steering wheel. The last thing he needed was for her to break down.

"Look, I'm sorry. I understand you've been traumatized by everything that's happened. But, Mallory, I am a cop. And I promise I'll keep you safe."

A tense silence stretched between them. She sniffled loudly and swiped at her eyes. When her chin came up again, he almost smiled, impressed by her ability to pull herself together. Mallory was obviously a lot tougher than she looked. "You better. It's only fair to warn you, I have a black belt in Tae Kwon Do, and besides, I can call 9-1-1."

When she actually punched in the buttons, prepared to make the call, he reached over to take his phone back. She didn't let go. In the brief tussle, she brushed her arm against the side of his chest.

"What is this? Are you bleeding?" She stared in horror at the stain on her arm.

He glanced down in surprise, feeling the dampness against his shirt. It wasn't easy to see in the darkness, but he could feel blood oozing through the dressing along the right side of his chest.

"Yuck. I faint at the sight of blood." She rummaged through her purse, pulled out a small packet of wipes and cleaned the stain from her arm before glancing over to frown at him. "Are you sure you're okay? Were you hit by a bullet back there?" The concern in her eyes was nice even though he didn't deserve it. He wasn't here just to save her life—he was here to close his case.

"No, I'm fine." He realized the fresh surgical incision located along his rib cage was throbbing painfully. There was ibuprofen in his duffel bag, which was all he was willing to take. "It's just an old injury that must have opened up a bit."

"We'll have to stop at a drugstore and get some bandages," she murmured. "Too bad I'm not Alyssa—you could probably use a nurse." She made a face as she placed a hand over her stomach. "I really am not much help when it comes to blood."

He gave a brief nod, even though he had no intention of stopping at a drugstore anytime soon. Right now, his reopened wound was the least of his worries.

First he needed to find a safe haven, somewhere they could stay for the next twenty-four hours. And then he needed to figure out a way to make Mallory trust him enough to tell him the identity of the man who was in charge of the money-laundering operation that had almost gotten them all killed.

Mallory sensed there was far more to the story regarding how Alyssa was injured than Jonah Stewart was telling her. But as much as she wanted to keep after him, she couldn't fight the wave of exhaustion washing over her, the adrenaline crash hitting hard. She wished she could talk to Alyssa.

She supposed it was logical that Gage wouldn't answer the phone in the middle of the night. And if Alyssa really had lost her cell phone, then there was nothing more she could do except wait until morning. She wondered how Gage and Alyssa were getting along. Jonah had made it sound as if they were a couple saying they were both worried about her. But Mallory knew better than to think Gage was worried—she could only hope he wouldn't let his personal feelings toward her get in the way of responding to her voice-mail message.

Back when Gage and Alyssa had started dating, she hadn't trusted Gage's feelings, especially the way he'd proposed so quickly. She'd shamelessly flirted with him as a way to test his feelings because, in her experience, men usually went for the easy, no-strings-attached type of relationship. But he'd surprised her by instantly shutting her down. He had claimed to love Alyssa, although just a short month later, she had returned his engagement ring.

Mallory suspected Alyssa still harbored deep feelings for Gage Drummond.

Since thinking about her past—and the way she'd messed up one relationship after another—was depressing, she concentrated on the present. Glancing over at Jonah, she focused on his wound. It wasn't easy to see the stain on his navy T-shirt, but she could tell the damp spot was spreading.

"Jonah, what happened? Why would an old wound bleed like that?"

"I had surgery about a week ago, and a few of the stitches must have popped open."

"What happened? Were you injured on the job?"

He clenched his jaw. "I was stabbed by a dirty cop Gage and I discovered was working for Hugh Jefferson."

Mallory twisted her fingers together nervously. The architectural firm she worked for had been awarded the design contract for the Jefferson Project—fancy high-rise condos overlooking the Milwaukee River. She was the firm's interior designer, and her boss, Rick Meyers, was the one who'd introduced her to Anthony Caruso.

Caruso had talked often to Hugh Jefferson. The mere memory of what she'd overheard made her stomach roll with nausea. "What are you saying? That you have proof Jefferson was involved with illegal activities?"

"Yeah. We have proof of how he was involved in a money-laundering scheme. But now he's dead."

Her mouth dropped open in shock. Hugh Jefferson was dead? "Are you sure all this happened while I was making my way to the cabin?" She hated thinking she'd left Alyssa in danger.

"I'm sure." Jonah's tone was terse. "Jefferson's yacht

caught on fire, and while Gage and Alyssa managed to escape, he and his cohorts didn't. All three of them died—Aaron Crane, the dirty cop, Hugh Jefferson and Eric Holden, the newly elected Milwaukee mayor. Well, technically, Holden died before he could be sworn into office."

She was disappointed that he hadn't mentioned Caruso. Listening to Jonah talk about the Jefferson Project confirmed that everything she'd suspected all along was true. There hadn't been some horrible mistake. Caruso really had sent that thug to kill her at Alyssa's town house, hoping to silence her forever. And then Caruso had found her again, at Uncle Henry's cabin. She licked her suddenly dry lips. "I'm relieved to know Alyssa and Gage escaped. But why were they even on the yacht in the first place? What possessed Gage to put Alyssa in danger?"

"Gage didn't put her in danger on purpose. In fact, he went to great lengths to keep her safe. But we didn't know exactly who she was running from, because of her amnesia."

She rubbed her temples, trying to make sense of what Jonah was saying. "I was the one they wanted to silence." She felt sick at the thought she'd inadvertently put Alyssa in danger. "They must have thought she was me."

"No, it wasn't that," Jonah said reassuringly. "Alyssa was working in the trauma room the night Councilman Schaefer was brought in with his stab wound. He told Alyssa that Jefferson was responsible. She believed him and reported the crime to Officer Crane, who happened to be working for Jefferson. He tried to kill her.

More than once. If not for Gage's help, he might have succeeded."

Mallory shook her head, unable to process what he was saying. Wave after wave of regret battered her. She'd been so worried about her own well-being, especially after Wasserman followed her to Alyssa's town house, that she'd never considered her sister might be in just as much danger. She'd left the urgent message—assuming Alyssa would drop everything to come out to meet her—then ditched her phone, worried that Caruso had the means to track it. If only she and Alyssa had been able to talk to each other. They could have disappeared together.

"So now, Mallory, it's your turn. We know why Alyssa was in danger, but we don't know what happened to you. Did you stumble onto something you shouldn't have? Did you find out about the money-laundering scheme?"

"I don't even know what money laundering is." She kept her tone even with an effort.

"It's taking money received from illegal activities and putting it into legal activities," he explained, not willing to be distracted from his purpose. "You left a lot of blood on the floor of Alyssa's town house, along with a blood-stained blouse."

She shivered, remembering that night all too clearly.

"Mallory, are you listening to me? I can't keep you safe unless you're honest with me. Tell me the name of the man you're running from. If you do, I'll make sure the DA knows you cooperated with our investigation."

She snapped her head up to glare at him. A flash of anger blurred her vision, forcing her to wrestle it back to maintain control.

"What do you mean you'll convince the DA I've cooperated with the investigation? I'm not involved in anything illegal. I'm the victim here. A guy named Kent Wasserman, followed me to Alyssa's town house and tried to kill me!"

"Yeah, maybe," Jonah said, his calm voice only fueling her annoyance. "But just a few hours ago, I was informed that Wasserman's body was found in an alley not far from your condo, and your fingerprints are on the knife in his belly. The ME has deemed his death a homicide. As a result, there's a warrant for your arrest."

She couldn't have been more surprised if the car had sprouted wings to fly. How could there possibly be a warrant out for her arrest? He was the one who'd tried to kill her! She'd fought with Wasserman, sure, but only in self-defense. She'd barely escaped. And she didn't touch the knife.

At least, not that she remembered.

"I didn't kill him," she whispered, the images she'd tried to forget crowding in her mind. Somehow, someway, she had to make him believe her. "I swear to you, Jonah, I didn't kill him. Don't you see? I'm being framed for murder!"

Jonah's mouth tightened, but he didn't say anything. And that was when she realized that Jonah Stewart hadn't just come to Crystal Lake to help find her. He'd come to take her back to Milwaukee.

To arrest her for a crime she didn't commit.

TWO

"Jonah, please. You have to believe me. I didn't kill him!" Mallory fought to control the fear that began to constrict her throat.

"I guess it's possible you're being framed," Jonah said slowly, in a tone laced with doubt. "But we'd have to prove it, which isn't going to be easy. You have to tell me everything, Mallory, from the very beginning. I can't help you if you hold back on me."

For a moment she stared through the darkness at the trees passing in a blur outside her passenger-side window. She didn't know if she could trust Jonah. What if she told him what she knew and he still arrested her? Caruso was a powerful man—she had no doubt he'd find a way to kill her even if she happened to be in jail. Yet if she didn't tell him, Jonah would take her back to Milwaukee and arrest her for sure.

A no-win situation, either way.

She took a deep breath and then let it out slowly. "I started dating Anthony Caruso a few months ago," she admitted, avoiding his gaze.

"Anthony Caruso?" Jonah interrupted with a frown. "Who's he?"

"He's an Illinois senator. I'm not normally into the political scene, but when I met him, I liked him. He told me he was providing Hugh Jefferson with capital for his condo project."

At the time, dating him had seemed harmless. Caruso had been older than most of the men she'd dated—thirty-nine to her twenty-seven—but he'd been charming so she'd figured, why not? Looking back, she wondered how she could have been so stupid.

"An Illinois senator," Jonah repeated under his breath, as if he couldn't believe it. "I recognize his name now. It's been all over the news. He's a big deal in Washington. Exactly how did you meet him?"

"My boss, Rick Meyer, introduced me to him at one of the meetings about the Jefferson Project." She glanced away, not wanting to see the censure in his eyes. "I— Things moved pretty fast. He literally swept me off my feet. Bought me gifts, took me to fancy restaurants and even flew me to New York to see a Broadway show." She felt like an idiot now, knowing she'd been blinded by the wealth. And power. Anthony Caruso wielded a lot of power—more than she could have possibly suspected. "I never, in a million years, suspected he would get involved with anything illegal."

She forced herself to look at Jonah. Sure enough, his eyebrows levered upward in surprise. "Caruso himself is involved? Seriously? Are you absolutely certain?"

He didn't believe her, and that hurt. Why didn't anyone take her seriously? She tilted her chin stubbornly. "Yes, I'm sure. I was leaving his office suite in the hotel after we'd had lunch but I forgot my purse. I went back in quietly so I wouldn't disturb him. I saw him standing out on his terrace by himself, talking on his cell. He sounded very angry. I paused and overheard him telling the person on the other end of the line to do whatever was necessary to make sure the condo project went forward as planned because he had too much riding on it."

"That statement isn't necessarily incriminating," Jonah pointed out. "Could be interpreted as having money on the line, which isn't illegal. Anyone would be upset with losing money on a business deal."

"I know. But then he said, 'My sources tell me Schaefer was alive when he hit the ER, so you better make sure our guy on the inside convinces the public his death was the result of gang violence.'" She remembered how horrified she'd felt in that moment, realizing the senator was actually discussing how to cover up a murder. "I retraced my steps, trying to sneak away, but I think he must have heard me. I caught a glimpse of his face as he came in from the terrace just as I closed the door behind me. I ran down the hall and avoided the elevator, choosing the stairs instead. I managed to get out of the building, but I couldn't go home. I kept calling Alyssa's place, but she didn't pick up. I eventually went to her town house, using my key to get in. I had this crazy idea of borrowing her identity, but then I heard someone at the door and assumed it was my sister. Kent Wasserman barged in, holding a knife. We'd briefly met a few weeks earlier through Anthony. I was shocked to see him at Alyssa's and knew he must have followed me. He lunged but I managed to get away, taking him down in the process. He fell on his knife."

"You took him down?" Doubt radiated from his tone.

She narrowed her gaze. "Try me." She didn't bother explaining she'd been training in martial arts since her senior year in high school—specifically, since the night of the assault that had changed her life forever. She had absolutely no intention of explaining the private horror of her past to Jonah.

Besides, her past was old news. She'd moved beyond the assault, and she'd get herself out of this mess, as well. If necessary, she'd figure out something on her own. But she wasn't going to allow any man to hold her helpless ever again. That included all of the thugs Caruso sent out after her.

And Jonah Stewart, who was perhaps the most dangerous of all.

Jonah tried to mask his surprise. First, he found it hard to believe a state senator could actually be calling the shots in the Jefferson Project. And then of course there was the rest of Mallory's story. Including the part where she claimed to have a black belt in Tae Kwon Do. But she didn't hedge the way people sometimes did when they were lying, and he found himself believing her.

"That's a very serious allegation, Mallory. You'd better be sure about this. Anthony Caruso carries a lot of weight on Capitol Hill. There's been talk about him being a candidate for vice president, or even for the presidency itself in a few years. I don't think many people are going to believe your word over his."

"I know." She twisted her hands together in a nervous gesture. "That's the reason I ran. But I promise you, I'm not lying about this. I know what I heard."

"I believe you. But we need proof, Mallory. If we're accusing a state senator of being involved, we need hard-core proof."

"I know," she murmured. Her face was grim and she

sighed heavily. "Up until that point, I had no idea Anthony was involved in anything shady. I'd been dating him for almost a month and I never heard so much as an inkling of anything dangerous. It was a total fluke that I heard that snippet of his conversation at all. But I knew Councilman Schaefer had been stabbed so it didn't take much to put two and two together."

Jonah nodded, discovering he didn't particularly care to hear about how she'd dated the guy.

Not that Mallory's personal life was any of his concern.

He told himself to get a grip. "Okay, so you left Alyssa's town house after being attacked by Wasserman and escaped to Crystal Lake. Then what?"

She lifted one shoulder in a helpless shrug. "Then nothing. I left Alyssa a message to meet me and hunkered down to wait."

"Anything out of the ordinary happen before tonight?" he persisted. "Anything at all to indicate Caruso had found you?"

"No. Not until I heard the guy sneaking through the cabin."

If nothing else, the guy in the ski mask helped reinforce her story about overhearing Caruso's conversation. There was no other reason for Caruso to try to kill her.

Unless there was far more to the story than she was telling him.

He didn't want to think Mallory may have been a part of the crime, but he couldn't totally discount the idea, either.

"Why didn't you go to the police with your story?"

In the darkness he saw her scowl. "Because Anthony

referred to *our guy on the inside*, making it difficult to know who to trust. Besides, I was waiting for Alyssa to meet me at the cabin. I guess I hoped we'd work together to figure out the next step."

Grudgingly, he had to admit her instincts were right. It was actually a good thing that Mallory hadn't gone to the police or Crane might have tried to silence her, too, the way he'd gone after Alyssa. "Do you remember anything else?"

"No. I wish I did. I wish I had proof I could simply hand over to you." She looked totally dejected. He found himself wanting to reassure her, to make her feel better.

Which was totally ridiculous.

Getting too close to someone in the case was unacceptable. Hadn't he learned that the hard way? It only took a fraction of a second to bring the image of his partner's widow to mind.

He'd failed his partner, Drew Massey, when he'd lowered his guard with a young drug runner. And when Drew's wife, Elaine, had accused him of causing Drew's death, he couldn't defend himself. Because she'd been right. Thanks to the eyewitness's cell-phone video, the whole world had been able to see how he'd failed his partner. Including his fiancée. Cheryl had wasted no time in leaving him.

"I'm sorry, Jonah," she said, interrupting his tumultuous thoughts. "I wish now that I had paid more attention."

"Don't worry about it. Why don't you try to get some sleep? I'm not planning to stop for a while yet."

"I'll try," she murmured.

She didn't sleep, but she didn't talk, either. He was

oddly relieved to discover Mallory wasn't the type to fill a silence with small talk.

No matter how much he told himself to keep an open mind, deep down, he believed Mallory's story. For the past twenty-four hours, he'd been hoping that finding her would be the key to blowing his case wide open. But overhearing a snippet of a conversation wouldn't get him anywhere close to pressing charges. If they couldn't corroborate Mallory's story, they had nothing.

Which meant not only was Mallory's life still in danger, but he was right back to square one.

Mallory yawned so wide her jaw popped. She scrubbed at her gritty eyes, trying to force herself to stay awake. Finally, just as dawn was breaking over the horizon, Jonah pulled into a motel with a flashing vacancy sign out front.

"Where are we?" she asked, realizing she hadn't even noticed the name of the town.

"Glen Hollow," Jonah replied as he shut off the car and opened his door. "Population less than nine hundred."

She slid out of the passenger seat. "Honestly, as long as there's running water and a shower, I don't care how many people live here."

He flashed a tired grin, and she was struck by how handsome Jonah was. He wasn't overly tall, just barely six feet in her estimation, but he was muscular. And she liked the way he wore his dark hair short. He opened the back door and rummaged around in a duffel bag. Before she could ask what he was doing, he stripped off his old shirt, revealing the blood-stained dressing covering the right side of his chest, before he pulled a black T-shirt over his head.

She turned away, feeling light-headed but unsure whether it was the blood or Jonah causing the sensation.

Must be the blood because she was immune to handsome men. She only dated men on her terms, determined to be the one in control. Never again would she let her guard down.

"Wait for me in the car," he said in a low voice. "I don't want the clerk to be able to identify you."

Unable to argue with his logic, she nodded and slid back into the passenger seat. It was only a few minutes before he returned.

"Here." He handed her a key. "We have adjoining rooms, numbers ten and twelve."

"Ah, okay." She was surprised he cared enough to respect her need for privacy. She couldn't remember the last guy who'd put her needs before his own.

She told herself not to place too much emphasis on Jonah's kindness. For all she knew, he was simply biding his time before he slipped handcuffs on her and hauled her off to jail.

If he tried that, he'd learn firsthand what it meant to be a black belt in Tae Kwon Do.

Jonah grabbed his laptop and his duffel bag from the backseat of his car. He caught Mallory eyeing his duffel with longing. Luckily he had plenty of cash—there would be time to pick up a few things for her later.

They went into their rooms. Jonah dropped his duffel bag on the bed and then crossed over to unlock the connecting door on his side of the two rooms. He was surprised to find that Mallory had already opened her side, too. He hovered in the doorway, not wanting to encroach on her personal space. The faint scent of juniper greeted him, as if Mallory had stashed a few Christmas trees inside. "I—uh—thought we'd head over to the diner for breakfast before we get some sleep."

"Sure." Her smile was weary. "But if you could stop at the front desk to get me a toothbrush, I'd appreciate it."

"No problem." He grabbed his computer and followed her outside.

She glanced at the computer in surprise. "Do you really think the café has Wi-Fi?"

"According to the desk clerk they do." He'd made sure there was an internet connection in the rooms, too. "Figured I'd do some research on your former boyfriend over breakfast."

Mallory didn't say anything in response, but followed him inside the café. He chose a booth in the back. But when he booted up the computer, Mallory slid in beside him.

"What are you doing?" he asked in alarm, trying to ignore her juniper scent.

"I'm not just going to sit there and watch you work," Mallory said in exasperation. "I can help."

He wished he'd brought more than one computer, to keep Mallory on the opposite side of the booth where she belonged. Yet he could hardly blame her for wanting to help. When the waitress came over with a pot of coffee, he stopped her from filling his cup. "Just orange juice for me, please."

"Me, too," Mallory chimed in.

While they waited for their order, he began to search for recent information about Anthony Caruso.

"Do you know what we're looking for?" Mallory asked.

"A needle in a haystack," he muttered. His computer skills were decent, but attempting to breach the security of a state senator's home computer probably wasn't smart, especially on a public network, so he refrained. Thinking clearly wasn't easy with Mallory glued to his side. He hadn't been this distracted by a woman in a long time.

And he shouldn't be now, while he was in the middle of a case.

They took a break from the computer search when their food arrived, and thankfully Mallory went back to her side of the booth. Neither of them said much as they ate. His original plan was to stay at the café and work while Mallory went back to the room to get some sleep. But exhaustion was already weighing him down.

Once they'd finished breakfast, Mallory again abandoned her side of the booth to slide in beside him.

"Why don't you cross-reference Caruso's name with Jefferson's?" she suggested.

He typed in the two names, and the first item to come up was a newspaper article regarding a charity event that had been held a week ago, down at the Pfister Hotel in Milwaukee. When a color photo bloomed on the screen, he heard Mallory gasp softly.

"What's wrong?" he asked. And then he noticed the slender woman in a deep blue gown standing off to the side. The photographer had only caught her back, but the woman's short, curly blond hair matched Mallory's. He glanced over at her as he lightly tapped the computer screen. "This is you, isn't it?"

"Yes. I attended the event with Anthony—he's in the photo, too, right here, but you can't see him very well." Her face had gone pale as she stared at the photo.

"Did you remember something from that night?" he pressed, watching her carefully. "Maybe another conversation you overheard?"

"Anthony was angry when this guy came by to take our pictures. In fact, at the time I thought he was completely overreacting when he had stomped over to the photographer, demanding the photo be erased from his digital camera. Of course the camera guy had refused, and Hugh Jefferson had come over to calm down Anthony. Anthony and Jefferson went off to talk, and the next thing I knew, the entire incident was glossed over. When I asked Anthony about it later, he told me not to worry about it, because Jefferson convinced the cameraman not to list his name."

He frowned and glanced back at the photograph he'd enlarged on the screen. "Strikes me as odd that the senator didn't want his picture taken. Normally politicians love to be splashed all over the media."

She nodded slowly. "Yeah, I thought it was odd, too. In fact, up until that point, I hadn't heard Anthony raise his voice to anyone. I think that was partially why I listened to his phone conversation the next night. He was always so smoothly charming."

He swiveled in his seat to stare at her. "Are you telling me this charity event was the night before you overheard him trying to cover up Councilman Schaefer's murder?"

"Yes. The benefit was on Thursday night, and I overheard the conversation the next day. We'd originally made plans to have lunch, but then Anthony backed out, saying something important at work had come up. Next thing I knew, he was talking about covering up a murder."

His gut clenched when he realized how lucky she'd been to get away from Caruso's thug not just once, but twice. He was thankful Mallory had managed to get away, or the outcome of Wasserman's attack could have been very different.

God was definitely watching over her. Watching over both of them.

And this time, he wouldn't mess up like he had the night his partner had died.

Please, God, give me the strength and the knowledge to keep Mallory safe.

He stared at the surprisingly clear photograph. It was easy to recognize Senator Caruso now that she'd pointed him out. But why would the guy go to a public charity event only to become upset when he was photographed? None of this made any sense.

Had something else happened that night? Something significant enough to put Caruso on edge? Something that may have sent the entire house of cards that Jefferson built tumbling to the ground?

His blood ran cold.

What if Mallory had become a target not just because she'd overheard Caruso's patio conversation, but because she saw or heard something with even more significance? Something so damaging, Caruso had no choice but to silence her forever?

THREE

Mallory rubbed the back of her neck. Holding her head at an awkward angle in order to read Jonah's computer screen was giving her a neck ache to match her headache.

They were crazy to think they might find something on the internet that would lead them to incriminating evidence against Anthony Caruso. She eased away from Jonah and reached for her orange juice.

She was too exhausted to do any more surfing and Jonah must have been, too, since he shut down the computer and pulled out his wallet to pay the bill.

"I have some cash, too, if you need some," she offered.

He scowled, apparently chauvinistic enough to dislike the idea of a woman paying her own way. "I'm fine. Let's go. We both need a couple hours of sleep."

She followed him out of the café and across the street to their motel rooms. He opened the door, checking to make sure the room was safe before he stood back and allowed her to go inside.

"Keep the connecting door unlocked, okay? Just in case."

Just in case what? She suppressed a shiver. "There's no way the ski-mask guy could have followed us, right?"

"No. But we can't afford to let down our guard, either. Just humor me, okay?"

She hesitated and then nodded. "Okay."

Jonah stared at her for a moment, as if he wanted to say more, but then he turned and disappeared inside his room. She partially closed the connecting door on her side, before testing out the running water in the bathroom—which was pure bliss—and then climbing into bed. She fell asleep the instant her head hit the pillow.

Mallory had no idea how long she slept, but much like the night before, a strange sound dragged her awake. She stayed perfectly still, straining to listen.

She heard it again. A muffled sound coming from Jonah's room. She climbed from her bed, pulled on her grungy clothes and pushed open the connecting door.

Jonah was talking in his sleep, thrashing on the bed, obviously in the throes of a nightmare. She crossed over to shake his shoulder. "Jonah, wake up. You're having a bad dream."

Almost instantly, he shot upward and grabbed his gun. She shrank away, holding out her hand to calm him down. "It's me, Jonah. Mallory. I was only trying to wake you up from your nightmare."

He slowly lowered his weapon, letting out his breath in a heavy sigh. "I'm sorry. I— You took me by surprise."

He avoided her gaze. A faint sheen of sweat covered his face and dampened the hair at his temples. Definitely a nightmare. "Jonah, who's Drew? You were muttering something about Drew."

His expression closed, and she sensed that whatever the source of his nightmare, he wasn't inclined to talk about it. "I'm sorry I woke you."

"No need to apologize." She noticed with surprise that the Gideon Bible was lying open on his bedside table. Had Jonah actually been reading the Bible? The only person she knew who'd ever read the Bible on a regular basis was Alyssa.

He must have noticed her gaze because he flashed a lopsided smile. "Renewing my faith helps me relax, especially in times of stress. You might want to give it a try."

She frowned and shook her head. "No thanks. Not after everything I've been through."

He frowned, but didn't look surprised by her attitude. "I'm sure you have your reasons for not believing, Mallory, but have you ever considered how God might help shoulder your burden rather than add to it?"

She wished there was a tactful way to change the subject. "You have no idea what I've been through. Having Anthony Caruso attempt to kill me isn't the worst I've suffered." She told herself to shut up before she found herself blubbering about her past.

The last thing she wanted or needed was Jonah's sympathy.

"You're right, Mallory. I don't know everything you've suffered. But I do know about my own experience." There was a long pause before he continued. "Drew was my partner. He was a few years older than me, and he taught me everything I needed to know about being a cop."

The stark agony in his eyes made her wish she'd

never asked about his nightmare. She knew, only too well, how reliving the past only made it harder to forget.

"One day, we caught this kid running drugs. He was young, barely eleven, and I wanted the guy who was pulling the strings on this kid. Drew wanted to haul him in, but I convinced him to try it my way first. The kid was so young, and he looked up at me with big eyes, telling me he'd show us where he was supposed to take the money. I believed him. Drew tried to talk me out of it, but I insisted. The kid led us right into a trap."

She gasped, the scene so vivid she felt as if she was right there with him.

"And when the shooting started, I instinctively protected the kid who'd betrayed us, leaving my partner open. He died as a result of my actions." Jonah's expression was grim as he faced her. "So while I don't know what you've been through, Mallory, I do know that God can help carry a heavy burden."

A long silence stretched between them, and she had no idea what to say. But she realized that Jonah's past was just as difficult to live with as hers.

Jonah reached out to touch the Bible. "Without faith, I would never have made it through the worst time of my life."

She gave a helpless shrug. "I guess I just don't understand how believing in God helps."

"It's hard to explain," he admitted. "But I can tell you that God doesn't abandon us when we need Him. He's there for us, always."

She didn't believe God was there for her. Not back when she was seventeen, or when Caruso's thug tried to kill her.

Unless God had sent Jonah to save her?

No, she didn't really believe that, and this wasn't the time or place to argue with Jonah over religion.

"Maybe at some point, you'll give it a try," Jonah said. "However, right now, we need to think of some way to get evidence against Caruso."

She was glad he let the subject drop. "I went back over the night of the fund-raiser, and there is one other thing I remember. Although I'm not sure it means much."

He leaned forward. "What is it?"

"There was a brief disagreement between Jefferson and Caruso. I didn't really pay much attention then, but looking back, it was right about the time Jefferson took a phone call. I think the news may have been about Schaefer."

"Can you remember exactly what was said? By either Jefferson or Caruso?"

"Caruso said something like, 'I wouldn't have to worry if you weren't such an amateur.'" She wished she'd heard what they were saying. "At the time, I assumed they were talking about investments, but now I'm thinking the conversation may have referred to having Schaefer stabbed and being forced to attribute the stabbing to gang activity."

"You could be right. Nice detective work, Mallory."

She blushed and shrugged off the compliment. No doubt Jonah was simply trying to stay on her good side. "So now what? Where do we go from here?"

He scrubbed his hands over his face. "Good question. Give me some time to pull myself together, and I'll try to come up with a plan."

"As long as your plan doesn't involve me turning myself in to the DA," she murmured as she turned away. No matter how good of a detective Jonah was, he couldn't possibly find proof she couldn't even be sure existed. And they couldn't stay on the run forever—they both had jobs, careers to get back to.

A wave of hopelessness washed over her. For a fleeting moment, she surprised herself and considered trying to pray. Except she didn't know how and didn't really think God would listen to someone like her even if she did.

She was better off relying only on herself—the way she'd always done.

Jonah examined his incision as well as he could in the mirror above the sink in the bathroom. It looked worse than he'd anticipated. He applied some antibacterial ointment before slapping a new gauze dressing over the area where he'd popped two stitches. At least the wound had stopped bleeding. He was glad Alyssa had forced him to bring first-aid supplies, although she'd no doubt be upset that he'd opened the wound. Belatedly remembering his antibiotics, he popped one, hoping the pills would be strong enough to ward off infection.

For a moment he stared grimly at his reflection in the mirror. What he really needed to do was call his boss and ask for someone else to watch over Mallory. Not only was he still recuperating from his stab wound and subsequent surgery, he also was too close to making the same mistake he had in the past—letting his emotions get in the way of his job.

He couldn't cross the line and begin caring about Mallory. He never should have accepted her help in finding evidence against Caruso. She wasn't a cop. What he needed to do was to convince his boss to put her up in some sort of safe house. A place where able-bodied cops could watch over her instead of a wounded warrior like him.

As he dressed, his cell phone rang. He picked up his phone to see who'd called.

He was expecting his boss, but it was Gage. Knowing Mallory would be thrilled to hear from her sister, he crossed over to gently tap on the door between their rooms. "Mallory? It's Gage. Do you want to talk?"

"Yes!" She eagerly took the phone. "Alyssa?" Her face lit up with joy, and he turned away to give her some privacy. "What happened?"

Jonah knew Alyssa would fill Mallory in on everything, in much greater detail than he had. He went back into his room and waited. When she was done, he'd call his boss.

Mallory didn't return for a good fifteen minutes, but when she handed him the phone, she was smiling. "Alyssa's fine. She told me everything and then offered to blow off her surgery to come up here. I convinced her to stay put and take care of herself. Thankfully, for the first time ever, Gage agreed with me."

"I'm glad." He took the phone and punched in his boss's number.

"Who are you calling?" she asked.

"My boss. Lieutenant Michael Finley."

Her jaw dropped open in shock. "Your boss? I thought you said Alyssa sent you. I didn't realize you were reporting everything to your boss." She'd trusted Jonah with her life and didn't appreciate how he'd held back important information.

"I'm keeping Finley updated. He knows the plan is to find the top guy involved in Jefferson's money-laundering scheme. Jefferson used way too much cash, and we were also able to trace his funds for the condo project to a Swiss bank account. I need to let Finley know we suspect Caruso."

The expression on her face indicated she wasn't happy with that news. "I thought you said there was a warrant out for my arrest."

"There is, but I think I can convince Finley you're being framed for Wasserman's murder. And I think he'll agree to put you up in a safe house."

"A safe house?" She glared at him with dismay. "Why would I want to do that? I'd rather stay with you."

He hardened his heart against the hurt reflected in her eyes. But he refused to let his emotions sway his decision. Putting Mallory in a safe house was the right thing to do. "Because you need to be safe, no matter what."

"Oh, yeah?" Her blue eyes narrowed with suspicion. "And what about you?"

He looked away. "Once I know you're safe, I plan to head back to Milwaukee or maybe even Chicago so I can find hard evidence against Caruso."

Mallory watched with helpless anger as Jonah went outside to make his phone call, obviously seeking privacy. She went over to the door but she was unable to decipher any specific words. Dejected, she went back to her own room, waiting in the connecting doorway for him to return.

What had she done to make Jonah so anxious to be rid of her? Apparently the closeness she believed might be growing between them was nothing more than her overactive imagination. No big surprise there. She couldn't help feeling hurt by the idea he'd leave her alone in a police safe house while continuing his investigation without her.

Apparently, Jonah preferred to work alone.

Granted, she didn't exactly have the skills or background that Jonah did, but she knew Anthony Caruso on a personal level. Certainly that knowledge alone gave her some value.

When Jonah returned to the motel room, his closed expression reinforced her deepest fears. She wanted to scream and yell that he couldn't leave her alone in some safe house, but knew instinctively that theatrics weren't going to sway him off course.

Through the open connecting doors between their rooms, she saw that he'd picked up the Bible. The way he settled down to read, as if he didn't have a care in the world, made her seethe with frustration. What was wrong with him? Didn't he have any feelings for her at all?

Of course he didn't, she reminded herself sternly. She wasn't the type of woman he could ever care about on a personal level. She didn't believe in God the way he did, for one thing. And she was part of his case against Caruso. A woman he was responsible for protecting. Until he could hand her over to someone else.

"Mallory? Are you all right?"

His soft question pulled her from her thoughts. "No, I'm not. But why would you bother asking? Haven't you already decided the next step without caring about what I want?"

When he glanced away, she knew her point had hit home. Being right didn't make her feel any better, though.

Jonah was silent for several long minutes. "'He will cover you with his feathers, and under his wings you will find refuge; his faithfulness will be your shield and rampart,'" Jonah murmured.

The phrase didn't sound the least bit familiar, but struck a chord deep within, nonetheless. "Is that really from the Bible? It sounds more like a poem." She was intrigued by the lyrical words.

"In a way. The Book of Psalms reads like a book of poems."

She was surprised to hear Bible verses actually read like poems. She'd always thought they were dry and preachy. Alyssa's friends had been involved in church activities, but she'd resisted going along, no matter how much Alyssa tried to convince her. Reluctantly curious, she walked across the threshold into his room to see for herself. As she approached, she caught sight of Jonah's car keys sitting on top of the dresser. Without giving herself time to consider the consequences of her actions, she silently swept them into her hand and stuck them into the front pocket of her sweatshirt.

"Here, start at the beginning," Jonah urged.

She took the Bible from his hands and tried to read but she couldn't concentrate. The car keys were practically burning a hole clear through the fleece to her skin. Finally, she handed the Bible back to Jonah. "Sorry, it doesn't really work for me."

The flash of disappointment in his eyes shouldn't have bothered her. She turned and tried not to rush as she made her way back to her room.

Once she was out of his line of vision, she paused long enough to take a deep breath. She looped her purse over her shoulder and tried to edge closer to the door.

She felt bad about leaving him here, but he'd called his boss, hadn't he? Someone would be here soon enough to rescue him. By that time she'd be far out of reach.

She didn't know how to explain to Jonah why she didn't trust anyone but him. Partially because Gage and Alyssa had vouched for his integrity. Partially because he believed in God.

And most of all, because she liked him. She couldn't remember the last time she had met a man she actually liked. A man she felt comfortable being around. She didn't need to constantly have her guard up with Jonah.

She crossed to the door and silently turned the handle. Holding her breath, she opened it, slipped through and tried to shut it quietly behind her.

But she'd only gone two steps when Jonah's door burst open. She was shocked speechless when he grabbed her hand, prying the car keys from her numb fingers. It happened so fast, she didn't have a chance to react, to strike out with a roundhouse kick or a blow to his arm.

Or maybe she just couldn't bring herself to hit Jonah.

"Nice try, Mallory," he said in a patronizing tone.

A red haze of fury blinded her. "Let me go! I'd rather be out there on my own than stuck in some safe house with someone I don't know!"

"Why?" he demanded, sliding the car keys deep into his pocket, far out of her reach. "I'm only doing this for your own good, Mallory. Can't you understand I want you to be safe?"

She ground her teeth together, fighting the urge to pummel him with her fists. Were all men this annoying? She'd never been emotionally involved enough to find out. "You said yourself that there was a dirty cop working with Jefferson, helping him from the inside. How do you know there aren't more? How do you know that Officer Crane, the cop who died, wasn't working with someone?"

He stood there, staring at her uncertainly. Sensing she might have an edge, she pushed a little more.

"Jonah, think about it. Can you live with your decision, knowing there is a slim chance Caruso might find me and kill me inside the safe house?" She held her breath, hoping, praying he'd understand.

Because the last thing she wanted to do was go off on her own—without Jonah Stewart.

FOUR

Jonah closed his fist around the car keys in his hand, barely feeling the hard metal edges cutting into his flesh. He'd been shocked to notice his keys were gone and had luckily caught Mallory before she could get away. As mad as he was, he couldn't blame her for trying to leave, any more than he could deny the truth underscoring Mallory's words.

But no matter how tempted he might be to sympathize with her, he couldn't allow himself to be swayed off course.

He couldn't live with himself if he failed Mallory. Logically, he knew stashing her in a safe house was his best option. A cop who wasn't recovering from a stab wound and surgery would be able to protect her better than he could. Whether she believed it or not.

"I'm sorry, Mallory. But the best course of action for me is to return to Milwaukee, and likely to Chicago, in order to find evidence against Caruso."

"Take me with you," she begged.

Feeling his resolve soften, he dragged his gaze away from hers. "I can't. You'll only slow me down. Besides, I need to know you're safe."

"And what if I'm not safe?" she challenged. "What if there's another dirty cop who finds a way to get to me?"

He couldn't bear to think of Mallory being in danger. But he also didn't think Aaron Crane had been working with another cop on the inside. From what little information he and his boss could piece together, they believed Crane had been working alone. "Lieutenant Finley assured me he'll find two men he can trust to stay with you at the safe house. I've been communicating with him since this mess started and I have no reason to believe he won't hold up his end of the deal."

She stared at him, stark resignation in her gaze. "Well, then, I guess there's nothing more to discuss." Her voice simmered with betrayal. She turned her back on him and returned to her room, closing the door behind her softly. Why he would have felt better if she'd slammed it, he had no idea.

For a moment he stared and then slowly made his way back inside, not at all surprised to discover Mallory had closed the connecting door.

Reminding himself he'd made this decision for her own good didn't make him feel any better. When his cell phone rang, he was thankful for the diversion from his thoughts. "Hey, Gage, what's up?"

"Not much, other than Alyssa is officially scheduled for surgery. They're going to operate first thing in the morning."

"Wow, that's fast."

"Yeah, although not as far as Alyssa's concerned. She's anxious for it to be done and over."

"I don't blame her. And I'm glad she and Mallory had time to talk." He was glad Mallory had already spoken to her sister, because he knew Alyssa would side with Mallory if the two of them talked now.

"Hey, when Mallory told Alyssa about Anthony Caruso, I did a little digging and stumbled across some information."

"Mallory told Alyssa about Caruso?" For some reason, that surprised him.

"Yeah, Alyssa was mad at herself for not recognizing him earlier, when she found a photo of the two of them together in Mallory's dresser."

He scowled, not exactly thrilled to hear Mallory had hidden a photo of Caruso in her condo. Was she upset about their broken relationship? He didn't sense she was grieving over it, but then again, he had the impression that Mallory was good at hiding her feelings. "Don't keep me in suspense, Gage. What did you find out?"

"I looked into who exactly supported Caruso's political career. Not surprisingly, Hugh Jefferson was on the list along with Eric Holden."

"You're right, that's not surprising." Too bad they hadn't stumbled across that connection much sooner, since Holden, a newly elected Milwaukee mayor, financially supporting Caruso, a U.S. state senator from Illinois, might have raised a red flag. Local politics were one thing, but why support someone in a different state? Unless you just happened to be in business together.

"The name that jumped out at me was Bernardo Salvatore, who owns a handful of Sicilian restaurants across the Midwest. From what I found online, he was planning to open a brand-new restaurant in downtown Milwaukee, less than a mile from Jefferson's condo project. However, now the plans are on hold, indefinitely."

Jonah could hardly suppress the buzz of excitement from the slim lead. The connection was worth investigating. "So Bernardo Salvatore is in league with Caruso."

"Possibly," Gage admitted. "At least it's something to work on. I wanted to let you know so you could start down that path, since Jefferson, Holden and Crane are all dead."

"Not your fault, Gage." Jonah knew his buddy was still blaming himself for allowing Alyssa to be caught and for inadvertently causing the fire on the yacht, which killed both Holden and Jefferson before they could get any information out of them. "We'll get Caruso, sooner or later. Maybe he'll make another mistake. If he thinks Mallory is the only threat at this point, he might be running his money-laundering scheme in a business-as-usual mode."

"I hope so. Jonah, be careful, okay?" Gage's concerned tone wasn't exactly reassuring. "One more death isn't going to weigh too heavily on Caruso's conscience. In fact, if Caruso somehow discovers you're involved with helping Mallory, you'll be marked as a threat he'll need to eliminate, right along with her."

"Won't be the first time some crook wants me dead," he said, downplaying his friend's concern. "Talk to you later."

"Yeah, later."

Jonah stared out the window, grimly realizing he'd made a mistake last night by allowing the ski-masked intruder to get away. Whoever Caruso hired to take out Mallory now knew she wasn't alone.

He fully believed that dirty cop, Aaron Crane, had attacked him on Jefferson's orders. And since Jefferson reported up to Caruso, he figured Caruso knew he'd escaped. How long before Caruso realized that he was the one who helped Mallory escape?

Several hours later, Jonah walked across the street to the gas station mini-mart to pick up additional medical supplies for his wound that wouldn't stop bleeding, along with a couple sandwiches and some chips. He'd decided against returning to the café, just on the off chance that someone had stopped by to ask about them.

There was a black Lab tied up outside but the dog didn't seem overly anxious about a stranger going inside. Apparently, the gas station was the main source of income for the town and the dog was accustomed to strangers.

After returning to the motel, he knocked on the connecting door between their rooms, hoping Mallory would accept his offer of peace.

A long minute passed, making Jonah wonder if she'd decided to ignore him, but then she opened the door, the expression on her face less than welcoming. "Has your replacement arrived yet?"

"Not yet." He lifted the bag. "I brought lunch."

She eyed the bag curiously, and eventually hunger won out over anger. She stepped back and allowed him to come in. He saw an open Bible on the bed, and he couldn't help crossing over to see what had captured her interest. "Are you reading the Book of Psalms?" he asked in surprise.

She lifted a shoulder in a shrug and color rose to her cheeks as if she were embarrassed. "They make more sense when you start at the beginning."

Humbled and pleased, he realized that he might be

helping her discover her faith. Of course, just reading the Book of Psalms didn't mean she would become a believer, but he couldn't help thinking he might be able to help sway her opinion if they had time to talk. Maybe attend church. Did the town have a church?

Maybe he shouldn't have called his boss for assistance so quickly. Was it possible God placed Mallory in his path not only to keep her safe from physical harm, but to assist her in finding her way to God?

If so, he was eager to accept God's calling. He closed his eyes and prayed for strength. Mallory watched him intently, but before he could pursue the issue, she changed the subject.

"Would you mind if I borrow your phone after we're finished eating? I'd like to find out how Alyssa is doing. She mentioned she had an MRI done of her ankle."

"Sure. In fact, I spoke to Gage earlier and he said everything went well." When he saw the annoyance flash in her eyes at being left out of the conversation, he quickly added, "Alyssa is scheduled for surgery first thing tomorrow morning. If you want to talk to her again, I'm sure Gage wouldn't mind."

"I guess there's no rush." Looking slightly mollified, she took another bite of her sandwich. "Jonah, would you consider sending me to stay with Alyssa and Gage instead? At least then I wouldn't be at the mercy of strangers."

He thought her statement was odd. Why would she feel she was at the mercy of strangers? Did she really think two cops posed some sort of threat?

"Mallory, if you go home, you'll be putting both Gage and Alyssa at risk. Especially Alyssa, who will obviously be unable to move very well after undergoing surgery." He'd left the hospital against medical advice right after the surgery to repair his deflated lung, and those first few days had been awful. Of course, running around the city chasing Jefferson hadn't exactly helped his recuperation.

"Okay, but couldn't they come to the safe house with me?" she persisted. "If this place is as safe as you think, they wouldn't be in danger."

He couldn't argue her point. And it was possible Gage could be persuaded to go along with her plan, if only to appease Alyssa. "We'll discuss the possibility with Gage, okay? If he agrees, then I'm happy to make the arrangements, once she's home from surgery."

"Great. Thanks, Jonah." Mallory's mood lightened considerably, and he couldn't help wondering what had happened in her past to make trust so difficult. "Do you mind if I ask you another question?" she asked.

He dragged his thoughts to the present. "Of course not."

"Do you really believe God forgives all sins?"

"Absolutely." Now he knew God really had sent him to assist Mallory in finding her way home. Her question touched him. "'Through Jesus the forgiveness of sins is proclaimed to you,'" he quoted.

She was silent for a long moment. "Even if the sins are really bad?" she asked in a voice so soft, he had to lean closer to hear.

"Yes, even if the sins are really bad. It's never too late to turn your life around, Mallory, never too late to accept God and your faith. But I find it hard to believe your sins are as bad as you claim."

She frowned. "You don't know enough about me to say that, Jonah." Avoiding his gaze, she leaped up from the table and began clearing away the mess from their meal. "I'd like to call Gage now, if you don't mind."

He silently handed her his cell phone. Feeling restless, he crossed over to his own room, standing next to the window and staring at the highway leading into town. A few dark clouds dotted the sky, but nothing too serious. He was surprised his replacements hadn't arrived yet.

Just ten minutes later, Mallory returned his phone. "Your boss called," she said.

"Did you get to talk to Alyssa?"

"Yes." Mallory flashed a brief smile. "She's a little worried about the surgery, but is thankful Gage will be there for her. I'm thrilled she's giving Gage a second chance."

"They're good together." He called Finley back, prepared for bad news. "Hi, boss, what's up?"

"I won't be able to free anyone up to relieve you until tomorrow. Stay right where you are, and I promise I'll have someone there first thing in the morning."

He sighed and rubbed the back of his neck. It was late afternoon, nearly four o'clock. "Okay, I suppose another sixteen hours won't make much of a difference."

"If anything changes, I'll let you know."

Jonah ended the call and crossed over to the connecting door between their rooms. "Make yourself comfortable. We're staying here for another night."

She didn't look overly disappointed. "Another night is fine with me. Maybe we could go to the hospital tomorrow to visit Alyssa?"

"Mallory, you know we can't take that risk." He didn't have the heart to remind her that Gage hadn't agreed to their plan yet, either. And even if Gage did agree, Alyssa wouldn't be ready for a few days. Better to give Mallory something positive to look forward to.

Now that he had extra time on his hands, he decided to keep digging into Caruso's and Salvatore's business holdings. There had to be another connection, besides just campaign support.

He worked on his computer for several hours, until the stupid thing died. With a scowl, he looked to make sure the power cord was plugged in. Was the outlet broken? The computer battery had gone dead, indicating the power had been off for a while, so he tried several outlets around the room, without success.

Was there something wrong with the power? He crossed the room, intending to flip on the switch to test his theory, but just then the black Lab outside the gas station began to bark.

Jonah crossed over to the window. The sun was low on the horizon, but there was still plenty of light to see. He could easily make out the image of the large black dog straining against the confines of his leash, staring in the direction of the motel.

The hair on the back of Jonah's neck rose in warning. Something was wrong. Very wrong. And then he noticed an orange glow reflected in the window of the gas station.

Their motel was on fire.

Grabbing the car keys off the dresser, he threw open the door between their rooms. "Mallory?" He crossed over to shake her awake. "Hurry, we need to get out of here right now."

To her credit, she didn't argue. She rose up off the bed, pushing her hair out of her eyes as she reached for her purse. "Why? What's going on?"

"The motel is on fire." He tried to open her door but it didn't budge. Panic surged as he tried the door again, putting more muscle into it.

Still, the door didn't give. He ran over to check his door, with the same results.

The fire was no accident. They were locked in.

Mallory's nerves were already on edge from the incessant barking of the dog, but when she realized they were trapped, her pulse soared. Illogically, she tried the door herself, as if she would be able to open the door that Jonah couldn't.

The distinct smell of smoke made her wrinkle her nose in distaste. "I don't understand. I didn't hear any thunder. Could lightning have struck the building?"

"No." He came out of the bathroom, two soaking-wet towels in his hand and another towel wrapped around his fist. "Take these and hold them over your face." He tossed the wet towels in her direction. "Stand back."

Before she could ask him anything more, there was a loud crash as he punched out the window. The dog continued to bark and she realized the black Lab may have saved their lives. Jonah swept the shards of glass out of the way, and for the second time in only three nights, he helped her escape.

Outside, the heat from the fire was intense. Glancing over her shoulder, she realized the entire second floor was burning. There wasn't a storm. In fact, there weren't even very many clouds in the sky. There was a loud crack and Jonah grabbed her arm, pulling her out of the way as the roof collapsed.

"Run," he urged, pulling her in the opposite direction from where their rental car was parked.

"The rental car is back that way," she argued, digging in her heels. Surely he didn't intend for them to leave this miniscule town on foot?

"Forget about the car," he said, dragging her along against her will. "We're going this way."

Jonah pulled her toward a cornfield. She tried not to think about the horror movie involving a cornfield she'd watched as a kid, as she followed him down between the rows.

"Try to be quiet," he whispered.

She couldn't help glancing back over her shoulder, gasping at how the orange glow from the fire lit up the sky. She shivered, in spite of the chill in the air. With the tall green stalks of corn surrounding them, her fear of tight places became overwhelming. "Jonah," she warned.

"What?"

"We have to get out of here—I'm claustrophobic." She struggled to control her breathing, but it wasn't easy. She was unable to ignore the corn husks surrounding them—they kept slapping at her arms, legs and face. Only bugs would have been worse. Spiders. Instantly her skin crawled with imaginary insects and she rubbed her hands vigorously over her arms.

"Hang on, Mallory, for just a little while longer."

She wasn't sure she could hang on. How could Jonah see where they were going? What if they got lost in the cornfields? She'd never survive if they had to spend the night here. Panic swelled. Maybe it was because she'd read the Bible earlier, but a prayer popped into her mind.

Please, Lord, guide us to safety.

Surprisingly, she felt calmer after her murmured prayer. She took a couple deep breaths and glanced up at the sky, hoping the sun wouldn't slip behind the horizon just yet. Seeing the open space overhead helped.

Jonah kept moving and, thankfully, seemed to know exactly where he was going. A good fifteen minutes later, they burst out of the cornfield.

Thank You, Lord, she whispered, stopping long enough to catch her breath.

Jonah stood close beside her, keeping a hand on her arm as if he were afraid he'd lose her. "Ready?" he asked.

"For what?" She glanced around, trying to figure out which direction the highway might be. "It's going to be dark soon, and we won't be able to find our way."

"We only have to go a little farther, Mallory," Jonah urged. "But we need to hurry."

She thought it was possible he was losing his mind, but since following him was better than standing in the middle of a field, she decided to go along.

There was a humming sound that seemed to gradually grow louder. "Come on, Mallory. Hurry."

Hurry? What on earth did he mean? It wasn't until she saw the train tracks that she understood what the sound was. "Is that a train?"

"Cargo train. I saw it go by earlier today." Jonah walked over to the edge of the train tracks and turned until he faced south.

The sound of the train engine grew louder, and suddenly she knew what Jonah intended. "No, I can't," she said with a horrified gasp.

"You have to," he insisted, his hand tightening around hers. "Mallory, if you want to get out of this place, we have to jump aboard the train."

She felt as if she were frozen in place as the light

of the train approached. The train was going too fast. Jonah was nuts if he thought they could really do this.

"Ready?" he asked, running alongside the train.

"No!" she shouted, the sound of her voice drowned out by the train as it went by.

"Now, Mallory!" he yelled directly into her ear. "Grab one of those railings! I'll be right behind you!"

Her heart lodged in her throat as she ran. She gauged the distance to the railing the way she would if she were about to do a jumping snap kick to break boards in Tae Kwon Do.

She took a deep breath, jumped and grabbed. She cried out in surprise as pain shot up her arm from being wrenched off her feet. Ignoring the pain, she found another handhold along the edge of the car, securing her precarious position.

She'd made it! She wanted to laugh and cry at the same time.

Feeling like Spider-Man clinging to the side of a building, she lifted her head and glanced to her left, peering intently through the darkness.

She'd made it safely on the train—but where was Jonah?

FIVE

Mallory tried to rein in her panic, taking several deep breaths. What if Jonah hadn't made it on the train? She wanted to believe he was farther back because he'd forced her to go first, but what if he had misjudged the distance and hadn't made it at all?

She was too afraid to move, even though she knew she couldn't just stay here like this forever. Would the train slow down at some point? Or did it keep going at the same speed until they reached their destination? And how many miles away was their destination anyway?

"Mallory!" Jonah's voice brought a rush of relief. She looked to the right and could have kissed him when she saw him standing in the opening, on a narrow metal ledge between the two cars. "Grab my hand."

She stared in terror as Jonah reached out for her. The thought of letting go of the metal railing only made her tighten her grip. "I can't."

"Sure you can. The distance is only about a foot. Let go of the railing with your right hand and reach out for me. I'll do the rest."

She looked at him across the distance, trying to trust him. Her eyes pricked with tears, but she told herself they were only watering from the force of the wind whipping past. Tightening her grip with her left hand, she took a deep breath and let go of the railing. When Jonah's fingers closed strongly around hers, she let out a gasp of relief.

True to his word, the rest was easy. With Jonah's guidance, she managed to find firmer footing on the small platform between the two cars. When his arms closed around her, she leaned against him, burying her face against his chest.

"It's okay," Jonah said, speaking close to her ear so she could hear as he rubbed a soothing hand over her back. "You were very brave, Mallory. We're safe now."

She wished she could believe the part about being safe. As far as she could tell, they'd have to keep running forever. She lifted her head to look up at him.

"What happened back at the motel, Jonah?" She had to speak loudly so he could hear over the noise of the train. "How could Caruso's thug have found us so quickly? Do you think he followed your car?"

Jonah's gaze darkened with anger. "I suppose he might have gotten the license plate number, but I'm more inclined to believe you were right all along when you voiced your fears about the possibility of another dirty cop. Considering I've only spoken directly to Lieutenant Finley, I have no choice but to believe he's another dirty cop working for Caruso."

Mallory's heart sank. If Jonah was right, they were in serious trouble.

Jonah could barely speak, he was so angry. He'd been betrayed by his boss! Finley was the one he'd called when someone had sneaked into his hospital room. Finley was the one who had ordered him to go after Mallory. And that story about no cops being available to relieve him was probably nothing more than a lie. Finley wanted him to stay put so he could send someone out to set the motel on fire.

Looking back, he realized how easily he'd been duped. Why would a boss send an injured cop out to keep a potential witness safe? If he'd been using the brain God gave him instead of relying on his emotions, he might have figured out Finley's true motives a lot quicker.

Mallory tightened her arms around his waist, giving him a warm hug that he felt all the way to the depths of his soul. "I'm sorry, Jonah."

He was amazed and humbled that she was trying to comfort him when he was the one who'd nearly gotten her killed. If not for the black Lab barking his head off, they might have succumbed to smoke inhalation.

God was truly watching over them.

"Mallory, I'm the one who should be apologizing to you," he said. "I should have been suspicious of Finley from the beginning. I'm sorry."

"We're safe on a train headed—somewhere far away from the burning motel, so there's no reason to apologize. You saved my life, Jonah. Twice. Three times, if you count forcing me to jump the train."

The way she chose to put a positive spin on things was a personality quirk that surprised him. Time to take lessons from Mallory. This wasn't the time to wallow in self-pity about being duped by his boss. Mallory had made a good point about the train's destination—he had no clue where this train was headed. In the motel, when he'd first noticed the cargo train, he'd tried to do a search online to figure out where it was going. But the map wasn't any help. There were dozens of trains using the same tracks going in both directions. It was like looking at a freeway and trying to figure out where each car was going.

"Jonah, I can tell you're upset, and I wish you'd give yourself a break. Look how many miles we've already gone. The train is going at least fifteen or twenty miles per hour, right?" Once again, she sounded downright cheerful. "Your idea to jump the train was brilliant. We can ride for days if needed."

"Unfortunately, we can't afford to wait that long. It's going to be dark soon and we need to get off before we lose all light. Keep an eye out for small towns, something not too far from the tracks since we have to walk."

He felt her sigh. "You think the bad guys will be waiting for us at the end of the line, huh?"

"I think it's a risk I'm not willing to take." He made sure his tone was firm. No way was he allowing her to talk him out of this one.

"Okay. Well, then, what about that place over there?"

There were lights just up ahead. For a minute he hesitated, worried that this town might be too easy to find. But maybe Caruso's men would assume they'd ride longer. After all, there were likely plenty of other towns along the way.

"Okay," he agreed, loosening his grip on her so he could turn and face the opening. As he scanned the area, looking for the best place to jump, he could feel Mallory edging closer behind him. He angled backward, so she could hear him better. "Do you want to go first?"

"Not really." She sounded less than enthused by the idea.

"There's no easy way to get off the train, just like

there was no easy way to get on. You're going to hit the ground, so keep your muscles loose—don't tense up. Tuck your head and roll, going with the momentum instead of fighting against it. Understand?"

"Tuck and roll," she repeated faintly. "Got it."

He hated the way he kept putting her in danger but he had to stay focused on what needed to be done. Soon, very soon, he'd have her someplace safe. "Okay, watch me." For a moment he closed his eyes and prayed.

Please, Lord, keep us safe!

He opened his eyes and crouched low, so he was closer to the ground. Gauging the distance carefully, he sprang off the train like a broad jumper, trying to use his feet to break the force of impact on the ground before going limp and rolling, his momentum sending him through several rotations. As soon as he stopped, he jumped to his feet, sparing only a quick glance at his shirt. The open stitches in his incision weren't going to heal if he kept doing acrobatics like this. Trying to ignore the ache in his side, he searched for Mallory.

He heard her cry out before he saw her. She'd apparently jumped right after he did—he caught sight of her rolling across the grassy embankment.

"Mallory! Are you all right?" He ran to her and dropped to his knees. He quickly ran his hands over her arms and legs, hoping, praying she didn't have any broken bones.

"Lost—my—breath," she wheezed, as she stared up at the sky. "But I'm fine."

He dropped his chin to his chest. "Thank you, Lord," he murmured.

"Amen," Mallory added.

He jerked his head up to look at her. Was she poking fun at him? At God?

"Why are you looking at me like that?" she demanded. "I thought you were supposed to say *Amen* at the end of a prayer." She shifted uncomfortably and ran a shaky hand through her hair.

He nodded slowly. "Yes. You're right. But I thought you didn't believe in the power of prayer."

She shrugged and glanced away as if intensely interested in their surroundings. At least the open fields covered in high grass wouldn't make her claustrophobic the way the cornfields had. "Honestly, Jonah, I'm so confused right now, I'm not sure what I believe anymore. I find it hard to accept that simply believing in God will actually help us, yet on the other hand, every time Caruso seems to get close, we manage to get away, relatively unscathed. Are we just plain lucky? Or is God really watching over us, giving us strength?"

"God is really watching over us and giving us strength, Mallory. I promise if you open your heart and your mind, you'll be rewarded. And there's no risk to believing, right?"

"I'll try," she promised. She groaned a bit and then frowned as she staggered to her feet. "Hey, why does the town look farther away now than it did on the train?"

"Hopefully the walk won't be too bad." The town seemed farther away now that they were on solid ground. "If you're sure you're not hurt, we'd better get going. The earlier we check into the motel, the better."

"Why do you assume I'm hurt when you're the one recovering from surgery? Maybe you should take a look, make sure it's not bleeding."

"I'm sure it's fine." He glanced down and checked his dressing beneath his shirt, trying not to grimace at the dampness of blood. He was glad blood hadn't seeped onto his shirt since he didn't have a change of clothes. A bloody shirt might cause the motel clerk to become suspicious. "I'll get more gauze and tape tomorrow." In the big scheme of things, his injury was the least of his concerns.

Mallory gamely fell into step beside him. When their fingers brushed by accident, he curled his fingers into fists to keep himself from reaching for her hand, forcing himself to put more distance between them instead.

He might be stuck in the role of Mallory's protector, since he no longer trusted Finley—or anyone other than Gage for that matter—but he couldn't afford to get emotionally involved.

Not if he wanted to keep Mallory alive and safe from harm.

Mallory stifled a yawn as they made their way toward the lights of the town. The adrenaline rush from jumping off the train had faded, big-time. She was tired and sore, and worst of all, she was keenly aware of Jonah walking beside her.

Just a few hours earlier, she'd begged him to let her stay. Now she'd gotten her wish, but they were on the run again. How could they investigate Caruso if they had to keep running? They didn't even have Jonah's computer anymore.

Jonah was holding himself distant now, as if this mess were somehow her fault, rather than his boss's fault. But on the train, he'd held her in his arms and she'd felt safe with a man for the first time in her entire life. She could have stayed there longer. Forever.

She told herself to be grateful for what she had. At least he wasn't turning her over to some strange cop. And he was probably just as tired and sore, too. No doubt his wound was bleeding again. Maybe after they both got some rest, things would look better.

When they finally saw the neon sign for the motel, she wanted to weep with relief. She couldn't imagine sleeping outside with the bugs.

Jonah opened the door for her and then followed her inside. The desk clerk was an older, unshaven man with gray-streaked, greasy hair who leered at them as he chewed on the end of an unlit cigar. Jonah greeted him politely. "Good evening, my sister and I would like two connecting rooms, please."

"Your sister?" Cigar guy smirked, raking a rude gaze over her. "Yeah, sure. That'll cost you a hundred bucks."

Jonah smiled, as if he wasn't the least bit offended by the cigar guy's leering expression. "We'd like to spread the good word of God to all His people. Maybe you'll grant us a few minutes of your time?"

Cigar guy took a step back as if Jonah carried some sort of contagious disease. "Fine—ninety bucks, and don't bother trying to convert me, Preacher Man. Leave me alone. Got it?"

"Thanks for your kind generosity." Jonah handed over the cash and picked up the two room keys. "God be with you, sir."

The clerk's terse "Good night" ended the conversation.

She waited until they were safely outside. "I can't

believe you said that, Jonah. He almost refused to give us our rooms."

"It's a good cover, Mallory, and besides, I couldn't stand the way he was looking at you."

For a moment she was stunned speechless. She was dressed in a sweatshirt and jeans—why would the cigar guy notice her? Jonah's anger on her behalf humbled her. When was the last time a man had stood up for her honor?

Never.

When they found their rooms, Jonah unlocked her door and flipped on the light. She flashed him a warm smile. "Thanks, Jonah, for everything."

He stared into her eyes, and for a tense second, she thought he was about to kiss her, but he abruptly turned away. "Make sure your side of the connecting door is unlocked, okay?"

She tried to hide the deep stab of disappointment. She should be glad Jonah hadn't tried to kiss her. "Okay."

"Good night, Mallory." Jonah unlocked his room and disappeared inside, closing the door quickly behind him before she could say anything.

Mallory took advantage of the facilities, enjoying the hot water against her sore muscles. But when she finally crawled into bed, she stared at the ceiling, unable to sleep.

She should be exhausted after running from a fire, jumping on a train, jumping off a train and walking for what seemed like miles. But her mind continued to race.

Should she try to pray? She closed her eyes and murmured the childhood prayer her parents had taught her, but saying the words as an adult felt silly, so she simply recited the Lord's Prayer.

Sleep continued to elude her. Her stomach was painfully empty and she sat up, reaching for her purse. She had a couple dollars, and she remembered there'd been a vending machine just outside the small office.

Jonah wouldn't like knowing she'd left the room, but the vending machine wasn't that far and she'd never get any sleep if she didn't eat something.

She pulled on her clothes, grabbed her room key and her money, and eased out the door. The area was only partially lit, as a few of the bulbs in the overhead lights were burned out.

She padded silently down the sidewalk and stood in front of the vending machine, trying to decide between the chocolate-chip cookies or the peanut-butter crackers. Finally, she bought both, smoothing the wrinkles from her dollar bills before feeding them into the slot of the machine.

"Well, now, looky here," a deep, nasally voice drawled. She froze as the cigar-chewing desk clerk came up close, invading her personal space so that she shrank back against the vending machine, the unyielding metal frame hard against her back. "If it isn't the pretty little preacher's *sister.*"

The cigar stench lacing his breath made her gag and for a moment she couldn't breathe, couldn't move as horrible memories of her past crowded into her mind. She opened her mouth but couldn't seem to make a sound.

"Let's say we have a little fun, huh?" He reached out to grab her and a flash of anger helped fuel her fighting instincts.

She swept her arm up to block his hand, knocking his arm upward as she kicked the lower part of his stomach, her aim true.

Stunned by her attack, he doubled over, his eyes bulging and grunts of pain gurgling from his lips. When he didn't move, she grabbed her cookies and crackers from the bin of the vending machine and ran straight to her room.

There were several long seconds as she struggled to fit the key into the lock, but she managed to slip inside, locking the door securely behind her before she sank against the door frame, her whole body shaking with fear.

The entire incident had taken place with hardly any noise, since she hadn't managed to yell the way her Tae Kwon Do instructor had trained her to do. But at least she'd gotten away.

She couldn't believe cigar guy had come after her like that. She'd done nothing, *nothing* to provoke him.

For the first time in years, she was forced to consider the possibility that maybe she hadn't done anything to provoke the sexual assault she'd suffered back when she was seventeen, either. After he'd assaulted her, Garrett Mason, the captain of the football team, had accused her of flirting with him. Of coming on to him. He'd told her that everything was her fault. And that no one would believe otherwise.

But now she wasn't so sure. Maybe some men, like Garrett and cigar man, were just evil, no matter how a woman looked or acted.

Right now, she was grateful she'd escaped. She closed her eyes and prayed. *Thank You, Lord, for keeping me safe.*

Opening her eyes, she was startled to feel a sense of peace. And she couldn't help but wonder if God had brought Jonah into her life to prove there were good men out there.

SIX

Jonah didn't sleep well, mostly because he kept thinking about Finley's betrayal. There was no doubt in his mind that his boss was working with Anthony Caruso. Why hadn't he figured it out sooner? No doubt Finley's plan all along was to send Jonah to find Mallory, and then once he had, send someone else to kill them both.

A plan that had almost succeeded.

The only issue was the timing of the ski-mask guy's arrival on the scene. Ski-mask guy had shown up at the cabin before Jonah had arrived so how could Finley have known where Mallory was hiding? Jonah thought back, piecing together a timeline of events. He'd stopped for dinner at Rose's Café in town and had casually asked about Mallory's uncle's place. Josie, the chatty woman behind the counter, had clued him in on where to find it. Was it possible Caruso's guy was there in the café, too? Had ski-mask guy overheard Josie giving him directions? It was the only way he could have beaten Jonah out there.

He tried to fit the pieces of the puzzle together. The only scenario that made sense was that the guy in the ski mask had planned to kill Mallory first, and then to hunker down and wait for Jonah to arrive. Luckily, ski-mask guy had underestimated Mallory's intelligence, strength and determination, just like Kent Wasserman had.

Jonah was more thankful than ever that he'd arrived just before Mallory burst out from the woods.

The minute the sun lightened the sky, he showered and headed over to the small lobby. The cigar-chewing clerk was just coming on duty, and when he caught sight of Jonah, he scowled.

"Checkout time is 11:00," he growled in his deep nasal tone.

"Thanks for letting me know," Jonah said graciously. "But we're thinking of staying another day."

"We don't got any rooms for you, Preacher Man."

"Really?" Jonah wasn't sure what this guy's problem was, but he wasn't about to get into the fight cigar guy was trying to start. He was glad he had his gun tucked in the back of his waistband, just in case. "That's interesting, because the sign outside says there's a vacancy."

The clerk reached out and flipped a switch on the wall next to him. Instantly the NO VACANCY light flashed on. "Not anymore."

Jonah hid a flash of anger. This guy was lying through his teeth, obviously willing to give up two paying customers to get rid of them. But why? Just because he'd claimed they were here to spread the word of God? He forced a smile. "I see. Well, then, my sister and I will make sure we're checked out by eleven. God be with you, sir."

The clerk only grunted in response and focused his attention on the small TV behind the counter. Jonah took several bagels from the continental breakfast buffet along with small packages of cream cheese and plastic knives, and went back to his room. He tentatively knocked on the connecting door. "Mallory? Are you awake? I have bagels for breakfast."

After a long minute, she unlocked the door. "Good morning, Jonah," she greeted him. Her hair was damp and curly from her recent shower.

The way she swept her gaze over the room, avoiding looking directly at him, caused him to frown. "Is there something wrong, Mallory?"

"No. Why do you ask?" Her gaze went up and to the right, a sure sign she wasn't being entirely truthful. In all his years of police work, he was amazed at how often people looked up and to the right when they were lying.

In a way, he didn't blame her for not trusting him. After all, he'd almost let his boss kill her in the motel fire. "Are you hungry?" he asked, gesturing to the food he'd brought from the lobby. "Please, help yourself. And if you're thirsty, there's orange juice, too. I'm happy to go back."

She crossed over and picked up a bagel, spreading a thin layer of cream cheese before taking a healthy bite. "I wouldn't mind some orange juice. Um—is that same desk clerk from last night working?" she asked.

He stared at her, dead certain her idle question was anything but casual. "Mallory, what happened?"

She flashed him a quick glance, full of guilt. "I don't know what you mean," she hedged.

Ignoring the bagel and his grumbling stomach, he crossed over to her, gently taking her slim shoulders in his hands. "Mallory, look at me. I can tell something is wrong. Why won't you tell me what happened?"

After a long pause, she reluctantly met his gaze.

"Last night, I went out to get something to eat at the vending machine, and cigar guy tried to grab me, so I kicked him in the stomach." She flushed and looked away. "I'm not up to seeing him again, that's for sure."

Jonah tightened his grip on her shoulders, raking his gaze over her as if searching for signs of injury. "Are you all right?"

"I'm fine. I was quick enough that he didn't touch me." She twisted out of his grasp and took a step back.

A red haze covered his eyes and he was tempted to march back to confront cigar guy himself. No wonder he'd wanted them out—he knew Mallory could press assault charges against him. When Mallory sank into a chair, he struggled to remain calm as he faced her. "Why didn't you tell me?"

She stared at her half-eaten bagel. "There was no reason to bother you, Jonah. I told you, I can take care of myself. When he doubled over in pain, I ran back to my room. End of story."

Jonah knelt down beside her, forcing her to look at him. "The clerks have master keys to these rooms, Mallory. He might have come back to hurt you, or worse."

"I know," she said softly. "I actually thought of that, but he knew we had connecting rooms, remember? So after about an hour, I figured he was smart enough not to pursue anything further."

For a moment he closed his eyes, wishing he had the right to take Mallory into his arms, hold her close and never let go. But she was a key witness in his case, and he needed to remember that. Emotions had a way of clouding good judgment.

Besides, maybe she didn't want him holding her in his arms. Hadn't she faced cigar guy herself, without saying a word about it? If he hadn't pushed her for information, he still wouldn't have known what happened.

Which begged the question, what else hadn't Mallory told him?

Mallory looked down at Jonah's bowed head and resisted the urge to reach out and touch him. Last night, after she'd lain awake for over an hour, waiting for cigar man to come back, she'd wanted so badly to wake Jonah, seeking comfort. But she'd talked herself out of it.

She set her unfinished bagel aside, feeling slightly sick when she remembered what had transpired out at the vending machine. She felt bad Jonah was so upset about what had happened, but wasn't sure how to reassure him that it wasn't his fault.

"What can I do to earn your trust, Mallory?"

His question caught her off guard. "What do you mean? I trust you, Jonah. You're probably the only man in the world, aside from Gage, that I do trust."

He was slowly shaking his head. "No, you say that, Mallory, but deep down, you don't trust me. Be honest—you weren't going to say a word about what happened last night, were you? If I hadn't pushed the issue, you wouldn't have told me anything."

She let out a small sigh. "But that's not because I don't trust you, Jonah. I just didn't want to burden you with my problems. Especially when they aren't significant to solving our case."

"Listen carefully, Mallory. Everything that happens to you is important to me. *Everything.* I want you to promise me that you'll come to me no matter how insignificant you think your problem is. Promise?"

His obvious concern for her well-being warmed her heart. Looking into his chocolate-brown eyes, she couldn't refuse his request. "I promise."

"Good," he murmured, his gaze never wavering from hers. Once again, she had the sense he wanted to kiss her, but in an instant, the moment was gone. He rocked back on his heels and rose to his feet. He walked over to the small plate of bagels. "After we're finished with breakfast, we'll have to find some sort of transportation out of here."

"We're leaving?" She was surprised Jonah didn't want to stay another day.

Jonah swallowed his food before answering. "Cigar guy has no intention of renting us rooms for another night. After what you told me, there's no way I'd agree to stay anyway."

"But what sort of transportation are we going to find here, in a small town?"

"I don't know, but I'm convinced we'll find something."

That something ended up being a small motorcycle that was propped near the street with a crudely written for-sale sign taped to it. Mallory watched as Jonah spoke to the guy selling the bike, and then started it up, to make sure the thing worked.

"Are you crazy?" she said under her breath. "We're going to run out of cash."

"Don't worry. I'll ask Gage to wire us some. Besides, this is a great deal." The broad grin on his face made her want to roll her eyes.

What was that saying? Something about men and their toys? Honestly, he looked like a little kid on Christmas morning, grinning from ear to ear as he straddled the bike and plunked a helmet on his head. "Come on, it'll be fun."

His idea of fun was very different from hers, but she took the second helmet and put it on her head, tucking in her hair. When she was ready, she climbed on the small seat behind him. "Are you sure you know how to drive this thing?"

"Ye of little faith," he scoffed. "Hang on!" Jonah revved the motor and then took off down the street. She gasped when she slipped backward in the seat, and clung tightly to his waist.

As they sped out of town, she was reminded of how he'd held her in his arms as they had ridden the train.

This was just as nice, she decided, as she leaned against Jonah's strong back and lifted her face to the wind. For a short while, she could pretend they were simply out for a ride, enjoying being together as the miles flew by.

Jonah took several different highways, heading toward Chicago. He hadn't ridden a motorcycle since he and Gage were in high school, and he couldn't deny he was having fun.

And he was far too aware of Mallory's arms wrapped tightly around his waist.

Every two hours they had to stop for gas to fill the motorcycle's small fuel tank. But they soon crossed the state line into Illinois.

At the gas station, he broke a twenty to use for the tolls. When Mallory groaned under her breath as she climbed on the back of the bike, he decided he'd find a place to stay outside of Chicago.

"Just another hour," he promised.

This time, he chose a nicer motel, one that boasted a small business center, which meant they'd have some computer access. He was glad there wasn't a sleazy motel clerk behind the counter this time, as he asked for two connecting rooms.

"Is there a fee for using the internet on the lobby computer?" he asked as he signed in as Jonah Adams and paid cash for the two rooms.

"Nope, but I'll kick you off if I catch you surfing anything inappropriate," the clerk said.

"No problem," he said quickly. "I just want to catch up on the latest news, that's all."

"Would you mind if I buy a T-shirt from the mini-mart across the street?" Mallory asked. "I've been wearing this same sweatshirt for two days."

Jonah hesitated, not liking the thought of letting her out of his sight, even for an hour of shopping. But no one knew where they were, not even Gage. He decided to take the risk.

Jonah took out his wallet. "Here, buy some stuff for both of us and we'll wash these clothes in the laundry facilities. Get some more gauze and tape, too. And a disposable cell phone."

"Anything else?" she asked drily.

"No, that should cover it." He handed her the cash he had and was glad she didn't argue about taking it.

"I'll be back soon."

"Good. I'll be here on the computer, waiting for you." When Mallory turned to go, he had to stop himself from reaching out for her. Letting her walk away alone was difficult.

The first thing he did online was send Gage a quick

email, letting his buddy know they were safe but unavailable by phone. He'd left his cell behind when they'd escaped from the motel fire. Besides, he wouldn't use his old cell phone anyway, knowing Finley had the ability to track it down.

He quickly explained his suspicions about Finley to Gage and warned his buddy not to go to the police for anything regarding this case. Jonah was surprised when he received a return email from Gage within fifteen minutes. Gage offered to wire him some money and Jonah agreed, making the necessary arrangements.

Once he'd gotten that out of the way, Jonah started reviewing the *Chicago Tribune* headlines. He scanned all the articles that even remotely discussed politics, but didn't find much information on Anthony Caruso.

He typed in both Caruso's name along with Bernardo Salvatore's name and got a hit. A newspaper article from three months ago mentioned briefly how Caruso was eating dinner at Salvatore's newest restaurant.

Jonah frowned when the article mentioned how Caruso was escorting a young model named Claire Richmond. When he blew up the photograph, he was shocked to realize Claire Richmond was tall, slender and had blond hair and blue eyes, just like Mallory.

Did Mallory know about the other women in Caruso's life? Or had Caruso already broken up with Claire Richmond by the time he'd met Mallory?

Somehow, he doubted it. He decided to do another search with both Claire Richmond and Anthony Caruso's names linked together, and dozens of articles came up.

His opinion of Caruso wasn't getting any better, that was for sure.

Jonah found several photos of Claire and Anthony together at various outings, but none of them recent. All the photographs were taken three to four months ago. Grudgingly he was forced to admit that it was possible Caruso hadn't been two-timing Mallory.

Still, he found himself wanting to show Mallory what he'd found. Ridiculous, really, because he doubted Mallory had any secret feelings for the man who was trying to kill her.

Jonah glanced at his watch. Where was Mallory? She should be back by now. How long did it take to buy a few articles of clothing?

He was tempted to go out looking for her, but an article caught his eyes in his search list as he scrolled down a few.

Missing Model: Runaway? Or Foul Play?

Missing? His gut knotted as he clicked on the link. The date on the article was just a month ago. Right about the time Mallory claimed she and Anthony Caruso had started dating.

He leaned forward and began to read.

> Claire Richmond had everything going for her: a million-dollar contract with Sports International and a powerful, handsome state senator as an escort. But less than two months after her breakup with Anthony Caruso, Claire Richmond disappeared. Her friends say she was heartbroken when Anthony broke off their relationship, despite the way she'd always put on a brave front. But she

failed to show up for a photo shoot and was reported missing.

Now that she's been gone more than five weeks, the police are starting to wonder if Claire Richmond ran away from the spotlight and the endless questions about her broken relationship with the senator, or if her disappearance is the result of foul play.

The small hairs on the back of his neck lifted as he read the article twice, making sure he didn't miss anything.

This couldn't be a coincidence.

"Hey, I didn't think you'd still be here," Mallory said, as she came into the lobby.

He turned to look at her, noting she was wearing fresh clothes. The bright orange T-shirt and jeans were nothing fancy, but Mallory was beautiful no matter what she wore.

"I was getting worried," he admitted slowly.

"Silly. I was perfectly fine." She frowned as she glanced over his shoulder at the computer screen. "Who's that?"

For a split second, he considered not sharing what he'd found. But he'd asked for her trust, so he needed to offer the same. "You'd better sit down, Mallory."

The color drained from her cheeks.

He glanced over to make sure the clerk wasn't paying attention. Thankfully, she was on the phone taking a reservation. "This woman is Claire Richmond, a young model who happened to be dumped by Anthony Caruso just a few months ago. She's been missing for the past five weeks."

Mallory stared at the photo in shock. He waited as she quickly scanned the article.

He put his hand on hers. "Mallory, I think Caruso had something to do with her disappearance."

Mallory turned toward Jonah and opened her mouth to speak just as she began to faint.

SEVEN

Jonah reached out and caught Mallory, lowering her into the chair beside him. "She looks like me," she whispered.

"Not really," he murmured reassuringly, although he couldn't deny there was a resemblance. "This other woman only slightly looks like you. And that doesn't mean anything other than Caruso obviously prefers to date beautiful blondes."

Her gaze remained troubled. "I don't understand. Do you think it's possible she stumbled across proof that Anthony was involved in something illegal, just like I did?"

"I don't know," Jonah admitted. "If that's true, it doesn't make sense that he'd wait almost two months after the breakup to get rid of her." He looked up Claire Richmond's last known address and then deleted the cache before he shut down the computer. "Come on, we need to get back to our rooms."

He put a supporting arm around her waist as they headed outside. Mallory walked beside him as if she were lost in a fog, her gaze unfocused and her breathing shallow. Maybe he shouldn't have told her about Claire Richmond.

He unlocked the door to his room and she immediately sank into the closest seat. After unlocking the connecting door between their rooms, he hesitated in the doorway and glanced back at her. "You did buy the disposable cell phone, right?"

She nodded. Turning his attention back to her room, he spied the bags sitting on her bed, the disposable phone sitting right on top. He grabbed the phone and returned to his room. Using the phone-book map, he pinpointed Claire's address.

"Who are you calling?" Mallory asked. Her voice was stronger and she looked a little less as if she was going to throw up. He was reminded again how Mallory was much stronger than she looked.

"The Chicago P.D. I'm going to find out what district is handling Claire's case and then I'm going to chat with the detective in charge."

She shook her head slowly. "You really think her disappearance is related to the Jefferson Project?"

"Claire's disappearance might not be related directly to the Jefferson Project per se, but I do think Caruso had something to do with it. For all we know, he's involved with other illegal ventures. Claire could have stumbled across something incriminating, like you said." Or simply been in the wrong place at the wrong time. He stared down at the map of the city, where he'd made a star at the point of her address. "I just can't believe her disappearance is a coincidence. And since our leads are few and far between, I think we need to probe further."

"But the article didn't say anything about Caruso being a suspect," Mallory argued.

"No, it didn't, which is why I want to talk to the detective in charge. Could be that Caruso's a person of interest in the case but that they don't have any evidence against him. Or that he has some sort of ironclad alibi." Depressing thought, but highly likely—Caruso wasn't the type to do his own dirty work. Hadn't he proved that by sending thugs after Mallory? He flipped open the phone and dialed.

It took him almost ten minutes of being transferred from one department to the next before he finally reached Detective Nick Butler.

"Detective Butler? My name is Detective Jonah Stewart and I work in Milwaukee's district six. We have a missing-person case here, a woman by the name of Mallory Roth. She's a young blonde who happened to be dating Senator Caruso just before she disappeared. I noticed you have a similar case involving the disappearance of Claire Richmond, so I wanted to talk to you in person."

"Stewart?" Jonah could hear computer keys tapping in the background. "What's your badge number?"

Jonah rattled it off, even though the last thing he wanted was for Butler to call and validate his identity with Finley. "Look, before you call the district to prove I really am MPD, you need to know my life is in danger. At the moment, I'm working off-grid."

There was a short pause. "How quickly can you get to Chicago?" Butler asked.

"Forty minutes."

Butler wisely didn't bother asking for specifics about his location. "Okay, let's say we meet in an hour at the coffee shop across the street from my district. I won't make any calls yet but make sure you bring your badge."

"An hour," he repeated. "Thanks. I really appreciate this." He shut the phone with a satisfied snap.

"Did you have to give him my name?" Mallory asked with a frown. "I mean, don't you think it's going to make us look bad when we meet him?"

He slowly turned to face her, knowing she wasn't going to like what he was planning. "You're not coming, Mallory. The only way I can pull this off is if I convince Butler that I'm investigating a missing person whose disappearance could be linked to his case. I need him to share what he knows, cop to cop, and I'll have to give him some information in return while pretending I haven't found you yet."

Her gaze narrowed. "An hour ago, you didn't want me to go shopping alone, but now you're just going to ride off to Chicago by yourself?"

He went over to kneel beside her chair so they were at eye level. "Mallory, I know you're upset, and if I could bring you along, I would. But this is important. We need whatever information Butler has about Caruso."

"And what if he doesn't have any information? This could be nothing more than a wild-goose chase."

"It's possible, but I think the Chicago P.D. has at least considered him a suspect at one point or another. So I can guarantee this trip won't be a waste of time. Just stay here and stay safe, okay? Please? For me?"

She let out her breath in a heavy sigh. "It's not like I have much of a choice, right?"

"I'll be back as soon as possible." Before he could stop himself, he pulled her into his arms in a quick hug. Once he realized he'd crossed the line, he hastily let her go and stood. "Don't open the door to anyone but me," he said as he grabbed his helmet and keys.

He avoided her gaze, leaving the motel room before she could say anything more. He jammed his helmet onto his head, telling himself he was an idiot.

He couldn't afford to get close to Mallory on an emotional level.

But he was beginning to fear that he already had.

Mallory imagined she could still smell Jonah's scent clinging to her new T-shirt long after he was gone.

She buried her face in her hands. She'd wanted to stay in his arms, to revel in his tender strength. Tears pricked her eyes and the small sign of weakness was enough to spur her into action.

She bounded to her feet. She would not cry over a man. Any man. Even one as nice as Jonah.

Returning to her room, she busied herself with unpacking the rest of the items she'd purchased, putting everything away.

Except for the second disposable cell phone.

Refusing to feel guilty for not telling Jonah she'd purchased two—after all, she'd used her own money for the second phone—she sat on the edge of her bed and began to dial Alyssa's number. Alyssa must have replaced her phone by now. She left a message, hoping Alyssa would get it.

Unfortunately, Mallory didn't know Gage's number by memory.

She hated not knowing what was going on with her twin. Was Alyssa all finished with surgery? Had everything gone well? She and Jonah had spent so much time running away from danger she'd barely had time to think about Alyssa.

After jumping to her feet, Mallory began to pace. She wasn't going to sit here and do nothing while she waited for Jonah. There had to be something she could do to help.

Maybe she should try to remember more details about the night of the charity event at the Pfister Hotel. If only she knew more about the people Caruso spoke to on a regular basis. But he didn't have a lot of family, his parents were dead, and he was divorced from his first wife and didn't have kids. Or so he claimed.

Wait a minute, what about his first wife? Was it possible she knew something? And if so, was she still in the Chicago area?

Mallory headed back to the lobby but there was a short, balding man seated at the computer, printing his airline boarding pass. She crossed her arms and tapped her foot impatiently. When he finally finished, she swooped in on the computer.

She found searching for people's names online wasn't as easy as Jonah made it look. But after fifteen minutes, she found the full name of Anthony's first wife—Rachel Camille Simon, a thirty-six-year-old blonde who just happened to be the heiress to the Simon estate. Her father was George Simon, the founder of the Simon Corporation, which had several diverse interests from pharmaceuticals to insurance.

Further searching revealed Rachel Camille Simon was following in her father's footsteps, working her way up in the company. Her pulse skipped with excitement when she realized the Simon headquarters was only about twenty minutes from the motel.

She wanted to talk to Anthony's first wife, but the woman was second in command at a multibillion-dollar corporation. What was she going to do, waltz in and demand to speak directly to Rachel? She'd be lucky to get two steps into the building before the security guards hauled her out of there, kicking and screaming. No, she needed to figure out a way to contact Rachel first and somehow convince the woman to at least talk to her. But how?

She went back to her room, called the general number for the Simon Corporation and asked to speak to Rachel Simon's assistant. "And what is the nature of your call?" the woman asked.

"I'm sorry, but it's personal."

There was a long pause, and Mallory was afraid the woman was going to refuse to put her through, but then the next thing she knew another woman was answering the phone. "Good afternoon, Edith Goodman speaking. How may I direct your call?"

"Ms. Goodman, my name is Mallory Roth and I need to speak to Ms. Simon about a personal matter that involves her ex-husband, Senator Caruso."

"I'm sorry, but Ms. Simon doesn't speak to reporters." The woman's friendly tone had cooled considerably.

"Wait! Don't hang up. I promise I'm not a reporter. I'm from Milwaukee, and I'm in danger. I believe her ex-husband is trying to kill me."

This time, the pause was even longer. Mallory figured it was a fifty-fifty chance that she'd be passed off as some kook or put through to Rachel's office. Finally Edith said, "I'll take your name and number and let Ms. Simon decide whether or not she'll call you back."

The answer was better than what she'd hoped for. She quickly rattled off her name and her new cell-phone number. "Thank you, Ms. Goodman, very much."

Mallory sighed and stared down at the phone in her hand. In truth, contacting Caruso's first wife was a total long shot. For all she knew, Caruso hadn't even gone down the path of corruption until after his divorce. Rachel might tell her she was crazy to believe her ex-husband would hurt a fly.

She tossed the phone on the bed and raked her fingers through her hair. How long had Jonah been gone? She checked the small alarm clock and winced. Not long. He wouldn't be back for hours yet.

She turned on the television, switching channels until she found the news. When her phone rang twenty minutes later, she was so startled she almost fell off the bed.

Her heart pounding, she grabbed the phone and flipped it open. On the screen she could see the caller was using a blocked number. Hesitantly, she answered, "Hello?"

"Is this Mallory Roth?" a female voice asked.

"Yes." She closed her eyes and pumped her hand in the air. Caruso's ex had returned her call! "Thank you so much for calling me back, Ms. Simon. I know you're very busy, but I desperately need to talk to you."

"You told my assistant that you feared for your life. Is that true?"

"Yes, Ms. Simon. It's true. I believe Anthony Caruso has already sent two hit men to kill me and I'm afraid he won't stop until he's succeeded."

There was a brief pause. "All right, I'll make time to meet you. But I'm warning you, if this is some sort of trick, I'll bury you so deep in lawsuits you'll never get out."

Mallory was light-headed with relief. "Agreed. I promise I'm not a reporter. Where would you like to meet?"

"Crabapple Park, at the merry-go-round. It's located about five miles northeast of our corporate office."

Mallory scribbled down the directions. "Okay, I'll see you there in thirty minutes." She scooped her purse off the bed and ran out of the motel toward the office to request a taxi.

If Rachel Simon agreed to the meeting, that meant she knew something about how dangerous her ex-husband was. Rachel hadn't sounded too surprised to hear Mallory feared for her life. Mallory could only hope that her meeting was just as productive as Jonah's.

And that she'd beat him back to the motel. It wasn't until she was almost all the way to the park that she realized she should have left Jonah a note.

Jonah stared at the report detailing Claire Richmond's investigation as Nick Butler downed the last of his coffee. The Chicago detective was in his late thirties and reminded Jonah far too much of Drew. He finished the report and sighed. "Just as I figured—he has the perfect alibi."

"Yeah, we called every person on his list to validate his story," Butler agreed. "We're pretty certain he could be involved, but there's been no way to prove it."

"Would a second missing person help?" Jonah asked. He began to fold his copy of the report, as Butler had agreed that he could keep it.

"Depends on what information you've found in the

course of your investigation. We had to tiptoe around Caruso the first time, because he's a state senator."

"I'm afraid I don't have much," Jonah confessed. Sensing Nick's growing impatience with the one-sided flow of information, he decided to give him what he could. "But we believe Caruso may be involved in money laundering in addition to attempted murder. We have two dead men, Hugh Jefferson and Eric Holden, who were both huge financial contributors to Caruso's last campaign. We have reason to believe they were involved in the money-laundering scheme, too. In fact, we think Caruso was the man in charge."

"Really?" Nick Butler's eyes had brightened with the news.

"I'm afraid I don't have a lot more, other than what I have already told you. They had at least one dirty cop working for them, and all three died in a fire on Jefferson's yacht. Just a few days before they all died, Mallory Roth went missing."

Nick leaned closer. "Do you really think you have a dirty cop still working for Caruso?"

"Yeah, I do. I went searching for Mallory Roth and the only person I'd been in contact with was my boss. I told him I had found her, and suddenly our motel is set on fire, the doors locked from the outside." Jonah didn't even like thinking about how close they'd come to dying that night. "We made it out alive, but I've obviously cut off all communications with him."

"Dirty cops make me sick," Nick muttered with a scowl. "But you found Mallory Roth?"

"Yeah, but I want to keep that information low-key for now. At this point we only have her word against his." Jonah wrote his new cell-phone number on a napkin and pushed it across the table. "If you find out anything else, will you call me? And I'll keep you in the loop of my investigation, too."

"Sure thing." Butler stuffed the napkin in the front pocket of his shirt. "I wish you luck, Stewart. If we're both right, Caruso's a slippery one. It's not going to be easy to take him down."

"I know." Jonah rose to his feet and held out his hand. "Take care."

Jonah straddled his motorcycle and started the engine. He hoped the traffic wasn't too bad—he was sure Mallory wouldn't be happy that he was gone so long.

But the trip hadn't been a total waste. For one thing, Nick had confirmed his suspicions that they'd considered Caruso a possible suspect. And that Caruso had been out of town in Washington D.C. during the twenty-four-hour time frame when Claire had disappeared.

So while he didn't find out a lot of new information, he felt as if they were on the right track.

He made good time getting back to the motel. As he drove into the parking space right in front of their rooms, he frowned when he noticed Mallory's window was dark. He could just make out the flickering light from the TV.

After parking his bike, he opened his door and pulled off his helmet as he strode to the open doorway between their rooms. "Mallory?"

No answer. He flipped on a light so he could see, even though it wasn't quite dark outside yet. He poked his head in the bathroom. No sign of Mallory.

He stood in the middle of the room, sweeping his gaze over her belongings. The bags from her recent purchases were still scattered on her bed, but her purse was gone.

Helpless panic surged. Where was she? Had she left on her own? Or had Caruso found her after all?

He never should have left her alone. Never.

EIGHT

Mallory's taxi driver dropped her off outside of Crabapple Park. She tipped him and asked for his card so she could call him when she was finished. Trying to look carefree, she ambled through the park, circling the merry-go-round twice before a woman dressed casually in jeans and a pink hoodie sweatshirt approached. "Are you Mallory Roth?"

Her heart sank as she turned to face the woman. She had blonde hair, but wasn't dressed in the corporate suit she'd expect of a VP. Rachel Simon must have sent someone in her place. "Yes, I'm Mallory."

There was a slight hesitation before the woman formally held out her hand. "I'm Rachel Simon. I believe you wanted to speak with me?"

Mallory stared at her for a moment, not sure if this woman was really Rachel or if this was some trick. "I'm sorry, but do you have your ID handy?"

There was a flash of annoyance, but Rachel obliged her. "I changed my clothes in case I was followed."

Looking past the clothes, the woman did resemble the photo on the internet, so she decided to trust her. "I would like to speak with you. Could we sit down?"

"Of course." Rachel Simon led the way over to an isolated park bench. She sat down at an angle so they could see each other as they spoke.

Now that she was face-to-face with Caruso's ex-wife, Mallory wasn't sure where to begin. She wished she'd waited for Jonah. What on earth made her think she could play detective? "I'm sorry, but I don't know where to begin."

"Why don't you start by telling me why Anthony wants to kill you?" Rachel bluntly asked.

Okay, then. "Because I overheard him discussing how to cover up a murder," Mallory admitted. "I was hoping you could explain why you divorced him."

Rachel shrugged and glanced away. "Suffice it to say we didn't want the same things out of life."

Mallory narrowed her gaze, her mind racing. Clearly Caruso's ex wasn't going to give him up easily. "Look, Ms. Simon, I'm in trouble. Caruso has already tried to frame me for murder, and he'll keep trying to kill me if I can't come up with some proof to use against him in court. Proof that he's involved in something illegal. So let's be honest with each other, okay? Did you divorce him because of his involvement with money laundering?"

"Money laundering?" The surprise in Rachel's dark eyes was all too real. She shook her head. "No, he must have gotten involved with that after we went our separate ways. Although I honestly can't say that I'm surprised."

A flicker of hope made her lean forward eagerly. "Why aren't you surprised? Did you discover other illegal activities he was involved in?"

There was a long silence as Rachel Simon stared

down at her clasped hands. "Yes, you could say that," she finally admitted. "I discovered that some of the high-powered supporters of his campaign had connections with organized crime. When I confronted Anthony, he laughed and told me to mind my own business."

"Did he try to hurt you?" Mallory asked, suspecting there was far more to the story than Rachel was letting on.

"I was afraid he might, so I went to my father's lawyer, who helped me put together an agreement that Anthony couldn't refuse. I'd stay silent about what I'd discovered if he'd grant me a divorce. Anthony wisely agreed to the terms."

The flicker of hope died. "So you can't help me."

Rachel smoothed out a wrinkle in her jeans. "I've kept silent all these years but after that woman disappeared, I began to wonder if it was worth it."

"You mean Claire Richmond?"

Rachel nodded. "One day, her body will be found but there won't be a shred of evidence linking her death to Anthony." Her tone was full of bitterness.

"How do you know he's involved?" Mallory asked. "I mean, suspecting him is one thing, but you would have had to see something to know for certain."

"I know because Anthony told me." Rachel lifted her head and looked Mallory straight in the eye. "Once the media picked up on her disappearance, I received a bouquet of red roses. The card read, 'If you ever break your promise, the same thing will happen to you and those you love.'"

Mallory sucked in a harsh breath. "He threatened you?"

"Oh, yes, he threatened me. And I believe him." Rachel stared over at the merry-go-round, where kids were squealing with joy. "Marrying Anthony Caruso was the biggest mistake I've ever made in my life. And even though we're divorced, I'll never be free of him. *Never.*"

"That's not true," Mallory said as she reached over to lightly clasp Rachel's arm. "You can be free of him. All we need to do is to find enough proof to get Caruso arrested. You need to work with us on this."

"Us?" Rachel tore her arm away and jumped to her feet, her accusing gaze harsh. "I thought you were alone. You didn't say anything about working with someone else."

Recognizing the stark fear in Rachel's eyes, she held out her hand in an effort to calm her down as she slowly rose to her feet. "I was saved from Caruso's thug by a Milwaukee police detective named Jonah Stewart. But he's not here now, and he doesn't know I'm meeting with you. I promise you, he doesn't know I'm here."

"I shouldn't have come," Rachel muttered, running a hand through her hair. "I'm sorry, but I can't help you."

"Wait! Please don't go. Don't you realize there's strength in numbers? Maybe you and I can't take Caruso down by ourselves, but together we can do this."

But Rachel was already shaking her head. "You don't understand. We have a nine-year-old son, Joey. Even if I wanted to help you, I couldn't. I'd never risk anything happening to my son. I'm afraid you'll have to find your evidence against Anthony without me."

"But—" Mallory watched helplessly as Rachel turned and began walking away. "Please, don't go!"

Abruptly, Rachel stopped and turned back to face Mallory. "Whatever you decide to do, be careful. Anthony is ruthless. You were right when you said he'd keep after you until he succeeded. He is not a man to mess with. But know this—if you repeat any part of this conversation to the authorities, I'll deny every word. I have staff members who will testify that I've been in a meeting with them during this exact time frame."

Mallory's shoulders slumped with dejection. Rachel might have agreed to meet with her out of pity, but she wasn't going to allow herself to become involved. And after learning about her son, Mallory couldn't really blame her.

Anthony hadn't told her about his son.

"I understand, Rachel. But please, if you change your mind, call me. You have my number, right? I promise we would do everything possible to keep you and your son safe."

"Don't hold your breath," Rachel advised before she turned and walked away.

Mallory let her go, her stomach knotted with despair. She'd probably blown the one chance they had to get the proof they needed to take down Caruso. And there was nothing she could do about it, except go back and tell Jonah what happened.

And hope he could find a way to forgive her.

The lights were blazing from her room as well as Jonah's when the taxi driver let her out in front of the hotel. For a moment she was tempted to jump back in to go somewhere else—anywhere but here.

Reminding herself she wasn't a coward, she paid the driver and then used her key to open the door. The minute she entered the room, Jonah came rushing through the open connecting doors, his eyes wild. “Are you okay? What happened? Where have you been?”

Knowing he was worried about her safety made her feel even worse. “I’m fine,” she hastened to reassure him. “I’m sorry I forgot to leave a note.”

Jonah raked a gaze over her, as if to check that she was really okay, before he crossed his arms about his chest and glared at her. “You shouldn’t have gone anywhere at all. What part of *being safe* don’t you understand, Mallory? Do you have any idea what I’ve been going through?”

“I already apologized,” she reminded him, keeping her tone even with an effort. “And yelling at me isn’t going to change what happened. If it makes you feel any better, I know I was wrong. And I won’t make the same mistake again.”

“What happened? You look upset.” Instantly, his anger turned to concern.

She dropped into a chair and sighed. “I went to meet with Caruso’s ex-wife. She knows he’s involved with something illegal, but she won’t help us.”

Jonah couldn’t have looked any more flabbergasted. “Caruso’s ex-wife? I didn’t even know he had an ex-wife!”

“He happened to mention his divorce, shortly after we first met,” she admitted. “And they’ve been divorced for a long time, almost ten years. Apparently she promised to keep his secret if he granted her a divorce.”

“And you expect me to believe Caruso went along with it?” Jonah scoffed. “I doubt it. He’d just silence her the way he has silenced everyone else who crossed him.”

“Her family is wealthy and powerful. He probably knew their word would carry a lot of credibility.”

Jonah stared at her for a long moment. "What's her name?"

"Rachel Camille Simon. And before you think you can leverage her cooperation where I failed, you should probably know they have a son. And she's convinced Caruso would kill his own son if he even suspected she broke her promise." When Jonah scrubbed his hands over his face, she knew just how he felt. Her clue had only led them to a dead end. "So, how did your meeting with the Chicago P.D. go?"

"About as good as yours," he said drily. "They have suspicions that Caruso is involved in Claire's disappearance, but no proof."

"So what should we do now?"

Jonah sighed. "I say we go out for dinner."

"Dinner?" she echoed incredulously. "That's it? We just go out for dinner?"

"We're going to eat at Salvatore's restaurant, in downtown Chicago. It's the only other link we have to Caruso at this point. And besides, I'm hungry."

Jonah's pulse still hadn't settled down by the time they'd arrived at the restaurant. He couldn't believe Mallory had actually gone off to talk to Caruso's ex-wife without telling him. Or waiting for him.

"Oh, look, outside seating." Mallory pulled off her helmet and ran her fingers through her hair. "It's a beautiful night."

"Actually, I'd rather sit inside. It's our best chance to find out something about the owner himself, Bernardo Salvatore," he said.

She shrugged but didn't say anything more as they walked inside. Thankfully, the place wasn't too fancy, although the food smelled heavenly. "This way," the hostess said in a soft Sicilian accent.

"Does Mr. Salvatore himself ever eat here?" Jonah asked as she stood by a small table for two and waited for them to take their seats. "I would love to meet him sometime."

The hostess's expression remained neutral, although he sensed she wasn't entirely pleased by his question. "Mr. Salvatore is very busy, but yes, he does occasionally stop in for dinner, although he prefers to be left alone." She quickly went on to describe the specials for the evening, and Jonah couldn't help but find her reaction curious.

Once the hostess left, Mallory leaned forward. "That was a little strange," she whispered. "I got the impression she was warning us off."

"Yeah, I know." Jonah glanced at the menu, wincing a little at the prices. They were getting low on cash. Even though Gage had agreed to get him more, he couldn't help wondering if this was a bad idea. What could they learn from eating here? He considered getting up to leave, but decided that would only fuel any suspicions the hostess already had. "What would you like to eat?"

"Spaghetti and meatballs," Mallory said, picking one of the cheaper items on the menu. "I'm in the mood for comfort food."

"Sounds good."

The server came by and introduced herself as Kate. She was young, blonde and slender, reminding him a bit of Claire Richmond. After she took their order, he flashed a warm smile and went with his gut. "Did you know Claire Richmond? She's an old friend of ours.

She used to work here, right? Before she landed her big modeling contract?"

Kate's bright smile dimmed and a hint of alarm flashed in her eyes. "Uh, no, I didn't know Claire."

"But she used to work here, didn't she?" he persisted, instinctively knowing he was on the right track.

Her gaze was a bit uncertain, as if she wasn't sure what to say, but then she shook her head. "I don't know. Excuse me but I need to place your order with the kitchen." The waitress couldn't get away from their table fast enough.

"How did you know Claire Richmond worked here?" Mallory asked in a low voice.

He shrugged and grinned wryly. "Lucky guess. Where else would a twenty-one-year-old meet a man like Caruso? And land a big modeling contract?"

"She looked scared," Mallory murmured, staring at the door Kate had disappeared through. "Maybe you should have told her you're a cop."

Jonah knew that sometimes people were more likely to open up to someone outside of law enforcement. "I'd rather pretend to be a concerned friend of the family."

Their dinner arrived in record time, and Jonah tried to catch the gaze of the young man who brought their food, but he simply dropped the plates and left. No one stopped by to offer freshly grated Parmesan cheese or ask how their meal was, which he also found very peculiar. Apparently, the management at Salvatore's was anxious to get rid of them because he'd asked too many questions.

Kate didn't return until they'd finished their meal. "Hope everything was all right. Are you interested in dessert?"

He looked at Mallory, who shook her head. "No thanks. Just the check, please."

"Certainly." Kate's perky smile and cheerful attitude were back in place, as if nothing had transpired earlier. But when she brought over the vinyl case holding their bill, she leaned close. "Abby knew Claire—she'll be outside," she whispered, before adding at a normal volume, "You can pay me whenever you're ready. Thanks for dining with us this evening."

"We enjoyed our meal, didn't we, honey?" he asked, beaming at Mallory like a devoted boyfriend. He placed cash in the vinyl folder and pushed it toward Kate.

"Absolutely." Mallory played along. "I'm so thrilled they're opening up a Salvatore's at home, aren't you?"

He quickly nodded. "Can't wait."

"Thanks again," Kate said as she walked away.

He stood and placed his hand against Mallory's back as she led the way outside. There were swarms of people crowding the sidewalks, so he stepped up against the building, glancing around for someone who apparently was willing to talk to them.

"Over there," Mallory murmured, nudging him. "She's staring at us."

Sure enough, a young brunette was standing across the street, smoking a cigarette and trying to catch their attention. "Let's go," he said to Mallory.

Mallory took his arm as they walked toward the waitress, keeping up the pretense of being out on a date. "Abby?" she asked as they approached.

The brunette crushed out the cigarette. "Next time, use a little finesse. We don't talk about Claire in the restaurant. Ever."

"I'm sorry," he apologized quickly. "I should have

been more subtle. We're just very anxious to find our friend. When was the last time you spoke to her?"

She gave him a disgusted look. "Drop the act. You're obviously a cop. I can spot one a mile away. I don't know what you think you're doing, but Claire is gone and she's never coming back. I spoke to her the night before she disappeared. Her plan was to go to the police with what she knew and then cash in the expensive jewelry he'd given her to relocate somewhere else, but then she was gone. Poof. Vanished. As if she'd never been here."

He couldn't believe she was telling them all this. "How do you know she didn't disappear on her own?"

"Because she was going to wait until after the weekend, since Friday and Saturday night are the highest-paying shifts." Abby looked at Jonah as if he were stupid.

That didn't make sense. "Why would she need to wait tables? I thought she had a big modeling contract."

Abby glanced away and shrugged. "She didn't think modeling was going to work out long-term."

Interesting. Had Caruso threatened to take the contract away?

"Did she say exactly what she wanted to say to the police?"

"No. And I didn't ask."

"Have you mentioned at least this much to the police?" Mallory piped up. "Do they know she was going to come to talk to them?"

"Yeah, right." Abby let out a harsh laugh. "You don't cross Salvatore or any of his friends. I need my job so don't ever come into the restaurant asking about Claire again. Understand? It's not exactly healthy, if you know what I mean."

Before he could thank her, she disappeared into the crowd of pedestrians.

"I don't like this, Jonah," Mallory murmured. "They're all so scared."

"She didn't give us much information. She never mentioned Caruso's name—she only referred to Salvatore's friends." He tried to ignore the surge of hopelessness. All of their leads were just dead ends.

"I hope we didn't cause either Abby or Kate any trouble," Mallory said as they walked back toward the motorcycle. "Do you think the hostess overheard us asking about Claire?"

"I don't think so. She looked pretty busy." But he wouldn't put it past a guy like Salvatore to bug the place. Something he should have considered sooner.

He put on his helmet and straddled the bike, waiting for Mallory to climb on behind him. She wrapped her arms around his waist and he vowed once again to find some other form of transportation. Being so close to Mallory was driving him crazy. He not only admired her, but genuinely liked her, far more than he should.

As he headed down the street, the front wheel on the bike shimmied a bit. He hoped it was nothing serious—the motorcycle was their only means of transportation. Concerned, he bypassed the freeway to take side streets, trying to avoid the more congested downtown area. When he found one that was less busy, he kicked the bike into the next gear.

The handlebars jerked hard in his hands, and he realized the front tire was loose. He tightened his grip, desperate to maintain control. "Mallory, jump off before we crash."

He felt her push away at the exact moment the tire flew off, sending him airborne. He hit the pavement with enough force to rattle his teeth and had only one thought before he slipped into unconsciousness.

Mallory.

NINE

Mallory screamed as she let go of Jonah's waist to jump free. She hit the ground with a hard thud, thankfully landing on the small grassy median before rolling onto the concrete.

Pain reverberated through her body and she lay flat on her back, staring up at the star-laden sky through her helmet while struggling to breathe. This tuck-and-roll thing was getting old. She decided right then she wasn't going to do it anymore.

Unlike the night she and Jonah had jumped off the train, he didn't come rushing over to see how she was. He'd stayed on the motorcycle until the last possible minute to save her. When she could breathe, she forced herself to sit upright, sucking in a harsh breath as her muscles protested. She tested her limbs, silently acknowledging that the aches and pains weren't anything too serious. Thankfully, her new hoodie and jeans had protected her skin. She took off her helmet, the crack in the side proof that it had saved her from a far more serious injury.

"Jonah?" She swept a gaze over the area, almost missing him, as he was lying in a crumpled heap at the side of the road beneath the back end of the motorcycle. Panic stabbed deep when she realized he wasn't moving.

"Jonah!" She stumbled to her feet and rushed over. With herculean strength, she lifted the bike off and then knelt beside him. "Jonah? Can you hear me?"

He didn't move for several long seconds. Then suddenly he groaned and turned onto his back. His right arm was literally covered in blood and dirt from the road. The sight was enough to leave her feeling sick and dizzy. She quickly averted her gaze, putting a hand to her stomach.

For a moment she closed her eyes, feeling helpless. *Lord, give me the strength to help Jonah.* She took several deep breaths and opened her eyes. The nausea had receded to a manageable level. Feeling more secure in her ability to help, she loosened the strap of his helmet and wiggled it off. She pulled open her purse in order to search for her cell phone.

"Mallory?" His hoarse whisper caused an overwhelming rush of relief.

"Are you hurt?" she asked, trying not to look at his bloody arm. His injuries were likely far beyond her capabilities. Her fingers closed around the small cell phone. "Stay right where you are—I'll call 9-1-1."

"No. Don't. I'm fine." Despite his assurance, he winced and groaned when she helped him to sit up. "Just give me a minute."

"Hey, are you two okay?" A middle-aged bald guy, as round as he was tall, had opened his front door to call out to them. "Don't worry, I've called 9-1-1!"

Jonah sighed heavily. "It's okay," he called out. "We're fine. Don't need an ambulance."

"I think it's too late for that," she muttered under her

breath when the man threw them a surprised look and then stepped back to shut his door. "Besides, it's best that you get checked out by a doctor, Jonah. That arm of yours looks pretty bad." So bad, she could barely look at it.

"Not an option." The firmness was back in his tone, and despite his injuries he struggled to stand. "We need to get out of here. But we obviously can't use the bike, so we'll have to call a cab."

She helped support his weight, placing her arm around his waist so he could lean on her. "We can catch a cab, but why are you being so stubborn about going to the hospital?"

"For one thing, there's still a warrant out for your arrest. And look at the bike for a minute." He lifted his chin in the direction of the seriously crumpled motorcycle. "See how the front tire came off the frame? That didn't happen by accident."

She stared in shock. "It didn't?"

"No. There was a little shimmy once we got on, and I should have stopped right then and there to investigate. I knew the tire was going to come flying off, which is why I wanted you to jump. Someone tampered with the motorcycle on purpose because we asked questions about Claire Richmond."

She swallowed hard, not wanting to believe him. But she couldn't deny how scared that waitress had looked when they'd gone out to talk to her.

She shivered, and not because of the cold. Was it really possible someone had just tried to kill them once again?

Jonah mentally kicked himself for not figuring out the bike had been tampered with sooner. Idiot. He should have known, or at least anticipated the possibility, especially after the way everyone at the restaurant acted so weird the minute he'd asked about Claire. Even Abby had tried to warn them.

Mallory looked scared, adding to his guilt. He put more weight on his right leg, relieved when the pain wasn't too bad. His right side had taken the brunt of the crash, but he didn't think he had any broken bones except for maybe a cracked rib—the right side of his chest felt as if it was on fire.

Thank You, Lord. Thank You for keeping us safe!

"I'll call a cab," Mallory said as she opened up her phone.

He put his hand over it, stopping her. "Not yet. Let's walk for a while first. I want to get away from here. The last thing we need is to answer a bunch of questions when the ambulance arrives. And besides, there's a good chance the police will be sent, as well."

"What about the motorcycle? Are you just going to leave it here?"

"I don't have a choice. Help me pull it off the road." He hated discovering he was more shaken up than he thought—it took both of them working together to drag the bike up over the curb. As they started down the road, he heard the wail of sirens growing louder and louder. A sense of urgency hit hard, there wasn't a moment to waste. "Come on, Mallory, we need to step on it."

"Maybe you should go to the hospital without me," she protested, even though she picked up her pace.

If he remembered correctly, there was a small strip mall just around the next corner. He tried to ignore the pain in order to walk faster. "Salvatore seems to have a far reach, and I'm convinced he could find me at the hospital, if he really wanted to." As they reached the corner, he gave Mallory a nudge. "Take a left—we're going to head back to the main road."

She didn't argue, for which he was extremely grateful. Every breath he took caused a stabbing pain in the right side of his chest. He tried to keep his breathing shallow, but that only made him light-headed.

Finally they reached the strip mall. And just in time. The lights from the ambulance raced toward them, and he quickly pulled Mallory into a doorway for a used bookstore. He wrapped his arms around her and buried his face in her hair. Her scent instantly filled his head.

She clung to him tightly as the ambulance rushed past. Even after it was long gone, he didn't move. Holding Mallory like this felt good. Felt right. And for a brief moment he wished things could be different and that she wasn't a potential witness he had to keep safe but that the two of them were just a couple on a date rather than on the run.

Mallory shifted in his arms, and he forced himself to loosen his grip. She lifted her head to look up at him but he couldn't tear his gaze away from her mouth. Before he could talk himself out of it, he lowered his head to capture her lips in a tender kiss.

Instantly she melted against him and his brain ceased all rational thought. He lost himself in the sweetness of her kiss until the shrill sound of sirens once again filled the air.

Reluctantly, he broke it off, breathing hard and looking over Mallory's shoulder as a cop car went whizzing past. It slowed in order to turn the corner, following the path the ambulance had taken to the scene of the crash.

Just as he'd suspected. "Let's go," he murmured, disentangling himself from the embrace. As much as he'd enjoyed the kiss, he knew full well he shouldn't have done it. Cops didn't do well with relationships. And getting emotionally involved with Mallory wasn't smart. He couldn't tolerate the thought of anything happening to her. If he wasn't careful, dividing his attention between her and finding the proof they needed just might get her killed.

They'd already had far too many close calls.

She stared at him for a second, as if she wanted to say something, but she simply turned away. Was she looking for an apology? He couldn't blame her if she was.

"Hey, there's a taxi," he said, catching sight of one slowing to a stop at the red light. "Come on, let's snag it."

Mallory surprised him when she put two fingers in her mouth and whistled loudly. He couldn't help grinning as she hurried ahead to catch the driver before he took off, leaving him to follow more slowly, holding his arm tight against his chest to minimize the pain.

It wasn't until they were both in the backseat that he allowed himself to relax.

They were safe for now. But they still didn't have any proof that Caruso was involved with anything illegal. And while it seemed Bernardo Salvatore was probably involved as well, chances were slim anyone would come forward to help them.

At this point, it was looking as if that proof they needed to clear Mallory might not exist.

Mallory huddled next to Jonah's warmth, trying to keep her teeth from chattering. Shock was beginning to sink in.

She wanted to go back to the brief moment when Jonah had held her in his arms and kissed her. She hadn't wanted to let him go.

But of course they couldn't just stand in the doorway of a used bookstore forever.

His kiss had surprised her but she told herself not to read too much into it. No doubt it had been a delayed reaction from surviving the motorcycle crash or just a tactic to divert attention. Besides, if Jonah knew the truth about her past, he'd likely run as fast as he could in the opposite direction.

She closed her eyes, wishing she could be the type of woman Jonah could love. But he deserved someone pure. Someone good. Someone like her sister, Alyssa. Not a fallen woman like her. Getting a tattoo under her collarbone wasn't the worst she'd done.

When the taxi driver pulled up to their hotel, she rummaged in her purse for the cash to pay the fare. It was telling that Jonah barely noticed, and she tried to hide her growing concern as she helped him from the back of the vehicle. He leaned against her, as if his strength was waning.

She opened her room door and flipped on lights as she helped Jonah to his room. He sank onto the edge of the bed, holding the right side of his chest. "I wish you'd go to the ER," she murmured. His right arm was still covered in blood and grit.

"I'm fine. Probably just a cracked rib. I'll feel better after I rest a bit."

A cracked rib? Her heart sank. She sighed, knowing there was no way to avoid the task at hand. She'd need to clean up his bloody arm. "I'll be right back with some water. Stay put."

“I think I can manage that.”

She took the plastic ice bucket into the bathroom and filled it with hot water. After tucking several washcloths and towels under her arm, she picked up the bucket and headed back to Jonah.

Hoping the spaghetti and meatballs she’d eaten for dinner stayed in her stomach where they belonged, she dunked the first washcloth in the warm water and glanced up at Jonah. “This is going to hurt,” she warned before gently placing the soft cloth over his bloody arm. Covering the blood helped minimize her nausea but when it came time to remove the cloth, her stomach lurched.

He held himself completely still as she worked on cleaning the blood and gravel from his wound. She imagined he was in pain and couldn’t bear to look into his eyes.

She doggedly kept at her task, emptying the ice bucket when the water became too red. As she worked, she grew relieved to discover the wound wasn’t as bad as it had originally seemed.

She lightly wrapped his arm with gauze, and once the open areas were covered, she began to relax. She risked a glance at Jonah, disconcerted to see he was staring at her. “Almost finished,” she murmured.

“Not bad for someone who claims she can’t stand the sight of blood.”

“Yeah, well, I think I’m starting to get used to it,” she responded drily. “But that doesn’t mean I want to keep bandaging you up like this. So let’s not make this a habit, hmm?”

“Mallory.” The sound of his husky voice saying her name made her shiver. Her hands stilled when he reached up to cup her face with his broad hand, his thumb lightly caressing her cheek. "I think you've been absolutely amazing through all of this."

She wanted to laugh and cry at the same time. He thought she was amazing? That was only because he didn't know the real Mallory Roth. She needed to tell him but the words strangled in her throat.

A smile tugged at the corner of his mouth. "Never thought I'd see the day when you were speechless."

She wanted to protest when he let his hand drop to his side. Finally, she found her voice. "Trust me, Jonah. I'm nothing special. I'm only doing what I have to."

His smile vanished and he looked almost angry. "Why do you keep doing that?" he demanded. When she stared at him blankly, he continued, "Every time I say something nice, you put yourself down. And there's no reason for it. You're a smart, beautiful, compassionate woman and whichever lowlife boyfriend told you otherwise needs his head examined."

His pop-psychological assessment was too close to the truth for comfort. She tore her gaze from his to concentrate on wrapping his arm. "Did it ever occur to you, Jonah, that you really don't know anything about me?"

"I know you, Mallory. I feel like I know the real you, not the person you've always pretended to be."

Avoiding his gaze, she rose to her feet and went back to the bathroom to empty the bucket. She wasn't used to people—men in particular—looking past the facade she presented to the world. Most men were satisfied with having her act as an arm decoration and nothing more. "I'll get some ibuprofen. I think you're going to need it."

She wasn't running away from him, she told herself as she rummaged through her things for the medication. She just wasn't comfortable with him being nice to her, that's all.

"Thanks," he murmured, as he took the pills she held out for him. He tossed them back and swallowed them dry.

"Yell out if you need anything, okay?" she said as she turned and walked back to her room.

"Only if you promise to stop putting yourself down," he said. "Otherwise I'll suffer in silence."

"Is that supposed to be a threat?" she asked, smiling in spite of herself. "Because if so, you could use more practice."

"Good night, Mallory."

"'Night, Jonah."

After everything that had happened, she would have thought she'd fall asleep the moment her head hit the pillow. But she kept hearing Jonah's words over and over in her head.

Did he really think she was smart, beautiful and compassionate?

Did he really know the true Mallory?

Why did that thought scare her more than anything else that had happened since she'd met Jonah Stewart?

Mallory spent a restless night, and she didn't even have cracked ribs to blame for her lack of sleep. As soon as the sun was up, she dragged herself out of bed. After a quick shower, she felt a little more human.

There was no sound coming from Jonah's room, so she decided to let him sleep while she went in search of some breakfast.

The motel lobby had a continental breakfast set out, so she helped herself to a bowl of Cheerios and half a bagel with cream cheese. A family of four left the room, leaving behind a newspaper, and she went over to their table, planning to read while she ate.

But the main headline splashed in big letters across the front page stopped her cold.

Woman's Body Pulled from Lake Michigan.

Overwhelmed with dread, she quickly read the article, fully expecting that the victim was Claire Richmond. But she was wrong. She had to read the sentence twice before the words could sink in.

The victim was identified as Abigail Del Grato, a young waitress who worked at Salvatore's. They were still waiting for the ME to determine cause of death, but there was bruising around her neck, indicating she may have been strangled.

Mallory let out a low sound, covering her face with her hands as she remembered the stark fear in Abby's eyes when they'd spoken about Claire.

Her stomach heaved, and she had to take several deep breaths. That poor frightened girl was dead. Because of them. The young waitress had died only because she'd talked to her and Jonah about Claire. She hadn't told them anything specific, but her killer hadn't known that.

Mallory wasn't sure just how much more of this she could take.

TEN

Jonah eased out of the bathroom, using the wall for support. His effort at showering was pretty useless as the physical exertion already had sweat beading on his brow. At least he'd managed to dress himself. Raising his arms up to pull a T-shirt over his head had almost made him pass out from pain. Too bad they were running low on cash or he'd ask Mallory to pick up some shirts that buttoned down the front.

He made his way across the room, feeling disgustingly weak. His open wound had started bleeding again. He kept forgetting to take the antibiotics and he was afraid infection may have already set in.

Gingerly, he lowered himself into a chair, holding his breath when pain shot through his chest. He couldn't figure out which hurt worse, having surgery or having a cracked rib.

At the moment, he would have said they were dead even.

"Jonah?" He glanced up in surprise when Mallory came barging through their connecting doors.

The alarm on her face made him jump back to his

feet, ignoring the stabbing pain. "What's wrong? What happened?"

"She's dead. Abby's dead!" She thrust the newspaper at him. "We killed her, Jonah. She's dead because she talked to us."

Dread twisted low in his belly as he recognized the name of the waitress who'd spoken to them outside Salvatore's. He took the newspaper, sank back into the chair and read through the article.

It didn't take long to realize Mallory was right.

He knew in his gut Abby'd been murdered because she had talked to them.

Knowing they hadn't forced her to talk to them didn't make him feel any better. He'd gone to Salvatore's restaurant on purpose. He'd poked the sleeping tiger with a stick, hoping for a reaction.

But he'd never anticipated something like this.

Dear Lord, forgive me. Please forgive me!

"What should we do, Jonah? Call the police?" Mallory's voice was thick with suppressed tears.

This time, he couldn't offer any comfort. Not when the acrid taste of bitterness coated his tongue. And especially not when the last time he'd held her in his arms, he'd been stupid enough to kiss her.

Feeling grim, he set the newspaper aside and scrubbed a hand over his jaw. "I'll call Detective Butler, the guy I met with yesterday."

"Maybe we should go back to Milwaukee." A small tear escaped from the corner of her eye, rolling down the side of her face. He resisted the urge to wipe it away. "I don't care if they arrest me for killing Wasserman. I can't do this anymore, Jonah. I just can't."

He didn't want to admit she might be right about

going back to Milwaukee. Abby's death proved the stakes in this game were high. Too high. He'd always known Caruso was playing for keeps, but he hadn't bargained for this. He couldn't bear knowing innocent people had already suffered as a result of their attempt to find proof against Caruso.

They needed help. Clearly, he couldn't break this case without assistance from someone within law enforcement. But he couldn't trust anyone within his district, either.

The only other contact he had was Rafe DeSilva, his buddy in the Coast Guard who'd helped him track Jefferson's yacht after Alyssa had been captured. Since he couldn't prove drugs were involved, and the crimes weren't taking place on the water, the Coast Guard didn't have any jurisdiction. But he hoped Rafe could get him in touch with someone who worked for the FBI.

At this point, he and Mallory needed all the help they could get. And then some.

Jonah made the call to Nick Butler, but the detective didn't answer so he left a terse voice-mail message asking for a return call. He was just about to call Rafe DeSilva when Mallory returned with a Styrofoam plate heaped with food.

"Please eat something, Jonah," Mallory urged, pushing the plate of food toward him. "You look pale."

"Thanks." He wasn't that hungry, but took a few bites of bagel because he knew he'd need his strength. He dialed Rafe's number, wincing at the early-morning hour.

Rafe sounded suspicious as he answered. "Yeah?"

"Rafe, Jonah Stewart calling. I'm sorry to wake you, but I really need your help."

"Do you have any idea what time it is, amigo?" Rafe demanded in his thick accent. "And this is my day off. I'm spending well-deserved time with my family."

"I'm sorry. But I promise this won't take long. I'm in trouble. Didn't you have a friend who left the DEA to work for the FBI?"

"Yes, Logan Quail. What do you need him for?"

"I have a problem and can't go to my boss. I need the Feds."

"I don't know if Logan will be able to help you. He's been on a special task force busting up organized crime."

Perfect. Logan Quail was exactly what he needed. His muscles relaxed as he realized he'd made the right call. "Yeah, well, organized crime is exactly why I need him. Can you give me his number?"

"Sure." Rafe rattled off the number while Jonah hastily scribbled it on motel stationery. "Is this about Hugh Jefferson by chance?"

"Yeah." He wasn't surprised Rafe connected the dots back to Jefferson. After all, they wouldn't have saved Alyssa and Gage without Rafe's help. They'd been forced to jump off the burning yacht, and Rafe's Coast Guard cutter had been there to pull them out of the water. "I'm trying to get evidence against the guy in charge of the whole money-laundering operation. Thanks, Rafe. Tell Kayla I'm sorry I disturbed you."

"No problem. Stay safe, my friend."

"I'll try." Jonah closed his cell phone and took another bite of his bagel.

"You're calling the FBI?" Mallory asked, her eyes wide. "Do you think they can help us?"

He shrugged. "I don't know for sure. The bureau likes to run things their way, and I'm not sure they'll believe your story. But it's possible this friend of Rafe's will help us off-grid."

"Off-grid? You mean unofficially?"

"Yeah. That's exactly what I mean." He stared at his phone for a minute before punching in the number Rafe had given him. He could only hope that calling Logan Quail wasn't another mistake.

Because if he put Mallory in danger one more time, he was never going to forgive himself.

Mallory wasn't sure she liked the idea of bringing more people into their investigation. Wasn't it bad enough that the one person who'd already talked to them was dead? She could remember, all too clearly, the stark fear in Caruso's ex-wife's eyes when they'd met at Crabapple Park. Too late now to undo any damage her impromptu request for a meeting might have done. She could only hope that Rachel Camille Simon and her son, Joey, would be safe.

The thought of anything happening to them made her feel sick to her stomach.

"Logan?" Jonah said into the phone. "Rafe DeSilva gave me your number. I need help bringing down the top guy in Jefferson's money-laundering scheme, but I don't want this information to go through the Fed's normal channels, at least not yet."

There was a pause while Jonah listened to the FBI agent. She leaned forward, trying to hear what was being said but she couldn't distinguish much except for the hint of a Southern drawl. Was it possible this Logan guy wasn't even close to them? For all they knew, he was down in Texas somewhere.

"I'm glad you're familiar with the Jefferson condo project. I also have some additional information you might find interesting but I don't want to go into everything now. I'm out here on my own and I need you to promise you won't bring the rest of your team into this until we have the proof we need."

There was another pause, shorter this time, giving her the impression Logan had indeed promised.

"That should work," Jonah agreed, glancing at his watch. "I'll figure out a way to get back to Milwaukee in the next four hours."

Four hours? What on earth was he talking about? She wasn't sure how they were going to get anywhere. And she doubted they had enough cash to take a taxi all the way back to Milwaukee.

The thought of going home filled her with a strange sense of dread. She hadn't been in her condo in almost a full week, yet it seemed more like a month. During those first few days at the cabin, she'd wanted nothing more than to go home. But that was then.

For some reason, she couldn't stand the idea of going back to her old job. Not that she minded her work—decorating was fun and she had an eye for color. But after everything that had happened over the past few days, she had a new perspective on life. Being an interior designer seemed so useless. A fluff job.

Truthfully, her entire life was useless. How much time had she wasted playing the role of someone she wasn't? Too much time. She was stunned to realize she wanted to do something more. Something important. But she couldn't be a nurse, like Alyssa. Or a cop, like Jonah.

Then what? She hated to admit she had no useful skills.

"Okay, thanks, Logan. See you later." Jonah snapped shut his disposable cell phone and finished off his bagel.

"You really think we can trust this guy?" she asked, dragging her mind back to the issue at hand.

"We don't have a choice. We can't do this without help, Mallory. You said so yourself. And if you remember, it was your idea to go back to Milwaukee."

Her thoughts were contradictory. Why was she so upset about getting more help? She should be glad they had another expert on their side, a federal agent no less. After all, it wasn't as if she'd been much help. "As long as Logan doesn't arrest me, I'll be fine."

"He won't." Jonah's phone rang and he looked down at the screen to see who was calling. "Detective Butler, thanks for calling me back. I need a favor. Will you give us a ride to the closest train station? I have some information to share on your latest floater."

She couldn't hear what the detective said on the other end of the phone, but he must have agreed because Jonah nodded. "We'll be ready. Thanks." He turned toward her. "Go and pack your stuff. Butler is going to be here in thirty minutes."

She crossed over to her room. There wasn't much to pack, aside from the new clothing she'd purchased. Since she had extra time, she went through her purse, cleaning out the junk she'd accumulated.

Way down at the bottom, she discovered a bracelet Caruso had given her in the first couple weeks of dating. She hadn't even remembered keeping it. She stared at the square-cut rubies and diamonds with distaste and seriously considered tossing the gaudy thing into the wastebasket.

But Abby's words from last night echoed in her mind. *She planned to go to the police with what she knew, and then cash in the expensive jewelry he'd bought her so she could start over someplace new.* Had Caruso given Claire jewelry the way he'd given Mallory this ruby-and-diamond bracelet?

"Mallory?" Jonah called from his room. "Are you ready?"

She dropped the bracelet back inside her purse, tugged its strap over her shoulder and picked up her bag. At the last minute, she added the Bible to her bag. "Yes. I'm ready."

There'd be plenty of time to get rid of the bracelet later. Besides, she thought, it was probably best not to leave anything too personal behind in the motel room anyway.

Jonah's coplike instincts were rubbing off on her. And so was his faith. She hadn't told him, but the few prayers she'd said had seemed to work so far. Maybe she was crazy for starting to believe, but she'd decided he was right when he'd told her believing in God couldn't hurt.

She murmured another quick prayer as she went out to join Jonah.

She didn't say much as Detective Butler drove them to the train station. She listened as Jonah explained what had happened the night before.

"Abby Del Grato actually said Claire was gone and wasn't coming back?" Detective Butler asked incredulously. "And that Claire was planning to go to the police with what she knew?"

Jonah nodded. "Yeah, but she didn't give us anything more. I'm convinced the reason she was killed was because someone caught her talking to us."

"Too bad she didn't come forward when we interviewed her along with the other employees." Butler sighed heavily before glancing at Jonah with suspicion. "And how did you know Claire used to work as a waitress at Salvatore's anyway? I didn't tell you that."

"It was a lucky guess on my part, but why didn't you tell me?" Jonah countered.

"I didn't even think about it." When Jonah didn't say anything, Butler shot him an exasperated glance. "Come on, you don't seriously think I withheld pertinent information on purpose?"

Mallory held her breath as the tension between the two of them rose to a palpable level. Maybe Jonah shouldn't have trusted the Chicago detective.

"I don't know what to think," Jonah finally muttered. "We spoke briefly to Abby outside the restaurant. And then our motorcycle was tampered with, causing us to crash. And we know Salvatore is a strong financial supporter of Caruso. So it just makes sense that this is all connected."

"Maybe Salvatore is the one who killed Claire, rather than Caruso," Mallory said, breaking into the conversation.

Both men swiveled around to stare at her. Detective Butler turned back to concentrate on the road, but she still had Jonah's attention. "What makes you say that?"

She shrugged. "I mean, we know Claire was dating Caruso, because there were pictures of them together, but she also worked at Salvatore's. Who knows why she was silenced? The fact that it happened a month after she and Caruso had broken up makes me think Salvatore is more likely to be the guilty one."

"You have a good point," Jonah agreed slowly. "Either way, it's obvious the cases are connected."

She thought so, too. When the detective pulled up to the train station, she gathered her belongings and opened the door.

"Thanks for the loan," Jonah was saying as Butler slipped him some cash. "I promise I'll pay you back."

"Don't worry about it." The detective waved him off. "Consider it payment for the help you've given me on this case. I think we're going to have to take another long look at Salvatore's business dealings, see if we can connect him to any other crimes."

"I'd like to stay in touch, if that's okay." Jonah shook hands with Butler.

"I'll count on it." With one last wave, the detective climbed back in his car and drove away.

Mallory followed Jonah inside the downtown train station, gazing around apprehensively. She'd taken the train to Chicago before, but her senses were hyperaware as she scanned the crowd of people milling about the station. After being on the run for so long, the crush of people was unnerving.

"At least this time we get to sit on proper seats," Jonah said as they prepared to board the train.

"True," she agreed with a small smile, remembering the cargo train.

As they settled in side by side, she pulled out the Bible and prepared to read. Just sitting and staring out the window would only drive her crazy.

"You took the Bible with you?" Jonah asked in surprise.

Warily, she nodded. "Is that a problem?" Stealing a Bible wasn't exactly a good way to connect with a God she wasn't completely sure she totally believed in, she guessed.

"Relax, Mallory. It's fine. The Bibles are there for people to take. I'm just surprised that you wanted to."

She didn't want to talk about the kernel of faith she was beginning to nurture. For one thing, it made her uncomfortable to talk about God and religion. For another, they were riding public transportation, where other people could hear them.

And while she liked reading the psalms and had murmured the occasional prayer, that didn't mean she was fully converted or anything. The last thing she wanted to do was to give Jonah the wrong impression.

Especially after that kiss.

"Here, try this one," Jonah said, taking the Bible from her hands and paging to a particular spot. "It's one of my favorites."

Glancing down, she realized he'd given her Psalm 23. She'd actually read it before, but this time, the words resonated in her soul.

"'Surely goodness and mercy shall follow me, all the days of my life, and I shall dwell in the house of the Lord forever,'" Jonah read softly.

His voice was mesmerizing. "I'd like to believe that's true," she murmured.

"Believe, Mallory," he urged. "Believe in God and it will be true."

His face was close to hers, so close she could see

the golden flecks circling the pupils of his eyes. She quickly averted her gaze.

Resolutely, she closed the book and put it back in her bag. "I'm a little tired. I think I'm going to rest for a while," she said.

She could feel disappointment radiating from him, but he didn't say a word. She wanted to tell Jonah the truth about her past, but couldn't think of a way to broach the subject. Talking about her feelings was never easy, and talking about faith was even harder, so she spent the rest of the ride thinking about Psalm 23 as she feigned sleep.

When the conductor announced the stop near the Milwaukee airport, Jonah nudged her. "Time to go, Mallory."

She rubbed her eyes and ran her fingers through her hair. She hadn't so much as touched makeup in days and knew she probably looked terrible. When the train came to a stop, she followed Jonah down the metal steps and through the crowd at the terminal.

"Do you have any idea what this Logan guy looks like?" she asked in a hushed tone.

"Yeah, I do." Jonah took her hand in his, drawing her out of the way of people trying to get past. She did her best to ignore the frisson of awareness at his touch. "Over there, the tall dude wearing a cowboy hat, frayed jeans and boots."

She saw Logan the minute Jonah described him, mostly because he stuck out like a sore thumb. He looked as if he'd ridden his horse into town for a rodeo. "I thought FBI agents all wore suits and ties," she whispered as they made their way toward him.

"Apparently not." Jonah held out his hand as the cowboy approached. “Hi there, thanks for meeting us. I’m Jonah and this is Mallory.”

“No problem.”

She thought it was odd that Logan didn’t offer his name.

“Let’s get out of here. I have a hotel room secured right across the street.”

Logan Quail had impeccable manners, opening doors for her and constantly calling her “ma’am.” She wanted to tell him to stop it—“ma’am” made her feel old.

It wasn’t until they were settled in a huge three-bedroom suite that Logan took off his hat, ran his fingers through his wheat-blond hair and faced them. “So, I hear you’ve gotten yourself in a bit of trouble.”

“Yeah, you could say that.” She listened as Jonah briefly summarized the events from the moment she’d run from Caruso to the latest victim being fished out of Lake Michigan. “We need proof that Caruso is dirty, but we don’t have anything solid,” Jonah finished. “Which is why we desperately need help.”

Logan didn’t say anything for a long minute. “Well, then, it’s a good thing Rafe sent you in my direction. Because we already have Salvatore in our crosshairs, but we didn’t know Senator Caruso might be involved. That bit of news takes the investigation to a whole new level.”

Hearing Logan actually believed them made her dizzy with relief. “I’m so glad,” she said, speaking up for the first time since Jonah had told their story. “Please tell us you have a plan.”

“Well, ma’am, now that you mention it, I do have a plan. But it’s risky.”

“I don’t care,” she said stubbornly, ignoring Jonah

when he began to shake his head, disagreeing with whatever Logan had planned. "And I think I already know what your plan is. You want me to call Caruso to set up a meeting with him, don't you?"

"No. No way. That's not happening," Jonah interrupted hotly.

"That's one idea," Logan said as if he hadn't heard Jonah. "But there are others to consider—"

"None as good as that one," she interrupted. "Let's go with what we think has the best chance of working." She held Logan's gaze, refusing to look at Jonah. He didn't understand that she needed to do this. Needed to end this nightmare once and for all.

Even if it meant putting her own life on the line to get it done.

ELEVEN

Jonah couldn't believe Mallory was making plans with Logan as if he weren't sitting right next to them. As if he weren't the cop leading this investigation.

Enough was enough.

"Listen up!" he yelled. Pain shot through his chest and he put a hand to his cracked rib as the two of them fell silent, staring at him in stunned surprise. He lowered his voice to a normal level. "Mallory is not going to call Caruso to set up a meeting, got it? There's no point when we don't have anything against him. He's too smart to talk in front of Mallory."

Logan's piercing green eyes seemed to look clear down into his soul. The agent might give the impression he was laid-back, but Jonah suspected his intense keen gaze didn't miss a thing.

And right now, he could tell Logan was wondering just how involved Jonah was with Mallory. An unspoken question he didn't want to answer.

Because he was already in too deep.

"If Salvatore was on your radar screen, Logan, then let's focus on him for the moment," he continued in a calmer tone. "Maybe once we have something solid against Salvatore, we can link him to Caruso."

"No," Mallory argued, the stubborn tilt to her chin all too familiar. He wanted to tear out his hair by the roots in frustration. "The last time we tried to investigate Salvatore, an innocent girl turned up dead. Caruso wants me—it makes more sense that we tap into him first."

Logan tipped back in his chair, glancing between the two of them with an amused expression on his face. "I'm not sure why y'all bothered to get in touch with me," he drawled in his exaggerated Southern accent. "Sounds like y'all got everything all figured out."

Jonah sighed and scrubbed his face with his hands, silently battling the pain in his chest. The thought of Mallory being in danger had made him forget momentarily about his cracked rib. He shouldn't have yelled, shouldn't have put up his arms. He took several slow deep breaths before speaking again. "You're right, Logan. Let's back up a minute. You mentioned Salvatore being on your radar screen. Rafe told me you're involved in a special task force investigating organized crime. Is there any way to link Salvatore to Abby's death?"

Logan dropped the chair back down on all four legs and leaned forward. "That's a good idea, Detective. I don't know what evidence they found on the girl because I've been in Chicago for the past few weeks. Only came up to Milwaukee today for a meeting with my boss."

"You're not going to call your boss, are you?" Mallory interjected in alarm.

"No, ma'am, I already gave you my word on that." For a second a flash of anger darkened the agent's eyes and Jonah realized that for all his cowboy charm, Logan wasn't a man to cross. "But as I was saying, we have a contact inside Salvatore's restaurant."

"Kate. Your contact is Kate, right?" Jonah asked.

Logan slowly nodded. "Yes, Kate Townsend. She called me last night, after the two of you left."

"Is she a cop, too? Was it Kate who convinced Abby to talk to us?" Mallory asked.

"No, ma'am," Logan said. "Kate isn't a cop yet. She's still in college studying criminal law. She contacted us when she first started working there, when she realized she'd stumbled into a haven for organized crime. We tried to convince her to quit, but she refused. She's been feeding us information ever since."

Jonah could tell Logan wasn't entirely thrilled with Kate being a source of information, but he also wasn't going to turn his back on whatever insights the young woman could gather. He remembered the pretty blonde waitress and had to admit the girl had guts. She was young—too young—to be putting her life in jeopardy like that.

"You need to get her out of there, Logan," Mallory said urgently, as if she'd read his thoughts.

"I've already made the call," Logan said slowly. "But she'd reported in for her shift tonight, so she's going to stick it out."

Jonah could see the stark fear in Mallory's eyes. "She needs to get out of there now," she urged. "She needs to walk away and never go back."

"Walking off the job in the middle of her shift would cause more suspicion," Jonah pointed out. "She's probably better off finishing."

Mallory still didn't look convinced. "But what if Bernardo Salvatore finds her after she quits?"

The flicker of fear in Logan's gaze was so brief, Jonah wondered if he'd imagined it. "Trust me, Mallory, we'll take care of Kate," Logan reassured her.

"What exactly did Kate tell you?" Jonah asked. "Did she uncover any details related to Claire's death?"

"Well, now, the waitresses don't talk about Claire much," Logan said. "And it took several months for Abby to confide in Kate at all. But when the two of you showed up last night, Abby told Kate that Claire was dead, and warned Kate not to mention the subject again unless she wanted to end up like Claire."

Disappointment stabbed deep. Jonah ground his teeth in frustration. "Is that all she said? We knew that much already."

Logan's expression turned grim. "No, that's not all. Claire's body hasn't been found yet, so we can't prove it, but according to what Abby told Kate, Claire Richmond was about three months pregnant."

"Pregnant?" Mallory stared at Logan in shock. She remembered the photos she'd found on the internet of Claire standing next to Caruso.

Jonah's expression was grim. "Pregnant? Do you really think that's true?"

Logan shrugged. "Why not? A pregnancy would be a really good reason to make sure her body doesn't show up somewhere."

"Unbelievable," Jonah muttered.

"So it's likely Caruso was the one who killed her," Mallory murmured. "The reason for the delay was because that's when he discovered she was pregnant. Maybe she threatened to go public with the news."

"Certainly one theory," Jonah agreed. "Although if

that's true, then her death may not have had anything to do with Caruso's money-laundering scheme."

"Maybe not, but murder is still murder, regardless of the motive," Logan said. "We get him on murder and we'll likely uncover proof related to his money laundering."

"But how are we going to prove it, considering we don't have a body?" Jonah asked.

"Good question. Caruso either destroyed the body somehow or buried it so deep we'll never find it," Logan pointed out.

The very thought made Mallory feel sick. She was appalled at the idea she'd gone out with a murderer. How could her instincts have led her so far astray? She was ashamed of herself, for the way she'd acted over these past ten years. She'd made the same mistakes over and over again. Why hadn't she seen Caruso for what he was? Why had she allowed herself to get involved with him? All he'd done was make her feel humiliated and betrayed.

Now she wanted more than anything to make things right.

"Maybe we should try to get a search warrant?" Logan asked.

"On what grounds?" Jonah demanded. "Abby is dead. Kate's statement at this point is nothing but hearsay. I doubt that will be enough to convince a judge that a well-respected senator murdered a possibly pregnant woman."

Logan didn't look at all fazed by the prospect. "Search warrants have been issued for less."

"Not against a senator," Jonah argued. "We absolutely have to do this by the book."

"Which takes us back to square one," Mallory murmured. "We don't have any other options than for me to contact Caruso. Jonah, let me confront him about Claire's pregnancy. He might be surprised enough to let something slip."

"No way," Jonah said again. "I already decided against you contacting Caruso as bait."

Logan pursed his lips and stared down at the toes of his cowboy boots. "I can tell you're not going to budge on letting Mallory help," he said finally. "You obviously don't want her in any danger. So what should our next step be?"

"I think we're better off using that plan as a last resort. Hey, what about Caruso's ex-wife?" Jonah asked, completely switching the topic of conversation. "Mallory, you met with her—what will it take to convince her to work with us?"

"Ironclad protection for her and her son," she answered without hesitation.

"We can offer her witness protection," Logan said.

Mallory shook her head. "That's not going to work, Logan. She's the vice president of a successful company. Why should she give it all up to testify against Caruso? Her wealth and position of power are the only things keeping her and her son alive."

A long silence hung heavily between them.

She leaned forward. "Jonah, listen to me. Allowing me to contact Caruso is our best option. Logically, you know it, too. I understand you don't want me in danger, but you're the one who told me to have faith. Well, I'm asking you to have faith, too, Jonah. I'm asking you to have faith in me."

"I'm not agreeing to anything until we've exhausted all options," Jonah said. "I still believe there has to be another way."

He hadn't agreed, but she suspected that he would if they didn't come up with anything better.

She didn't feel an overwhelming sense of relief. Instead, her stomach churned with turmoil. She gripped her fingers together, so he wouldn't know how deathly afraid she really was.

Fear didn't make her any less determined, though. She was the one who'd blithely gone into a relationship with Caruso. It was only right that she should be the one to help bring him down once and for all.

Jonah unrolled Logan's map, racking his brain to come up with an alternative to using Mallory as bait to lure Caruso.

Okay, maybe he was too emotionally involved. So what? If it meant keeping Mallory safe, he was perfectly fine with that. This time, he didn't intend to make any mistakes. And he knew allowing Mallory to set up a meeting was a mistake.

Especially when he wasn't exactly in top physical form to keep her safe.

"My source tells me these three warehouses are abandoned," Logan said, pointing to them on the map. Jonah was irritated at the way Mallory's gaze clung to Logan as she listened intently. "The property was purchased by a company called Green Speak, with the intent of leveling the warehouses to make room for a new structure they planned to use for building wind turbines. But after the real-estate market crashed a few years ago, they put their plans on hold. We could easily get a team in place prior to the meeting between you and Caruso."

"Okay, so we need some reason for Caruso to agree

to a meeting at an abandoned warehouse," Jonah said with a heavy sigh. He wasn't agreeing to Mallory being the one to set up the meeting, but hadn't yet come up with another way to get Caruso there.

Logan opened his mouth to say something but was interrupted by his cell phone. He glanced at the screen with a frown. "It's Kate," he murmured before bringing the phone up to his ear. "Hello?"

Jonah glanced warily at Mallory as they listened to Logan's one-sided conversation.

"Okay, listen, we'll be there in an hour."

"What's going on?" Jonah demanded.

"Guess who's having dinner at Salvatore's tonight?" Logan's eyes gleamed with anticipation.

"Caruso?" Jonah couldn't believe their luck.

"Yes, with Salvatore himself. But not until eight o'clock."

"I don't want Kate anywhere near them," Mallory said forcefully.

Jonah knew Mallory was traumatized by Abby's murder and put a reassuring hand on her arm. "Kate has been working at the restaurant for several months, Mallory. There's no reason for Salvatore to suspect her at this point."

"Let's go." Logan's attitude was all business now. "We can discuss the best plan of action on the way down to Chicago."

Jonah nodded and they headed down to the main level, to Logan's vehicle.

He couldn't help feeling thankful that the ridiculous idea of using Mallory as bait to draw out Caruso had been put on hold.

As far as he was concerned, the plan would stay on hold, indefinitely.

* * *

Mallory didn't have much to add to the conversation between Jonah and Logan about listening devices and other gadgets that might be of some use to overhear the conversation between Salvatore and Caruso.

She wrapped her arms around her waist to keep from shivering. The summer-evening air was actually very nice but she couldn't seem to shake the feeling of impending doom.

When they arrived in Chicago, Logan pulled into the parking lot of a fancy hotel. He flashed his ID and the parking attendant waived him through. "You're staying here?" she asked incredulously.

Logan nodded. "Yeah, it's all part of my cover story. I own several oil wells in Texas, which means I have to live the part of being wealthy."

"You didn't mention you've been working undercover," Jonah accused. "Have you already met with Salvatore? Do you actually have business meetings with him?"

"We've met, but no, I haven't had any business meetings with him." Logan's tone held a note of exasperation. "We've been on this task force for months, but it's slow and painstaking work to build a case like this."

"Sorry," Jonah muttered. "I know better than anyone how tedious law-enforcement investigations can be."

Logan parked his Jeep in the underground parking lot and then went around to the back and opened the door. Curious, Mallory followed, surprised to discover the rear of his vehicle looked as if he had robbed an electronics store.

"You're not really thinking of bugging Salvatore's table, are you?" Jonah asked.

"Do you have a better idea?" Logan drawled.

The burgers they'd eaten along the way sat like a rock in Mallory's stomach. "Sounds risky," she said. "If they suspect Kate, she'll end up dead, like Abby."

"We'll talk about this inside," Jonah said, as Logan put several electronic items into a small duffel bag before tossing it over his shoulder and slamming the car door shut.

None of them spoke as they made their way up to Logan's room. Once inside, Logan set the duffel bag on the table and opened it up. "Salvatore always sweeps the restaurant for bugs before he comes in to eat, so we only have a couple options. We can wire Kate, but it's not likely they would say anything incriminating in front of her so I'm not in favor of that option."

"You can bug the table, but Kate would have to do that once they're already seated," Jonah said, catching on to Logan's train of thought.

"Exactly. It's more risky, but we have the best technology Uncle Sam has to offer." Logan opened a container the size of a ring holder and revealed a small black disk that was slightly thicker than a dime yet a bit smaller in circumference. "Kate can place this right under the table and remove it as soon as they're finished eating, with no one being the wiser."

"Great idea," Jonah said with renewed enthusiasm.

Mallory wasn't so sure. "Seems too easy," she said with concern. "Have you already tried this? You know it'll work?"

"We've used it once before and it worked beautifully," Logan assured her, closing the box with a snap. "There's no reason to think it won't work again."

Mallory didn't bother to hide the doubt on her face.

"Except for the fact that Abby was killed late last night simply because she spoke to us."

"Mallory, it's very possible that there were other things that happened late last night that caused Abby's death," Jonah pointed out. "We don't know for sure that it's only because she spoke to us."

"Trust me, I'm not going to let anything happen to Kate Townsend," Logan said firmly. "We're going to do this tonight, and tomorrow, my team is going to relocate Kate someplace safe."

Mallory sighed, knowing there was no way to talk either of the men out of this. Both of them were convinced they couldn't fail. She wished she had the same certainty.

Helplessly, she closed her eyes. *Dear Lord, please keep Kate Townsend safe in Your care.*

Jonah knew Mallory was distressed over their plan to bug Salvatore's table, but while he understood her apprehension, he also felt a deep sense of anticipation.

This plan of Logan's could work. And if they managed to get some sort of incriminating evidence against Caruso tonight, this entire mess would be over soon. And Mallory would be completely safe at last. He didn't like thinking about how his priority had changed from simply closing the case to clearing Mallory.

Jonah took the earpiece Logan held out to him and the small ring box containing the black disk to the other side of the room. He opened the box and then spoke in low tones but Jonah could hear every word plain as day.

"Amazing," he said in admiration. "When are you going to get in touch with Kate?"

"We're going to hand over the disk outside the restaurant while she's on break," Logan said, glancing at his watch. "Which should be in about fifteen minutes."

Considering it was already seven-fifteen, the timeline was a tight one. "And where are we going to sit and listen?"

"We're going to stay in the Jeep right where it's parked," Logan said. "The restaurant is only half a block away."

"Won't the concrete walls interfere with the signal?" Jonah asked.

"The signal was clear last time I parked on that same level, but we'll test it again to be sure." Logan took the disk out of the ring box and put it in a small, clear plastic sheath that was no bigger than a nickel. "Here, you take these two sets of earpieces and go sit in my Jeep. I'll take this out to the restaurant and you can let me know if you don't hear anything."

"How do we let you know?" Mallory asked.

"Text me." Logan settled the cowboy hat on his head and flashed a grin. "I'm going to bump into Kate and make a big deal out of apologizing as I hand her the disk."

"Sounds good." Jonah waited a few minutes after Logan left before he led the way down to the parking structure. Once they were seated in the backseat safely behind Logan's tinted windows, he showed Mallory how to put the earpiece in.

Amazingly, they could hear the traffic noise on the street, as Logan walked down to Salvatore's. "Testing," he drawled in a low tone.

"It's so clear," Mallory whispered.

"Yeah." Jonah couldn't help being impressed. He quickly texted Logan to let him know the listening device worked fine.

It was getting close to Kate's break time, and he wished he could see Logan as well as hear him. The minutes ticked by slowly. Then he heard a muffled gasp, and Logan's deep drawl came through crystal clear. "My apologies, ma'am, I didn't mean to step on your foot."

"Well, maybe you should watch where you're walking, big guy," a young female voice said with sharp annoyance.

"Yes, ma'am. I guess I'm used to wide-open spaces like we have in Texas, not the crush of people here."

"Whatever." Kate's annoyance radiated through the listening device. "I have to get back to work."

There was no more talking, only the sound of traffic and people's voices in the background. Apparently Logan didn't head back to the parking garage right away because it took time for him to return. Jonah figured he must have walked around the block before returning to the hotel.

Logan finally slid into the Jeep. "We're all set. Nothing more to do except wait."

Jonah knew from long experience that waiting was the hardest part of a stakeout. Kate must have had the device in her pocket because they could hear the sounds of dishes being stacked and menu items being discussed. Then they heard Kate's voice.

"Mr. Salvatore, how nice to see you again. We were expecting you at eight."

"Our meeting ended early. Do you have our table ready?"

"Yes, sir, right this way."

"I'd like my bodyguard to check out the place first," they heard Salvatore say.

"Of course, sir. Excuse me for a moment while I let the chef know you've arrived earlier than planned."

Jonah glanced at Logan. "She's pretty good, knew enough to get out of the way of the bodyguard sweeping for bugs."

"No, Kate, don't go." Salvatore's sharp tone came through the earpiece. "I'd like you to stay."

There was a long pause before they heard Kate's voice. "Yes, sir."

"Logan, do something," Mallory whispered tersely. "Kate's in trouble!"

Logan's expression turned grim, and Jonah understood. There wasn't anything they could do now except wait for this to play out, hoping and praying Kate wouldn't get caught.

TWELVE

Mallory couldn't breathe. Her heart pounded so hard against her ribs that she put a hand to her chest to ease the ache. She couldn't bear knowing that, any minute, the bug they'd handed to Kate would be found.

"All set now?" Kate's voice asked politely.

"Yes." Salvatore's tone was curt and they could hear the sounds of the two men settling into their seats. "Send the wine steward down to bring us the usual."

"Right away, sir."

Mallory momentarily closed her eyes with relief. Kate was safe. At least for now. She reached over and grasped Logan's elbow. "How is it possible that Salvatore didn't find the bug?"

"The disk I gave Kate uses a completely different frequency than the normal listening devices," Logan explained.

"You knew she'd be safe," Mallory said, feeling foolish for being so worried.

Logan's grin faded. "No, ma'am. I hoped she'd be safe, but I couldn't know for sure. Salvatore has deep pockets and I had no way of knowing if he'd upgraded his technology, too."

Slightly mollified she sat back in her seat, listening to the background noises that were coming through her earpiece. "Sounds like Kate is still in the kitchen," she murmured.

Logan nodded. "She can't place the bug until she takes their order for dinner without raising suspicion."

"How does she know to do all this?" Mallory asked as her stomach once again knotted with anxiety.

Logan's expression turned grim. "Apparently, she has a knack for undercover work," he muttered.

She hid a smile. It was clear Logan had a soft spot for the young waitress and didn't like using Kate's talents even though she obviously was good at her chosen career.

Too bad she didn't have the same skill set. Mallory's stomach was so upset she feared she'd end up with a bleeding ulcer if she had to do what Kate was doing.

Mallory strained to listen, although with all the background noises it wasn't easy. The minutes dragged by slowly, until finally they heard Kate addressing the restaurant owner. "Are you ready to order, Mr. Salvatore?" she asked.

The two men took their time ordering their food. When she heard Caruso's voice ordering the Chilean sea bass—his distinct northern nasal tone a direct contrast to Salvatore's deeper voice carrying a hint of his Sicilian heritage—she shivered.

The man was cold. He'd murdered at least one person and attempted to murder her, yet he still sat leisurely eating an expensive dinner as if he didn't have a care in the world.

"I'll have the chef prepare your food right away, Mr. Salvatore," she heard Kate say.

Again there was no response from either man, as if it were beneath them to respond personally to the hired help. But when they began to talk in low voices, she realized Kate had succeeded in placing the disk beneath their table.

"Have you found her yet?" Salvatore asked.

"No. She has help, which has made her much more difficult to find," Caruso answered with annoyance.

Mallory experienced a surge of satisfaction when she realized the two men were discussing her. She was fiercely glad that, with Jonah's help, they'd managed to elude Caruso.

"I'm not pleased at how you've managed to drag me into your mess for the second time, Tony." The implied threat underlying Salvatore's tone was unmistakable. "To have them show up here is inexcusable. I will not tolerate incompetence."

"Don't threaten me. I've helped make you a rich man, Bernardo."

"And you wouldn't be in office without me."

"I know, I know. Don't worry. I'll take care of my loose ends the same way you've taken care of yours."

Jonah glanced back at her, and she knew he was thinking about Abby's body floating in Lake Michigan. But while the two men obviously were discussing their various crimes, they were careful enough not to say anything blatantly incriminating.

A wave of helplessness washed over her. What if this was all for nothing? What if the two men didn't give them anything to work with?

"Your soup, Mr. Salvatore and Senator Caruso," Kate said. Mallory had the impression Kate mentioned both names on purpose. "I hope you enjoy your meal."

"Where is the ground pepper?" Salvatore asked sharply. "Is this the service you provide? I expect better, or this will be the last meal you serve."

"Yes, sir," Kate murmured in apology.

There was a long silence as the men ate their food. The next bit of conversation centered on the restaurant business. It wasn't until the two men had been served the main course that their conversation turned back to important matters.

"Tell me, Tony, what is the next step in solving your small problem?"

"I told you not to worry. I have a contact inside the MPD helping me track them down."

Mallory gasped. Jonah was right—his boss really was helping Caruso.

"And is that all?" Salvatore asked softly. "You're just going to sit back and wait for someone else to find her for you?"

"What do you expect?" Caruso asked with clear annoyance. "I have to be back in Washington by the middle of next week for the Senate vote on the budget bill. I can't ignore the obligations of my career, Bernardo."

"Perhaps it's time to use her sister as leverage."

Mallory reached out to grab Jonah's arm. "We have to do something to keep Alyssa safe!" she hissed in a low tone.

"Drummond is with her constantly. She's never alone," Caruso said. "And besides, the Feds are watching them. I'm not about to walk into a trap."

The Feds? Really? Mallory relaxed back in her seat.

"Idiot," Salvatore mumbled beneath his breath. "Tony, have you forgotten how to bluff? If your ex-girlfriend is on the run, she won't know that her sister is safe."

"You have a point, Bernardo."

Mallory could easily imagine how Caruso's mind was exploring the possibilities. And despite knowing the Feds were watching over Alyssa, she couldn't help but worry.

"I have a couple other options, too," Caruso continued. "But rest assured I will have everything taken care of before I leave for Washington. Including hiding all evidence so that it doesn't wash ashore to be discovered quickly."

The subtle dig did not go unnoticed.

"Watch yourself, Anthony," Salvatore said in a soft yet dangerous tone. "Your public position is extremely vulnerable, while I have the support of the family behind me."

There was a tense silence and Mallory imagined they were glaring at each other as they exchanged their veiled threats.

"Bernardo, you worry too much. I will have everything taken care of. I managed to eliminate the earlier threat, didn't I?"

"After you were stupid enough to get her pregnant."

"Because she lied to me." Caruso was clearly backpedaling, trying to make amends. "And I learned from my mistake. Our goals are still the same, Bernardo. We both want to be rich. Trust me to make that happen."

There was another pause. "All right, then, I will grant your request for five days," Salvatore said. "But I expect results by next Wednesday, understood?"

"Of course."

Within a few minutes, Kate returned. "Are you both finished, Mr. Salvatore?" she asked.

"Obviously," he replied in a snide tone.

Mallory could hear dishes being stacked, and then suddenly, there was a loud yell followed by the sound of dishes breaking.

"You imbecile!" Salvatore shouted. "Clean up this mess!"

"Yes, sir. I'm so sorry sir!" Kate's voice was full of horror. "I'll clean it up right away, sir!"

"You're fired!" Salvatore shouted. "Get this woman out of my sight!"

"Right away, Mr. Salvatore."

"I'm sorry. I'm sorry," Kate sobbed. Once again, the sounds of voices in the background along with dishes clanking together made it apparent that Kate had retrieved the bug from under the table and put it back into her pocket. They could hear someone telling Kate to put her stuff together and get out.

Logan ripped the earpiece out of his ear, jammed the key into the ignition and started the SUV.

"Where are we going?" Mallory asked, barely having time to buckle her seat belt before he barreled out of the parking garage.

"To pick her up," Logan replied tersely. "She must have set that whole scene up so that she'd get fired."

Mallory's jaw dropped in surprise. "She did? You mean that wasn't part of the original plan?"

"No," Logan spat the word with annoyance as he cranked the steering wheel with more force than was necessary before turning onto the street. "That wasn't part of the plan."

Mallory grinned. She was looking forward to meeting this Kate, who obviously had a thing or two to teach her.

* * *

Jonah glanced down at the notes he'd taken. He felt good knowing that their suspicions had been confirmed, yet he was just as disappointed that the two men hadn't said anything more damaging than veiled innuendos.

He glanced up as Logan drove well beyond the restaurant, miraculously finding a place to park. Logan slammed out of the car, muttering that he'd be right back.

Jonah exited the passenger seat, opening the back-right passenger door to slide in next to Mallory. Within a few minutes, Logan and Kate returned, obviously arguing.

"You should have followed the plan," Logan said.

Kate tossed her blond hair. "My way was better." She turned in her seat, holding out her hand. "Hi, I'm Kate Townsend."

"Jonah Stewart, and this is Mallory Roth," Jonah said, making quick introductions as Logan pulled back into traffic. He shook her hand, as did Mallory. "Thanks for your help back there."

"No problem." The gleam in Kate's eyes gave him the impression she had enjoyed every moment.

"I told you this isn't a game," Logan snapped. "You're lucky all he did was fire you."

Kate rolled her eyes and then turned back in her seat so she could buckle her seat belt. "Don't be such a worrywart."

Jonah hid a grin as Mallory choked back a laugh. Despite the seriousness of the situation, the relief of knowing they'd pulled off their mission was enough to give them a rush of adrenaline.

"So you're Anthony's ex-girlfriend?" Kate asked, glancing back at Mallory as Logan made his way to the interstate. There was no doubt he was planning to take Kate to Milwaukee, far from Salvatore.

"Unfortunately." Mallory scowled and Jonah knew she regretted the decisions she'd made. "And you're the detective wannabe."

Kate laughed. "Yep, that's me. Actually, I graduate at the end of the semester, so my career is well within reach. And it's also why I'm not packing up to leave town the way the cowboy keeps demanding."

"I told you, we'll make arrangements to transfer your college credits to another institution," Logan said, inserting himself in the conversation.

"But I'll lose a semester if I do that," Kate argued.

"How long have you worked for Salvatore's?" Jonah asked, hoping to sidetrack the argument brewing between Logan and Kate.

"Just over a year." Kate let out a heavy sigh. "Too bad I had to quit—I made good money working there."

"How did you figure out Salvatore was involved with organized crime?" Mallory asked.

"They didn't exactly keep it a huge secret," Kate said. "Honestly, if I'd have known, I wouldn't have applied for a job there in the first place. But my roommate was working there and gave me a good reference."

"They must not have known you were studying criminal law," he said, "or there's no way they would have hired you."

"I'm pretty sure they assumed I knew what was going on there because of Angela, my roommate. Salvatore is her uncle on her mother's side. Angela is studying business but she's made it clear she plans to get a job with her uncle when she graduates." Kate wrinkled her nose. "Talk about keeping business within the family."

"You took a huge risk tonight," Jonah pointed out. He understood why Logan was so frustrated with Kate. Even now, she was acting as if this was nothing more than a game, when in fact it was anything but. Salvatore and Caruso played for keeps.

"I didn't have much choice, once I knew what was going on in there." Kate shrugged off his praise. She turned to sit back in her seat. "Did you get anything useful from them?" she asked Logan.

"They confirmed our suspicions but didn't give us any new information," Logan admitted.

Jonah leaned forward. "Is it true the bureau is watching over Alyssa and Gage?" he asked.

Logan lifted a shoulder. "I'll check to be sure, but I wouldn't be surprised. To be honest, I think they might have been waiting to see if Mallory would show up."

Mallory reached over to tightly grip Jonah's hand. "Please check right away, Logan. I need to know Alyssa's safe."

"She'll be fine," Jonah murmured, helpless to defuse the tension radiating from her. "Gage won't let anything happen to her."

"I know, but he's not a cop and he can't possibly sit with her 24/7, either." Mallory worried her lower lip between her teeth, and he wished he had the right to draw her into his arms, hold her close and kiss her.

"Don't panic until we know what we're dealing with," Jonah reassured her. "Caruso isn't going to make a move toward Alyssa until he's exhausted a couple other options first."

"I hope you're right, Jonah." Mallory's wobbly voice betrayed her fear. "I really hope you're right."

The trip back to Milwaukee seemed to take forever.

It was late by the time they all trooped back up to the large three-bedroom suite Logan had obtained for them.

"Kate, I'd be happy if you shared my room," Mallory said, indicating the large bedroom containing two queen-size beds along with its own private bathroom. "That way we'll have some privacy from these guys."

Kate quickly nodded. "Sounds great. Thanks."

The two women disappeared into the bedroom, closing the door behind them. Jonah glanced at Logan. "I don't like the deadline Caruso created for himself. I'm afraid he might make a play for Alyssa to bring Mallory out of hiding."

"I hear you. Let me make a couple calls tonight, but it could be that we won't hear anything until tomorrow," Logan said.

"I understand. But I think we should strike first. And I have an idea."

"Let's hear it," Logan drawled.

Jonah shook his head. He needed some time to think through the details. "No, make your calls first. It's late—we'll have plenty of time tomorrow to talk it through."

Logan nodded and went to make his phone calls.

Jonah went to his room and closed the door, going over the steps in his mind. There had to be a way to make his idea work. Because he refused to put Mallory in the center of danger.

He cared about her far too much.

Mallory awoke early and glanced over at Kate, who was still asleep. They'd been sharing the room for two days now, and she was reminded of the early days when she and Alyssa had shared a room while growing up.

She missed her twin so much. And she was determined to do whatever was necessary to keep Alyssa out of this.

Her stomach grumbled as she showered and dressed, making her remember she hadn't been able to eat much of the meal they'd ordered from room service last night. The four of them had spent the entire day considering various plans but had not been able to come to an agreement.

Of course, Logan had wasted almost half the day trying to convince Kate to go into witness protection, to no avail. Mallory had admired Kate's ability to stick to her guns, and selfishly, she'd wanted Kate to stay.

She eased open her door, silently entering the main living area of the suite. The other two doors were closed, so she knew she was the first one up.

In the small kitchen area, she made a pot of coffee and nibbled on some of the leftovers from the night before. But her stomach cramped and she gave up pretending to eat.

She glanced down at the map Logan had left on the table as she sipped her coffee. There were some drawings on it but she didn't understand exactly what the scribbles meant. The guys had stayed up late, trying to decide what their next steps would be.

When Jonah's bedroom door opened, she was so startled her hand jerked, spilling coffee on the table.

She jumped up to get a napkin to clean up the mess. "You scared me."

"I'm sorry," he murmured.

She took a deep breath, trying to slow her racing heart. She didn't know why her nerves were on edge; it wasn't as if they'd agreed to implement anything today.

But at the same time, time was running short. They had to do something, and quick. "Would you like some coffee?"

"Uh, no thanks. I'm going to church."

She blinked in surprise and frowned. "Church? It's Sunday?" How could it be Sunday already?

He smiled. "Yes, it's Sunday. There's a small church down the road that offers an early service. Let everyone know I'll be back in a couple hours."

Mallory couldn't remember the last time she'd attended church, mostly because she'd never wanted to. But as Jonah walked toward the door, she jumped up. "Do you mind if I come with you?"

He froze, and for a moment she thought maybe he was looking for time alone, but when he turned to face her, there was no denying the pleased surprise on his face. "I'd like that. It's about a mile away, though, and I was planning to walk. Is that all right with you?"

A walk sounded perfect. Better, really, than sitting through a church service. "I don't mind at all." She glanced down at her casual attire. "I don't have anything else to wear," she said by way of apology.

"Under the circumstances, I don't think God is going to mind," he murmured.

His comment made her smile and relax. Her preconceived notions about God and church were obviously a bit outdated.

"Are you ready?"

As they walked outside into the cool summer air, she lifted her face, enjoying the breeze and her surroundings. The sky was a prettier shade of blue than she'd seen before and the white puffy clouds were the kind little kids would see as animal shapes. Being outside without fearing for her life was a novelty. For the first time in what seemed like forever, she felt like a normal person. As if she and Jonah were the only two people on the earth.

The church was picturesque—brown brick on the outside with a tall steeple and beautiful stained-glass windows. It wasn't elaborate but it was beautiful in its simplicity. Funny how she'd never considered a church to be noteworthy before now.

As Jonah approached the steps leading up to the front door, she hesitated, gripped by a sudden surge of panic. She fought the urge to turn and run all the way back to the relative safety of the hotel room.

Going inside to attend church services was a big step for her. A step made even more important because she was going with Jonah.

She slowly realized that becoming closer to God would impact her relationship with Jonah.

Irrevocably changing her life—forever.

THIRTEEN

Mallory kept her head down as she entered the church, feeling like a fraud. She avoided eye contact with the other parishioners as she slid into the pew beside Jonah.

The early-morning service didn't have a strong showing, but there were more people than she'd expected in attendance. The members of the choir didn't seem to mind—they sang the opening hymn with gusto and the rest of the church members quickly joined in.

Including Jonah.

His deep baritone was soothing and helped Mallory relax. If she had a decent voice she might have joined in, but she was content to read the words in an attempt to follow along. She shouldn't have been surprised that Jonah knew every word of the song—after all, attending church wasn't a foreign event to him the way it was to her.

Church music wasn't normally her thing but she had to admit the song was more upbeat than she'd expected. Jonah belonged with the rest of the choir, she thought with a flash of pride—his voice was absolutely amazing. She was surprisingly disappointed when the last verse of the song ended. When he kept his hymnal in his hands, rather than putting it back into the holder, she followed suit, holding on to hers, too.

As the pastor started his sermon, Mallory thought she'd be bored out of her mind, expecting the usual fire-and-brimstone type of preaching she'd seen in movies. No doubt she'd hear about the perils of being a sinner, a situation she was all too familiar with. But surprisingly, her attention was snagged, almost immediately, by the pastor's viewpoint on the topic of forgiveness. She had the uncanny feeling he was speaking directly to her. And when he quoted from the Bible, the words resonated deep within her.

"'Therefore, my friends, I want you to know that through Jesus the forgiveness of sins is proclaimed to you. Through him everyone who believes is set free from every sin, a justification you were not able to obtain under the Law of Moses. Take care that what the prophets have said does not happen to you.'"

For a moment Mallory sat in stunned silence, thinking about her own sins and whether or not God would really forgive them. Jonah had told her all along that God would forgive her, but hearing the words from him was one thing. Hearing them from the pastor was something different. She hadn't been sure she could really, truly believe.

Until now.

When Jonah reached down to pick up the hymnal that had dropped from her nerveless fingers, she gave him a tight smile. "Thanks," she whispered.

His brows were furrowed with concern. "Are you all right?" he asked in a hushed tone.

She swallowed hard, amazed at his perceptiveness. She nodded and glanced away. How could she explain her feelings? Jonah had told her about his partner's death—had bared his soul—but she'd never confided her own deepest shame.

Yet maybe this was God's way of telling her the time had come to do just that.

Jonah could feel how tense Mallory was beside him, and he prayed for strength and understanding so he might help her with whatever burden she carried.

When the church service ended, Mallory didn't get up to leave like the rest of the parishioners. He sensed she wanted to talk but maybe didn't know how to start.

"Mallory, why don't you tell me what's bothering you?" he asked gently. "I could tell the pastor's sermon meant something to you but I'm not sure I understand. Why is it that you think you don't deserve forgiveness?"

"Because deep down, I've always thought he was right," she confided. "That what happened was really all my fault."

His breath froze in his chest as he digested her words. Was she saying what he thought she was saying? "Who was right, Mallory? What do you mean?"

She toyed with the strap of her purse for several long seconds. "Garrett Mason, the quarterback and captain of our high-school football team." Her voice was so low he had to strain to hear what she was saying. "During our senior year of high school, I had a huge crush on him, but he didn't know I existed. One Friday night, I asked Alyssa if we could switch identities. I wanted to work her shift at the Burger Barn, because the team was planning to go there after the game."

Jonah's gut knotted with anger as he slowly began to understand where her story was going.

"I shamelessly flirted with Garrett, making it clear I wanted to go out with him. I even told him my real name and the joke I'd played on the manager, pretending to be Alyssa. He laughed and told me I obviously like to live dangerously. I blithely agreed. When he offered to wait for me after the end of my shift, I was ecstatic. My plan had worked."

She paused and as much as he didn't want to hear the details, he knew she needed to tell him. To let go once and for all. "Then what happened?" he forced himself to ask.

"He drove me back out to the high-school stadium so we could sit under the bleachers. I was thrilled, especially when he kissed me, but then—" Her voice trailed off.

Red-hot anger surged, momentarily blinding him. It took all the control he possessed to keep his feelings from showing. The last thing he wanted to do was to scare her. "Whatever happened wasn't your fault, Mallory. No matter what he said, he's the one who broke the law, not you."

"Logically I understand that. I knew what the term *date rape* meant. But when I remember how I acted back then, I can't deny my actions started the chain of events. And I have to own up to them. I'm the one who switched places with Alyssa, just so I could see him and talk to him. I'm the one who flirted with him. Maybe I did give him the wrong impression, but I didn't mean to."

"I know, Mallory. I know. It's his fault, not yours."

She shook her head as if still unable to believe that. "Afterward, I was—shattered."

He could only imagine what she must have gone

through. He placed his arm around her and hugged her close, wishing he could go back and change the past. No woman should have to suffer like she had. His heart ached for her lost innocence. "I'm sorry, Mallory. I'm so sorry," he murmured.

"I didn't tell anyone, except Alyssa." Her voice was muffled against his chest. "She tried to convince me to go to the police, but I couldn't. I was afraid everyone would believe what Garrett said, that I asked for it."

"You didn't," Jonah repeated, fighting to keep the rage from his tone.

"That's when I signed up for Tae Kwon Do. And as I became stronger, I grew angry and bitter. I turned my back on God. I also decided that I'd never let any man get the upper hand, that relationships would be on my terms. That I'd never let myself get emotionally involved." She shifted in her seat and looked up at him with tearful eyes. "Except I ended up doing the same thing all over again, by dating Caruso. Maybe he didn't assault me like Garrett did, but he wants to do something worse."

"You couldn't possibly know Caruso was involved in criminal activity," Jonah protested, brushing away a damp strand of hair from her cheek. "Cut yourself a little slack, Mallory. Everyone makes mistakes."

She let out a harsh laugh. "Not the kind of mistakes I've made. And besides, that's not the worst of it." Now that she'd started talking, it seemed as if she couldn't stop. "Listening to the pastor today, I finally believed God would really forgive my sins. Except as we were saying the Lord's Prayer at the end of the service, I realized it wasn't good enough. I have to forgive Garrett for what he did to me, don't I? Not only Garrett, but

Anthony, too." There was a long pause before she whispered in a low, agonized tone, "Honestly, I'm not sure I can do that, Jonah."

He didn't know what to say because he wasn't so sure he could forgive the two men, either, even though he knew he should. God expected him to forgive them and anyone else who trespassed against him.

He pulled her close and held her for a long time, offering what meager comfort he could. And he wondered humbly if God had sent him Mallory, not just so that he could help her believe, but so that she could help him become a better Christian.

"Your note said you were attending church, but you were gone so long, we were starting to worry something had happened to you," Logan drawled, his eyes glittering with a pent-up anger that wasn't reflected in his laconic tone.

"Why didn't you invite me?" Kate asked from where she sat curled up on the sofa.

"Sorry," Mallory murmured. Jonah hoped the two of them wouldn't notice Mallory's reddened and puffy eyes. "We stayed longer than we anticipated."

"I take full responsibility," Jonah quickly interjected. "We talked for a while afterward. I should have called to let you know we were on our way."

"Next time, I'd like to go with you," Kate said.

Logan lifted his eyebrows as he glanced at Kate, as if surprised to know she'd have wanted to go along, but he didn't say anything other than, "I ordered breakfast if y'all are hungry."

Jonah glanced over at the array of breakfast items Logan had ordered from room service, in quantities that would support a small army, realizing his appetite had returned. He glanced at Mallory, relieved to see she appeared anxious to eat something, too.

Neither of them had said much on the walk back, mostly because he couldn't think of a way to tell her how much he admired her strength. He took solace in the knowledge that Mallory looked better, as if finally telling him the truth had given her some peace.

Knowing what he did now, he understood Mallory's actions better than ever. All along, he'd suspected that she'd hidden her real self from the world behind a facade, but now he knew for certain.

He somewhat understood the choices she'd made and knew she'd learned from her mistakes. And most of all, he was thankful she'd come into his life when she had.

Dangerous thoughts, he warned himself as he headed over to the table Logan had cleared for their meal. He could admire Mallory from afar, but he'd already crossed the line once by kissing her. He couldn't allow a lapse like that to happen again.

He was a cop and would always be a cop. He knew, better than anyone, the type of stress his career had on families.

But he was glad when she took a seat next to him at the table, leaving Kate to sit beside Logan. Jonah bowed his head and asked for God's blessing, thanking Him for the food they had to eat and for keeping them safe from harm. The way Mallory and Kate both murmured, "Amen," warmed his heart.

Logan didn't add to the prayer, but he waited for Jonah to finish before digging in. There were several long moments of silence as everyone concentrated on eating. Jonah was tempted to tease Logan about the way he dug into his food, as if he had a stomach the size of Texas. But he refrained, since he was doing his part in putting a large dent in the meal.

When Logan finished, he pushed back from the table, picked up a mug of coffee and eyed Jonah over the rim. "Do you want the good news? Or the bad news?"

Mallory froze at his words, her fork halfway to her mouth. The quick flash of fear in her eyes seared his soul.

"Don't play games, Logan." Jonah knew he was overreacting, but after everything Mallory revealed less than an hour ago, he wasn't in the mood for Logan's teasing.

"The good news is that I heard from one of the guys on my task force. He confirmed Alyssa and Gage do have FBI agents keeping an eye on them. The bad news is that the two agents are probably going to be pulled off by tomorrow. Apparently they're convinced Mallory isn't going to return, as that would put her sister in danger."

"No!" Mallory jumped to her feet. "They can't leave them alone. Caruso will find them!"

Jonah's heart went out to Mallory. "Take it easy. We're not going to let that happen. Remember, we still have twenty-four hours before they're in any danger."

"Jonah's right, but we need to decide on a plan and move forward today," Logan said. "Kate knows the names of two guys who are for sure working for Salvatore."

"James Kiefer and Kevin Graves," Kate said. "They both come in a lot to talk to Salvatore when he's there."

Jonah's eyes brightened. It was exactly the opening he'd been looking for. "Then let's use them to lure Caruso to the warehouse. I'll place a call to Caruso pretending to be one of Salvatore's men, claiming I caught Mallory sniffing around Salvatore's restaurant, and say I'm holding her at one of the abandoned warehouses."

"Except he knows you and Mallory were at the restaurant together. It's why he killed Abby," Logan argued.

"But maybe he'll believe I went back later and saw something I shouldn't have," Mallory agreed slowly. "I think we can make this work."

Logan scowled. "But that was forty-eight hours ago. Why would the guy wait?"

"Maybe we could make Caruso believe I escaped and he just got me back," Mallory said, her eyes betraying her inner fear.

Jonah reached out to take Mallory's hand. "Don't worry. We can make this work without putting you in any danger."

He turned toward Logan. "We need backup if we're actually going to trap Caruso."

It was Logan's turn to be silent. "Well, now, I'm not so sure about that idea," he drawled.

Jonah's gaze narrowed suspiciously. "Why not?"

"Because Salvatore himself is the main target of the FBI task force, which means my boss isn't going to go along with this plan, especially if there's any possibility it will risk our chance to nail Salvatore." When Jonah kept glaring at him, he added, "You asked for this to be kept off-grid, and I agreed. I knew all along that helping you and Mallory trap Caruso would ultimately blow my cover, putting my career in jeopardy. Rafe is a good friend, and you sounded like you were in trouble, so I decided to take the risk."

* * *

Mallory pushed away from the table and began stacking up the dirty dishes, hoping neither Jonah nor Logan would notice her shaking hands. She'd thought for sure Logan's plan would work.

But now she was plagued with doubt. And fear.

"You told me you have a team," Jonah insisted hotly, not bothering to hide his anger.

"I have some guys who will help us off-grid," Logan insisted. "I told you I had backup."

Jonah still looked tense, as if he wasn't reassured. "You're sure these guys are trustworthy? It's not just our lives, but Mallory's and Kate's on the line."

"You don't have to remind me," Logan said testily. He let out a heavy sigh. "I don't know them that well," he finally admitted.

"I need you to be sure, Logan. I've already been betrayed by one of my fellow officers."

"What do you want me to say, Jonah? Do you want me to call this whole idea off?"

"No," Mallory said sharply, whirling around to face them. "We're not going to call this off. We need to do this. We can't risk placing more innocent people in danger."

For a moment Jonah's gaze held hers, and she was shocked at the agony reflected there. He was worried about her. Truly worried.

"She's right, Stewart," Logan said. "We don't have time to waste. If we're going to do this, we need to agree on a plan and get the ball rolling, ASAP."

"I'll be your backup," Kate offered.

"You're not a cop!" Logan shouted, his face red with anger.

"Kate and I will be fine together," Mallory spoke up. "Kate knows how to use a gun. Let's just finish this, okay? We'll be fine." She refused to consider any other option.

Ironic how she hadn't trusted a man to get close to her over all these years, but now she was putting her very life into these two men's hands.

"Let's go down to the SUV and pull the equipment we'll need," Logan suggested. "We'll need to plant listening devices in the warehouse."

"I'm going to call Alyssa while you're getting the equipment," she said to Jonah. "She needs to know what's going on."

He nodded and the three of them left the hotel room. She quickly dialed Gage's number, and luckily, she finally got through to him.

"How is Alyssa?" she asked. "Did the surgery go okay? Is she feeling better?"

"Yes, she's fine." Gage's voice changed subtly. "Is Jonah there? I'd like to talk to him."

"Why? Did something happen?"

"Nothing you need to worry about. Just have him call me."

She tried not to take it personally that Gage didn't trust her enough to pass on the message. "No problem. I'll have him give you a call."

"Okay," Gage said, although his tone clearly indicated he wasn't thrilled with the delay. "Hold on while I get Alyssa."

"Mallory?" Tears filled her eyes when she heard her twin's voice. "Are you really okay?"

She blinked the tears away with an effort. "Yes, but listen to me, Alyssa. You and Gage need to be careful. I just found out that the FBI has been watching you both, waiting for me or Caruso to show up. But starting tomorrow, they're not going to be watching you anymore. I want you and Gage to go someplace safe, understand?"

"Yes, I understand." Alyssa's tone seemed to grow stronger knowing there was a potential threat. "I'll let Gage know."

"I'm sorry, Alyssa." Mallory wished more than anything that she could be with her sister. "We're going to try to finish this once and for all, but I don't want you to wait. Get out now, okay?"

"We will. But, Mallory, you need to stay safe, too. What has Jonah gotten you into? He promised me he'd keep you safe."

"He's determined to protect me. He's the one going into danger, not me. Just take care of yourself, okay?" Mallory closed her eyes, wishing she could tell Alyssa everything. How she'd gone to church and opened up to Jonah. That he hadn't run away from her, even after hearing the truth. That he'd held her hand as they'd walked back to the hotel. That she had fallen for him.

But this wasn't the time. "I love you, Lyssa," she said instead.

"I love you, too, Mal," Alyssa replied. "Call me every day, okay? I want to know you're safe."

Mallory swallowed against the hard lump in her throat. "I will. Take care, Alyssa."

"You, too, Mal," her twin murmured, her voice fading. The pain meds must have caught up with her.

Mallory closed her phone and spent a few minutes pulling herself together. She had to be strong. She could face anything if it meant keeping her sister safe.

She opened Logan's laptop computer, and on an impulse, she did another search on Claire Richmond.

The same photographs and articles came up as before, only this time, she examined the pictures more closely, trying to see if there was any evidence of Claire's pregnancy.

But there was no betraying bump in the woman's slim figure. Based on the timeline, she figured Claire was only about twelve-to-fourteen weeks along. Was Claire's pregnancy the reason she thought her modeling career wouldn't last? No wonder she hadn't totally given up her waitressing job at Salvatore's.

Her gaze rested on a familiar bracelet circling Claire's wrist. Her stomach knotted as she zoomed in to get a better look.

The picture was grainy, but there was no mistaking the square shape of the emerald-cut rubies and diamonds. She blinked and ran over to dig through her purse for the bracelet, hoping she wasn't mistaken.

She wasn't. She held the bracelet Caruso had given her next to the photograph and realized it appeared to be the same piece of jewelry. Caruso had claimed it was a one-of-a-kind piece. She'd believed him, as the designer's initials were engraved on the back of the clasp.

Seeing the same bracelet around Claire's wrist seemed too much of a coincidence.

Hadn't Abby said that Claire was going to sell an expensive piece of jewelry to start over? Was this bracelet the item she was going to sell? The two girls had talked the night before Claire had disappeared.

If this bracelet was the exact same one he'd given to Claire then didn't the bracelet prove that he'd seen Claire the night before she'd disappeared?

She imagined the struggle as Caruso tried to kill Claire. Had the bracelet fallen off? Or had he taken it? Either way, he must have gotten the bracelet back, either right before or right after he'd killed her.

She stared at the bracelet, suppressing a shiver of distaste. How horrible to think she had worn the same bracelet as a murdered woman. Did Caruso plan to give it to his next girlfriend, after he'd killed her?

They had to stop him before that happened. All they needed was a way to prove her theory.

FOURTEEN

Mallory quickly saved the photo of Claire wearing the bracelet onto Logan's hard drive. Was it possible there were other photos of Claire wearing the bracelet after she and Anthony had broken up? She tried several other general searches without success.

What she needed was some photos of Claire with her friends. Curiously, she logged on to Facebook, just to see if Claire had ever had a presence there. She discovered there were a lot of Claire Richmonds listed, but eventually she found a Claire Richmond in Chicago whose photo looked familiar.

When she clicked on the photo, she discovered Claire had a page that her family and friends must have created as a way to honor her memory. Several had posted heartfelt messages saying how much they missed Claire, and others begged Claire to come home.

For a moment, Mallory was overwhelmed with sadness. Seeing the photos of the young, smiling blonde only emphasized the loss. Deep down, she knew Abby had been right. The pretty girl wasn't coming home ever again.

She painstakingly went through all the photos where

Claire was tagged. Unfortunately, most of them were head shots, so there was no chance of even seeing a bracelet.

But then she found one where Claire was dressed up in a cocktail dress, standing beside another woman at what appeared to be a fancy restaurant. Her heart leaped into her throat when she could make out the same bracelet around Claire's wrist. But when was the photo taken? There was a date listed as to when the photo was uploaded, but that didn't necessarily mean the photo was taken at the same time.

The uploaded date was just five days before Claire's disappearance. She sat back, her mind whirling with possibilities. There had to be some way to track down when the photo was taken. Did either Jonah or Logan have ways of finding the woman in the photo with Claire? She wasn't tagged, so she must not be on Facebook.

If they could find a way to prove the date of the photograph, they would have something they needed to implicate Caruso in Claire's disappearance. And maybe, just maybe, that would be enough for the authorities to believe her side of the story over Caruso's.

She picked up the bracelet again and carefully put it in a zippered compartment of her purse for safekeeping as she anxiously waited for Jonah, Kate and Logan to return.

"Get the door, will you?" Jonah said, balancing the box of electronics in his arms.

Kate obliged, as Logan was also carrying a similar box.

"You're back!" Mallory exclaimed, leaping off the

sofa. "Come here and look at what I found," she said, gesturing toward the computer screen.

He and Logan set their boxes on the floor and then crossed over to the coffee table where she had the laptop set up. He immediately recognized the photo of Claire Richmond. He frowned. "I don't think it's big news that Claire had a Facebook page."

"See this bracelet here around her right wrist?" Mallory said, pointing at the screen. "That's the same bracelet Caruso gave me on our third date."

Logan's head jerked up at that comment. He was standing on the opposite side of the computer and leaned over to get a better look. "Well, now, are you sure about that?"

Mallory pulled the bracelet out of her purse and set it on the table next to the computer. Logan whistled in surprise but Jonah could only stare at the bracelet in shock. As Mallory explained how she saw the same bracelet on another photo of Claire standing next to Caruso, he could barely contain his excitement.

"It's possible Caruso took it back from Claire and gave it to me," Mallory was saying. "He claimed it was a one-of-a-kind item. If we could nail the timeline as to when this photo was taken, we might be able to prove that Caruso saw Claire shortly before her disappearance."

"Unbelievable," Jonah murmured. Leave it to Mallory to find the clue they needed. He wanted to leap up and pump his fist in the air. "This is it, Mallory. We can easily use the bracelet itself as a way to get Caruso's attention."

"I don't understand," she said.

He glanced at Logan. "What if we changed the plan

a bit? We can call my boss, who we know is working for Caruso. We can let him know we have this bracelet to set up a meeting. Once we have Finley, we'll use him to get to Caruso."

Logan grimaced and nodded. "I see what you're saying, but remember, the bracelet is only circumstantial evidence at this point. It's not a murder weapon or DNA found at the scene of a crime. It also might not even be the same bracelet." Logan shrugged. "Mallory is still the key witness who overheard him covering up a murder."

"Yeah, but don't you see that this way is safer? Finley doesn't know why I cut off all communication with him. He has no way of knowing I suspect him of being dirty. I'll let him know I want to discuss the bracelet as evidence and provide Mallory's testimony. He'll be anxious to get his hands on both the bracelet and Mallory—he won't be able to say no."

Deep in his gut, Jonah knew this was the way to go. It was the only way to keep Mallory away from Caruso.

"I don't know if I like that idea," Mallory said slowly. "To be honest, I'd rather face Caruso than your boss. What if Finley arrests me despite what you tell him? Caruso could easily find a way to have me killed in jail."

"Don't worry, Mallory. I wouldn't actually turn you in. This would just be a way to get to Finley." The more he thought about his plan, the better he liked it. Finley deserved to be used as bait to get to Caruso. And Mallory would be totally safe.

"And what if Finley isn't the dirty cop, but someone above him is?" Logan asked.

"Finley is the only one I've been talking to since we discovered Crane was dirty. He reports directly to the chief of police. I find it difficult to believe the chief is involved in this."

Logan was silent for a long minute. "Your decision," he said grudgingly. "If you want to try that route then count me in."

"Me, too," Kate added, earning another scowl from Logan.

He felt light-headed with relief. All along, he'd been so worried he'd fail Mallory, the same way he'd failed Drew. He'd tried not to become emotionally involved, but he knew he was. He cared about Mallory, far more than he should.

As much as he wanted to, he knew he couldn't pursue his feelings. She might see him in a positive light now, but how long before the extended hours of his job and the horrible things he saw every day wore on their relationship? He couldn't bear to see the same look in Mallory's eyes that he'd seen in Cheryl's, right before she'd walked out on him.

He knew his feelings were for real, but he understood that Mallory was dependent on him for safety. She was embracing her faith, but that didn't mean she cared about him, specifically.

He shook off his uncertain thoughts. Time enough to worry about the future later. Right now, they needed to plan out the next step. For the first time in the past twenty-four hours, Jonah felt good about the direction their investigation was going. He knew they were finally on the right track.

And he firmly believed God was guiding them.

Mallory wasn't sure she agreed with Jonah's plan, but she couldn't deny she was glad they were doing something. Glancing at the clock, she was surprised to realize it was only an hour since she'd spoken to Alyssa.

According to Jonah, Gage had already taken Alyssa someplace safe, which was a relief.

"Call your boss and set up the meeting in this warehouse here," Logan said, pointing to the map. She leaned closer to see it was the one located farthest to the east. "We'll have our surveillance cameras and bugs set up well before he can get there."

"All right." Jonah took a deep breath and pulled out his cell.

"He's not going to answer on Sunday," Kate said.

"His office phone sends messages to his cell phone," Jonah explained. He turned his attention to the phone call. "Lieutenant Finley, this is Jonah. I have something important we can use against Caruso. Meet me at the warehouse on Fourth and Harper tonight—I don't want to come in because I'm being followed. Call me back as soon as you can." He quickly rattled off the new number.

Jonah snapped his phone shut and looked at Logan. "The trap has been set."

"Guess we should head down to the warehouse, then." Logan settled his cowboy hat on his head as he started toward the door. "Kate and Mallory can wait for us here."

She opened her mouth to protest, but surprisingly, Jonah beat her to it.

"The women are coming with us, Logan. We need to stick together."

Logan narrowed his eyes and crossed his arms over his chest as he glared at Jonah. "Why expose them to danger?"

"We stick together," Jonah repeated. "When I was

helping Gage stake out Hugh Jefferson's yacht, we left Alyssa back in the motel alone to keep her safe, except she was anything but. We didn't realize Crane had found her until we saw him leading her to the yacht at gunpoint. I'm not going to make that same mistake. We all go together."

Mallory hadn't known that detail. She crossed over to place a hand on Jonah's arm. "Thanks, Jonah."

"Three against one," Kate piped up cheerfully, apparently not the least bit fazed by the deep scowl creasing Logan's brow. "We outnumber you, Logan."

Logan lifted his hat long enough to swipe a hand over his hair before settling it low on his brow as he glared at Jonah. "Fine, we'll do this your way. But I still think bringing them along is a bad idea."

"Your objection is so noted," Kate said smartly, and Mallory coughed to hide a grin.

The four of them left the hotel suite and headed down the stairs to the main lobby. As they walked outside, Jonah wrapped a protective arm around her waist.

She smiled up at him, wishing she could tell him how she felt. Opening up to him after church had lightened her heart and soul more than she could have imagined. And while she was still working on the forgiveness angle, at least as far as Garrett and Caruso were concerned, she was amazed that Jonah didn't seem to hold her past against her.

Of course, his being nice to her could be nothing more than friendly consideration for what she'd gone through. It didn't mean he cared about her on a personal level.

Except there had been that kiss.

She and Kate slid into the backseat, leaving Jonah and Logan up front.

"Earlier, you mentioned Alyssa and Gage. Who are they?" Kate asked.

"Alyssa is my twin sister, and Gage is her boyfriend." Thinking about her sister made her smile. "Although I guess they could be engaged by now."

"Wouldn't surprise me," Jonah muttered.

"You have a sister? Is she your identical twin?" When Mallory nodded, Kate grinned. "Did the two of you ever switch identities to fool people?"

Mallory's smile faded but amazingly, her stomach didn't cramp painfully at the mention of that night, the way it used to. Because of Jonah. And her newfound faith in God. "Not very often, no."

Kate seemed oblivious to the subtle change in mood. "I would have loved to have a sister and especially a twin. But I only had brothers. Three older brothers, all in various types of law enforcement."

"Figures," Logan said drily. "And I bet you drove them crazy."

Kate laughed. "Not hardly. They were the ones who tortured me, not the other way around."

"There's the warehouse," Jonah said, bringing an abrupt end to the lighthearted conversation.

"I see it." Logan didn't stop but kept driving. Both men were peering intently through the windshield. Mallory did the same, craning her neck to check out the area surrounding the warehouses. The one they were looking at using had two separate garage doors in the front covered with graffiti. There was only one streetlamp out front, providing just enough light for her to see that all three buildings looked pretty dilapidated. She couldn't imagine why they hadn't been leveled a long time ago.

"They look abandoned," Jonah murmured.

"Looks can be deceiving," Logan grimly pointed out. "Let's hope they're not currently being used as gang hangouts."

"Maybe we should go around the block, just to be sure," Kate spoke up from the backseat.

From Mallory's angle in the back, she could see Logan's jaw tighten with annoyance, but he obliged Kate's request, making a big circle so that they saw the warehouse from different angles.

"There's a narrow driveway between the two warehouses there, leading around to the back," Jonah said. "If we park there, the car will be tucked out of sight from the street and away from the streetlight."

"Exactly what I was thinking," Logan said, making a left turn into the narrow driveway. He pulled around so that the building completely blocked the view of the SUV from the road. He put the vehicle in Park but kept the engine running as he turned around in his seat to look at her and Kate. "I'd like you two to wait here for a minute, at least until we verify the place is empty."

"No way," Kate said, trying to open her door. But it was locked, because Logan hadn't turned off the SUV.

"I'm in agreement with Logan on this one," Jonah said. "We just need five minutes to make sure the place is empty."

Mallory nodded, putting her trust and faith in Jonah. "All right."

Kate threw up her hands in disgust. "Okay, five minutes. But I'm going to be ready to drive away if they're not."

The two men climbed out of the vehicle. They stopped at a door on the side of the building and tested the handle, but it must have been locked, so they headed for the front. Mallory watched them until they disappeared from view. Time passed with excruciating slowness.

When Jonah tapped on her passenger window a few minutes later, she jumped from surprise, her heart leaping into her throat. Kate bailed out of the car and Mallory followed more slowly, admiring the younger girl's apparent nerves of steel.

Clearly, a career in law enforcement wasn't in her own future.

"Are you okay?" Jonah murmured, as they walked around to the rear of the vehicle.

"Of course." She'd rather be here than waiting at the hotel, but she couldn't totally hide her nervousness.

Jonah opened the back of the Jeep. "The place is empty, so our plan is to plant a few of these bugs."

"We can help," Kate offered.

"Take this inside to Logan," Jonah said as he thrust the small box into Kate's hands. He tucked the last box under his arm rather than giving it to Mallory.

"I'm not helpless. I can help, too," Mallory said testily.

Granted, Kate was studying criminal law, but she wasn't a cop any more than Mallory was. Yet the men seemed to treat Kate as more of an equal.

"You've helped us a lot already," Jonah said. "Finding the bracelet in photos of Claire Richmond was pure genius."

She hadn't been looking for a pat on the back so she dropped the subject and followed Jonah inside the warehouse through the open garage door. The interior was dark thanks to the grime coating the windows, and she glanced around, wondering where the light switches might be located.

Next to a tall stack of crates, Kate and Logan were crouched over the box of supplies, going through the contents. Jonah was on the other side of the building, setting crates up to use as a makeshift ladder, so she began examining the walls for a light switch. She finally found one, right near the side door.

Just as she was about to flip the switch, Jonah shouted, "Wait! Everyone freeze!"

"What's wrong?" Logan demanded.

Afraid to move, Mallory slowly turned her head to look over at Jonah.

"We need to get out of here," Jonah said grimly. "This place is wired to blow."

FIFTEEN

Mallory quickly dropped her hand from the light switch. What if the switch was the dynamite trigger? A chill spiraled down her spine. She could have easily killed them all.

"Are you sure?" Logan demanded as he rose to his feet. He held out a hand to help Kate up but she ignored it, crossing her arms over her chest.

"Yeah. I'm sure." Jonah slowly backed away from the pile of crates. "But if you want to see for yourself, go ahead."

"It's possible the owners were planning to blow these up in order to build their new wind-turbine plant," Kate said, as if trying to find a logical reason for what Jonah had found.

"I don't think so." Jonah's expression was grim. "Demolishing existing buildings with explosives is a detailed and precise process, with small amounts of dynamite placed in strategic locations." Jonah was continuing to back up slowly until he stood in the center of the room. "I'm not an expert, but from what I can tell, there's enough dynamite here to blow up the entire neighborhood. Far more than would be needed to bring down three abandoned warehouses."

Everyone fell silent for a moment as the implication of Jonah's assessment sank in. Logan was scowling deeply, and Mallory knew he was probably feeling guilty for suggesting they use these warehouses for a meeting in the first place.

"Well, if it isn't Detective Stewart. You arrived earlier than I expected."

At the sound of a strange voice, Mallory shrank back against the wall near the side door. From where she stood, she could just barely make out the tall figure standing in the open area where they'd left the garage door open.

"Chief Ramsey? What are you doing here?" Jonah asked, trying to hide his surprise.

"Meeting you, of course." Dread curled through her stomach as the chief of police stepped forward, his weapon leveled dead center on Jonah's chest. She glanced at the side door, wondering if she'd have time to slip through and escape before anyone noticed. "Lieutenant Finley was kind enough to let me know you'd contacted him. Keep your hands where I can see them, or I won't hesitate to shoot."

Both Logan and Jonah went still at his words, and Mallory understood why. Was it possible the police chief didn't know the building was wired to explode? Apparently not, as he'd surely realize one gunshot would be enough to ignite the dynamite.

Unless he was trying to bluff? Either way, they couldn't take a chance on any weapons being fired.

From the corner of her eye, Mallory could see that Kate had melted backward, disappearing behind a small stack of crates. And just in time, as Ramsey narrowed his gaze as he glanced at Logan. "Who are you?"

Mallory watched Logan turn his body so that he was facing Ramsey while helping to cover Kate's hiding place. Jonah mirrored Logan's move, trying to block Ramsey's view of her. Taking the bit of coverage he provided, she moved closer to the door, relieved to feel the handle pressing into the small of her back.

"Special Agent Logan Quail with the FBI," Logan replied in his deepest Southern drawl. "But I can't say it's a pleasure to meet you, sir. Why don't you put the gun away so we can talk this out? I'm sure we can reach a mutually acceptable agreement."

While Logan was speaking, she silently flipped the lock open and turned the handle. Thinking of Kate hiding behind the crates gave her a surge of grim satisfaction. The four of them against one chief—there should be no reason they couldn't find a way out of this.

"FBI?" Ramsey echoed in shock. "I don't believe you. You're bluffing."

"No, he's not bluffing," Jonah said.

"Keep your hands up!" the police chief shouted, when it looked as if Logan was reaching for his pocket.

She chose that moment to open the door a crack and slip through, using the darkness as a cover. Thankfully, clouds covered the moon. She quickly and silently closed the door behind her and then stood for several long seconds, her heart pounding in her chest as she waited to be discovered.

When nothing happened, she wanted to collapse with relief. But instead, she forced herself into action. She needed to call for help. She grabbed her phone and inched along the wall toward the back side of the warehouse where they'd left Logan's SUV. She couldn't call 9-1-1 so she quickly texted Gage.

The minute she turned the corner, she gasped when strong hands gripped her shoulders painfully. Horrified, she looked up into Anthony Caruso's leering face.

"Gotcha," he said with a cold, empty smile.

Jonah faced the chief of police. He knew Mallory had just slipped out and he was worried about what she might find out there. He had to move this along and go after her. "It's time to give up, Chief. It's over. We have the evidence we need against Caruso. I'm sure if you cooperate the DA's office will go easier on you."

Ramsey took a step back, keeping both men easily within firing range. "I don't think so," he said. "All I have to do is kill both of you and I'm off the hook. I've worked hard to hype up the gang killings in the area, so it won't be a stretch for me to ensure your deaths are attributed to gang warfare. Especially since you've been so accommodating, coming down here to an abandoned warehouse. This will play out perfectly in the media."

Jonah realized he'd made a huge mistake. He'd automatically suspected Finley rather than thinking about the possibility that the dirty cop could be someone higher up the chain. He'd told Finley to meet them at the warehouse, but he should have anticipated that Finley—or in this case, Chief Ramsey—would come early, too.

His mistake that could easily get them all killed.

He couldn't believe he'd once again let his emotions get in the way of doing his job. He'd been so concerned with protecting Mallory that he'd allowed himself to be distracted from what was truly important. Solving this case.

His fault. They were standing in a warehouse full of dynamite at gunpoint because of his foolish mistake.

"You can't shoot both of us at the same time," Logan pointed out, calling Ramsey's bluff. "Is it really worth risking your life? Let's talk this through."

Jonah quickly added to what Logan was doing, trying to keep Ramsey talking. "Tell us how you got mixed up with Caruso," he invited. "If he blackmailed you into helping him, then we can probably keep you out of jail."

Ramsey shook his head. "Nice try, Stewart, but it's not going to work. Drop your weapons and get over there to stand closer to your FBI friend."

Jonah hesitated, not sure what to do. If he refused to move, Chief Ramsey might fire in an attempt to convince him to move. And that would likely set off the dynamite hidden behind the crates. Yet moving toward Logan would mean giving up their advantage. Because no matter how good Ramsey might be with a handgun, there was no way he'd be able to shoot both of them if they were far apart.

"I said, move!" Ramsey yelled.

"Keep your voice down," a second voice said from somewhere behind Ramsey. "This might be an abandoned section of the manufacturing district but there's no sense in taking foolish chances. But you've already blown it anyway. How could you be so stupid as to let this woman escape right under your nose?"

Jonah's heart lodged in his throat when he saw Senator Caruso with his arm locked around Mallory's neck and a knife pressed against her side. He forced her to walk into the warehouse, her back arched at an awkward angle as he kept her body solidly in front of his.

Mallory's eyes were full of silent apology as she met

his gaze across the room. But once again, he accepted full responsibility for this mess. He'd all but encouraged Mallory to escape. Right into Caruso's hands.

"Let her go, Caruso," he demanded angrily.

"You're not the one calling the shots here," Caruso replied. "Now tell me where the bracelet is."

Jonah fell silent, caught off guard by Caruso's demand. He was fairly certain Mallory had put it in her purse, which was likely in Jonah's SUV. But she could have just as easily left it back in their hotel suite.

"If you don't answer, I'll start cutting her up until you do," Caruso threatened. He saw Mallory wince as Caruso pressed the point of the knife harder against her side. The chilling expression in the senator's eyes convinced Jonah he wouldn't hesitate to make good on his threat.

"He doesn't know where the bracelet is," Mallory said, apparently trying to sound brave, as much as she could manage with Caruso's arm locked around her neck. "I'm the one who hid it. Let me go and I'll show you where it is."

Logan pretended to be confused by Caruso's abrupt demand. "Why do you care about a stupid bracelet?" he asked.

"Because I haven't gotten this far without being meticulous about loose ends," Caruso replied tersely. He tightened his grip around her neck, making Mallory's face grow red as she struggled to breathe. "I'm not letting you go, Mallory, so save yourself some pain and tell me where the bracelet is."

Jonah desperately wanted to rush over and yank Mallory out of harm's way. But he could only watch helplessly as Caruso used Mallory as a pawn in his deadly game.

"The bracelet..." Mallory's voice came out as little more than a croaked sound since he was holding pressure against her windpipe. Caruso obliged by loosening his arm around her throat. Mallory gulped in several breaths of fresh air. "I have it in a safe place back in our hotel room," she finally admitted. "I'll take you there."

Jonah wanted to yell out in protest. No way did he want Mallory going anywhere alone with Caruso. "I'll take you," he interjected. "I know right where she put it."

"No, you don't," Mallory argued, shooting him a glare that silently implored him to shut up and trust her. "I hid it after you left."

Jonah knew she wasn't being entirely truthful. He was equally torn between stalling for time and getting them all out of the rigged warehouse. The more Ramsey and Caruso talked, the more he was starting to believe that neither man knew the warehouse was a bomb waiting to blow.

"Forget about the bracelet," Chief Ramsey said in a curt tone. "I'll make sure my officers find it and I'll get it to you."

Caruso hesitated, as if considering the possibility. Jonah could tell Caruso didn't like letting Ramsey call the shots, especially since the bracelet was evidence that could be used against him. "I want the bracelet," he said. "And I don't believe she left it in some hotel room. Give me a couple minutes to search their vehicle, okay?"

Ramsey scowled. "Make it quick."

Jonah glanced at Logan, knowing that they were going to have to make a move, and soon. Their only hope was to distract Ramsey and Caruso enough for them to rush them head-on. A risky plan at best, with the dynamite surrounding them.

Yet it was one step above getting shot point-blank.

"You're right," Mallory suddenly said. "I do have the bracelet with me." Her gaze was locked on his and Jonah was trying to understand what she was silently trying to tell him. Her hand was tucked inside her sweatshirt pocket—was it possible she'd managed to make a call before she was grabbed by Caruso?

He was almost afraid to hope. He tried to figure out how long they'd been standing there. It seemed like forever, but he knew it couldn't have been more than five to ten minutes.

At that moment, a tower of crates came crashing to the floor. The sound made everyone jump in surprise, including him. But when Logan headed straight for Ramsey, he realized that Kate had provided the distraction they needed.

He ran toward Caruso at the exact moment Mallory used the element of surprise to leverage Caruso's arm up just enough to duck underneath. He rammed his head into Caruso's torso, causing them both to crash to the ground. He heard Mallory cry out in pain.

Out of the corner of his eye, Jonah could see that Logan and Ramsey were wrestling for the gun. He paid dearly for allowing that brief look. Caruso hit him square in the face. He jerked backward, his head bursting with pain. For a moment darkness threatened, but he fought back against Caruso, exchanging blows, doing his best to ignore whatever was going on around him.

He hoped Mallory and Kate would run for help, but of course they didn't. He had the slim advantage of being on top, pinning Caruso to the concrete floor. But

Caruso wasn't going down easily. He stretched his arm out wide, and Jonah realized the senator was reaching for the knife he must have dropped.

Jonah leaned forward, putting more pressure against the man's throat. Mallory's foot swept the knife well out of reach, sending it skittering across the room. He wanted to shout at her to get into the SUV, but he was distracted by blood.

Bright red blood.

Dripping onto the concrete floor right where Mallory was standing.

Caruso had stabbed her.

Mallory could barely tear her gaze from where Jonah and Caruso struggled on the floor. She was feeling more light-headed by the second and knew she was losing too much blood.

Please, Lord, grant Jonah the strength to get away from Caruso!

"Mallory!" Kate called from the other side of the room. Her arms and legs didn't want to work very well, as she turned toward the other woman. "Grab a piece of crate!"

In the distance Mallory could hear the wail of sirens and she hoped and prayed that help was on the way, since she'd texted Gage asking for help and giving their location. She took a piece of crate that Kate thrust in her hands, but found that she lacked the physical strength to lift the board high enough to hit Caruso.

But she noticed Kate didn't have the same problem, as she hit Chief Ramsey on the back of his head. Logan grunted as the chief collapsed and he managed to wrestle the gun away without the weapon going off.

Logan tossed the gun outside, far out of anyone's reach, before he went over to help Jonah. Mallory blinked when Kate came up beside her.

"What's wrong?" Kate asked.

She held her hand against her side. "I have to sit down," she murmured.

"You're bleeding!" Kate exclaimed. "Why didn't you say something sooner?"

She shook her head, finding it difficult to concentrate. She didn't even notice that Jonah and Logan had managed to knock out Caruso.

"Come on, we need to leave here," Jonah said, putting his arm around her for support. She clung to him, hating the fact that she didn't have an ounce of strength.

Jonah must have realized how bad off she was because suddenly he swung her into his arms. "Let's go!"

"The car is this way," Logan said, hanging back.

"The car won't help if the building blows," Jonah said, breathing heavily. "Come on!" he insisted. She felt him crane his neck back to look behind them. "Caruso's trying to get up!"

She tucked her head in the hollow of his shoulder, trying to ease the bouncing as he ran. When Logan and Kate came up beside them, she tried to get their attention. "He has cracked ribs."

"Give her to me," Logan said, understanding her concern.

Before Jonah could reply, an earsplitting boom filled the night, shaking the earth and sending all four of them airborne.

SIXTEEN

Jonah couldn't breathe—he felt as if he had a knife stabbing his heart. But he still crawled frantically on his stomach toward Mallory.

Please, Lord, keep her safe. Let her live—please.

He finally reached her, several feet from where he'd landed. She was unconscious, but he wouldn't allow himself to believe the worst. He caught her wrist, closed his eyes and concentrated on feeling for a pulse.

Finding the faint beat almost made him weep with relief. The sirens were louder now, and he had to believe they were coming for them.

"Jonah?"

Hearing Logan's voice made him raise his head and glance around. "Over here!"

Miraculously, both Logan and Kate didn't appear to be badly injured, judging by the way they rushed over to Mallory's side. "Is she okay?" Kate asked anxiously.

"She has a pulse," Jonah said, ignoring the deep stab of pain that accompanied every word. He couldn't be sure, but he thought maybe he'd broken his rib to the point that the bone was poking into his lung. "But it's fast and faint. She's lost too much blood."

"She'll be fine. Medical help is on the way," Logan assured him.

"Don't give up, Mallory," he murmured, reaching over to brush her hair off her cheek. He couldn't bear to think about losing her. "Don't give up on me—on us. Do you understand?"

Mallory stirred, and his heart raced with hope, but she didn't open her eyes. He wished the ambulance would get here faster.

"Press this against the wound in her side," Kate said, stripping off her hoodie and handing it to Jonah.

He took the fabric. "Logan, help me. I don't have the strength to hold pressure."

Logan stepped up and used his weight to press against Mallory's side. Jonah couldn't allow himself to think Mallory might not make it. He had faith in God and in Mallory's own will to live.

The paramedics arrived and shoved him aside in order to assess Mallory.

"He's injured, too," Kate said, pointing at Jonah.

"I'm fine. Take care of Mallory first," he insisted.

The paramedic brushed away his concern. "We have two teams here and more on the way so stop playing hero. You're girlfriend is being well cared for. What happened?"

He craned his neck, trying to see what was going on with Mallory. "She's been stabbed," he called out. "There's a knife wound in her right side."

"Buddy, I'm trying to help you here," the paramedic said, clearly exasperated. "I need to know what happened to you."

"Cracked ribs, maybe broken now," he reluctantly admitted. "And a surgical incision that may have opened up again."

"Where does it hurt? Here?" The paramedic pressed against his lower left side.

Excruciating pain shot through his chest. Despite his best efforts to battle the pain, Jonah passed out cold.

When Jonah awoke, he was already in the hospital. He didn't remember anything about the ambulance ride, which made him wonder if the guy had given him something to knock him out.

He turned his head on the gurney but didn't see Mallory. "Where's Mallory?" he asked the nurse.

She turned toward him. "Hello, my name is Susan. How are you feeling?"

"Fine. Where's Mallory? Mallory Roth?"

"Calm down," she urged, putting a hand on his arm. "I don't know who Mallory Roth is, but I'll try to find out, okay?"

"Logan!" he bellowed, annoyed with the nurse who was trying to placate him.

"Excuse me, ma'am," Logan said, appearing in the doorway to his room. He flashed his badge for the nurse. "I'm with the FBI and I need to talk to this witness."

"Fine. But you need to keep him calm. We just reinflated his lung and repaired the surgical incision he did his best to ruin."

"I promise I'll keep him calm," Logan drawled, flashing his most charming grin.

"Where's Mallory?" he asked, unable to concentrate on anything else until he knew she was okay. "Have you seen her?"

"Mallory is fine. She has a minor concussion and

they've already stitched up the wound in her side. They're giving her a couple units of blood to replace what she lost."

"She went to surgery?" He was appalled to know that she'd undergone surgery while he was unconscious.

"No, they took care of everything right in the trauma room," Logan assured him. "I swear to you, she's fine. Resting for now and waiting for a hospital bed. They want to watch her overnight to make sure her head injury doesn't get worse."

He saw the truth in Logan's eyes and allowed himself to relax. Mallory was alive. She was going to be okay.

Thank You, Lord.

"I want to see her," Jonah said. He put a hand to his chest, feeling the bulky dressing along his left side. "Help me up."

"No way, not until the doctor gives the okay."

"I'm fine," he insisted. The pain was bad, but he didn't care. He wanted to see Mallory.

"Knock it off, Jonah," Logan said in an exasperated tone. "One of your broken ribs punctured a lung, and so help me, if you don't stay put, I will help hold you down while that nurse gives you a sedative."

Jonah glared at Logan, but his colleague didn't back down. He ground his teeth in frustration. "Then get the doctor in here to clear me. I doubt I'll need a hospital bed."

"Don't count on that," Logan muttered drily. "Listen, it's time for me to report all this, so humor me for a minute, okay? As soon as you've answered my questions, I'll get the doctor in here."

He narrowed his gaze but he nodded. "Fine. Ask your questions."

"How did you know the warehouse was going to blow up?" Logan asked. "I wanted to get the car, but you made us run in the opposite direction. If we'd have gone to the car, we'd all be dead."

Despite the pain, he flashed a crooked grin. "Chief Ramsey didn't seem to know the place was wired with dynamite, since he showed up with a gun. But Caruso had a knife. I suspected there was a possibility he might be planning to double-cross the chief by blowing all of us up with the warehouse once he had the bracelet. When he was trying to get up but collapsed onto his stomach, he reached for his pocket and I was afraid that he might trigger the explosion by accident, so I wanted to put as much time and distance between us and the warehouse as possible." Thankfully, God had guided him in the right direction.

"But how did you know Caruso was the one who'd wired the warehouse in the first place?" Logan persisted.

Now Jonah understood what was bothering Logan. Logan was the one who'd suggested the warehouse as a meeting place and he couldn't understand how it had been used against them. "You'll have to help me answer that one, Logan. You mentioned you had a contact who told you about the warehouse. Is it possible your contact planned on double-crossing you, too?"

"Bruce Dunlop," Logan said with disgust. "We sent him to work undercover in Salvatore's business. He's the one who gave me the idea of using that particular warehouse and he's the one who was supposed to be helping us from the inside."

Jonah shook his head. "Plenty of guilt to go around, Logan. I'm the one who left the message with Finley telling him we wanted to meet him at the warehouse in the first place."

"No matter when you told Finley the meeting spot, he would have told the chief anyway, to keep him in the loop."

Maybe, but by then they wouldn't have been trapped inside with the chief holding a gun on them. Jonah hated the way he'd made so many mistakes. "You were right, Logan. I should've considered the possibility that the corruption went higher than Finley."

"It's all over now, Jonah. We made it out alive. Unfortunately, both the chief and Caruso died in the explosion."

Jonah nodded. "Yeah, and I still don't know for sure if Finley is dirty, too. I'd like to think not, since the chief showed up without him, but let your boss know so that there can be a full investigation."

"You got it," Logan agreed. He held out his hand and Jonah solemnly clasped it. "Thanks, Jonah. I'll be in touch. And I'll get the doctor to come in and talk to you now."

"Thanks."

The doctor insisted on admitting him to a hospital bed, and he agreed only if he could be on the same floor as Mallory.

It was several hours later before he was settled in his room on the third-floor surgical unit. Getting out of bed with the IV pump and all his tubing wasn't easy. But he insisted on walking in the hall, so the nurse and the aide reluctantly helped to disconnect him.

"You can't stay off the suction too long," the nurse warned him. "We need to make sure your lung doesn't collapse again, okay?"

Since he didn't particularly want that, either, he nodded. "Just a few minutes. I promise."

With the IV pole in tow, he made his way out to the main nursing station. He found Mallory's room number, inwardly groaning as he realized she was on the opposite side of the floor.

Walking wasn't bad as long as he didn't breathe too much. When he reached Mallory's room the door was closed. He lightly tapped.

"Come in."

He pushed open the door. She was lying in bed, looking pretty good except for the blood dripping through her IV and the dark bruises shadowing her eyes. He crossed the room toward her.

"Jonah!" She looked happy to see him. "Are you okay?"

"Yeah, I'm fine. Just need to make sure my lung stays good, and if it does, they'll take this chest tube out tomorrow morning and let me go home." They'd mentioned the possibility of needing more IV antibiotics but he was sure he could convince them to give him pills instead.

She reached out her hand toward him and he gingerly sat in the chair next to her bed so he could grasp it without too much pain. "Jonah, I'm glad you're here. God has answered my prayers. I was so worried about you."

"I was praying for your safety, too. But I wasn't the one who had surgery in the trauma bay," he pointed out.

"Not true. Logan told me that you had minor surgery but that you were insisting on going home."

"The doctor wouldn't let me. They agreed to put me on the same floor as you so I decided not to argue." Her hand felt so dainty in his, but he knew Mallory was so much stronger than she looked. The blood transfusions had brought color back to her cheeks, and aside from the bruising, she looked great. He silently thanked the Lord again for keeping her safe. "How's your head?"

"Hurts," she admitted. "I feel sick to my stomach, too, but that could be just from seeing the blood." She kept her gaze on his face, and he realized she didn't like watching the blood transfusion drip into her arm. "Can't wait till this one is finished."

He grinned and gently squeezed her hand in reassurance. "It's all over, Mallory. Caruso can't hurt you anymore. I'm sure we'll get a search warrant to go through his house and garage. We'll find out what happened to Claire Richmond. You're free to go home once you're released from the hospital."

"And what about you, Jonah?" she asked, her gaze serious. "Will I ever see you again?"

He stared into her blue eyes and knew the best thing for her would be for him to walk away. Cops weren't a good bet in relationships. His own fiancée had walked away—what if Mallory eventually did the same thing? She deserved better than a wounded warrior.

"I'm sure we'll see each other again," he said slowly, sidestepping the real meaning of her question. "But for right now, I think you should call your sister. I know Alyssa will want to be here for you."

"She's on her way." Mallory stared at him for a long moment, her gaze full of hurt.

He needed to get out of here, and soon, or he'd change his mind. Time to let Mallory go, so she could move on with her life.

"I better get back to my room," he said finally. He had to drop her hand so he could hold on to his injured side as he stood. "The nurses warned me that I need to keep this chest tube hooked up to suction until to-morrow."

"I understand," she murmured, although her puzzled expression tore his heart. He clamped his jaw shut and pushed the IV pole toward the door.

"Jonah?" she called out, stopping him before he could open the door.

Steeling his resolve, he turned back to her. "Yes?"

"Thanks for showing me the way to our Lord," she said humbly. "Believing in Him has helped me work through my past. I never trusted men, but I want you to know I trust you. I trust that someday, you'll come back to see me. And I want you to know I'll be waiting for you. Because I love you."

He stared at her, feeling as if she'd sucker punched him in the gut. He struggled to breathe without hurting himself. "Mallory, you don't have to say that. You have a concussion. We've been through a lot over this past week and sometimes emotions run high—" He forced the words out, even though he desperately wanted to believe she did know her true feelings.

Her smile was sad. "Jonah, please don't belittle how I feel. I would never say something I didn't mean, al-though I certainly understand if you don't feel the same way. I—I know that I'm not the sort of woman a man like you might want to become involved with. But that doesn't change how I feel. I love you. And I want you to promise me you'll take care of yourself, okay?"

He wheeled his IV pump around and came back over to her bedside. He couldn't possibly let her believe that he was walking away because of what happened to her. "Listen to me. This isn't about you and your past. I care about you, far more than you can possibly realize. But you don't have any idea what it means to be with a cop. The stress of the job puts a huge strain on our relationships. Our loved ones watch the news in terror. It's not fair to you, Mallory. Now that you've found God, I'm sure you'll find another man to care for."

The last sentence almost got stuck in his throat. Because he didn't want her to find someone else. He wanted her. He loved her. He loved her!

How could he have been such a fool? All this time, he'd acted as if he was protecting Mallory from being with him, when in reality, he was protecting himself. Protecting his heart from being hurt the way he'd been when his fiancée walked away.

Surely if Mallory could overcome her fears, he could do the same?

"You're dooming our relationship before even giving us a chance. Yes, your job is dangerous. But I can't believe there aren't police officers out there who manage to make a relationship work."

She was right about that. There were a few cops who had faith and somehow their marriages survived. "Some, yes, but it's an uphill battle."

"Maybe it is, but isn't that where our faith is supposed to help us? Weren't you the one to convince me that God's strength helps us to shoulder our burdens? I thought you were a true believer."

He thought so, too. But hadn't he known for a while now that God had brought Mallory into his life to strengthen his own faith? She was thanking him for showing her the way to their Lord, when he should be thanking her.

She was the best thing to happen to him, and now

that he'd faced his deepest fears, he couldn't let her go. He lowered himself gingerly back into the chair beside her bed and reached over to take her hand again. "You're right, Mallory. I have a confession to make. I love you. I love you so much, it scares me. I feel like I don't deserve such a precious gift."

Her beautiful blue eyes filled with tears. "Crazy man, we both deserve this precious gift of love. God loves us just the way we are. Which means He'll watch over us and protect us, too."

Jonah couldn't find the words to respond, so he simply reached over and kissed her, vowing to make sure she never regretted loving him.

EPILOGUE

Mallory stood next to Alyssa in the back dressing room of the church, amazed that the wedding gowns they'd chosen were so similar in style. Once they'd dressed completely opposite, but not anymore.

"Are you ready?" Alyssa asked.

Mallory nodded, hoping and praying she wouldn't start crying like a baby, ruining her makeup. Because if she started crying, Alyssa would, too. And then they'd both be blubbering idiots walking down the aisle.

The double wedding had been Alyssa's idea, and Mallory was secretly relieved she didn't have to walk down the aisle alone. They'd agreed that since their parents were gone, they would walk together to the church altar. Gage would be waiting on the left side of the church, and Jonah would be waiting on the right.

"I love you, Alyssa," Mallory said. "Thanks for always being there for me."

"Likewise, Mallory," Alyssa said with a tremulous smile. "Now, don't get too mushy on me or we'll both be crying on a day we should be rejoicing."

"I'm happy," Mallory insisted, although she could feel the threat of tears pricking her eyes. "Truly happy."

"Me, too." Alyssa linked her arm with Mallory's. "Come on, they're playing our song."

Mallory took a deep breath and nodded. Together, they left the dressing room and approached the aisle. The church was surprisingly packed with family and friends. Mallory couldn't get over how easily the members had welcomed her into their community.

They paused at the end of the aisle and she smiled when she saw Jonah staring at her in awe. Gage had a similar expression on his face, and she knew in that moment, she and Alyssa were the luckiest women on earth to find two guys like Gage Drummond and Jonah Stewart.

She smiled at Jonah, keeping her gaze locked on his, determined to show him just how much she loved him. Jonah's smile held her steady as she approached the altar. He surprised her by stepping forward to meet her, taking her hand in his. "You look beautiful, Mallory," he murmured.

Her heart swelled with love as they turned to face the pastor. As they recited their vows, she knew there was nothing on this earth that would keep them apart.

* * * * *

Dear Reader,

I've always been fascinated by twins, especially identical twins. I've seen TV documentaries about twins separated at birth who have the same careers, the same medical problems, even the same hobbies. But what if you had identical twins with completely different personalities?

Alyssa and Mallory are twins, but due to a traumatic event when Mallory was younger, they lead very different lifestyles. Until danger forces them to take each other's personalities.

You met Alyssa and Gage in *Identity Crisis. Twin Peril* is Mallory and Jonah's story. Mallory is running for her life and doesn't trust men, until she meets Jonah Stewart, a Milwaukee police detective. Jonah knows better than to get emotionally involved with a potential witness, but he can't help responding to Mallory, anxious to help her find faith in God.

Forgiveness is the theme of *Twin Peril* and I hope you enjoy Mallory's story. I'm always thrilled to hear from my readers and I can be reached through my website at laurascottbooks.com.

Yours in faith,
Laura Scott

UNDERCOVER COWBOY

In their hearts humans plan their course,
but the Lord establishes their steps.
—*Proverbs* 16:9

This book is dedicated to my editor, Tina James.
Thanks for being so wonderful to work with!

ONE

"Kate, I'm in trouble," Angela Giordano, her former college roommate, whispered urgently through the phone. "You have to help me!"

Kate Townsend frowned and tried to ignore the churning in her stomach. She tightened her grip on the subway pole as the Chicago train lurched around a curve. "What kind of trouble?"

"I think my uncle is trying to kill me."

She sucked in a harsh breath, but couldn't say she was surprised. Angela's uncle was Bernardo Salvatore, suspected Chicago crime boss. "Why? What happened?"

"I can't tell you now," Angela whispered. "I need you to meet me here in the back of the restaurant. Hurry!"

No way was she going to the restaurant owned by Salvatore. Talk about walking straight into the lion's den. "Try to remain calm. I'll help you escape, but we have to meet someplace else." She tried to think logically. They needed to meet out in the open, in neutral territory. "I'm on the red line, heading north. Let's meet at Stanton Park. It's not far from the restaurant."

There was a long pause. "I'd rather wait for you to

get here." Angela's voice had dropped so low Kate almost couldn't hear her. Had someone come outside to find Angela? Someone spying for her uncle? Salvatore wasn't the type to do his own dirty work.

"Stanton Park," Kate insisted, glancing at her watch. "I can meet you by the northeast corner of the building in forty minutes."

"Okay," Angela agreed, before quickly hanging up.

Kate clutched her phone, trying to calm her racing heart. She was worried about her former roommate, but she also hoped this might be the break she needed. Now that Angela was in danger, too, there was no reason for her to protect her uncle. Surely Angela would cooperate, giving the authorities inside information about Bernardo's activities.

And maybe, just maybe, Kate would find a solid link to her father's death. His murder. Her chest tightened painfully and the grief she'd tried so hard to keep at bay threatened to erupt.

She took several deep breaths, battling back the wave. She missed him so much. She still had trouble believing he was gone. The pastor at their church reminded her he was in a better place, but that knowledge didn't stop her heart from aching. Didn't stop her from crying herself to sleep at night.

From being determined to seek answers.

In the four weeks since her father's death, she'd become obsessed with trying to find a way to link Salvatore to the crash that had claimed her father's life. But she wasn't getting any help from official channels. According to the police report, her dad, a Chicago cop, had been on the way to the courthouse when he was killed in a motor vehicle crash. His driver's-side door was

T-boned at a busy intersection. A witness had come forward claiming it was a tragic accident, and based on that statement, the cops were willing to close the case.

But Kate wasn't buying that story. For one thing, the driver of the other vehicle hadn't been hurt at all, and when she'd tried to track him down, it seemed as if he'd vanished without a trace. She couldn't find proof that a person with that name and address had ever existed. Also, she had thought it was suspicious that her father had died on the way to the courthouse to testify against Dean Ravden, one of Salvatore's goons. But since the only charge against Ravden was a DUI, no one believed that her father had been the victim of a mafia hit.

Not even her oldest brother, Garrett, who was also a Chicago cop. He'd listened patiently to her theory, but then told her she was imagining things. Their father's unexpected death couldn't possibly be the result of a professional hit. Garrett told her the mafia wouldn't bother to stage a car accident—they would have simply shot him in the head. Or the heart.

Still, she knew deep down that somehow, someway, Salvatore was responsible. With Angela's help, she might be able to prove it. Turning her grief into grim determination wasn't easy, but she steeled her resolve and focused on the upcoming meeting with Angie. It was nearly eight o'clock in the evening, which meant that it would be dark by the time she reached the park. She needed to arrange some sort of backup.

For a moment she considered contacting FBI Special Agent Logan Quail, but almost as soon as the thought formed, she rejected it. She'd only talked to Logan once in the six months since she'd been his informant while working as a waitress at Salvatore's restaurant. With his help, she'd left the mafia-owned restaurant without raising Salvatore's suspicions.

But once she'd recognized Dean Ravden during a news story, she'd called the number he'd made her memorize. Much like her brother, Logan had listened while she explained how she had seen Ravden meeting with Salvatore at the restaurant and why she thought her father was murdered. But while Logan thanked her for the information, he also told her in no uncertain terms to stay out of the investigation. He seemed distant and impatient with her for calling, so she simply agreed and hung up.

She shouldn't have been surprised at the way he'd shut her down, since Logan didn't think much of her goal to become a police officer. He'd made it clear he didn't believe women belonged in law enforcement.

During the few days they'd worked together, six months ago, she'd felt close to him, but once they were out of danger, he'd walked away. To be fair, he'd first tried to convince her to go into a safe house. When she refused, he left barely saying goodbye.

After Logan bruised her heart, she decided it was better to keep her distance. She'd thrown herself into her schooling, finishing up her criminal justice degree.

Being a cop was all she had ever wanted to do. Her grandfather, her father and her three older brothers were all in law enforcement. She'd intended to try out for the police academy, but then her father had died. And her world had spun out of control.

Now it was time to get back on track. She grimaced and pulled out her phone to call her eldest brother, Garrett. He hadn't believed her before, but surely he'd come through for her now that she had Angela as a potential witness. Maybe Angie could even verify that Ravden was one of her uncle's thugs.

For the first time in days, she felt a quiver of anticipation. She quickly dialed her brother and waited for him to answer.

"Katie? What's up?" Her brother's deep voice helped calm her nerves.

"I need your help. My old roommate Angela needs to get away from her uncle, Bernardo Salvatore. I'm heading over to meet her now. How quickly can you get to Stanton Park?"

"Are you crazy?" Garrett shouted in her ear, so loud she winced and pulled away the phone. "No way, absolutely not. It's too dangerous." Her brothers were always overprotective, but she couldn't remember the last time Garrett had yelled at her.

"But she might be able to give us key information," she pointed out, striving to remain calm. "I can stall until you get here."

"I'm more than an hour away and can't leave in the middle of my shift. Don't go, Kate. I mean it. I forbid you to go!"

Forbid? Since when did her brothers forbid her to do anything? She was so upset and shocked she could barely speak.

"Katie, please." Her brother's tone softened, as if he'd sensed he'd gone too far. "We'll meet her first thing in the morning, okay? Call her back and let her know we'll meet with her then."

"What if tomorrow is too late?" She knew only too well how Salvatore got rid of people. He murdered them in cold blood and then dumped their bodies into Lake

Michigan. At least that's what he'd done six months ago, when a waitress at the restaurant had crossed him.

"Tell her we'll meet her later tonight then. I get off work in a couple of hours. Just don't meet her alone," her brother insisted.

"All right, I'll call her back." She hung up on her brother and then dialed Angie's number, but the call went straight through to voice mail.

She sighed and chewed her lip as she considered her options. Her brother didn't want her to meet Angela alone, but she wasn't helpless. She knew basic self-defense moves; her brothers had taught her well. She'd picked the location, not Angie. Therefore, she had the upper hand.

Again, she considered calling Logan Quail, but knew his reaction would be very similar to her brother's. She tried Angie one more time, and when she still didn't pick up, Kate decided she had no choice but to go to the park as planned. Her brother called, but she sent the call to voice mail. She didn't have time to argue with him, and besides, he was too far away to help her, which was why she'd called him in the first place.

When the subway stopped near the park, she elbowed her way past the crowds to exit the train. Stanton Park wasn't far from Old Town, a short distance from Salvatore's restaurant. She walked quickly, avoiding direct eye contact with any of the other patrons.

She arrived at the park a good ten minutes early, and made sure she wasn't followed as she wound her way to the back of the park, where the recreation center was located. She'd thought a public place would be safe, but because of the late hour, there weren't many people around. Still, she rested against the side of the brick building before sending Angela a quick text.

I'm here. Where r u?

She waited a few minutes, but didn't get a response from Angela. Her stomach knotted with worry. First no response to her phone calls, and now no response to her text message. Had something happened? Had Salvatore or one of his men caught her at the restaurant before she could leave? Was Kate too late to help her?

Please, Lord, keep Angela safe.

Kate stood with her shoulder pressed against the brick wall, peering cautiously around the corner toward the front of the building, scanning the area. Her heart thudded painfully, as the seconds passed with agonizing slowness.

The area in front of the recreation center was unusually quiet. Time passed slowly, until it was ten minutes past their arranged meeting time. She silently vowed to wait another ten minutes before heading back to the subway.

Then she saw Angela, dressed in the familiar Salvatore's waitress uniform of black skirt, black apron and crisp white blouse, walking briskly up the sidewalk toward the building. Kate let out her breath in a sigh of relief.

"Kate?" Angela called softly. "Where are you?"

For a moment she hesitated, the tiny hairs on the back of her neck lifting in sudden alarm, but before she could move the cold steel barrel of a gun pressed through into the center of her back. "Step forward very slowly," a low male voice said from behind her. "If you try to run, I'll shoot."

A trap! Stunned speechless, she could hardly wrap her mind around the fact that Angela had actually set her up. How else would the gunman have known she was here? Kate glared at her former roommate in horror as she followed the gunman's demand to take several steps forward.

Angela's eyes had widened in shock. "What are you doing? You promised you wouldn't hurt her!"

"Go back to the restaurant. This isn't your concern," the gravelly voice said. Battling her fear, she listened intently to the hint of an Italian accent in the gunman's voice. Her mouth went desert dry as she realized it wasn't likely Salvatore himself behind her, when he delegated the dirty work. He had plenty of hired muscle to do these kinds of things for him.

Like kidnapping her. Or flat out killing her. Feeling helpless, she thought of how upset her brothers would be to lose her. And for a moment, Logan Quail's broad grin, as he tipped the brim of his cowboy hat, flashed into her mind. He wouldn't be at all happy if she died here tonight. Especially since he'd gone out of his way to help her escape Salvatore six months ago.

Angela gave Kate one last helpless glance before turning and running back in the direction from where she'd come. Kate tried to slow down her breathing, assessing her escape options, which admittedly looked grim. If she ran, she had no doubt the gunman would follow through on his threat of shooting her in the back.

Obviously, she'd been a fool to believe her former roommate had really been in trouble. Angie knew what her uncle was, and went to work for him at the restaurant anyway. Convincing Kate to join her, no less. Kate foolishly had taken the job, only to find out the place was run by the mafia. She'd been so glad Logan had helped her get out of there. Yet all for naught, considering she was being held at gunpoint.

Swallowing a lump of fear, she briefly closed her eyes and prayed. *Please keep me safe, Lord!*

Feeling calmer, she lifted her hands up higher in the air as a gesture of surrender, as she addressed the gunman. "Tell me what you want. Money? Information? I'm sure we can come to some sort of understanding."

"I don't want anything, but Salvatore wants *you*."

Oh, boy. She didn't like the sound of that. Why would Salvatore want her now after all this time? She didn't know what Salvatore wanted, but there was a slim chance of surviving this if she could keep the gunman talking long enough. If Garrett had figured out she hadn't listened to his advice, maybe, just maybe, he'd send a police cruiser to the park to help her. "I'm surprised to hear that since he's the one who fired me. Does this mean he'll give me my waitress job back? I could use the money, the tips were great."

The tip of the gun jabbed the area between her shoulder blades, making her suck in a harsh breath. "Don't play dumb. Turn around and walk to the back of the building."

Never go to a second location. The knowledge reverberated in her mind, but what choice did she have? With the gun prodding her, she walked slowly, twisting her neck in an attempt to get a glimpse of the gunman. But when the gun barrel dug painfully through her T-shirt into her skin, she gave up.

She would stall as long as possible so she could remain at her last-known location.

"I'm not playing dumb. I don't know what's going on. Mr. Salvatore fired me because I was so nervous I dropped dirty dishes into his lap. Surely he hasn't held a grudge all this time? I mean, is killing me over dirty dishes really worth it?"

As they reached the back of the building, the gun barrel pressed even harder, making her bend forward at the waist in an attempt to ease the pressure. "Down on your knees," he said in a harsh tone.

No! Was he really going to kill her right here in the park? She'd thought Salvatore wanted her alive, but maybe he only wanted her dead. She sank to her knees, closed her eyes and silently recited the Lord's Prayer.

"Well, now, who's this little filly?" The familiar Texan drawl made her eyelids snap open.

Logan?

"What are you doing here, Tex? This isn't your business."

"Seems I just made it my business. She's a pretty little thing. I'm willing to pay for her. Name your price." His exaggerated Southern drawl took on a hard edge.

If she hadn't been 95 percent sure the man offering to pay for her was FBI agent Logan Quail, she'd take the bullet instead. She had to force herself to breathe as the seconds stretched into a full minute.

"I'd let you have her if I could, but Salvatore wants her alive," the gunman said. "He has a few questions for her."

"Oh, yeah? That's funny, 'cause it looks like you're about to shoot her in the back," Logan pointed out casually, as if he could care less about her fate. "Why not let me have a little fun with her first? Salvatore won't care as long as I bring her back unharmed."

"Why are you here, anyway?" the gunman demanded. "Are you following me, Tex?"

Terrified, she caught her breath as a tense silence stretched out between them. "No!" she abruptly shouted. "Don't sell me to the stranger, please. I'll talk to Salvatore. I'll tell him whatever he wants to know."

Her attempt to cause a diversion may have worked because suddenly she heard a scuffle and the pressure of the gun against her back disappeared. She caught herself before her face hit the dirt. She twisted around, scrambling backward in a crablike crawl in time to watch Logan wrestle away the gun from Salvatore's thug. Logan hit him with enough force to send the shorter, heavier guy sprawling to the ground. One more fist to the jaw and he slumped, unconscious. Logan grabbed the thug's gun before turning to her.

"Come on, let's get out of here," Logan commanded, yanking her to her feet and dragging her away from the injured gunman.

As she followed Logan, she thanked the Lord for sending him to rescue her, yet also vowed to protect her heart from being bruised by him once again.

Logan ground together his teeth with frustration, knowing he'd blown his cover in order to rescue little miss cop-wannabe, Kate Townsend, from Salvatore's hired gun Russo. Nine months of work, and hundreds of thousands of dollars, down the drain.

What was wrong with the woman? Six months ago he'd done his best to convince her to relocate somewhere far away from Salvatore, but she'd refused. She insisted on finishing her degree at the University of Chicago and it had taken all his willpower to stop from throwing her over his shoulder, physically carrying her far away and dumping her in a safe house himself.

But in the end, he'd let her go, knowing he had a job of his own to do. As part of the FBI task force focusing their efforts on eliminating organized crime, he'd had a key role to play. It had taken a long time, too long for his taste, but he'd finally gotten close to Salvatore. Had managed to earn the man's trust.

Until now.

Once Salvatore found out he'd rescued Kate from Russo, his cover would be useless. You would think she'd have enough brains to stay far away from Bernardo Salvatore, but no, here she was, trying once again to get herself killed.

"Where are we going?" she asked, as he ruthlessly dragged her through the trees and shrubs lining the back side of the park, to the road.

His jaw hurt from clenching his teeth so hard. He unclamped them and mentally counted to ten, even as he kept a wary eye out for any of Salvatore's men.

"You're hurting me," she hissed in a low voice, and he immediately loosened his grip on her wrist.

He led the way down the street and around the corner. "In here," he said, indicating the large black truck he'd parked on one of the side streets a few blocks from Stanton Park.

She climbed up into the passenger side, and he slammed the door shut behind her before getting in beside her.

"Where are we going?" she asked as he pulled out onto the street.

Since he wasn't sure, he didn't answer. The hotel where he was registered under his alias, Tex Ryan, a rancher and rich oil magnate who'd expressed an interest in investing some money into Salvatore's new horse-racing business, was too close to Salvatore's restaurant for comfort. But now that his cover was blown, he needed to get his stuff out of there, ASAP. Especially the high-tech surveillance device he'd been using to spy on Salvatore. He'd been forced to hide the disk in his suite earlier this morning, when Bernardo had made a surprise visit. The technology was top secret and he didn't dare let it fall into Salvatore's hands.

He should have kept it with him at all times, but he also couldn't guarantee he wouldn't be searched by one of Salvatore's goons. Hiding it in his room had seemed like the best idea at the time.

"Thanks for rescuing me," Kate said softly, breaking into his thoughts.

"What on earth were you doing there with Russo?" he demanded harshly.

"Russo?"

"Salvatore's thug."

She was quiet for a moment. "Angela called claiming Salvatore was trying to kill her." Kate rubbed her arms, as if she were cold. As angry as he was, he still reached over to crank up the heat for her. "But she set me up, instead."

"Why?"

Kate shook her head, helplessly. "I don't know. You must have more information than I do. How did you manage to find me?"

"I was following Russo." He scowled, not happy about this new twist. What had gone wrong? Why did

Salvatore suddenly want to question Kate now? She would have been easy enough to find over the past six months.

His gut knotted in warning at the abrupt turn of events. He'd been so deep undercover that he didn't know what was going on back at the FBI headquarters, which made him feel as if he was completely in the dark right now.

Pushing the speed limit as much as he dared, he headed for the concrete driveway leading down to the hotel's underground parking garage. He parked in the farthest corner, not too far from the exit ramp, yet away from the main walkways. He got out of the truck, and Kate followed, close on his heels.

"Why are we here? Is this where you're staying?" she asked, as they wove a path between the parked cars.

"I was, but as of this moment, Tex Ryan is checking out." His boss, Kenneth Simmons, would be furious when he heard how Logan blew his cover, but what else could he do? Stand there and let Russo take her away at gunpoint? Or shoot her in the back? Just seeing her on her knees before Russo was enough to make his blood boil. For a brief moment, he'd thought he'd convinced Russo to hand her over. But then Russo had questioned his motives for following him. Thankfully, Kate had chosen that instant to beg for mercy, which had provided enough of a distraction that he'd been able to get the jump on Russo.

As they rode the elevator up to the penthouse suite, Kate remained thankfully silent. His instincts were screaming at him to hurry. "Pack up the laptop for me," he directed. "And make sure you get all the USB drives, too."

For once, Kate did as she was told. He went into the master bedroom and retrieved the disk from where he'd taped it beneath the lamp. Once he had the disk, he tossed his clothing, including his cowboy hat and his shaving kit, into the large suitcase. Better to take everything at this point. Within minutes he was rolling the suitcase into the living room.

"Ready," Kate said, throwing the strap of his laptop case over her shoulder. As usual, she was dressed casually in a long-sleeved T-shirt and jeans, which now sported grass stains on both knees from her near miss behind the recreational center. The reminder of how close he came to losing her made him angry all over again.

"Give it to me," he said, taking the case from her. She looked so tiny and fragile with her slim build and long, honey-blond hair that he had to remind himself Kate was tougher than she looked. But no matter how strong she thought she was, he absolutely refused to let her carry his bags. "Let's get out of here."

She narrowed her gaze, clearly annoyed with him, as they rode back down the elevator to the parking garage. When the elevator doors opened, he held her back for a minute, scanning the area for any sign of Russo. He had hit Russo hard enough to keep him out for a while, but he wasn't taking any chances.

"Stay behind me," he commanded in a low voice. Astonishingly she actually fell back a step, so that she was mostly covered by his larger frame.

They'd only gone a few yards when he suddenly spied Russo walking through the rows of cars to their left. "Get down," he whispered, yanking Kate behind the cover of a midnight-blue minivan.

Kate's eyes were wide with fear, but to her credit she didn't make a sound. He pulled out the gun he'd taken from Russo, the one with the silencer, and tried to assess their options.

Russo was either planning to trap him up in the hotel suite or wait down here to ambush him by the elevator. There was also the possibility that Salvatore's men had staked out his truck, but with all the vehicles parked in the underground garage, he had to believe his truck wouldn't be that easy to find, especially since he'd made sure to stay away from the main aisles and walkways.

Had Russo called for reinforcements? Were Salvatore's men already covering the lobby and the exits?

Adrenaline surged and he knew they didn't have time to waste. He peered through the rows of cars until he saw Russo. The guy was heading toward the elevator. It was now or never.

He moved as silently as possible and stashed the suitcase under a car. Keeping only the laptop and of course the disk, he threaded his way through the rows of cars, zigzagging away from the elevator. Kate stayed right at his side, moving quietly. He couldn't let himself think about how they might be trapped down here.

The flash of headlights, followed by the sound of a car engine, filled the parking garage. He pushed Kate down behind a silver Camry, away from the beam of its headlight.

Did the vehicle belong to Russo's backup? Or another hotel guest?

He didn't dare believe the latter. Fearing the worst, he waited a moment and then picked up the pace. Speed was nearly as important as stealth. When they reached the truck, he opened the driver's-side door, the sound extraordinarily loud. He urged her to get in and then climbed in after her.

"Maybe we should wait here for a bit?" Kate suggested in a hoarse whisper.

"We can't. We'll have to risk it. Buckle up." He understood her concern, but there wasn't another option. They absolutely needed to get out of the parking garage.

He tucked the gun in his lap and took a deep breath. The moment he started up the engine, he'd give away their position.

With a twist of his wrist, he cranked the key and the engine roared to life. He threw the truck in reverse and backed out as fast as he dared. In less than ten seconds, he shifted gears and surged toward the ramp leading to the exit.

Shouts penetrated the air and screeching tires echoed through the garage.

Russo and his men were coming after them.

TWO

"Keep your head down," he shouted. A car hurtled toward them from a perpendicular row. Another car clipped his back end, but the smaller vehicles were no match against his oversize truck. He floored the accelerator, the truck surging forward, eating up the distance between them and the exit.

Just when he thought they'd made it, the back window of his truck shattered. "Stay down," he shouted. He hunched over the steering wheel. He hadn't heard gunfire, so Russo must have gotten his hands on another weapon with a silencer.

He ignored the bullets peppering his truck as he took a sharp curve, scraping his side mirror against the wall. They finally reached street level.

He blew through a stop sign, veering directly into the stream of traffic. Several drivers leaned on their horns and swerved out of his way.

He ignored them and kept going, switching directions often and keeping a close eye on his rearview mirror in case he picked up a tail. He headed north toward the Wisconsin border, hoping that Russo would expect him to head south toward his home state.

Twenty minutes later, when he finally left the city limits, he relaxed his deathlike grip on the steering wheel. He glanced over to where Kate was sitting low in her seat, wedged in the corner between the bucket seat and the door.

"Are we safe now?" she asked, straightening enough in her seat to glance through the back window.

He slowly shook his head as he dragged his gaze back to the road. As much as he wanted to reassure her, he refused to lie. "You know better than that. We're not going to be safe until both Salvatore and Russo are locked up behind bars."

Or until the mafia boss and his right-hand man were dead.

Logan didn't dare contact his superior or anyone else within the downtown Chicago FBI headquarters, although he knew he wouldn't be able to put off the confrontation for long. Right now, he and Kate needed a place to stay, at least until he could come up with a plan.

He ran his fingers through his hair, already missing his cowboy hat. In Texas, a guy was expected to wear a cowboy hat, but not so much in Chicago. Now that he'd been forced to ditch his Tex Ryan persona, he needed to blend in as much as possible.

Which meant he needed to get rid of the cowboy boots, too. Not to mention the big black pickup truck riddled with bullet holes. Especially since he knew there was a good chance Russo had already put out a trace on his license plate number.

All because Kate couldn't stay away from Salvatore. She knew, better than most, how the mafia boss was dangerous, but did that fact keep her away? Obviously not. Just the thought of the way she'd put herself in danger made him simmer with fury.

"Why don't you start at the beginning?" he asked, trying to remain calm as he took the next exit off the interstate, intending to hide among the anonymity of suburban Chicago. There were a string of hotels not far from the large amusement park and he hoped they could find somewhere to stay that they wouldn't be noticed. "How do you know that Angela set you up on purpose? Maybe Russo followed her?"

"Nope. She called my name seconds before I felt the gun at my back. And then she said something like, 'What are you doing? You promised not to hurt her.'"

Logan didn't even want to think about how close he'd come to losing Kate. A fact that didn't do anything to soothe his temper. "And then what happened?"

Kate let out an audible sigh. "He told her to go back to the restaurant. I couldn't believe it when she simply turned and ran away."

"You believed she was really in danger?" he asked, unable to hide his skepticism.

She winced and nodded.

He let out a heavy sigh. "Why would she do something like this now? It's been six months since the night Salvatore fired you. There was plenty of time for them to come after you if they suspected you were feeding us information."

Kate hunched her shoulders defensively. "I don't know. She sounded scared and upset. What was I supposed to do, ignore her? I couldn't. Not when I know how her uncle gets rid of people who cross him." She paused and he kept quiet, sensing there was far more to this story than she was telling him. Finally she added,

"And I thought she'd be willing to talk, to tell us what she knows about Salvatore."

Bingo. This was exactly what he'd suspected. Nothing was ever simple with Kate Townsend. "You've been investigating your father's death." It wasn't a question.

Her lips thinned but she didn't deny the allegation.

Mentally he counted to ten, again, seeking patience. He'd told her to stay out of it. He'd thanked her for the information and had specifically instructed her to leave it alone.

But she'd ignored him. And now, months of work had been blown to smithereens.

She had no idea the cost. Not just in dollars. But to him, personally. Jennifer, his fiancée, had died as the result of a drug bust that had gone bad. The source of the drugs had been traced to Salvatore. It was the biggest reason he'd agreed to join the FBI task force. But now, Kate had ruined his chance to avenge his fiancée's death.

And he wasn't sure he'd be able to forgive her for that.

Kate could feel Logan's anger radiating through the confines of the truck. Deep down, she knew she deserved some of his anger, but how was she supposed to know she couldn't trust Angela? It wasn't as if she'd stayed in contact with her former roommate.

Although maybe that was exactly why she should have gone in better prepared. Why hadn't she listened to her brother's advice?

Her phone vibrated in her pocket. She reached for it, but Logan's hand shot out to prevent her from answering the call.

"It's probably my brother," she said. "He's a cop and

I told him how Angela wanted to meet with me. He'll be worried if I don't answer."

"No calls," Logan said tersely. "Especially not to your family."

Her jaw dropped open in shock. "I have to, Logan. He didn't want me to meet with Angela, and I need to let him know I'm okay."

Logan's grip didn't relax around her wrist. "But you're not okay. Salvatore wants you. He sent his thug Russo after you. Do you really want to drag your brothers into this mess?"

No, she didn't, not if her brothers would be in danger. Except she'd already called Garrett. Worry curled in the center of her gut. "How about if I just send him a quick text message?" she pleaded.

Logan finally released her. "Fine. But then shut off your phone. We can't risk someone tracking you through it. I'll buy you a new one."

Her fingers were trembling, as she quickly texted her brother.

Don't worry, I'm safe. Don't trust Angela, she tried to set me up. I'll call soon.

She sent the message and then powered down the phone.

"I thought I told you that I'd follow up on the information you gave me about Dean Ravden," Logan said.

She couldn't bear to meet his gaze. "You did," she acknowledged. She didn't add the part where she'd sensed he was annoyed with her for contacting him at all. Which was why she'd called Garrett earlier this evening instead.

Logan pulled up in front of a chain motel and threw the truck in park, turning in his seat to face her. "Yet you couldn't leave it alone, could you? My cover has been blown. Do you have any idea the significance of that? Thanks to you, thousands of dollars and months of hard work have been flushed down the drain."

His accusation lashed over her skin like a whip. "I already apologized, Logan. What do you want me to say? Maybe it was naive of me to believe Angela was really in trouble, but I couldn't take the chance that hers would be the next body found floating in Lake Michigan. I couldn't bear to have her death on my conscience."

Logan let out a heavy sigh and scrubbed his hands over his face. She felt awful about what happened, but rehashing the past wasn't going to help them now. They needed to move forward.

"Okay, wait here. I'll get two connecting motel rooms."

She didn't say anything as he slammed out of the truck. She huddled in the corner of the passenger seat, wrestling with guilt. Even though she hadn't done it on purpose, he had every right to be angry.

She closed her eyes, tears pricking her eyelids as she thought about her father. Her mother had died during her senior year of high school, and her father had been a rock of support during that difficult time. Especially for her, the baby of the family. Her brothers were already out on their own, and for a couple years it was just her and her dad. She couldn't believe he was gone.

Dear Lord, please keep my father's soul safe in Your care.

When Logan returned, she sat up and brushed away the evidence of her tears. There was nothing she could do to change the recent events, despite how much she desperately wanted to. Maybe she shouldn't have told her father what little she knew about Bernardo Salvatore. She glanced through her window as Logan drove around to the back of the building.

The hour was late, and she shivered in the cool night air as they headed inside. Logan handed her one key and used the second key for the door to his room.

"Ten minutes," he said gruffly, before disappearing inside.

A spark of annoyance pushed away her grief. She'd grown up in a household of domineering males, and didn't appreciate his tone. Obviously he wanted to talk, but she'd open her side of the connecting doors when she was good and ready and not one second earlier.

Since she didn't have any luggage, it didn't take her long to get settled. She splashed water on her face and ran her fingers through her tangled hair. Since waiting longer than the ten minutes he gave her seemed juvenile, she went ahead and strode over to unlock her side of the door.

Logan was leaning against the door frame, waiting for her. "Okay, I need to know exactly what happened with your father," he said.

"I already told you most of it," she said, crossing her arms over her chest defensively. "Dad was scheduled to appear in court to testify against a guy named Dean Ravden. He'd pulled Ravden over on a routine traffic violation and busted him for driving under the influence."

"Your dad told you this?" he interrupted.

"Yes, we talked about his cases sometimes and we had dinner together the night before. The name didn't ring a bell with me, not at first. It was only after dad's car was T-boned at the intersection that I caught a glimpse of Ravden on the news. As I told you over the phone, I recognized him as one of the men Salvatore met with at the restaurant."

"How can you be so sure?" Logan asked, his tone full of doubt. "That was a long time ago."

She narrowed her gaze and thrust out her chin. "I'm sure. I recognized his long greasy blond hair, his scruffy sideburns, his thin lips and the tiny scar buried under his left eyebrow."

"Okay, so you recognized him. What did you do then? Who did you talk to besides me?"

She tried to think back to that dark time. "I talked to my oldest brother, Garrett, first. He didn't believe me, said that the mafia wouldn't bother to make it look like a car crash."

Logan's expression tightened. "Maybe, maybe not," he muttered. "They would if it suited their purpose."

She was ridiculously pleased that he'd agreed with her, believed in her when Garrett hadn't. "Garrett may have mentioned my theory to our brothers, too. But the only other person I spoke with was my dad's boss, Lieutenant Daniel O'Sabin."

Logan frowned. "Daniel O'Sabin and Garrett Townsend. What are the names of your other brothers?"

She scowled at him. "My brothers aren't a part of this."

"Look, Kate, for all we know one of your brothers trusted the wrong person. The Chicago P.D. is known to have ties to the mob."

She didn't want to think about how some men would do anything, even sell out their brothers in blue, for a quick buck. But she knew Logan was right. "In order, oldest to youngest, Garrett is first, then Ian and then Sloan. My dad's name was Burke, if you want to verify anything on his accident report. And I only mentioned my suspicions to my brother. When I talked to O'Sabin, I asked if he was sure the crash was an accident. I begged him to do a thorough investigation just in case it wasn't. He said he would, but then told me later that they'd closed the case as an accidental death."

Logan nodded slowly. "If he's dirty, that request alone may have been enough to make him suspicious."

"I didn't mention Ravden," she pressed, wanting Logan to understand she'd been cautious. "He couldn't know that I recognized Ravden from the restaurant."

"And you only saw Ravden on the news? Not in person?"

"Only on the news. And really, they flashed his mug shot on the screen for less than ten seconds. The only reason they had him on camera at all was because my father died on his way to testify against him."

"A fact that makes it even less likely that the mob was behind your father's accident," Logan drawled. "Why draw attention to Ravden if they didn't have to? A DUI isn't that big of a deal. Salvatore's lawyer surely would have gotten him off without a problem."

She suddenly shivered despite the warmth radiating from the heater. "Because of the cash," she whispered. She swallowed hard and dragged her gaze up to meet Logan's. "My father told me Ravden had a lot of cash on him. Enough to make him wonder if he was into drug dealing or some other illegal activity."

For a moment they stared at each other in silence. Then Logan pushed away from the door frame. "Stay here and get some rest. I'll be back in a while."

She tensed. "Where are you going?"

"I have to ditch the truck and get another set of

wheels." His expression was grim as he turned away. "Keep your door locked and don't let anyone in except for me."

"Okay." She moved back and started to close the connecting door between their rooms.

"Kate?" he called.

She stopped and peered around the edge of the door. "What?"

"Don't use your cell phone, okay? Don't call or text your brothers until I pick up new phones."

"I understand," she said before closing the door with a soft click.

For a moment she closed her eyes and leaned against the door, hoping and praying that she hadn't already put her brothers, especially Garrett, in danger. She was tempted to text him again, asking him not to say anything to Ian or Sloan, but she'd promised Logan. So she kept her phone off and prayed, instead.

Please, Lord, keep my family safe from harm!

Logan headed out to the truck, and quickly slid into the front seat. He needed to get far away from the hotel before he dumped it, but he also needed to get new transportation.

Thankfully, he had a backup vehicle stashed not far from here, outfitted with traveling cash, a change or two of clothes, including his running gear and shoes. He could share the sweatshirt and sweatpants with Kate. Even the FBI didn't know about the car he'd hidden in the event of a crisis.

And this was about as big of a crisis as he'd faced since going undercover as Tex Ryan. Not that there hadn't been plenty of close calls.

Logan battled a wave of helpless fury at the way he'd been forced to abandon his cover. Yet how could he blame Kate for going to rescue Angela when he'd basically done the same thing by rescuing her? Very simply, he couldn't.

He sighed and thought through everything Kate had told him. While he didn't think it was likely her brothers were involved, he made a mental note to do some checking up on them once he returned to the motel. And then there was her father's boss, Lieutenant O'Sabin. O'Sabin might not be dirty, either, but it was likely he'd reported Kate's request up the chain of command.

And he knew only too well how high corruption could reach. To the chief of police and even state senators. In his experience no one was immune. The lure of greed and power was strong.

When he passed a well-known box store that was still open, he pulled in and quickly purchased two new disposable phones, and basic toiletries to replace what was in his left-behind luggage. From there, he drove several hours before ditching his truck in the parking lot of a large outdoor mall. He hoped the truck would go unnoticed for a while, but if Salvatore had cops working for him, they'd no doubt find it sooner than he'd like.

There was no choice but to head back on foot. He'd walked about a mile before a semitruck driver pulled over and offered him a ride. Logan gratefully climbed in, and let the older guy talk his ear off as the truck ate up the miles.

Several hours later, he drove his replacement car up to the motel and dragged himself inside. He was exhausted, but forced himself to plug in and activate the phones before booting up his computer. Refusing to feel guilty, he did a quick search on all three of Kate's brothers.

Nothing popped out at him, but he'd only done a cursory review. He'd need to do more, but right now he was so exhausted, he was swaying in his seat. As he shut down the computer, headlights flashed against the curtained window of the motel room.

He tensed, his previous exhaustion vanishing with the sudden surge of adrenaline. Was someone out there, looking for the bullet-ridden truck? He rose silently to his feet, reaching to douse the lamp, plunging the room in darkness. Moving slowly, he crossed to the window overlooking the parking lot. He didn't move the curtains, but peered through the slim crack to see what was going on.

A basic black car, much like the type Salvatore preferred, glided slowly through the parking lot. His heart thudded painfully against his ribs. Was he overreacting? Was the driver of the black car just looking for a parking spot close to their room?

He held his breath as the auto swung in a wide curve and then headed back out to the main road.

The knot in his stomach tightened painfully and he quickly moved away from the window. He didn't believe for one moment the driver was a guest at the motel.

Logan jammed the computer in its case and then walked to the connecting doors. He opened his side and was relieved that Kate had left her side unlocked. He called her name softly as he pushed it open. "Kate? Wake up!"

In the dim light he saw her bolt upright in bed. "What is it? What's wrong?"

"We need to get out of here. Now."

She scrambled out of the bed, thankfully fully dressed, except for her shoes, which she quickly donned without bothering to untie the laces. "What happened?"

"A black car swept through the parking lot. I'm pretty sure the driver is one of Salvatore's men, looking for us." He was glad he'd gotten rid of the truck, but now realized they should have moved to a different motel, too. The one saving grace was that they wouldn't have a way to track his replacement vehicle. "We need to leave, before they return."

"I'm ready," Kate whispered, coming over to stand beside him, so close he could feel the warmth of her arm against his.

It struck him that for the first time in months, he wasn't alone. There was someone to work with. Someone to bounce ideas off. Having Kate with him was both a blessing and a curse.

He couldn't fail her. Not the way he'd failed Jennifer. He refused to let Salvatore take another person from him.

Grimly, he took Kate's arm and swept a glance over the parking lot to make sure there weren't any of Salvatore's goons around before he hustled her out to his car, a nondescript sedan with blackened windows for added privacy.

As he climbed into the driver's seat beside her, he silently vowed to do whatever it took to protect Kate.

No matter what cost.

THREE

Kate shivered when the cold night air washed over her skin, but she didn't say anything when Logan pushed her toward a dark gray four-door. The car didn't seem to have the same power as the big black truck, but if Salvatore didn't know about it, they'd obviously be far safer inside this vehicle.

She was grateful when Logan reached over to crank up the heat. He kept his gaze on their surroundings, so she did the same, looking for anything or anyone that seemed out of place. Thankfully, she didn't see anything suspicious.

Logan went in the opposite direction from the highway, taking several back roads to get away from the area. She waited until they'd ridden for several minutes before she relaxed her vigilance.

"How did they find us?" she asked. "I mean out of all the motels in all the suburbs outside Chicago, how did they look for us there so quickly?"

His mouth tightened into a grim line. "The best I can figure, they either tracked us by tapping into the GPS of your cell phone, since you didn't turn it off right away, or they had some sort of tracking device on my truck." He didn't look happy about either option.

"I'm sorry," she whispered, thinking of everything she'd done wrong since she'd received that first call from Angela. She wished she'd listened to her brother. "It must have been my phone," she said softly. "They trusted you up until tonight, right?"

He lifted his shoulder in a half shrug. "About as much as they trusted anyone, which isn't saying much. But even if it was your phone they tracked, there's nothing to worry about now. I've ditched the truck, and as long as you keep your phone off, they can't track it. Besides, I should have switched motels right after I ditched the truck."

With a spurt of frustration, she retrieved her old cell phone, opened her window and tossed it out into a farm field. Getting rid of the thing only made her feel marginally better. Truthfully, she was surprised Logan had let her off the hook so easily, considering she'd been nothing but trouble from the moment they'd met. "Where to now?" she asked, peering through the darkness.

He let out a heavy sigh. "Good question. At present we just need another place to stay. But sooner or later I'm going to have to call my boss, to let him know…" He trailed off but she knew what he'd left unsaid.

She shivered again, and not because of the cold. She couldn't imagine how angry Logan's boss would be when he discovered Logan had blown his cover and maybe risked that of the task force at large.

For her. To save her life.

She wished there was something she could do to make it up to him. But she had more questions than answers at this point. Even if she could prove that Ravden was one of Salvatore's thugs, she'd need more to link her father's death to the mob.

"Do you think we could stop at my place to pick up some stuff?" she asked hesitantly, knowing the answer because all police procedure would agree on this point. However…

But Logan was already shaking his head. "That's the first place they'd look for you."

"They might have already been to my apartment, but that doesn't mean they're staked out waiting for me," she argued gently. "I should have brought a jacket," she muttered half under her breath.

She could feel Logan's gaze rake over her. "We'll get you some stuff tomorrow."

It wasn't just warm clothing she wanted. After her dad had died, she'd been going through his things at the house, and there were family photos that she wanted. "Logan, my dad kept notes at home."

"Notes? What kind of notes? You mean about his cases?"

She winced at his incredulous tone. "Yes, but they're in a safe, way down in the basement. I found them when I went through some of his legal papers after he died."

"Any recent cases?" Logan asked.

"I didn't go through everything, but I didn't get the impression much of what he had was recent. Except I did find a newspaper clipping that I thought was odd."

"About what?"

"Remember last year, when the gaming commissioner died of a heart attack? For some reason my dad saved the article in his safe."

"John Nelson," Logan mused. "I shouldn't tell you this, but the FBI didn't think Nelson's death was an accident. Especially when the new gaming commissioner was named. William Sheppard didn't waste any time throwing his support behind the new racino bill."

"Racino?" She wrinkled her nose at the unfamiliar term. "What's that?"

"A combination of a racetrack and casino." He glanced at her. "The state of Illinois doesn't allow gambling casinos in general, not like the state of Nevada does. But this new bill granted special privileges for owners of racetracks to allow slot machines and other casino games."

"Do you think my dad might have been looking into John Nelson's death?" she asked.

"I doubt it," Logan said bluntly. "I mean, he wasn't a homicide detective, was he? What reason would he have to be investigating anything related to Nelson's death?"

"No, he wasn't a detective." Her dad had prided himself on being a beat cop, on his role of protecting the general public from danger. He'd enjoyed his work for the most part, but now she wished she'd spent more time looking over the old case files that he'd had in his safe. Much like Logan, she'd brushed them off as unimportant, since there was nothing recent. The most recent item was the clipping, and that was a year old.

Except now, she couldn't get the possibility out of her mind. What if she'd been wrong about that, too? What if those random events that had happened in the past, information her dad had kept, were in fact linked to the present?

To Salvatore and his illegal activities?

Maybe it was too late to go tonight, but somehow she needed to convince Logan to take her back to her father's house so they could get his notes out of the safe.

They couldn't afford to ignore any possibility, no matter how remote, of bringing down Salvatore's organization.

* * *

Logan found a motel just over the Indiana border and secured two more connecting rooms, thinking that it was a good thing Tex Ryan had been known for flashing a lot of cash.

Money his boss wouldn't be too happy to discover was used to hide Kate from Salvatore, instead of furthering his cover.

He made a mental note of the amount he'd have to pay back to the FBI. They both needed to get some sleep, but after a few hours, he got up and went back on the computer, searching for the article that Kate's father had kept related to John Nelson's untimely death.

He reviewed the story again, and as before, nothing jumped out at him. His boss had been convinced that Nelson's death was part of Salvatore's plan, but Nelson did have a history of heart disease. And he knew the autopsy report had been clean, so it wasn't as if Salvatore had drugged or poisoned him.

After he saved the article on his hard drive, he then went searching for information on Kate's father. The image of Burke Townsend bloomed on the screen, and he had to admit that Kate's father was an imposing figure in his full dress blues.

"What are you doing?" Kate asked.

He swiveled in his seat to look at her, upset with himself for not hearing Kate come through their connecting doors. "You have your father's hazel-green eyes," he said.

For a moment he thought she'd burst into tears. But then she pulled herself together and came closer, her gaze riveted on his laptop computer screen. "Irish mud," she murmured. "My dad used to call them Irish-mud eyes."

They were beautiful to him, but he refrained from stating that fact. “There’s a quote from the witness in the newspaper article.”

She nodded. “The oncoming green truck sped up in an effort to get through the yellow light, but the small red car just drove ahead as if the driver didn’t see him,” she quoted, almost verbatim.

“But you still think it’s suspicious?” he asked. He wouldn’t put it past the mob to stage a car crash, but considering the witness statement, he couldn’t ignore the niggle of doubt that crept in.

“For one thing, the driver of the green truck apparently walked away from the crash unscathed. And I’ve tried to find the guy except I keep hitting dead ends. The name and address seem to be fake. I couldn’t validate either one. The guy does have a police record now. The system shows he has a speeding ticket and reckless driving ticket pending. But what good is that when the name and address appear to be bogus?”

“You’re right. I think we should look into that a bit more,” he admitted. He could use FBI resources to track down the guy. Or prove that he was using a fake identity.

“And they didn’t name the witness,” Kate said, dropping down into the chair across from him. “Not even in the police report. Don’t you think that’s odd? Why withhold the witness’s name? Especially when they used the witness statement as a reason to call Dad’s death an accident?”

She had another valid point. “No good reason that I can tell,” he admitted. “Officially the name should be there.”

“Name and address,” Kate added with a dark frown. “I can’t help feeling that the document was faked. That someone made it up and then purposefully withheld the guy's identity so no one could verify whether or not the statement was truthful."

It was a potential angle to consider. "I can't think of a legitimate reason to withhold the identity of the witness," he mused. "And surely there was more than one?"

"Unfortunately, Chicago is a lot like New York. People don't always stick around to help out when something happens. Everyone just keeps going on their merry way."

He'd noticed that, too. Very different from where he grew up in South Texas. There everyone knew everyone else's business and not one person would have left the scene of an accident. Unless, of course, that person had something to hide.

"Logan, couldn't we please go to my father's house? I really want to look through the notes he left in his safe."

He suppressed a sigh. "You know it's not likely his old case notes have any bearing on Salvatore, right? It's a huge risk for very little payoff."

She scowled, her eyes dark with anger. "It is really that big of a risk? I spent lots of time at his house over the past few weeks since his death. It's not like Salvatore sent his men there to get me. They drew me out through Angela."

"All the more reason going there would be nothing more than a fool's errand." When her face fell, he felt himself caving. "Okay, fine. We'll take a look. But not until we get something to eat."

She gazed at him with relief. "Thanks, Logan. I know you're just humoring me, but I'm still grateful."

He powered down his computer and shut the lid. He wasn't sure why he'd agreed to go back to Chicago, to her father's house, except that he was fairly certain he was looking for any excuse to avoid talking to his boss.

A strategy that was working out quite well for the moment, but wasn't something he could do for much longer.

They stopped at a secondhand shop along the way to buy Kate at least one change of clothes, then ate at a truck-stop diner not far from the motel where they'd stayed. Kate wasn't surprised when Logan had checked them out of the motel. They'd have to pick someplace else to stay for the upcoming night.

"Eat a lot," he advised as he scanned the menu. "We won't be stopping again for a while."

Seeing as they served extra-large portions, judging from the plates nearby, she approved of his strategy. After the waitress brought their order, she leaned forward, capturing Logan's gaze. "I have an idea."

He lifted his eyebrows, never pausing as he dug into his Paul Bunyan–sized meal. "Yeah?"

She licked suddenly dry lips. "What if we contact Angela? Wait a minute, just hear me out first, okay?" she quickly added when he frowned at her. "I know she lured me to Russo, but she also mentioned how he'd promised not to hurt me. I think that if I talk to her, I can convince her to come with us. To turn in her uncle."

He took his time, apparently savoring his hotcakes before responding. "She also left you alone with an armed man," he said. "And you told me that she knew about her uncle long before she started working at the restaurant. Before she convinced you to hire on there."

"You're right, all that is true. But maybe she was being naive, too? Maybe she had some sort of glossed-over idea of what her uncle was really involved in? She looked shocked to see Russo holding a gun on me. Maybe if she knew the truth—"

"Assuming she doesn't already know the truth," he interrupted with the barest hint of sarcasm. "You need to know, the women in the mafia are just as ruthless, if not more so, than the men."

She didn't doubt that he knew more than she did about it, but he hadn't been there when Angela had witnessed Russo holding her at gunpoint. Her former roommate had been truly shocked. "I was there, Logan. Angela isn't cold or ruthless. I honestly believe she's in over her head."

"Let's focus on one thing at a time. First, we'll get your father's notes out of his safe. Then we'll decide where to go from there."

She dropped the issue, hoping he'd at least consider her idea. Maybe they couldn't totally trust Angie, but could they turn her against her uncle? She wanted to believe they could.

When they were finished eating, Logan paid the bill at the cash register before leading the way out to the car. She was a little surprised he took the interstate to Chicago. "I take it this car isn't registered in your name?"

"You're right, it's not." He seemed preoccupied by his thoughts, and she hoped he wasn't thinking of ways to get rid of her. She'd had trouble sleeping last night, worried that he'd force her to go into a safe house. "Don't worry, this car can't be traced back to me."

She hadn't really thought it could. "Is it okay to call my brother again?" she asked, pulling out her new, disposable cell phone.

He grimaced, but then slowly nodded. "I guess, but

whatever you do, don't tell any of your brothers where you are or that you're with me."

She rolled her eyes as she opened the phone and turned it on. "I'm not stupid, Logan. I just don't want them to worry."

"I never said you were stupid," he muttered. "But right now, you can't trust anyone. Not even your family. Your brothers wouldn't betray you on purpose, but they could accidentally say something to a cop who's secretly working for Salvatore."

"I know. I hear you." She wasn't about to do anything to put her family in additional danger. She took a deep breath and dialed her eldest brother's number. Garrett answered the phone before it even rang.

"Hello?" he answered warily.

"Garrett, it's me. Kate." She was surprised he'd even picked up since he wouldn't have recognized the phone number.

"Katie? Where are you! We've been worried sick!"

"Didn't you get my text message?" she asked, taken aback by another uncharacteristic emotional outburst. Garrett had always been the calm, stable brother. He'd been married, but his wife had left him a few years ago. He'd grown even quieter after his divorce, holding himself aloof from the rest of the family. "I told you I was fine."

"You didn't answer your phone and now you're calling me from some unknown number. What's going on, Katie? You need to get home ASAP."

"Look, I only called to let you know that I'm fine. You're not going to hear from me for a while, okay? Tell Ian and Sloan not to worry."

"Katie, come home," Garrett pleaded. "Between the three of us, we'll keep you safe."

Her throat welled with emotion, and she wanted nothing more than to be with her family. But Logan was right. Salvatore was after her. She couldn't bear for her family to be dragged into this mess. "My staying away is the best way to keep the three of you safe. I promise I'm fine. I'll check in as often as I can, okay? But don't call me. Wait for me to contact you."

Garrett sputtered, obviously unhappy with her response, but she cut him off. "I love you, Garrett. I love all of you. I'll talk to you later, okay?" She quickly hung up the phone and then powered it down.

Logan glanced over at her. "Are you all right?" he asked.

She forced herself to smile. "I'm fine. They're just a bit protective, which is nothing new."

Logan nodded again, and fell silent. She was relieved to have some time to pull herself together. Talking to her brother had shaken her more than she cared to admit.

They made good time on the way back to Chicago, and within an hour and a half, they were back inside the city limits. "You'll need to give me directions to your father's house," he said.

She pointed out turns and soon they were in the familiar neighborhood where she and her brothers had grown up. They hadn't had a lot of money, but there had always been an abundance of faith and love.

"There, the small white house with the black shutters, house number 824."

"I see it." Despite his words, Logan drove right past it, taking a left at the next intersection.

She bit back a cry. "Where are you going?"

"We need to make sure the house isn't being watched," Logan said, as he made another turn, as if heading back toward her father's place.

She batted down a flash of impatience. "I think if Salvatore was going to make a move on my father's house, he would have done it four weeks ago, right after his death."

"Kate, he's still searching for you," Logan said.

She let out a breath, knowing he was right. Did Salvatore have enough manpower to waste time staking out her apartment and her father's house? She doubted it, but kept her eyes peeled for anything that might seem out of place. She caught sight of an elderly woman walking a small white dog. "That's Mrs. Gordon and her dog, Mac. They live two houses down from my dad."

Logan drove around the block again, going a different way this time. And then he surprised her by pulling over to the curb. "We're going to walk from here."

She knew he meant through the backyards, as her father's house was located directly behind the green-and-white house.

They climbed from the car. She made sure she had her key in hand as they quickly darted under the old apple tree, using it as cover on their way through the yard.

Just as they reached the edge of her father's property line, a loud explosion rocked the earth. She cried out as she was thrown backward, into Logan. She hit the ground hard and could only stare in shock as her father's house went up in flames.

FOUR

"Are you all right?" Logan hissed in her ear. She barely managed to nod before he hauled her up to her feet. "Let's go."

She tried to dig in her heels, wanting to resist as Logan dragged her back the way they came. "Wait, we have to check," she protested. She wanted to see what she could salvage from her father's house before the fire took everything.

"No way. We have to get out of here before one of the nosy neighbors sees us."

She had little choice but to follow him to the car, the scene from the explosion replaying over and over through her mind in excruciating slow motion. The faint wail of sirens could be heard, slowly growing louder. Numb from shock, she barely managed to buckle her seat belt as Logan stomped on the gas pedal, heading out of the neighborhood where she'd spent her early years.

"I don't understand," she whispered, trying to gather her scattered thoughts. "Why would someone blow up my dad's house?"

Logan didn't answer right away, and when she

glanced over at him, she could see the tense angle of his jaw, his eyes glued to the road. After several long moments, he finally responded. "Good question. Who else knew what your father had in the basement?"

She shook her head, unable to believe that Salvatore would have blown up her father's house over a few notes. "Other than me and my brothers? No one."

"Not his boss, Daniel O'Sabin?" Logan pressed. "Are you absolutely sure?"

She closed her eyes and rubbed her throbbing temples. No, she wasn't sure. She wasn't sure about anything anymore. "I don't think so. There's no reason for my dad to confide in his boss. But it doesn't matter, because no sane person would blow up a house because of a few notes. Why not send someone in to steal them? Wouldn't that make more sense?"

"You mentioned he had a safe," Logan said with a frown. "Is it possible that someone planted dynamite beneath the safe? The explosion knocked us off balance but we weren't seriously hurt. Could be that the source of the explosion was down in the basement."

"Maybe." She was forced to agree, even though she still thought Logan's theory was a stretch. "But the safe isn't that big. Salvatore could have had his guys steal it in order to take it someplace else to crack it open."

The farther they got from her dad's house, the more Logan relaxed. She could hear him draw in a deep breath and let it out slowly. Was he remembering a similar explosion from six months ago? This was the second time they'd managed to escape by the skin of their teeth.

Thank You, Lord! Thank You for sparing us!

"Maybe the dynamite served a dual purpose," he

murmured. "First to get rid of whatever evidence your father might have saved and second to scare you."

She shivered, staring sightlessly out the window as Logan headed to some new location. She didn't like to admit that he might be right.

She hated the thought that Salvatore was constantly one step ahead of them. Almost as if he knew what they were going to do before they did it. And despite the faith she had in Logan and in God, she couldn't fight the sense of overwhelming despair.

Logan kept shooting glances at Kate, sensing she was far more upset than she'd let on. And he couldn't blame her, not when everything in her father's house—photographs, other personal items—were all likely gone forever.

He knew they shouldn't have gone back there, although he never once considered that their lives would be in danger from an explosion. No, at the most, he'd figured they'd need to dodge a few of Salvatore's men.

Even though Logan had provided a logical explanation to Kate about why her father's house had been blown up, he had trouble believing it himself. Granted, he knew better than most that Salvatore was unpredictable, but at the same time, it seemed like overkill to draw such attention to Kate's father's house, when Salvatore had gone to great lengths to make Burke's death look like an accident.

None of it made any sense. Unless the explosion wasn't a warning for Kate at all, but for Logan?

A warning for both of them, most likely, as Salvatore probably figured out they were working together against him. And Logan felt slightly sick knowing that Salvatore had endless resources to keep coming after them.

When the orange fuel light went on, he pulled into a small corner gas station. As he filled the tank, he tried to come up with another plan of action. He was well overdue to call his boss, but he didn't want to do that, yet. Not until he had something more on Salvatore.

He needed to be able to redeem himself. And he needed desperately to find a way to bring Salvatore to justice.

After he paid in cash for the gas, he climbed back into the driver's seat. When he started the engine, Kate put her hand on his arm as if to stop him. "Wait. We need to head back to Chicago, to try to find the guy who hit my father."

The warmth of her hand surprisingly helped him relax. "Kate, you were right, okay?" he said gently, turning partially in his seat to face her. "I believe you. I believe Salvatore sent one of his goons to kill your father. But trying to find the driver has already proven to be a dead end. If he used a fake name and address, we won't find him."

"So what are we going to do?" she asked, her Irish-mud eyes wide and fierce. "How can we prove it?"

And wasn't that the million-dollar question? "Maybe we need to focus on Dean Ravden."

Her eyes widened and then gleamed with anticipation. "Yes, that might work. Maybe we should get a copy of the original police report my father filed?"

"You read my mind," he drawled. "And we can use my laptop to research him, as well."

She let her hand drop from his arm, and he found he missed the warmth of her touch. Which was ridiculous because he wasn't interested in anything that resembled a relationship. Not now, not ever. Now with anyone, but especially not with Kate.

Kate was too young. Too stubborn. And too intent on becoming a cop.

Three strikes and you're out.

He didn't say much as he headed once again toward downtown Chicago. They would have to request a copy of the police report, and he knew they wouldn't just hand it over right away, since the cops loved to tie everything up in red tape.

When they arrived at the small precinct where Burke Townsend had worked as a beat cop, he reached over to stop Kate from getting out. "I need you to stay here."

Immediately, her eyes narrowed. "What for? You can't think we're in danger at a police station?"

He strove for patience. "Look, normally they make you wait up to five days for a copy. I'm going to flash my FBI badge to get it right away."

Comprehension dawned in her green eyes, but her scowl only deepened. "So I can't come with you because I don't have a badge?"

"Exactly." He left the car running, just in case. "Stay here. Hopefully I won't be long."

She folded her arms over her chest and gave a terse nod. He walked inside, not at all convinced his badge was going to help him. Although he needn't have worried since the gum-chewing, bubble-blowing young woman behind the counter was more than impressed and almost fell over her feet to get him a duplicate of the report.

"Thank you, ma'am," he drawled, laying the Texas

accent on a little thicker than normal as he folded the report. “Much obliged.”

“Oh, no problem,” she gushed. “If you need anything else, don’t hesitate to ask.”

He gave her a nod, missing his cowboy hat and boots more than ever as he left the police station. He refrained from rolling his eyes when he saw that Kate had climbed into the driver’s seat.

“Did you get it?” she asked eagerly.

He nodded. “Move over, I’m driving.”

“Chauvinist,” she muttered before awkwardly scooting over the console and back into the passenger seat.

“It’s my car,” he pointed out, tossing the folded police report into her lap. “Besides, you have to read through that, since you know your father better than I do. Let me know if anything jumps out at you.”

She fell silent, scanning the pages as he pulled away from the curb and turned into traffic. He headed toward Indiana, to find another innocuous motel to stay the night, preferably one with internet access.

Kate sucked in a harsh breath, causing him to glance over. “What is it? What’s wrong?”

“This doesn’t make sense,” she murmured, half under her breath.

“What?” he demanded. “What doesn’t make sense?”

“The timing. My dad normally worked day shift. After all, he had thirty years in and they always fill shifts by seniority. Everyone wants day shift.”

“Yeah, that makes sense.”

“But this police report states that my dad pulled Dean Ravden over at 0422. Almost three hours before the normal start time of his shift.”

He didn't think that was any big deal. "Obviously he switched shifts with someone."

Kate was shaking her head. "No, I don't think so. Why would he? The rookies work graveyard and he wouldn't agree to switch, staying up all night without a really good reason. Certainly not just to do some rookie a favor."

Maybe she had a point. "So then why would your dad be out on the streets in a squad car in the wee hours of the morning?"

"There's only one reason that makes any sense," she said slowly. "I think my dad must have been following Ravden."

The more Kate thought about the possibility, the more she grew convinced she was on the right track. It was the only thing that made sense, and she was irritated with herself for not figuring it out sooner.

Her dad had led her to believe he was on his regular shift when he'd told her that he'd pulled Ravden over on a suspicion of a DUI.

"What possible reason would he have to follow Ravden?" Logan asked in a tone that made her believe he was more than a little skeptical. "You recognized him because you saw the guy talking to Salvatore at the restaurant, right? After your father had already given him a ticket. There's no way your father could have known Ravden was working for Salvatore before then."

Logan's words resonated in her head, making her stomach clench with dread. "He could have known, if he was watching Salvatore," she said, forcing the words from a throat tight with guilt.

There was a long, heavy pause. "You actually told

him your suspicions about Salvatore?" he asked in disbelief.

Yes, she had. Tears stung her eyes, and she blinked them back with an effort. What was wrong with her? She deserved Logan's disgust and anger. Logically, she knew she probably shouldn't have mentioned Salvatore to her father. But she'd wanted her dad to be careful, as his beat included Salvatore's restaurant. Had wanted him to know the truth so that he didn't stumble into something dangerous. She'd known that Salvatore had cops on his payroll and had wanted her father to be aware of the potential danger.

Instead she'd caused his death. She buried her face in her hands and rocked back and forth, trying not to drown beneath the tsunami wave of guilt and sorrow.

"Kate, don't. Come on, it's not your fault."

But it was. She knew it was. Even Logan knew it was, or he wouldn't be trying so hard to comfort her.

"Kate, please. I can't stand to see you like this."

His hand was on her shoulder, but she couldn't bring herself to look at him. She sensed the car wasn't moving. He must have pulled over to the side of the road.

Her fault. Her father's death was ultimately her fault. And somehow she hadn't even realized it until now.

She felt Logan gathering her into his arms, no easy feat with the console between the bucket seats. For a moment she allowed herself to lean against him as she tried to pull herself together.

He smelled wonderful. His aftershave mixed with his unique musky scent managed to soothe her raw nerves. For a moment she wanted more than anything to be the type of woman Logan might be attracted to. Someone beautiful and glamorous, who hadn't spent her entire life wanting to be a cop.

But she wasn't that woman. And Logan wasn't the man for her. For one thing, he'd already bruised her heart. And besides, he was a cop, too. She'd tried dating a cop, Sean Parker, one of her brothers' friends, and that had been a total disaster. She knew she needed to find a guy with faith, someone who would support her dreams rather than trying to change her into something she wasn't.

Taking a deep breath, she let it out slowly. Then silently begged for forgiveness.

I'm sorry, Lord. I'm so sorry. Please forgive me!

"Kate, please don't do this. You haven't done anything to feel guilty about."

She realized she must have spoken out loud. Somehow, she found the strength to lift her head and face him. "Yes, I do. For telling my father about Bernardo Salvatore. For believing Angela was in danger. For blowing your cover." Her voice was husky from crying and she sniffled loudly, desperately wishing for a tissue. "I've done nothing but make mistakes."

"Here." Logan pressed a packet of tissues into her hand. As she blew her nose, he smoothed damp strands of hair from where they were stuck to her cheek. "You didn't make mistakes, Kate. I'm sure you told your father about Salvatore in order to warn him, right? And you believed Angela, mostly because you didn't want her death on your conscience. And you didn't try to get captured by Russo. Salvatore obviously must have targeted you because you were poking into the truth around your father's death. One of the cops working for him must have tipped him off. So don't you see? Salvatore is running scared, from you."

A ghost of a smile tugged at the corner of her mouth at the thought of big, bad Salvatore running from little ole her. But Logan had a point. Salvatore had reacted in a big way, to her quest for truth.

She looked up at Logan at the same time he'd lowered his head toward her and for a long, heart-stopping moment she thought he was about to kiss her.

But then he eased back, and the brief moment of opportunity vanished. Which was good, because she couldn't afford to allow herself to get sidetracked.

"Wait here, I'll get us two connecting rooms." Logan quickly opened the driver's-side door and hopped out, striding toward the main office of the Motel 6 he'd obviously found while she was wallowing in her misery.

She used a few more tissues while she waited, trying to repair the damage she'd done. She pulled down the sun visor to peer in the mirror, grimacing at the red blotches on her face, which matched her lovely red nose.

"Pathetic," she told herself as she flipped up the visor. She needed to be strong if she was going to find the proof she needed to lock Salvatore up for good.

The evil man deserved no less than life in prison. And she vowed to do whatever was necessary to help put him there.

Logan was relieved that Kate looked better when he returned with two motel room keys. He climbed in beside her and tossed her one. "We're in rooms eleven and twelve, on the other side of the building."

"Great." Her smile didn't reach her eyes, but he wasn't going to complain since watching her fall apart had unnerved him badly enough. Kate was always so strong, so stubborn, that watching her dissolve, her shoulders shaking with sobs, had wrenched his heart.

And then he'd almost messed up everything by kissing her.

He was anxious to get settled into their respective rooms; he could use some distance.

She disappeared into room twelve, while he let himself into room eleven. Even though he hadn't unlocked the connecting door between their rooms, he thought he could still smell the distinct scent of vanilla that followed her everywhere.

He scrubbed his hands along his face, the overnight growth of his beard starting to itch. They still had the few supplies he'd picked up at the store before they went on the run, so he dug for the razor.

He felt more human after he shaved. It was too early to eat dinner and too late to eat lunch, so he booted up his computer to start a search on Ravden.

After ten minutes of not hearing any sound from Kate's room, he set aside the computer and went to the connecting door. He unlocked and opened his side, then lightly tapped on hers.

"Just a minute," she said and he heard her footsteps as she approached the door. When she opened it up, he was relieved that she wasn't crying again. "What's up?"

"Aah, nothing, really. I just wanted to make sure you were okay." *Lame, Quail, really lame.* "I didn't hear anything. I thought you might be sleeping."

"So you decided to wake me up?" she asked and he found himself smiling at her tart tone. "I was reading the Bible, which is obviously just as quiet as sleeping."

Now he really felt like a fool, because he'd forgotten

that Kate was a Christian. Not that he was an atheist or anything; he just didn't display his religion, or lack thereof, for everyone to see. "I thought we'd eat dinner around six if that's okay with you?"

She cocked her head and leaned on the door frame. "Changing the subject, Logan?"

No, he wasn't changing the subject. He was avoiding it. "Get some rest," he advised. "I'll let you know if I find anything."

She straightened and her gaze zeroed in on his computer. "I forgot about your laptop," she said, pushing her way past him to enter his room. "Are you searching for Dean Ravden? Have you found anything yet?"

"Yes and no," he said with a sigh, as he followed her toward the small table where he'd been working. "Look, I just told you that I'll let you know if I find anything. Two people and one laptop won't work."

"I'll just sit and watch you work." He wanted to groan when she plopped into the chair next to his. "I won't disturb you."

She was already disturbing him, but he didn't let on as he returned to his seat. He'd started with the FBI computer program, but hadn't found anything on Ravden. He thought it was too early to get data about her father's house explosion, but he went to the local media webpage anyway. The explosion had made headline news, and he clicked on a live camera link where a reporter stood in front of Burke Townsend's house.

"We're here live, outside a quiet neighborhood still reeling from the shock of an explosion at the house belonging to former police officer Burke Townsend. As you know, Burke Townsend died several weeks ago, on his way to testify in court on an alleged DUI case. As you can see, there is a lot of activity going on behind us between the police and the firefighters, and we have confirmed reports of a person being inside the home when the explosion hit."

"What?" Kate whispered in shock. She leaned forward as if she could see past the news reporter. "I have to call my brothers."

Logan hadn't thought of her brothers, and nodded as she fumbled with the phone. But when the news reporter continued, he put a hand on her arm to stop her.

"The police have not confirmed the identity of the body at this point. However we have a source claiming the deceased is Dean Ravden, the suspect that Officer Townsend was planning to testify against in court."

"I can't believe it," Kate said, dropping her phone in her lap. "Do you really think that's true? That Ravden was actually inside my dad's house when it blew up?"

"I think that it's entirely possible that Salvatore used the explosion to get rid of Ravden," he said slowly and with grim certainty.

And he knew this was just another message from Salvatore, letting them know he was playing for keeps.

FIVE

Kate dialed her disposable cell phone with shaking fingers. She desperately needed to talk to her brothers, to make sure they were okay. To make absolutely certain none of them had been inside their father's house.

Logan was still searching for information on Ravden, although if the guy was really dead, then there wasn't much point. It wasn't as if Ravden could lead them to Salvatore now.

"Kate?" Garrett answered on the first ring. "Are you all right? Where are you?" he demanded.

"I'm fine." She winced, knowing she should have called earlier, right after the explosion. No doubt her brothers had been worried. "Have you spoken to Ian and Sloan? Are they both okay?"

"Thank You, Lord," Garrett whispered. "Katie, you have no idea how worried we've been." Her brother sounded truly rattled, as if he was hanging on the end of his rope.

She knew how protective they were and didn't plan to tell any of her brothers how close she'd been to their dad's house when it exploded. "What about Ian and Sloan? I need to know they're okay, too."

"They're fine—trust me. I've spoken to both of them. They want to call you, Katie, and talk to you themselves. They want to know you're all right. And they want you to come home."

Home. For a moment tears threatened but she ruthlessly shoved aside the remorse. She'd always considered her father's house *home*, but now it was gone. There was nothing left but charred walls, smoke and ashes. "You'll need to convince them I'm fine, Garrett. I already told you, I won't put any of you in danger. Look, I have to go but I promise I'll be in touch."

"Katie, wait," Garrett said, but she snapped shut her phone and powered it off. Disposable phones were harder to trace than personal cell phones, but not impossible. Who knew what sorts of resources Salvatore had at his fingertips? She knew Logan expected her to keep it off except for emergencies.

"Are you all right?" he asked.

"Yeah." She forced a smile, even though the previous peace she'd found by reading the Bible had vanished after the horror of the newscast. "I was worried one of them might have been at my father's house, but they're all fine."

"I know." He put his arm around her shoulders and gave her a gentle hug.

She savored his embrace for a moment, before reluctantly pulling away. She knew from her criminal justice classes that getting an accurate ID on a dead person took time. And if the body was burned, fingerprints weren't going to help. They'd need dental records or other DNA evidence. All of which took lots and lots of time. "How do you think they managed to ID the body as Ravden so fast?"

"I suspect they found some sort of ID that was planted at the scene," Logan said slowly. "And I also think some dirty cop let the information leak on purpose."

She didn't like the thought of a corrupt policeman, but she knew he was probably right. "Salvatore is still trying to scare me, huh?" she asked, striving for a light tone.

"Yes, he is." Logan's tone was blunt.

Okay, then. No sugarcoating that one. She squared her shoulders. "Then we have to be smarter than he is," she said with conviction. "And find a way to keep him on the defensive."

Logan nodded, although she knew that was all easier said than done. "You mentioned you couldn't find the driver of the green truck that barreled through the intersection, hitting your dad. Let's see if we have better luck using the FBI resources at our disposal," Logan said.

She nodded, and Logan motioned to the police report that he'd handed her earlier. At least the trip to the police station hadn't been a total bust. She still couldn't believe Dean Ravden was dead.

Once again, she wished she could convince Logan to call Angela. If she could talk to Angie, maybe she could convince her to turn on her uncle. And even if her former roommate didn't know anything that would really help them, at the least she would like to have Angie safely away from harm.

She was very worried Angie's body would be the next one they stumbled across.

Logan glanced at his watch when his stomach grumbled loudly, not surprised to see the hour was well past six. “Let’s go,” he said, shoving away from the computer. “My eyes are starting to hurt from staring at the computer screen anyway.”

Kate nodded, but didn’t say anything as they grabbed their stuff to leave. She’d been unusually quiet over the past hour or so.

“I thought we’d eat at the steak house that’s located just down the road a ways,” he said, with a quick check outside before holding the door for her to move past him. “If you don’t mind steak?”

She lifted a shoulder. “Steak is fine.”

He scowled, longing for the return of her feisty attitude because, even though she’d often driven him crazy, he preferred that attitude over this new subdued passiveness. Once they were both settled in the car and on the highway, he asked, “What’s your favorite food?”

Finally, she smiled. “Italian, but I don’t mind steak, either.” There was a pause before she suddenly asked, “Are you really from Texas?”

He glanced at her in surprise as he pulled into the parking lot of the restaurant. “Yes, why do you ask?”

“Just curious.” She fell silent again as they got out of the car and walked inside. Thankfully, there were plenty of available seats for a Thursday night.

They were seated in a booth near the back, and Logan sat so that he was facing the door. “I figured you could tell just from my accent. In fact, my parents still live on the ranch where I grew up.” Everything in his real life had helped in creating his cover as Tex Ryan.

Her smile dimmed and he mentally kicked himself for bringing up his parents, now that hers were both gone. “That’s nice,” she murmured, staring down at the menu.

Time to change the subject. He glanced at his menu, although it didn't take long for him to figure out what he wanted to have. "The T-bone sounds good."

"I doubt they have Texas-sized portions," she teased, as she closed her menu. "I'm having the New York strip."

The waitress returned to take their order. He was surprised when Kate ordered her steak medium rare. "Brave woman," he said. "You know it will be red on the inside, don't you?"

"I learned to eat medium-rare steaks from my dad. He used to say, 'Walk it slowly through a warm room.'" The fleeting smile on her face made his chest hurt.

"Sounds like you miss him," he said.

She gave a little sigh. "More than you could possibly know." She was quiet for a moment and then pulled herself together. "Enough wallowing in the past. Tell me, what do your parents think of your career? I'm surprised you didn't want to take over the ranch, keeping it in the family."

Normally, he didn't like talking about himself, but in this case, since she was clearly missing her dad, he obliged. "My younger brother, Austin, has already pretty much taken over the ranch, the Lazy Q, and since that was what he always wanted, I figured he deserved it." He took a long gulp of his water and looked around for the waitress, hoping she'd bring refills. "Ranching is tough—long hours and backbreaking physical work."

"And your current career is so much easier?" she teased.

He didn't want to talk about his current career, especially since he wasn't even sure he still had one. Still, he responded, keeping his tone light. "Sure. Piece of cake."

"What made you want to go into law enforcement?"

"My uncle was the sheriff of our town. I knew early on that I wanted to be a cop."

"Similar story to mine, I see." Before he could argue that point, she asked, "Have you talked to your boss yet?"

"No. And I don't plan to, until I have some good news to share."

"Listen." She leaned over the table, dropping her voice low so their conversation couldn't be overheard. "I want you to reconsider talking to Angela."

He scowled, wishing she would drop it already. Why in the world was she so set on getting in touch with her roommate? "No."

Her gaze narrowed, but she refrained from saying anything more when their server brought over their meals.

He was about to dig into his meal when Kate clasped her hands together and bowed her head to pray. Feeling like an idiot, he bowed his head and waited for her to finish, before picking up his fork. He was too hungry to care that the steak wasn't exactly done as he'd ordered it. Close enough.

"God would want us to forgive her, and to help save her from Salvatore," Kate said, between bites. "And what if she has information that could help us?"

Information that would implicate them, more likely, but he didn't voice his skeptical thoughts. "I'm impressed you can forgive her so easily. And I understand you're worried she's going to end up dead, but we have no way of knowing whether or not she wants to be saved."

The way she looked at him, with something akin to

pity shadowing her gaze, only made him mad. Didn't she understand how much trouble he was in already? How many rules he'd broken by bringing her along as he searched for evidence to use against Salvatore? And how many others in the task force may now be under greater scrutiny, at bigger risk?

"I guess you don't believe in God," she said as she scooped up a forkful of mashed potatoes.

"I never said that I didn't believe," he responded testily. She was going from one sore subject to another and he wished she'd just drop them both.

"Really?" She looked happy at the news. "That's wonderful."

"Not really, considering I haven't been to church since my fiancée died."

"Oh, Logan," she whispered. "I'm so sorry."

He didn't answer, keeping his attention focused on his food. And thankfully, she did the same, without asking a dozen more questions.

Questions he had no intention of answering.

Kate wanted to ask Logan more about his fiancée, but knew from the closed expression on his face that he wasn't going to satisfy her curiosity.

When they'd finished their meal, they headed back to the motel, and she found herself wishing they had two laptops so they could both search.

Watching Logan work wasn't very much fun, yet at the same time, she couldn't make herself leave.

"What do you know about Steve Gerlach?" he asked, after he booted up his computer.

"You mean other than he's the officer who responded

to the scene of my dad's murder?" she asked drily. "Not much, why?"

"I've discovered that the driver of the truck that hit your dad used a fake name. The real Joseph E. Canton was sixty-seven years old and died three years ago."

"I knew it!" She was relieved to discover her instincts hadn't failed her, after all. When no one had believed her, she'd thought maybe she was losing her mind. "I knew it wasn't an accident. Too many things felt wrong."

"What we need to know is whether or not we can trust Officer Steve Gerlach," Logan said grimly. "Because either he neglected to write down the name of the witness, or someone else scrubbed it from the report."

The idea of some dirty cop going to such lengths made her feel sick to her stomach. A cop who had turned his back on a fellow officer, no less. "I've heard my dad talk about him, which isn't that surprising since they were both on day shift. I could also ask my brothers," she offered.

"No, let's just call him, see what he says on the phone." Logan picked up his disposable cell phone and dialed the police station. "This is FBI agent Logan Quail, I need to talk to Officer Steve Gerlach, as soon as possible."

She leaned close in an attempt to hear what the dispatcher said. "He's not working this evening, I'll put you through to his voice mail."

"Do you have his cell number? Because I need to speak to him right away."

"I'm not supposed to give out personal cell numbers," the dispatcher said. "Can you provide confirmation that you're with the FBI?"

"Call my boss at the Chicago office to verify my identity if you need to," he offered. "I'll wait."

"No, that's fine. I'll give you the number." There was a brief pause and then she rattled it off. "Gerlach, 555-2920."

"Thanks, I appreciate your cooperation."

"I can't believe she did that!" Kate exclaimed. "She's not supposed to give out those numbers and she couldn't know for sure you weren't bluffing."

"Actually, I kind of was," he said.

"Wait," she said, as he typed in the number. "I think I should call him. For one thing, I'm a cop's daughter and I think I can use my brothers as leverage if needed. If he hears you're a Fed, he'll clam up."

Logan reluctantly handed her the phone. She took it and pushed the button to make the call. She half expected it to go to voice mail, but he picked up on the third ring, his voice deeply masculine. "Hello?"

"Officer Gerlach, my name is Kate Townsend and my father was Burke Townsend. You probably also know my brothers, Garrett, Ian and Sloan. I'm sorry to bother you but I have a quick question about my dad's accident report."

"Oh, yeah? I knew your dad, he was a good cop. What kind of question?"

At least he hadn't hung up on her. "You didn't write down the name of the witness."

"That's not a question and besides, you're wrong. I did write down the name. I clearly remember taking her name and her address."

The witness was a woman? She glanced up at Logan, gauging his reaction. "Do you remember her name?"

"Something common, like Jones or Smith. Her first

name ended in a *Y*, like Sally or Mary. I don't remember the details. It was like a month ago, although maybe it will come to me."

"Tell him we want to meet, tonight if possible," he whispered.

"Officer Gerlach, would you be willing to meet me tonight? You can pick the place and the time."

She practically held her breath, hoping he wouldn't refuse. "Tonight, huh?" There was a pause. "You familiar with the Oakland Cemetery?"

"Yes, I am." She'd heard about Oakland from her brothers. it wasn't far from the fifth district cop shop and sometimes the rookies would meet there after working the graveyard shift before grabbing breakfast.

"Meet me in the southwest corner at eleven o'clock."

She thought it was odd he wanted to meet there, although the cemetery wasn't that far from the fifth district police station and maybe he felt it was safe enough. "All right. Thanks again."

"Don't thank me. I'm only doing this out of respect for your dad and your brothers," he said curtly before hanging up.

"I can't believe he agreed," Logan murmured when she handed him his phone. "Although why he would choose to meet in a cemetery is beyond me."

"I think it's a cop thing," she said, turning toward the computer screen. "We only have an hour before we need to hit the road, so let's see what else we can find."

But further searching proved fruitless. "Come on, let's go," Logan said, pushing away from the computer. "We need to get there early anyway."

She grabbed her sweatshirt and the police report before heading outside. As Logan navigated the dark streets of Chicago, she hoped and prayed that Officer Steve Gerlach could remember the name of the witness that somehow failed to be listed on the official police report.

Because right now, it seemed that every lead they managed to uncover only resulted in a dead end.

Logan didn't like meeting in the cemetery, but since Kate had agreed, there wasn't much choice but to go along with it. He was slightly relieved to discover it wasn't located too far from the police station, as promised. But it was pitch-black, no lights whatsoever. At least the darkness helped cover them just as it provided cover for the bad guys.

And he wanted desperately to believe that Steve Gerlach wasn't one of the bad guys.

He parked on the opposite side of the cemetery from the designated meeting spot, and made sure his weapon was loaded as they prepared to walk through the graveyard.

"Stay behind me," he murmured, as they slipped past several engraved headstones.

For once she didn't argue, but fisted her hand in the back of his dark sweatshirt. He concentrated on moving slowly and silently, avoiding the grave markers as much as possible.

He froze when he heard something, but after several long moments there was nothing but silence, so he continued toward the southwest corner of the cemetery.

They were pretty much on time when they reached the proposed meeting spot. He hunkered down behind a large crypt. "Stay here," he whispered.

Kate's fingers dug into his arm in protest, but he

didn't plan to leave her there. He only wanted to peek around the corner, searching for signs of Gerlach.

His eyes had grown accustomed to the darkness, and he swept his gaze carefully over the area. But if the cop was there, he wasn't in plain view.

The center of his back itched with warning, and he tightened his grip on his gun. "See that smaller crypt over there?" he asked, keeping his mouth close to Kate's ear. When she nodded, he continued, "That's our destination, but stay low."

When she nodded a second time, he crouched down and moved as quietly as possible over to the smaller crypt. When he got there, he stumbled over something soft. Human.

"Look out," he whispered urgently, grabbing Kate's arm so she wouldn't trip over Gerlach's prone figure. And now it was clear why the cop wasn't in plain sight.

She gasped, and he leaned over to feel for a pulse, not entirely surprised to discover the officer they were supposed to meet was dead. There was a bullet hole in the center of Gerlach's forehead. Ordered by Salvatore? Or was the scene simply set up to make it look like a mafia hit?

"I can't believe he's been murdered!" Kate whispered in horror. "How did this happen? Was he followed? How could anyone know he was meeting us here?"

He pulled the officer's phone from his pocket at the same instant he heard the sound of a silencer. "Get down!" he cried, yanking on her arm just as a bullet whizzed past his head.

SIX

Logan threw Kate down on the ground and covered her body with his, protecting her as best he could. Whoever had killed Steve Gerlach was still out there, only now he and Kate had become the targets.

Thankfully, they'd managed to get behind the small crypt. But how long did they have until the gunman came looking for them? Probably not long. They had to move. Now.

"Can't breathe," Kate whispered in a hoarse voice.

He tried to shift his weight to the side, lifting his head as much as he dared in order to assess their surroundings. He couldn't see any sign of the hit man, but the cemetery provided a lot of cover.

Cover that would work both ways—hiding the killer and helping them escape.

He gauged where the shooter might have been based on where he heard the *poof*ing noise and the angle of the bullet whizzing past his ear. The shot had come from the northwest. Even if the guy was on the move, they had two options, to head farther east or farther south.

Or stay put, but he didn't like that option. Considering the shooter had already pinpointed where they were. They needed to move, the sooner the better. Their vehicle was located to the east, so that's where they needed to end up.

"You're going first. Fifty feet in front of us and slightly to the right are two large headstones. Head that way and use them for cover," he whispered in Kate's ear. "I'll be right behind you."

She hesitated, but then nodded. He moved enough so that she could get to her hands and knees, gathering herself so that her feet were beneath her. She took a calming breath and waited for him to give the signal before she sprinted from behind the crypt. He was impressed with her speed, and made sure he was directly behind her as he followed, in case the gunman fired at them.

But even after they ducked down behind the headstones, there was nothing but the sound of their ragged breathing and his heart hammering in his chest.

"Do you think he's gone?" she whispered, her eyes wide in her pale face as she braced herself against the back of the tombstone.

He shook his head. Just because the gunman hadn't fired at them, didn't mean he was gone. In fact, he could have been hiding, waiting for them to move. And if he'd done that, he might know just where they were now. What they needed was some sort of distraction.

He tightened his grip on his weapon. Before using it, he glanced around to determine their next hiding place. "See that tall crypt, about twenty feet to your right? That's our next spot," he said in a low voice.

"Okay," she agreed.

He took a deep breath, and then stood and shot in the direction from which the silencer sound had come. After he shot, the shrill sound echoing through the night, he gave Kate a nudge, and they darted out from behind the tombstones, crossing over several graves.

As they ran, he heard another *poof*ing sound seconds after they both ducked behind the tall crypt. Only once they were safe did he become aware of a sharp pain in his left arm.

Dazed, he reached up with his other hand to investigate and discovered his sleeve was damp. When he pulled away his hand, dark smears stained his fingertips.

Blood. He'd been hit by that last bullet.

Kate did her best to swallow her fear, her heart beating so fast she was becoming dizzy. Flattened against the cold concrete structure, she rested her forehead against the unyielding stone, realizing she'd have to get used to being shot at once she graduated from the police academy.

She closed her eyes for a moment, wondering how her brothers faced this every day. Was Logan right? Was she cut out to be a cop?

Dear Lord, keep us safe!

Logan was moving beside her so she lifted her head and glanced over at him. "What are you doing?" she whispered.

"I need you to tie this around my arm," he said, pulling the string free from the hood of his sweatshirt. "As close to my armpit as you can."

It took several moments for the meaning to sink into her tired brain. "You're hit?" she whispered, unable to hide her horror.

"It's not bad, but hurry. We have to keep moving."

She wasn't a nurse, had no clue how to fix a gunshot

wound, but at the moment all she needed to do was to apply a makeshift tourniquet. So she took it from his hand and looped it around his bicep, tying it snugly as high as she could. "Is that too tight?" She could barely see what she was doing in the dark.

"No, it's fine."

A gunshot wound wasn't *fine*, but there wasn't time to argue. They needed to get back to the car so Logan could get to a hospital. Now that she knew he was wounded, the sense of urgency was almost unbearable.

Her mind raced. Twice now, the gunman had gotten close, too close, to hitting his target. "He must be holed up somewhere, watching us," she whispered.

In the darkness, she could see a faint smile. "Good deduction, Sherlock."

His attempt at humor, in the face of danger, and being wounded to boot, gave her a boost of badly needed confidence. "We need another diversion."

"The last one didn't work so well," he pointed out.

No, it hadn't. But she refused to give up. She scanned the area, searching for—something. Anything.

And then she saw it. A metal cross anchored on top of a small crypt, the one where they'd first taken cover. She took out her cell phone and gauged the weight in her palm.

Thanks to her older brothers and four years as captain of her high school softball team, she had a decent arm and a good eye. She could imagine how the scene might play out, the brief diversion possibly buying them enough time, if she could convince Logan to go along with her plan.

"We have to split up," she whispered.

"No way." Despite the whisper, his tone was fierce. "I'll keep covering you."

She ground her teeth in frustration. "He can't shoot both of us at the same time. Splitting up will confuse him." And maybe, just maybe, they could get far enough away that they could call the police station across the street for help. The dispatcher couldn't trace a cell phone signal like they could a landline, which meant she'd have to be able to speak loud enough for them to hear and understand what she was saying, without giving away her position to the gunman.

She prayed that the cops who responded weren't the ones on Salvatore's payroll.

"I'm going to hit that cross with my phone, and the noise will help distract him as we both head in different directions. From there, he won't be able to watch all three spots, which will help us get farther away. We'll both move every few minutes, keeping him off balance." Her plan could work, if he'd just trust her.

"Use this, instead." He pressed a decent-sized rock into her hand. "Hang on to your phone."

The rock was perfect, so she nodded. "You go east and I'll go north."

"You go east, *I'll* go north," Logan responded. East was closer to the spot where they'd left the car, and clearly Logan wasn't going to give on this one. Even though he was the wounded one.

"Fine. Get ready." She picked out her next hiding spot and then took a steadying breath. She peeked around the corner and took aim, throwing the rock on a wing and a prayer.

There was a loud clang, and they both darted off, heading in different directions. As soon as she was safely behind the protection of another tall headstone, she became acutely aware of how much she missed Logan's reassuring presence.

The darkness seemed more oppressive, more sinister without him beside her. She tried to focus on the reassuring sounds of the crickets and frogs.

She couldn't let herself think of the fact that Logan might be hit again. Or losing blood despite the tourniquet she'd placed. After waiting just thirty seconds, she moved again, this time with more stealth, as she slid on her belly over the ground to the next crypt.

A muffled noise made her freeze, but she realized the sound was probably from Logan. She darted to the next crypt, and then saw the dim glow of the streetlight.

Their car was less than fifty feet away.

She clutched her cell phone, wondering if she were far enough away from the shooter to call the police station. But after opening her phone, she realized the number was on Logan's phone, not hers. They'd used his phone to call the station, asking for Steve Gerlach's number.

There was the option of calling 9-1-1, but she couldn't be sure that the officer sent by the dispatcher wasn't on Salvatore's payroll.

Her brother Garrett's number was in the phone, but he wasn't close enough to help. No, their best bet would be to get to Logan's car. She moved to another gravestone, and then decided to go straight for the car.

It wasn't until she was within arm's reach of the vehicle that she remembered Logan had the keys.

Logan ignored the throbbing in his arm as he moved as silently as possible from one tombstone to another.

As much as he hated to admit it, Kate's plan was a good one. He hadn't heard any more *poof*ing sounds, which made him think their shooter was confused as to where they were hiding, exactly the way Kate had anticipated.

He'd gone north at first, but then angled toward the street where he'd parked the car, grimly realizing he should have given Kate the keys.

No point in berating himself. He quickened his pace, hoping to meet her there, only to trip over a dead tree branch lying between tombstones. He managed to catch himself before he fell, pain zinging up his injured arm.

He froze, plastering himself against the tombstone, hoping that the gunman hadn't heard the noise. When there was nothing but silence, he moved steadily toward the next tombstone.

The nagging itch in the center of his shoulder blades eased, and he thought it was possible the gunman had given up and left, but he didn't break from cover, unwilling to risk his life on gut instinct. So he continued moving toward the road. And when he saw Kate dashing toward the car, he couldn't help feeling a surge of relief.

Safety and freedom were just a few yards away. He grabbed the key fob from his pocket and unlocked the car, the soft beeping noise echoing loudly in the night.

Kate threw a glance over her shoulder in his direction as she opened the car door and dove inside.

He could see her sitting low in the driver's seat, the top of her head barely visible as she waited for him. The minute he reached the car, he tossed her the keys as he scrambled for the passenger seat. She fumbled for a moment before jamming the key into the ignition, turning it and stomping on the gas.

As she peeled away from the curb, he closed his eyes, partially because she was driving like a maniac, but mostly because he was so thankful they'd made it out of the cemetery alive.

And for the first time since his fiancée had died, he found himself praying. *Thank You, Lord! Thank You!*

Kate drove as fast as she dared, putting mile after mile between them and the cemetery. Imitating Logan, she turned several times, in case anyone was trying to follow them. But this late at night, there weren't too many cars on the road and it was easy to see no vehicle was tailing them.

She glanced over at Logan, more worried than she wanted to admit when she saw him sitting calmly in the passenger seat with his eyes closed. She racked her brain for the location of the closest hospital.

"Go back to the motel," he said, as if he'd read her mind.

"Logan, you need a doctor." She glanced around anxiously. Where were those little blue H signs when you needed them?

"No hospital. You know gunshot wounds have to be reported."

His eyes were open now, and she relaxed her death grip on the steering wheel. "So what? We need to report this, Logan. And we need to call the police about Steve Gerlach."

Now that they were safe, the images came flooding back. Steve Gerlach's prone body lying on the ground with the horrible dark bullet hole in the center of his forehead. How did they find him? Why did they kill him?

But of course she knew why he was dead. And it

was her fault. She'd called him, asked about the witness that had described her father's car accident. The witness whose name had been mysteriously erased from the police report.

Steve Gerlach had been killed so she couldn't prove the entire so-called accident that had claimed her father's life was nothing more than an elaborate setup to hide the truth.

The truth about her father's murder being linked to Bernardo Salvatore.

"Kate, turn left up at this next intersection," Logan said, breaking into her thoughts.

She turned, and then realized they weren't that far from the motel. She glanced at him to find that he was loosening the string she'd tied around his arm. "What are you doing?"

"I need to assess the damage," he said calmly, as he somehow maneuvered his left arm out from the sleeve of his sweatshirt.

The T-shirt he wore beneath the sweatshirt was short sleeved, giving her a far-too-vivid view of the angry red gash on his arm. She quickly averted her gaze, gluing her eyes to the road. "How bad is it?" she asked, almost afraid to hear the answer.

"Not nearly as bad as I feared," he said. "Not deep enough to have hit an artery or vein, so the tourniquet was overkill. The bullet tore through some muscle, that's all."

Tore through some muscle? "Sounds painful," she murmured, fighting to keep her tone steady. Cops were expected to stay cool under pressure, right? And while she wasn't a nurse, she knew basic first aid. She should be able to handle this.

Not that a bullet wound qualified as first aid in her mind, but she had to admit he was right about going to the hospital. Who knew if the cops who came to investigate would be on Salvatore's payroll? Maybe if she could arrange for one of her brothers to investigate? But no, they'd have to call the district where the incident occurred.

Incident. As if being hunted through a cemetery in the dead of night by a mafia gunman was nothing more than an incident.

"Kate? Are you all right?" Logan asked.

"Yes. Fine. Why?"

"Because you just passed the motel."

"Oh." She scowled, because he was right. She pulled into the next driveway and made a U-turn. This time, she managed to pull into the motel, driving around the building and parking in the spot in front of their connecting rooms.

She turned off the car, feeling an overwhelming sense of exhaustion. But she couldn't afford to cave under the pressure. There was still too much to do.

Gathering every ounce of strength and willpower she possessed, she handed Logan the keys and slid out from behind the steering wheel. By the time she came around to the other side, Logan had opened his motel room door and held it for her with his good arm.

She ducked inside, and then waited as he closed and locked the door behind him. He plopped down on the chair closest to the door, as if he were as weary as she was.

Sending him a tired smile, she grabbed the yellow plastic ice bucket. "Stay there, I'll get some hot water and towels."

Without waiting for a response, she disappeared into the small bathroom, gathering everything she'd need. They didn't have any bandages or gauze, though, so the washcloths would have to work until the stores opened in the morning.

She returned with her arms full, to see Logan sitting with his head leaned against the wall, eyes closed and legs stretched out in front of him. He looked so peaceful. The blood trickling down his arm was the only indication of the day's violence.

When she set down the bucket, water sloshed over the side. "Are you ready?" she asked, even though he looked as comfortable as she was nervous.

"Yes. Have at it, Nurse Nancy."

There he went again with the lame jokes. She flashed an eye roll before taking one of the hand towels and dipping it in the hot water and using it to clean the wound.

He flinched, but didn't protest. She tried to work quickly, making sure the entire area was clean before she used the washcloth as a bandage and then wound a larger towel around it to keep the smaller cloth in place.

"All finished," she murmured. She took the bucket of red-stained water and the bloody towels back to the bathroom.

When she returned, she almost smacked right into Logan, as he was standing just outside the bathroom door. He caught her shoulder with his right hand and then hugged her. "Thank you, Kate," he whispered against her hair.

She closed her eyes and leaned against him for several long moments, sinking into the embrace, even though she knew he only meant to offer comfort. And friendship.

"You're welcome," she whispered against his T-shirt. His chest was strong, yet supple, the beat of his heart beneath her ear reassuring. She could have stayed like that for the rest of the night, and despite her desire to protect her heart from being hurt again, she found herself lingering in his arms.

But this wasn't the time to relax, reveling in the fact that they were alive and safe. There was still work to be done. She reluctantly stepped away, intending to remind him that they had to call the police about finding Officer Gerlach, when Logan caught her off guard by tipping up her chin and lowering his mouth to hers in a heart-stopping kiss.

SEVEN

Kate couldn't help succumbing to Logan's kiss, even though she knew it wasn't smart. Logan was going to walk away from her once this was over, the same way he had six months ago.

But she didn't possess the strength to pull away from him. Instead she moved into the kiss, enjoying the way he hugged her tightly, exploring her mouth with his.

When he finally lifted his head, she gasped for air and leaned against him, her knees week. All too soon, he eased her away. Glancing up at him, she saw regret reflected in his eyes.

"I shouldn't have done that," he said in a low, husky voice.

Knowing that he regretted the kiss they'd shared only made her mad. Dropping her arms but not moving, she said, "Thanks, that makes me feel so much better."

He winced at her caustic tone. But what did he expect? She'd enjoyed his kiss, even though it was clear he didn't feel the same way.

And she needed to accept he never would. Which was just fine with her. She didn't need another domineering male in her life. She wanted someone who would partner with her, not try to control her. Was it too much to be accepted for who she was? Seemed all the men in her life wanted to change her into something else.

But this wasn't the time to worry about her personal life. Or lack thereof. She waved her hand. "Never mind about that, we have to call the police and tell them about Gerlach," she said, changing the subject. "And about being shot at in the cemetery."

"Look, I'll call in an anonymous tip about Gerlach, but as far as going in to give statements about what happened tonight? No way." Logan's expression was grim. "Especially not after hearing how Gerlach's accident report was tampered with. Salvatore doesn't have the ability to change a police report. But a cop working for Salvatore from inside does."

He was right, but that didn't mean she had to like it. The very thought of dirty cops on Salvatore's payroll made her sick to her stomach. "I could call my brothers. They could help investigate."

"Kate, do you really want to drag them into this? Gerlach is dead because he talked to us. Or because someone knew he was going to talk to us."

Guilt squeezed her chest, making her light-headed. "I still can't believe he's dead. I feel so helpless," she murmured.

"Get some sleep," Logan said firmly. "I'll call one of the guys on the FBI task force to let them know about Gerlach. I'll make sure they understand the officer's death is related to Salvatore."

She nodded her agreement with his plan and eased around Logan to head to her own room. But in the doorway, she paused and turned back toward him. "Do you really think it is?" she asked. At his frown, she added, "That Gerlach's death is really linked to Salvatore?"

"Yes, I do. You were right all along, Kate. Your father's death wasn't an accident. He was killed so that he wouldn't blow the whistle on Salvatore."

She nodded and stepped over the threshold into her own room. Hearing the conviction in Logan's tone made her feel better. She wasn't in this alone anymore. Logan believed her.

She needed to believe that, together, they'd find a way to prove it.

And hoped and prayed they wouldn't die trying.

Logan did his best to ignore the pain in his arm so that he could sleep. But it wasn't easy. For one thing, he couldn't get comfortable.

And when he closed his eyes, he kept seeing the dead cop he'd stumbled over. Officer Gerlach.

Who'd killed him?

He figured that Gerlach must have called someone. Maybe the second officer who'd come to the scene of Kate's father's car crash? Or his partner?

As possibilities whirled in his mind, he must have drifted off to sleep.

"No, stay back!" he hissed, putting out his arm to stop Jennifer in her tracks, pressing her back against the building. "I'll take care of these guys."

She nodded, holding her gun at the ready, her eyes wide.

He vowed to convince Jennifer to quit the DEA once they were married. He couldn't take having her exposed to danger this way. But right now, they were on their own. They'd stumbled upon the drug deal going down, giving him no choice but to intervene. He'd called for backup, but there wasn't time to waste. These guys wouldn't be here long.

Taking a deep breath, he waited for the drugs to exchange hands before he made his move. "Stop! Police!"

The two guys sprang apart, and he followed the one with the money. But the guy with the drugs shot at him. He ducked beside the parked car and by the time he peered around the bumper, he saw the man was facing Jennifer, both of them pointing their weapons at each other.

Shoot him, *he silently urged. But Jennifer seemed frozen, unable to move. No! He brought up his weapon but too late. Jennifer crumpled to the ground. He pulled his trigger and watched the man with the drugs fall, while the guy with the money managed to get away. He rushed over to her side.*

Except that it wasn't Jennifer lying there on the ground in a pool of blood. It was Kate, her long blond hair stained red. His heart squeezed in his chest as he screamed her name. Kate! Kate!

"Logan? What is it? What's wrong?"

His heart was pounding in his chest as he forced away the remnants of the nightmare. He looked up at Kate, hoping his mind wasn't playing tricks on him again. "You're alive."

She frowned and reached up to feel his forehead, as if checking for a fever. "Yes. And so are you. You must have had a bad dream."

Yeah, that was putting it mildly. She had no idea. "I'm fine," he said in a low, husky voice. "Sorry to wake you."

She shrugged, and moved away as if uncomfortable

being alone in his room in the darkness. It took everything in him not to ask her to come back. "No problem," she said lightly. "Just try to get some sleep, okay?"

"Sure. You, too." He waited until she returned to her own room before getting up to drink a glass of water. It helped, but he knew with sick certainty nothing was going to erase the image from his mind of Kate lying on the street dead.

He buried his face in his hands, trying to shake off the effects of the dream. He had to keep Kate safe. Because he wouldn't survive another innocent death on his conscience.

The next morning, Kate woke up to find the sun streaming through the motel room window. She staggered up and out of bed, amazed to realize it was almost nine o'clock in the morning.

Falling asleep after Logan's nightmare hadn't been easy. But she'd managed to get some sleep after all, and could only hope he'd been able to, as well.

She quickly showered and dressed, wrinkling her nose at having no choice but her wrinkled clothes. When she heard a loud thump from Logan's room she rushed over to open the connecting door.

"What happened?" she asked, when she found Logan braced against the wall. "Are you all right?"

"Yeah, I'm fine." He straightened and carefully made his way to the small table. "I tripped over my own two feet."

She narrowed her gaze at the way he avoided looking at her. First the nightmare last night and now this. Was his injury worse than she'd realized? She fought a sense of panic. "I need to go to the drug store to pick up some bandages and antibiotic ointment. I'll be back in a few minutes, okay?"

"Sure, I'll be here." A faint smile tipped his mouth. "Bring back some breakfast, too, okay?"

"No problem. But I'll need some cash and the car keys."

"Right." Logan dug into his back pocket and pulled out his wallet. He handed her a twenty and the keys she'd returned last night. "Stay safe."

His concern grated a bit on her nerves. She was going to the drug store, not something that could be considered dangerous by any stretch of the imagination. "I'll be back soon."

Despite being out in broad daylight, she couldn't help watching the rearview mirror like a hawk, to make sure she wasn't followed. She'd hoped to enjoy the few minutes of normalcy, but instead found herself hurrying to return to Logan. She was worried about him, and the thought of facing the danger of Salvatore alone was terrifying.

Picking out the dressings took longer than she'd anticipated. Afterward, she stopped at the first fast-food joint she saw to pick up egg sandwiches on the way back to the motel. Thankfully, no one seemed to pay her any attention.

She used her key to get into her room, and then tapped lightly on the connecting door. "Logan? Are you hungry?"

"Yeah, come in, it's open."

She wasn't sure if it was a good thing that Logan was still sitting at the small table where she'd left him. Then she relaxed when she realized his hair was damp from the shower. "Let's eat first while the egg sandwiches are still warm, then I'll look at your arm." She was glad he had another towel wrapped around the wound.

She set the bag of food on the table between them, closed her eyes and put her hands together. "Dear Lord, thank You for providing us food to eat, and please keep us safe from harm. Amen."

"Amen," Logan echoed. She glanced at him in surprise. He'd never done that before when she'd prayed. She found herself hoping that Logan had a relationship with God after all, as she dug into her meal.

They both ate in silence, and she wondered if she should have gotten two sandwiches for Logan when he devoured his in record time. "I can go out for more," she offered.

"No need, I just want to finish up here and get back on the road."

Back on the road? She frowned. "Why do we need to leave?"

"Because we can't afford to stay too long in one place," he said curtly. "I need to make sure you're safe. Check out time is eleven o'clock."

She suppressed a sigh as she finished her sandwich. When he began unwrapping the towel from his arm, she went to fill the plastic ice bucket once again with hot water.

The injury to his bicep looked a little better, at least from what she could tell. The deep furrow was starting to scab over a bit and didn't look infected. Still, she washed it again and spread a liberal layer of antibiotic ointment over it before she lightly wrapped gauze around it, more to keep the area from being irritated than anything else.

"We should have split up earlier," she said as she finished. "Then he wouldn't have hit you."

Logan's mouth thinned. "Or maybe he would have hit you," he said harshly. "Did you think of that possibility?"

"You act as if I'm helpless," she said, struggling to understand what was driving his seemingly single-minded determination to keep her safe.

"And you're acting as if you're already a cop. But you're not. So don't try to compare yourself to me. And if I had my way, you never would be. Women shouldn't be cops."

For a moment she was shocked speechless. Logan had never spoken to her this bluntly about his views before. He was worse than her brothers! How could he be so chauvinistic?

And then she caught a glimpse of the sheer agony in his eyes, and realized there must be more going on with him than what he was saying. Was this the root of his nightmare? She strove to keep her tone light. "What was her name?"

His scowl deepened. "I don't know what you're talking about."

She wasn't put off by his attitude. "Your fiancée. I know you loved her, but now I'm thinking that she must have been someone you worked with. A partner maybe?"

He winced and turned away, and she knew she'd hit the nail on the head. She'd known he'd lost his fiancée but she hadn't realized, until right now, that she had also been a cop.

Just like Logan.

No wonder he felt the way he did.

She couldn't stop herself from reaching out to him. "Logan, you're not alone. I'm here. And don't forget, God is with you, too, if you're willing to believe and to lean on His strength."

He let out a harsh sound, something between a laugh and a groan. "That's just it. I don't believe. Otherwise, why would God take Jennifer away from me? Why didn't He take me instead?"

She ached for him and wished he'd tell her what had happened. Although did it really matter? His fiancée was dead. And he'd obviously loved her very much. "It's not up to us to question God's will, Logan. But I believe He has a reason. One that just hasn't been revealed to us yet."

He shook his head, showing his disbelief, and pulled away, rising to his feet. "Grab your stuff from your room. We have to hit the road."

She reluctantly returned to her room to pack her meager belongings. So, Logan's dislike of her chosen career wasn't personal, but was related to Jennifer, the woman he'd loved and lost. She didn't know if that made her feel better or worse.

And she was troubled by his lack of faith. She slid into the passenger seat beside him and silently vowed that while he helped her find her father's murderer, she would do her best to help him rediscover his faith.

Logan drove to the other side of town, keeping to the less-traveled back roads and wishing he'd kept his mouth shut.

Why had he blabbed about Jennifer? Kate didn't need to know about his personal life. Besides, he'd lost Jennifer well over two years ago. He should be over it by now.

And he was over Jennifer's death. But in his dream, or rather his nightmare, Jennifer wasn't the one who'd died.

Kate was.

He gripped the steering wheel tightly as he navigated around a large tractor rambling in front of him on the long stretch of county highway. He couldn't afford to be distracted by the dream.

They had to figure out their next move.

"I think we should call Angela," Kate said, breaking the silence. "We're pretty much out of options."

"I have Gerlach's cell phone," he said, avoiding her comment about Angela. He was still angry about her former roommate setting her up in the first place. No matter what Kate said, he wasn't about to trust the woman. "I went through his call history and wrote down all the numbers."

"Why didn't you say so sooner?" she demanded. "Where's the list?"

"There's only one other number he called after we contacted him," he said, pulling a piece of paper out of his pocket and handing it over. "It's the last one on the bottom."

"I don't recognize it," she murmured, staring at the motel stationery he'd used for his notes. "But we should try calling it."

"No!" He shot out his hand to stop her. "Not yet. Not until we do a little investigating first."

She frowned, and then nodded. "Okay, I can see your point. We don't want to tip him off, do we?"

The band of fear that had tightened around his chest eased enough for him to breathe. "No, we don't. Once we get settled, I'll boot up the laptop and see what we can find. There were a few text messages there, too, but they were pretty cryptic. Nothing so obvious as a name or anything."

"Okay, I'll try to have patience. Although we already know that it's a local number, based on the Chicago area code."

Yeah, he'd already noticed that much, too.

"'See you later,'" she murmured, reading through the text messages. "That one came in shortly before we contacted him."

"Yeah, and from a number that shows up on his call list a lot," he added. "Probably a girlfriend."

"Do you think she might know something?" Kate asked excitedly.

"I don't know." And truthfully, he was loath to find out. The last thing he needed was to drag any more innocent bystanders into this mess.

Having Kate here beside him was bad enough. Maybe he liked working with a partner more than he'd thought, but he'd rather have another FBI agent instead of a woman he was starting to care about.

A woman he'd kissed.

A woman he wanted to kiss again.

Grimly, he dragged his concentration back to the issue at hand. Hopefully, the phone numbers and text messages he'd taken from Gerlach's phone wouldn't turn out to be another dead end.

Because the sooner he brought Salvatore to justice, the sooner Kate would be safe. And he desperately needed to know that she was out of danger. Before he moved on to the next case.

EIGHT

Kate spent some time in the uncomfortable motel armchair going over the text messages, but there really wasn't much to be gleaned from them. It wasn't a surprise that Steve Gerlach had a girlfriend. Kate wanted to talk to her, to see if she knew anything important.

Although there was a strong chance she wouldn't know anything that would help them. Kate knew from her brothers and her father how a lot of cops didn't like to bring the ugly aspects of their jobs home to their families. It was only when Kate had made it clear she was pursuing the same career in law enforcement that her father had started opening up to her.

Grief stabbed deep and she momentarily closed her eyes, remembering the way her dad had looked the last time she'd seen him, with his green eyes crinkling at the corners when he smiled. The way he'd hugged her at the end of their dinner together, engulfing her in the comforting scent of his Old Spice aftershave.

She swallowed hard and took several deep breaths to get her emotions under control. She had to remind herself again that her dad, a devout Christian, was up in heaven now, finally reunited with her mother. Their pastor was right—he was in a much better place.

She swiped the moisture from her eyes, sniffled loudly and tried to focus again on the phone numbers Logan had written down. Her gaze kept lingering on the number Gerlach had called about thirty minutes before their scheduled meeting in the cemetery. Something about it was vaguely familiar.

And suddenly she figured it out. "Logan, I know this number Gerlach called right after he talked to us! It's one of the numbers in the third district police station."

"The third district?" he echoed in surprise. "Are you sure?"

"I'm sure. My brother Garrett works there. All the phones in that district have the same first three numbers. I didn't recognize it at first, because I don't call him there often. I normally use his cell phone."

"At least that will be easy enough to check out. But Gerlach worked out of the fifth district, didn't he?"

"You're right, Gerlach did," she echoed, staring at the phone number with a deep frown. "So why would he call someone in another district? That doesn't make any sense."

"Could be that he has a friend there," Logan mused under his breath. "A friend who just happens to be dirty."

"Maybe," she agreed. All along she'd assumed that Gerlach had died because he'd talked to them, but there was another possibility. "Or maybe he was the dirty cop." She didn't want to think that of him, but it was an avenue that had to be considered. "Maybe he called someone else to let them know I was asking questions."

"Then why kill him?" Logan asked. "Why not just wait for us to get there and take us both out of the picture?"

She glanced at the makeshift bandage she'd applied to his arm. "That was part of their plan, obviously."

"But killing Gerlach before we got there doesn't make sense."

She could almost imagine how it might have gone down. "It does if Gerlach balked at killing us. Maybe he made it clear to the dirty cop that he'd meet with us and try to shake us off the trail. But the dirty cop wanted us to be silenced forever, and Gerlach wasn't keen on that approach. So the dirty cop killed him, and then waited for us to show up, and then tried to take us out."

"It's possible," Logan said slowly. "I guess at this point, anything is possible."

"So many deaths," she murmured. "I just don't understand. Is there no value to human life? How is it possible that money is more important?"

Logan glanced at her and shrugged. "Money and power, the two go hand in hand."

She knew he was right, but she simply couldn't comprehend it. Salvatore's men, even the cops he had on the payroll, had to know the mobster didn't value human life. Was the risk really worth the benefit? Were they so blind they couldn't see that they were disposable?

She rubbed her eyes and then leaned back against the seat cushion. She'd started down this path to avenge her father's death, but that wasn't the driving force any longer. Salvatore had to be stopped. Soon.

Because it was just a matter of time before he killed again.

Kate barely glanced at the name of the motel Logan had picked for their next hideout. It didn't really matter much. They'd be here for forty-eight hours at the most.

Idly, she wondered just how much cash he had left to keep getting motel rooms like this. Granted, they were staying at cheap places, but still, how long could he afford to keep throwing away money?

She couldn't shake the feeling of helplessness. It seemed that for every step forward they took on the investigation into her father's murder, they slid back three.

"I managed to get two connecting rooms again," Logan said when he'd come back out to the car. "Here's your key."

"Thanks." She took the small plastic card. "Logan, I know I've mentioned this several times already, but don't you think it's time to call Angela Giordano? It's a long shot to think we'll be able to figure out who Gerlach called at the third district. We need someone who knows Salvatore. Like Angela."

He narrowed his gaze. "You do remember how she led you to Russo, right?"

"Yes, and I clearly remember her saying something like 'you promised you wouldn't hurt her.'" She couldn't explain the deep need she had to try to save her former roommate. "Just let me call her. Please?"

He stared at her for a long moment, before giving a terse nod. "Fine, call her. But we're going to use Gerlach's phone. I don't want her to have your number."

"It's a deal." She went into her own room first and opened the windows to get rid of the musty smell. Not that she was complaining. Clearly these were the sorts of places that took cash with no questions asked.

She splashed water on her face and then headed over to open her side of the connecting door. Logan already had his ajar, so she knocked lightly before crossing the threshold.

"Here's Gerlach's cell phone," he said, handing it to her. "The battery is already half-gone so we'll need to keep it off when we're not using it since we don't have a charger."

"We might be able to buy one," she said as she punched in Angela's number. The phone rang several times before going to voice mail. "Angie, this is Kate. I want to help you stay safe. Call me back at this same number as soon as possible." She hung up and glanced over at Logan. "Can I leave it on for a few minutes?"

"Sure." He was reading something intently on the computer screen, so she moved closer to see what had snagged his attention.

"Is this the racino you mentioned?" she asked, tapping the photo on the screen. The picture of the racetrack looked like something you would see if you went to the Kentucky Derby.

"Yeah, that's it all right. The Berkshire Racetrack."

And a casino. *Racino.* "Are the slot machines inside the building?"

He nodded. "And blackjack tables." He grimaced. "Perfect way to get rid of dirty money."

"It's not right that Salvatore can get away with it," she muttered, scowling darkly. "Is the public really so blind that they can't figure out it's partially owned by the mafia?"

He shrugged. "Who knows? Gambling is much like any other addiction. Easy enough to keep a blind eye to the parts you don't want to see."

She couldn't understand what anyone saw in gambling. Especially if you didn't have money to lose in the first place. But Logan was right. The people who spent a lot of time gambling probably couldn't care less who owned the place.

The phone in her lap vibrated and rang simultaneously, making her heart leap into her throat. She grabbed it, recognizing Angela's number. "Angie?"

"Kate, I'm so glad you're all right. How did you escape Russo?"

It was on the tip of her tongue to let Angie have it for setting her up, but that was in the past. Time to move forward. "Never mind that now, I want to make sure you're safe. You need to get away from your uncle, Angie. Before it's too late."

"I know. I'm so sorry, Kate. I didn't know…" Angie's voice trailed off.

"It's okay, Angie, we all make mistakes." Hadn't she made the biggest one of all, by mentioning Salvatore to her father in the first place? "Just get away from the restaurant. Find someplace to hide."

"I will. Actually, your brother Garrett called me. I'm going to meet him in a few hours."

"Garrett called you?" She didn't bother to hide her surprise. Logan just frowned. "That's great. He's a cop. He'll keep you safe."

"Yeah, well, he did promise that, too. But the main reason he wants to talk to me is to find out what I know about my uncle," Angie said drily. "He was not pleased with me."

"No, he wasn't at all happy that you allowed Russo to capture me," Kate murmured. Logan's snort was probably heard through the phone by Angie.

"I'm sorry, Katie. Honestly, he said he just wanted to talk to you."

Angie should have known better than to believe her

uncle's thugs would simply talk to anyone. But that wasn't the point. "Do you have information on Salvatore? Because if so, I'd like to hear it, too. Where are you meeting Garrett? I'll join you."

Hearing this, Logan stood over her, shaking his head for emphasis.

"I don't know anything," Angie said in a weary tone. "You know what it's like working at Salvatore's. We see the customers who come in here, but they're pretty good at not talking in front of us. And I wish I did know more about my uncle's business associates. All I know is that he's tried to kill me."

Kate caught her breath, even though she shouldn't be shocked to hear the news. Hadn't she feared this all along? It was the main reason she'd agreed to meet Angie at the park in the first place. "What happened?"

"He sent Russo after me. But I'd already left my apartment, was just inside the stairwell when I saw him kick his way inside. I've been on the run ever since."

"Garrett will help you, don't worry," she soothed her. "I'd still like to hear from you, too."

"All right. Look, I have to go. I've been riding the subway all day, and I need to change trains. I'll talk to you later."

"Sounds good. Bye, Angie." She snapped Gerlach's phone shut and then turned it off to preserve the battery. "She's safe, at least for the moment."

"Why did your brother get in touch with her?" Logan asked.

"Probably because he's trying to help by getting information about Salvatore," she told him. She held up her hand to keep Logan from interrupting her next words. "We need to meet up with them to convince

Garrett to back off." She'd warned her brother to stay out of it, but he hadn't listened. And suddenly, she was very afraid that Garrett would somehow end up just like her father.

Dead because of her.

"There's no reason for us to meet. He can fill us in on whatever he finds out. Besides, I told you all along that Angela probably doesn't know much," Logan countered.

"How do you figure? I found out quite a bit while I was waitressing at Salvatore's," she pointed out. "If you remember, that's when I called you."

How could he forget? Six months ago, Kate had discovered that she was working in a mafia-owned restaurant and offered to be an informant for the FBI. She'd been sharp enough to figure out how to piece together the fragments of conversations she'd overheard into something useful. Especially after one of her coworkers, another waitress at the restaurant, had disappeared, only to end up floating in Lake Michigan.

He'd been ecstatic to get Kate out of there. But after they'd worked together to bring down Anthony Caruso, the state senator who was working with Salvatore, she'd flatly refused to go into a safe house.

So here she was, six months later, still in danger. And no matter what she thought, there was no way Angela would have been able to figure out anything nearly as valuable as what Kate had discovered.

As much as it pained him to admit the truth, Kate had strong investigative instincts. Somehow, he didn't think Angela was nearly as good.

"Angie might not even realize what she knows," Kate was saying. "But we can ask her questions, see if she remembers seeing Dean Ravden there, meeting with Salvatore. Putting the two of them together would be helpful."

He raised a brow. "Even if Ravden is dead?"

She scowled. "*Especially* because Ravden might be dead. First of all, we don't know for sure he was the one who died in my father's house. But if he was, then we can add that to the case we're building against Salvatore."

"Circumstantial at best," he murmured.

"It's a place to start."

He stared at the picture on the screen of the new Berkshire Racetrack. Linking Ravden's death to Salvatore might be a place to start, but somehow he knew that the new racetrack was the way to finish it.

He just needed to figure out how to accomplish that minor feat, especially now that his Tex Ryan connection to Salvatore was exposed.

Logan didn't like the thought of meeting up with Angela and Kate's brother, but he didn't think they had a choice. According to the article, the new Berkshire Racetrack was scheduled to open the following Friday night. Today was Saturday, so they had less than a week.

As part of his Tex Ryan cover, he'd given Salvatore a large sum of money to be used as an investment in the racetrack. Logan's boss was hoping the partnership would create a bond of trust, so they could find out more about Salvatore's illegal activities.

Now Logan wondered if Salvatore had established another partnership for the racetrack. Or was the mobster moving forward on his own? The racino as an investment opportunity was a sham since the payouts they were to receive for their investments would be paid with laundered money.

Logan's boss had wanted to trace the money through the process, in order to bring down Salvatore. But that wasn't going to be possible, now that his cover was blown. So they needed a plan B.

Too bad he was drawing a blank on that one.

He realized Kate was turning on her disposable phone. "What are you doing?"

She flashed him an exasperated look. "Calling my brother Garrett. I told you we're meeting up with him and Angie. I have to find out where."

"Okay, but make it quick."

She rolled her eyes in a show of annoyance, but then frowned when her call went straight to voice mail. "Garrett, it's me, Kate. I just spoke to Angie, thanks for bailing her out. Call me ASAP to let me know where you guys are meeting so I can join you."

"Do you really think he'll call?" he asked.

She stared at him. "Why wouldn't he?"

"I don't know—maybe to keep you safe?" He understood she wanted to avenge her father's death, but he wished she valued her own life just as much.

Kate volunteered to get them something to eat for lunch, mostly because sitting around while Logan did internet searches was driving her crazy.

She glanced at her phone for the zillionth time since she'd left Garrett that voice mail message. Why wasn't he calling her back? What could possibly be taking so long?

She went to the closest fast-food restaurant, the place where she'd picked up breakfast, to get a few burgers.

She was tired of fast food, but it wasn't as if they could afford to get a hotel room that was equipped with a kitchen. Even if there were time to cook a meal, which there wasn't.

After she'd paid for their food, her phone rang. She pulled out from the drive-through window, juggling the food and the steering wheel. She quickly turned into a vacant parking spot and grabbed the phone, hoping it wasn't too late. "Hello? Garrett?"

"Kate, I think something has happened to Angela."

"What?" She gripped the phone tightly. "Why? What happened?"

"She was supposed to meet me thirty minutes ago, but she didn't show. And now she's not answering her phone." Garrett's voice was harsh with fear mixed with frustration. "I think Salvatore must have found her."

No! She didn't want to believe that. "I spoke to her a few hours ago, Garrett. She was riding the subway. It could be just that it's taking her longer to get there."

"Maybe." He didn't sound the least bit hopeful. "Stay away from here, Katie, do you understand? If I find Angela, I'll let you know."

"Wait!" She didn't want her brother to hang up on her. "Why won't you tell me where you are?"

"Remember how you didn't want to get me involved? Well, the same holds true for me. I took a gamble contacting Angela, and I lost. Just stay away from here, Kate. Promise me!"

"Okay, I promise." What else could she do? It wasn't as if she could trace his cell phone to get his location. "But, Garrett, you have to keep in touch. Why didn't you answer your phone?"

"I was in the middle of something and trying to

hurry so I could meet Angela. I have to go. I want to make another sweep of the area here, just to be on the safe side."

"All right, call me as soon as you hear anything." She hung up the phone and sat for a few seconds, staring blindly out through the windshield of Logan's car.

Where was Angie? Had Russo or Salvatore found her before she could get to Garrett? Or was she still hiding somewhere, trying to get to the meeting place?

She was about to put the car in gear, when she spotted a kid on a skateboard heading toward her. She wanted to call Salvatore's restaurant but not with her own cell phone, so she opened her car door and flagged down the kid.

"What's up?" he said, eyeing her suspiciously.

"I'll give you a dollar if you let me borrow your cell phone to make a quick call."

"A dollar?" His upper lip curled in disgust. "Man, you gotta make it worth my while."

"Okay, five bucks!" She held out the bill, waiting impatiently for him to hand over the phone.

He seemed to debate whether or not he could get more, but then grudgingly handed over his smartphone.

With shaking fingers, she dialed the number for the restaurant, practically holding her breath. Was it possible Angela was there? That maybe her former roommate had planned to set up Garrett, the same way she'd done Kate?

The phone on the other end rang several times before someone picked it up. "Salvatore's, may I help you?"

She recognized the falsely polite tone of Suzanne, the hostess, who no doubt knew exactly what sort of boss she had. "May I speak with Angela Giordano?"

There was a long pause. "I'm sorry, but Ms. Giordano doesn't work here anymore."

The sharp click of Suzanne hanging up on her seemed almost as loud as a gunshot. Numbly, she handed the cell back to the skater. "Thanks."

The kid shoved the phone in the pocket of his baggy cargo shorts and she thought he muttered "weirdo" under his breath as he skated away.

She didn't care. There were bigger issues to worry about. She slid back into Logan's car and drove as fast as she dared back to the hotel, battling another wave of helplessness.

She didn't want to believe the worst, but deep down, she knew the truth. They were too late to save Angie. Salvatore must have gotten to her.

How many more would die before they managed to arrest him?

NINE

Logan pushed away from the computer and rubbed his eyes to ease the strain. The grand opening of the brand-new racetrack was the key, but he couldn't think of a way to trap Salvatore without help.

Broodingly, he sat back in the chair and stared out the motel room window. Kate should be back any moment and he was no further ahead than when she had left to pick up lunch.

Maybe it was time to call his boss. Ken Simmons wouldn't be happy to know what happened days ago and how he was just getting around to contacting him now. But what other choice did he have? He needed help, beyond Kate. He needed resources—and not just money, although they only had enough cash to last for a few more days.

He had the listening device, but he would need to figure out how and where to plant it so that he could get the most valuable information.

Maybe at the racetrack itself? He spun back toward the computer, intent on reviewing the floor plans once again. Maybe, just maybe, there was a conference room of some sort where the "investors" would meet and discuss business. He knew that Salvatore had gone there once before, so it was possible that the mafia boss would go again.

He'd found exactly what he was looking for when Kate returned. She came in through her motel room door, carrying the bags of fast food, her expression grim. He frowned. "What's wrong?"

She set down the bag of food on the table and dropped into the empty chair. "Angie was supposed to meet my brother Garrett, but didn't show. And she doesn't work at the restaurant anymore, either. I think—Salvatore silenced her once and for all."

Kate looked so devastated, he wanted to reach over and take her into his arms. But he feared he'd be tempted to kiss her again, so he forced himself to stay where he was. "I'm sorry, Kate," he murmured, aching for her. Maybe they should have contacted Angela earlier? Although he still wasn't sure the woman could be trusted. And there were other possibilities, as well. "It could be that she's just running late, though, right?"

"I don't think so," she said wearily. "The meeting was well over an hour ago."

"But it's possible, right? Say, for instance, that she thought she was being followed? She'd go out of her way to lose a tail before going to meet your brother." It wasn't like him to offer false hope, but he couldn't stand to see Kate looking so defeated. Especially when he knew that Angela would have had a better chance to escape if he'd agreed to contact her right away, when Kate had asked him to.

"Maybe," she said, sitting up straighter in her chair. "I'm going to keep my disposable cell phone on, because Garrett promised to call if he had an update."

"No problem." He wasn't in the mood to deny her anything right now. "Let's eat before the food gets cold, okay?"

She grimaced a little, as if she didn't have much of an appetite, but reached for the hamburger bag nonetheless. He took the sandwich she held out to him, and then waited before unwrapping his food, because he knew she was going to pray. He found it unsettling the way he'd fallen into Kate's routine.

She set her burger in front of her and then closed her eyes and bowed her head. "Dear Lord, thank You for this food, we're grateful to be able to eat when others go hungry. Also, please keep Angela Giordano safe in your care and forgive whatever sins she may have committed, Amen."

"Amen." He was touched and a little amazed that she'd included Angela in her prayers. And he remembered how he'd prayed during those life-threatening moments in the cemetery. Was God really watching over them? He wished he could believe that were true, but then why had God taken Jennifer? Kate said that God always had a plan, and that they had to trust in Him, but it wasn't easy. Not when Jennifer had been young and innocent. He couldn't fathom why her life on earth had to be cut short, while he was still here.

"What are you looking at?" Kate asked between bites, her eyes glued to his computer screen. "Is that a floor plan for the Berkshire Racetrack? How did you get that?"

He dragged his thoughts away from the painful past, taking a healthy bite of his burger to ease the hunger pains in his stomach before taking the time to answer. "I still have access to the bureau's search engines." He lightly tapped the screen. "I think this room is where I'm going to plant the listening device."

Her eyebrows lifted, and he knew she was remembering how they'd used it six months ago to listen in on Salvatore's dinner conversation with the late Senator Caruso. Salvatore had all kinds of power in his back pocket. "Not a bad idea."

He munched a French fry and shrugged. "It's a long shot, but worth a try."

She sighed and nodded. "That's about all we have left, isn't it?"

"Hey, we have a lot of options left," he said, despite thinking the same thing just a few minutes ago. "Don't give up hope, Kate. We're going to nail Salvatore. He will be punished for his crimes."

"I hope so," she said softly.

They finished the rest of their meal in companionable silence. He was struck again by how nice it was to have Kate nearby to bounce around ideas with. After eating, Kate changed the dressing on his arm, and then Logan discussed plans to get the listening device inside the not-yet-opened racetrack.

"I think we should go in late at night. Fewer people around," Kate said.

"Agreed, although we'll need to make sure there aren't any security guards in place yet."

"Can you pick the lock to get inside?" she asked.

"Well, now, I'm hurt that you doubt my ability," he drawled, laying on thick his Texas accent.

When she smiled, he caught his breath and looked away. This was not the time to think about how beautiful she was. They had things to do. Plans to make.

And he couldn't afford to think about anything beyond bringing Salvatore to justice.

Logan was glad that Kate agreed to stay near the trees outside, covering him as he crept up to the Berkshire track in the darkness. The hour was well after midnight, and he was anxious to get in and out as soon as humanly possible. They were both dressed in black from head to toe, with ski masks to hide their pale faces.

There weren't guards, but there were security cameras—especially in the parking lot, in the front atop the main doors and at the back where the horse stalls were located. Messing with the security cameras would only raise suspicions, so he crouched behind a tree and used his binoculars to see if there was another way in. The proposed racino had a kitchen, nothing fancy, but enough of one to serve hot dogs, hamburgers and chicken sandwiches. Luckily, the kitchen door didn't have a security camera stationed anywhere he could see—a lapse that would work in their favor.

He stayed low, moving in the darkness until he reached the kitchen door. After picking the lock, he headed inside, imagining the floor plan in his head. The small conference room nestled between the offices was located way on the other side of the building.

There was no way to know if there were cameras inside or not, so he stayed in the darkness as much as possible, at least until he reached the conference room. Once there, he used the small penlight to find the best hiding spot. The technology used to make this listening device was state-of-the-art and wouldn't be picked up by regular bug sweepers.

He was half-afraid there wouldn't be any furniture

yet, but there was a beautiful maple conference room table with six cushy chairs surrounding it. He didn't waste any time planting the bug beneath the center of the table. The moment he had it affixed, he turned off the penlight and made his way out to the kitchen, using nothing but touch.

When he slipped back outside, crossing over to where Kate was waiting, he couldn't help but grin. "Mission accomplished," he whispered.

"Thank You, Lord," she murmured. "Now let's get out of here."

He wasn't about to argue. They kept as far away from the cameras as possible as they cut across the small field to get to the hiding spot where they'd left their car.

After they had put several miles between them and the Berkshire Racetrack, he heard Kate let out a heavy sigh. "I don't think I'd like being a burglar. Too stressful."

He glanced at her. "Being a cop isn't any less stressful, you know."

"I hope you don't mind, but I'm planning to attend church in the morning," she said, completely changing the subject.

"Church?" He mentally switched gears to catch up, not surprised that she'd dodged his comment about her career. Was tomorrow, or rather, today, really Sunday? "Where?"

"There's a small church located a few miles from the motel. If you don't want me to drive, I'll walk."

He didn't like the thought of her going anywhere alone. He hadn't been in a church since he had lost Jennifer, but it looked as though he was going to break his streak by going along with Kate. "I'll go with you."

She glanced at him in surprise. “You will?”

“Yes, I will.” Going to church didn’t mean he was going to embrace religion the way his buddy Jonah Stewart did. Back when he was young he’d found sermons to be dull and boring, and he doubted that had changed much. But he could use the time to plan out their next move, while making sure Kate stayed safe.

Besides, it was only an hour or so. He could put up with anything for that long.

After they returned to the motel, they both retreated to their separate rooms, keeping the connecting door closed for privacy. They only had a few hours to sleep before the service Kate had chosen to attend would start.

When his radio alarm clock blared good ole country music in his ear, he groaned and turned over, wincing as he inadvertently squashed the wound on his arm. The pain had him instantly regretting his offer to go to church, if it involved getting up now. The music lightened his spirit, though. Maybe he had had to give up his cowboy boots and his Stetson, but at least he had country music to remind him of his Texas roots.

He was more than a little tempted to back out of attending the service. Kate could easily go alone. She could take the car and he’d enjoy another hour of sleep before she returned.

But even though he turned off the radio alarm clock and closed his eyes, he knew he wouldn’t be able to fall back asleep. So he reluctantly got up and headed into the bathroom.

After he showered, shaved and changed the dressing on his arm, relieved to note that it didn’t look infected, he went to the connecting door between their rooms. He knocked lightly, and Kate answered right away, as if she'd been waiting for him.

"Ready?" she asked. "Do you need me to change your dressing first?"

"No, I already took care of it. Let's take everything with us—we'll need to find a new place to stay anyway." He grabbed his computer case and the few clothes he had before he followed her outside. Once they were both settled in the front seat, he started the car and headed toward the road. "Which way?"

"Left. It's just a mile or two down the road."

Sure enough, the steeple could be seen almost immediately, above the trees. He had to admit, it was a beautiful church, all white with small but colorful stained-glass windows. He was reminded of the church he'd attended as a youngster.

Once they were seated inside, the choir broke into song, and he sat listening to the music rather than using the time to plan their day.

When the pastor began his sermon, he thought for sure he'd be bored, but the subject of the sermon was everlasting life to those who believed, no doubt because of the recent Easter holiday.

"Listen as I read from Acts 11:16–18," the pastor said before looking down at his Bible. "'Then I remembered what the Lord had said: "John baptized with water, but you will be baptized with the Holy Spirit." So if God gave them the same gift he gave us who believed in the Lord Jesus Christ, who was I to think that I could stand in God's way?'"

Logan sat in stunned silence for a moment, the last few words resonating deep within. Kate was right. Who was he to think he could second-guess God's plan? Jennifer was a better person than he was. She believed in God, and as the pastor's sermon went on, he found himself listening intently.

"And we learn this from 1 John 5:12–14," the pastor said after turning to another page in the Bible. "'Whoever has the Son has life; whoever does not have the Son of God does not have life. I write these things to you who believe in the name of the Son of God so that you may know that you have eternal life. This is the confidence we have in approaching God: that if we ask anything according to his will, he hears us.'"

For the first time since losing Jennifer, Logan felt a strange sense of peace. And he understood now what Kate had been trying to tell him. That Jennifer was in a better place, up in heaven. She wasn't suffering the way he was. Maybe he'd had it backward all this time. God had chosen to bring Jennifer home, but had left him behind on purpose. To hurt and suffer.

Because he hadn't believed? Because Jennifer was a better person than he was?

The truth was suddenly very clear. So he closed his eyes and the prayer came from deep within his heart. *Dear Lord, forgive me for not understanding Your will. Please guide me along the path You've chosen for me. And please give me the strength to keep Kate safe from harm.*

Kate was amazed by how attentive Logan was during the pastor's sermon. She'd expected him to either look bored or preoccupied with Salvatore.

Yet he was following along with the Bible readings, as if discovering them for the first time. He had mentioned his parents taking him to church as a child, but he'd made it clear that he hadn't sustained a close relationship with God over the years.

Especially after losing his fiancée.

Yet here he was standing beside her, Bible in hand. She was pleased that he'd not only attended church with her today, but appeared to be taking the sermon to heart.

Or was that nothing more than wishful thinking?

She hoped not, because she ached for him. For his loss, so similar to her own. The sermon was exactly what she needed to cherish her father's memory.

"Lastly, my friends, I leave you with this final word from the book of Psalms, Chapter 91, Verse 1. 'Whoever dwells in the shelter of the Most High will rest in the shadow of the Almighty.' Now please join me in reciting the Lord's Prayer."

Logan took her hand and she couldn't help reveling in the warmth of his fingers surrounding hers as they prayed together. And once the sermon was finished, she wrapped her arms around him in a brief hug. "Thank you for coming with me today, Logan. Attending church today was exactly what I needed."

"My pleasure," he murmured, returning her hug and keeping ahold of her hand as they walked back outside. She squinted a bit in the bright sunlight, even as she enjoyed the warmth against her skin.

Her smile widened as he held open the passenger door for her. "My dad would always hold a door for me," she said as she slid inside the stuffy car. After the sermon, she could think of her father without the crippling grief that had haunted her since he'd died.

"My mother drilled manners into me and my brother," he said, turning on the car and opening the windows to let out the stifling heat while she buckled her seat belt. "Old habits are hard to break."

She was glad, and wanted to tell Logan how much her father, if he'd still been alive, would like him. But she kept her thoughts to herself, afraid of making him uncomfortable and breaking the sense of camaraderie that had settled between them.

As Logan steered the car out of the church parking lot and back onto the highway, she noticed a tan car parked on the side of the road, the driver's head buried in a map. When they'd passed him, though, she noticed he instantly set aside the map and then pulled out behind them.

Immediately, the tiny hairs on the back of her neck rose in alarm. "Um, Logan? Check out the tan car behind us."

"I see him," Logan said, although his gaze didn't lift up to the rearview mirror. "If he's really following us, then I'll lose him."

She tried not to stare into her side-view mirror at the car behind them, but it wasn't easy. "I don't understand. How could they possibly have found us?"

"Good question. Tracking our disposable cell phones would be nearly impossible, since I paid for them with cash."

Her stomach churned. "I didn't turn mine off last night," she confessed softly. "I was waiting to hear good news from Garrett and forgot about it."

He glanced at her, but didn't look angry. "As I said, it would be hard to trace us through the disposable cell phones. A more likely scenario is that someone spotted our car last night, during our visit to the Berkshire Racetrack."

"How? You told me this car couldn't be traced to you, and besides, we parked far away from the cameras," she protested.

"I don't know," Logan said grimly. He turned onto a less-used country road, and the car behind them followed.

The knot of dread in her stomach tightened painfully. "I don't like this, Logan. What if that guy is another of Salvatore's goons?"

"Don't worry, I'll keep you safe."

She braced herself by holding on to the door handle, but he didn't increase the speed of the car. In fact, Logan acted as if they didn't have anywhere pressing to go.

She told herself to take deep breaths, relax and trust in Logan's experience, but it wasn't easy. The country highway they'd taken twisted and turned but there wasn't any traffic, so the car following exactly two car lengths behind them was only that much more noticeable.

It couldn't be good that the guy didn't even try to hide the fact that he was on their tail. Was he planning on killing them both in the bright light of day?

Without warning, Logan stomped on the brakes and yanked the steering wheel to the right, tires squealing as he turned onto a dirt road that disappeared into a wooded area that looked to be private property.

"What are you doing?" she squeaked.

"Get out!" He slammed on the brakes and opened the driver's-side door the same time she opened hers. "This way." He came around the car, grabbed her hand and pulled her into the trees just thirty seconds before she heard the sound of the second car turning down the same dirt road.

She barely had time to think as Logan pushed her down into the bushes, hiding her from view. He pulled out his weapon, which he must have been carrying even while they were in church, she realized grimly. He kept his hand on her back as he crouched beside her, waiting for Salvatore's goon to come after them.

TEN

Kate struggled to control her breathing so that she wouldn't inadvertently give away their location. She concentrated on listening, and after the other car's engine stopped, she heard the soft *snick* as the driver opened the car door.

Every muscle in her body tensed. She trusted Logan, but the impending danger made her acutely aware of the vulnerability of their position. The guy in the tan car was the hunter and they were the prey.

Logan remained motionless beside her, his gaze intent as he stared through the brush. And then slowly, very slowly, she saw him raise his weapon.

She grabbed his arm. "Don't," she whispered urgently. She couldn't bear the thought of Logan shooting the guy following them in cold blood.

But then she heard a gunshot and ducked as the tree branches rustled overhead.

Logan returned fire and she heard a soft cry, indicating Logan had hit his target.

"Stay here," he whispered, but she clutched his arm, preventing him from leaving. "I wasn't shooting to kill,

I only wanted to wound him. I need to know who sent him after us."

"No. We either stay here together or we move forward together."

A look of impatience flashed across his face at the same time they heard the sound of a car engine.

"He's getting away," Logan said, yanking from her grasp and charging out of the brush. She pushed aside the leaves and branches, staying right behind him, instinctively knowing that Logan would want her to follow. When they reached the dirt road, the other car was gone.

Without a word, she jumped in the passenger seat and closed the door as Logan went around to the driver's side. Within moments he backed out of the dirt road, while she kept an eye out for the tan car. She was very much afraid that the guy would pull the same trick they'd just performed, hiding and waiting for them to show themselves.

She needn't have worried, because by the time they reached the paved road, there wasn't any sign of the other car. The country road took a curve about a mile to the right, so she wasn't surprised when Logan headed that way.

"Do you know where you hit him?" she asked.

"Somewhere along his right side," Logan said. "My goal was to get him to talk." He eased up on the gas as they went around the curve, only to see a fork in the road up ahead.

He brought the car to a stop at the intersection, but even looking both ways, she couldn't see any sign of the tan car. "I can't believe we lost him," she muttered.

"Me, either," Logan admitted. "If I'd have known there was an intersection this close, I would have kept going."

She reached out to put a hand on his arm. "He got lucky, that's all. I don't suppose there's any hope he would get treated at a hospital and we should alert the local authorities?"

"Maybe. I have to call my boss anyway," he said slowly. "Although if the guy works for Salvatore, then there's a chance he'll be able to get medical treatment from someone on the mafia's payroll."

The idea was frustrating beyond belief. "Does he have someone from every profession in his pocket?" she asked harshly. "Doctors are supposed to uphold their Hippocratic oath. They shouldn't be swayed by criminals."

Logan didn't respond right away as he turned the car around in the intersection and headed back the way they'd come. "Money and power go hand in hand, remember?"

She did remember, but that didn't mean she had to like it. She sat back in her seat and let out a heavy sigh. It was easy to see why cops eventually became jaded and callous. For every crook they put away, there were dozens more to take their place.

Which made her only more determined to join the fight—as a police officer. Just like her dad and her brothers. She was convinced this was the work she was meant to do. Once she and Logan were safely out of this mess, she would try out for the police academy.

And refuse to consider failure an option.

Logan headed west, intending to find a place to stay on the other side of the racetrack. As he drove, he kept a sharp eye on the road behind them, hoping they wouldn't pick up another tail. The fact that someone had managed to follow them to church had badly shaken him. He couldn't stand the idea of Kate being in danger.

As soon as they'd found a motel, he'd call his boss. Enough of trying to do this on their own. That had been a close call back there. If he hadn't taken everything out of the motel room, including his weapon, the situation could have turned out very differently.

He wasn't sure the guy he'd hit would have told them much, but he felt certain the puppet master pulling the strings had to be Salvatore. Still, something about this latest scenario didn't quite add up.

He searched his memory, retracing their steps outside the racetrack. They'd stayed away from the cameras, but had there been others that he'd missed? Or had they been followed even last night? But if so, there's no way he would have gotten inside the building. He and Kate hadn't been in a hurry at all. In fact, they'd taken extra precautions to make sure that they wouldn't be discovered. Plenty of time for someone to take them out, if they had in fact been followed.

No, that scenario didn't play for him. Which left only two options: that somehow they had been on a hidden camera, or someone was tracking Officer Gerlach's phone, even though it was mostly turned off.

Neither option was particularly reassuring.

And regardless of who had come after them, one thing was certain. Their vehicle was compromised. They needed a new set of wheels, the sooner the better.

Too bad he wasn't sure how to get what they needed.

About three hours later, he found the perfect motel, just ten miles away from the Berkshire Racetrack. He rented two rooms for him and Kate, and then placed the call to his boss.

"Where have you been?" Simmons demanded. "You've missed several check-ins!"

"I know. Things have gone downhill in a big way." He tried to think of a way to soften the news, but couldn't come up with one. "My Tex Ryan cover is blown. Salvatore has set his goons after me."

There was a long silence and he could almost imagine the fury that was etched in his boss's craggy features. "What happened?"

The last thing he wanted to do was talk about it, especially since Kate had come into the room. He glanced at her and flashed a lopsided smile. "Look, a lot has happened, and there isn't time to go over everything right now. You need to put out an alert with the area hospitals. I wounded a guy following me earlier today. I also need a new set of wheels, and more cash. Can we meet somewhere?"

"More cash?" He could hear the tense anger vibrating in his boss's tone. "Do you have any idea how much money we've wasted on this investigation so far? And what do we have to show for it? Nothing. Nada. Zip! Logan, you blew your cover!"

Ken Simmons didn't understand that Logan felt guilty enough. Adding more wasn't going to make a difference. "I have something," he protested, even though he knew the argument was weak. "I was able to plant the high-tech bug in the conference room of the new racetrack. If Salvatore holds another meeting there, we'll be ready."

"If? *If?*" Simmons's tone rose, incredulous. "I'm supposed to bank on a long shot? Is that what you're telling me?"

He pulled the phone away from his ear with a wince. "Get me new transpo. Something that can't be traced. Help me out, and I will get you the evidence you need to bring Salvatore down."

"You'd better," Simmons said in a threatening tone. "Because if I go down because you bungled this job, then you're going with me."

"I know." He wouldn't have expected anything else. "When and where can we meet?"

"Are you in Chicago? Or closer to the racetrack?"

"Let's pick someplace halfway in between," he suggested, sidestepping his boss's question. They weren't far from Chicago Midway International Airport, but he didn't want to give out his exact location. He searched his memory. "There's a statue of Louis Armstrong in the center of Maplesville Park. Send someone to meet me there. With cash and keys."

"Maplesville Park? Okay, but it's going to take some time. I probably can't get anyone there until seven o'clock this evening."

He glanced at his watch, surprised to realize it was already almost three in the afternoon. "No problem. Seven is perfect."

"Don't mess this up, Quail," his boss muttered. "Neither of us can afford to fail."

"I hear you." He disconnected the call and glanced at Kate, who'd been listening to his side of the conversation. "He's not very happy with me, but he'll come through with what we need."

"I figured as much. I'm starving. Do we have time to eat before we meet him at the park?"

He stifled a sigh as he turned to unpack his computer case. "I don't suppose I can convince you to stay here and wait for me?"

"No, you can't. We're a team, Logan. So far that's been working out well for us, hasn't it?" Her green-brown Irish-mud eyes implored him to agree.

He didn't want to admit she was right. Not when their recent near escape was still so fresh in his mind. But he'd worry about her, whether she was here waiting for him or not, so he might as well keep her close. "Yeah, sure." He paused and then added, "Give me a few minutes to check the various routes on the computer, and then we'll go. We'll have time to stop and get something to eat. I want to arrive at the park early, to make sure everything is on the up-and-up."

Her eyes widened in surprise. "Surely you don't believe your boss would set us up?"

"There is no *us*, as far as he knows. I didn't tell him about you, as there will be plenty of time for that later. And no, I don't think he'd compromise us. I'm trusting him to bring me a new vehicle and some cash. But I'm not willing to go in blind, either. There's always a risk." He couldn't deny he'd become highly suspicious of everyone and everything over the six months he'd been working on the Salvatore case. Maybe because he'd seen more than a few important people who'd aligned themselves with criminals, like State Senator Anthony Caruso and the Milwaukee chief of police. No one was immune, and he wasn't about to take any chances.

Especially not with Kate's life.

Kate stared down at her phone, which she'd turned off after their near miss with the guy who'd followed them after church. She hadn't heard from Garrett and she was certain that couldn't be good.

Had she put Garrett in danger, too? He'd told her to stay away from him, so she had to think so. Although she certainly hadn't told him to get ahold of Angela Giordano, either.

She wasn't sure why Garrett had contacted her former roommate, but it was probably to get them inside information on Salvatore. She could imagine Garrett getting frustrated with being unable to help Angie and deciding to work the case from another angle.

Nibbling her lower lip, she pushed the button to turn on her phone. The small screen lit up and she practically held her breath as she waited to see if there was a voice mail message or text waiting for her.

But there was nothing. Since Logan was preoccupied with staring at the map of Maplesville Park, she sent a quick text message.

AG show up yet?

There was a long pause, and she was about to turn off her phone again, when her brother responded.

No. Where r u?

She couldn't tell him, so she avoided his question.

Safe, but can't talk, will call later.

Turning off her phone was difficult when she would have given anything to see her brother. Or at least talk to him, hear the sound of his voice. Being isolated like this, away from her family, was horrible.

But temporary. Something she needed to remember. Something to hold on to.

"Ready?" Logan asked, straightening from the computer. She belatedly realized he was in the process of shutting down the machine.

"Yes." She ignored her emotional and physical exhaustion. "Are you bringing the computer along?"

"Bring everything. We'll be exchanging vehicles."

"Which means we'll need to find a new place to stay." It shouldn't matter, but this constant changing of motel rooms was wearing on her.

"Afraid so." Logan slung the computer case over his shoulder and held open the door. "Don't worry. We'll find something just as convenient."

She nodded and followed him outside. "How about we eat at that Mexican place we passed on the way here?"

He grinned. "Why not? Mexican it is."

Kate sat back in her chair with a groan. "I should have stopped at two burritos," she moaned.

He chuckled and pushed away his plate. "I'm stuffed, too. But I'm afraid we need to get going."

"I'm ready when you are."

The waitress came at Logan's signal and handed them the bill. She winced when she saw Logan's dwindling amount of cash. "Do we have enough?"

"We're fine." He tossed down the bills and stood. "Come on, let's hit the road."

The drive to Maplesville Park took a good hour and a half. But they still had almost another hour before their scheduled meeting. Dark clouds swirled in the sky, and she watched them warily, hoping the rain would hold off until after they had their new vehicle and more cash.

Logan insisted on parking far away and walking in from the south. Since she hadn't studied the map the way he had, she didn't argue. As they walked along the sidewalks, she noticed that there weren't many people around. She saw one jogger, heading past them as if on the way home, and a couple kids on Rollerblade skates.

She pulled together her hoodie, as the temperature had dropped. A storm threatened. They walked past the bronze statue of Louis Armstrong, the famous jazz musician, to make their way through the rest of the park.

There was nothing remotely suspicious anywhere, but she was still tense, unable to get rid of the strange sense of heightened awareness.

"Let's sit here for a moment," Logan said, interrupting her thoughts as he gestured to a park bench. "And then I'd like you to go back and wait for me in the car."

"No way." She glared at him. "If you don't want your boss to see me, I'll hide. There was a good-sized tree not far from the statue. I'll keep watch for anything out of the ordinary."

"We've just gone through the entire park. I think we're as safe as can be."

How could she explain her deep sense of foreboding? "Please? I'll go crazy sitting in the car."

"All right, you can sit behind the tree. But you'll have to go now and you'll be tired and cramped being there for the next twenty minutes or so."

"I don't care." She was willing to do whatever was necessary to keep him safe. "I'll go now, and make sure no one sees me."

There was the slight rumble of thunder in the distance, and Logan grimaced. "I doubt we'll have to worry about that—everyone will be heading home to beat the storm."

Everyone except the two of them. She gave him a fleeting smile, and then rose to her feet and ambled down the sidewalk, back toward the statue.

She didn't pass anyone on her way back, and it was easy enough to slip off the sidewalk, cutting through the wooded area until she reached the large oak tree. She walked around it, checking several spots for the best view, before she hunkered down, making herself comfortable. She glanced at her watch and grimaced. Still eighteen minutes before the scheduled meeting time.

Patience wasn't exactly her strong suit.

After ten minutes, her legs started to go numb so she shifted a bit, making sure she didn't make any noise. She removed the large rock from beneath her hip, and immediately felt much better. It wouldn't do Logan any good if she were physically unable to help him. Or to run.

Another four minutes passed before she saw Logan slowly approach the bronze statue from the area to her left. She was glad she'd kept the tree to her right so she could easily keep him in view.

Out of the corner of her eye, she saw something move. She eased from behind the tree, trying to get a better view. There was an old homeless guy, dressed in multiple layers of clothing, a tattered hat pulled low over his eyes, pushing an old rusty grocery cart.

As she watched him, she noticed he was muttering to himself under his breath, his shoulder twitching every few minutes.

He was likely harmless, but the uneasy feeling that she'd had ever since arriving at the park was growing stronger. She knew she should be watching Logan, waiting for either his boss or someone else from the FBI task force to show up, but she couldn't seem to tear her gaze from the homeless guy.

The shopping cart hit a rock, and teetered precariously. The homeless guy grabbed it, preventing the cart from toppling over and spilling all his worldly possessions on the ground.

In that instant she saw a flash of silver on his wrist. A watch? On a homeless guy?

Her heart leaped into her throat. She picked up the rock she'd dug out of the ground a few minutes ago, and abruptly stood. "Watch out!" she shouted to Logan, before lobbing the rock toward the homeless guy.

She managed to hit her target in the shoulder, and he flinched away from the impact, even as Logan dove behind the statue. The homeless guy straightened and that's when she saw it.

"He has a gun!" she shouted, drawing the fake homeless guy's attention from Logan to herself. He swung the weapon toward her at the same time Logan popped his head up from behind the statue and took aim.

She ducked behind the tree, as the sound of gunfire echoed through the night.

ELEVEN

Dear Lord, keep Logan safe! Kate prayed as she pressed her back against the tree. She should have looked for more rocks, or branches—anything to use as a weapon. Another crack of thunder rumbled above, followed by an abrupt downpour of rain.

The leaves on the tree above protected her somewhat, but not enough to keep her dry. She listened, trying to figure out what was happening with Logan and the guy in disguise. She heard the rustle of leaves from her left and tensed, only to relax when she recognized Logan.

Thank You, Lord!

"Are you all right?" he asked harshly.

"Yes. What about the fake homeless guy?" She could tell, by the grim expression etched in Logan's features, the news wouldn't be good.

"He's still alive, but I'm not sure for how long. He moved as I was shooting and I ended up hitting him in the stomach. We need to get out of here."

She peeled herself away from the tree, her skin indented from the pattern of the bark. He put his arm around her shoulders and she leaned gratefully against him for a moment.

"Can you walk?" he asked with concern.

"Of course I can walk." She told herself to stop being a wimp, and moved away from Logan. "Did your contact show up from the FBI?" she asked as they made their way back out of the park to where they'd left the car.

"I think I saw him, his name is Jerry Kahler, but the moment you yelled he took off in the other direction." The fierce expression on his face matched his frustrated tone. "So close."

Too close. She couldn't help thinking about what might have happened if she hadn't noticed the flash of silver on the gunman's wrist.

"This way," Logan said, tugging on her hand.

She frowned. "Our car is this way." She pointed in the opposite direction.

"I know, but I'm looking for the vehicle left by the fake homeless guy. It has to be somewhere close to the park."

"How do you know he left a car?" she demanded. "And I have to call 9-1-1, Logan. He needs medical attention."

"I put a pressure bandage on his wound, so he'll be okay for a few minutes. We'll call 9-1-1 as soon as we find his car."

She kept pace with him as best she could, but the rain made it difficult to see very well. Just when she thought that maybe they were lost, she heard Logan say, "Yes! There it is."

She didn't see anything, until the headlights flickered and she heard a beep. She turned to look at Logan. "You found his keys?"

"And a bit of cash, but no wallet or ID," he said as they approached the car. "Stay back, in case it's wired."

"Wired?" She wiped the water from her eyes. "You mean like with a bomb?" Was he crazy? "Logan, don't—"

"Just give me a few minutes, okay?" he interrupted. She stood uncertainly as he pulled out a small penlight and then dropped to the ground to crawl under the vehicle.

She was soaked to the skin and now that the adrenaline had worn off, she began to shiver, almost uncontrollably. She hugged herself and lightly jogged in place in an attempt to stay warm. After what seemed like forever, but was probably less than ten minutes, Logan scooted back out from beneath the car and motioned her over. Now that she was closer, she realized it was an SUV.

"It's clean. I've already disabled the GPS. Come on, let's get inside."

She wasn't going to argue. Being out of the rain helped, but she was still freezing. As if he could read her mind, Logan put the key in the ignition, turned on the motor and then cranked the heat on high.

"You'd better call 9-1-1 for the guy back there," he said as he pulled away from the curb. "I'm going to get our stuff, and then we're getting far away from here."

She nodded, forcing her frozen fingers to push the buttons on the phone. When the dispatcher came on the line, asking what her emergency was, she took a deep breath. "There's a man with a gunshot wound in Maplesville Park near the Louis Armstrong statue in the center. Please hurry."

"Wait, don't hang up…" the dispatcher started to

say, but Kate pushed the end-call button regardless, knowing that the dispatcher would still send a squad to check it out.

"They're going to have your voice on tape," Logan pointed out.

"And my cell number." As much as she hated to admit it, she'd need to ditch the phone. With a sigh, she opened the window of the SUV and tossed out the disposable phone, barely able to hear the *ping* as it hit the ground.

Within a few minutes, he'd pulled up to the car they'd left behind. "Wait here," he said before getting out.

It didn't take him long to grab their stuff from the vehicle, stashing the computer case and their clothes into the backseat of the SUV. He tossed a sweatshirt in her lap. "Use this to warm up."

She did, even though putting it on over her wet clothes would only get the sweatshirt damp, too. They'd have to find a motel with a laundry, she thought with a weary sigh as Logan headed north.

"Now what?" she asked, feeling depressed. "Where do we go from here?"

Logan didn't answer right away. "I need help, and clearly going back to my boss isn't an option."

"You don't think your boss turned on you, do you?"

He shrugged. "I don't know what to think. But I can't trust that it wouldn't happen again."

She could see his point. "Do you want to call my brother Garrett?" she offered.

"No, but there's a Chicago Detective that I worked with six months ago, a guy named Nick Butler. He knows about Salvatore because he worked on a related missing person case."

She tried not to feel hurt that Logan would prefer to use this Nick Butler's help rather than her brother's, but it wasn't easy. "If that's true, why haven't we contacted Nick Butler before now?" she asked.

Logan scrubbed his hand over his jaw. "It's not like I'm anxious to call him, Kate," he said, a sharp edge to his tone. "Do you think I want to put anyone else in danger? I don't want to draw your brother or Nick Butler into this, but I don't have a choice. We need help. And Butler is one of the few guys I can trust."

Now that he put it that way, she could admit she didn't want to pull her brother further into this mess, either. She wanted her family safe from harm. She didn't know Nick Butler, but for some reason, she'd rather he be included instead of Garrett.

She frowned when Logan made a fast right-hand turn into a busy truck stop, dragging her attention from her brothers.

"Gotta change plates. Give me a sec," he explained as he parked out back in a dark area and again suffered the rain.

"By the way, nice aim back there," Logan said as he reentered the vehicle. "That's the second time you hit exactly what you were aiming at. First in the cemetery and now here. Thanks to you, he was knocked off balance."

She couldn't help but grin. "I played four years of fast-pitch softball in high school," she admitted. Pride was a sin but she couldn't help but add, "We went to state my senior year and I pitched the winning game."

"Hard to imagine you playing sports," Logan drawled. Meanwhile, he dug in his computer case, pulled out a roll of black electrical tape. Ripped off a few inches.

She lifted a brow. "Why not? My brothers were all involved in sports, and I wanted to follow in their footsteps. I was too short to be any good at basketball and volleyball, but I found my niche with softball. We had a lot of fun."

He felt along the steering column, felt the raised impression of the VIN and placed the tape over it. Logan's answering smile made her heart flutter in her chest. "I owe you for saving my hide," he said quietly. "Thank you."

"No thanks necessary," she replied lightly. "You've saved me several times. I'm simply returning the favor."

He nodded thoughtfully and reached out to take her hand in his, gently wrapping his fingers around hers. "I was praying like I've never prayed before back there," he confessed.

"Really?" The news warmed her more than the heat blasting from the vents. "I'm so glad, Logan."

"Me, too."

She smiled and looked down at their clasped hands for a long moment, before relaxing back in her seat. She didn't pull away her hand.

And neither did Logan.

Logan found another small motel a little farther from the racetrack than he wanted, but was satisfied that no one would find them this far off the highway. He pulled up in front of the lobby and reluctantly released Kate's hand, wondering why he'd felt the need to tell her about how he'd prayed back at the park. He wasn't normally one to bare his soul to anyone, and especially not to a woman.

But Kate wasn't just any woman. The more time he spent with her, the more he liked her. Admired her. And was grateful she'd been a star player on her high school softball team. Throwing that rock at the guy had given him the time he needed to duck for cover.

God's will? Or pure luck?

Surprisingly, he was leaning toward the former.

"I'll be right back," he said as he climbed out of the SUV. He felt guilty for taking it even though it belonged to a guy who'd tried to kill him.

He paid for connecting rooms and went back to where Kate was waiting in the SUV. He drove around to park near their rooms. He reached back to grab the computer case, and the action caused the skin around his arm wound to pull sharply. Instantly, he felt something warm trickling down his arm.

"You're bleeding again," Kate said, grabbing a spare T-shirt to wrap around his arm. "Luckily we still have gauze and antibiotic ointment left."

"I'll be fine," he said gruffly.

"Don't be stubborn, Logan. You should have let me check it out this morning."

From what he could see of the wound, it had been scabbing over nicely—no doubt his actions today had helped open it again. But the wound wasn't anything serious. He'd suffered far worse in his career. There was no reason to let Kate hover over him.

No matter how much he liked it.

"Sit down," she said, after they'd gotten settled into their respective rooms.

Realizing she wouldn't relent, he gave in and sat in

the chair. She'd already had fresh towels, warm water and their first-aid supplies set out on the small table. He let her unwrap the blood-soaked bandage, trying to ignore the fact that they were still sopping wet from the storm.

"I don't suppose this place has a Laundromat?" she asked as she worked.

"No, they don't. Just set your wet clothes over the wall heater. They'll be dry by morning."

She wrinkled her nose. "I guess that will have to work," she agreed. Using the washcloth, she cleaned his wound and then dried it with a towel. "This doesn't look too bad," she said as she spread more antibiotic cream over the area. "Although it would look better if you hadn't ripped off half the scab."

"I'll try to keep that in mind," he murmured drily.

She wrapped gauze around his arm and then stepped back to clean up the mess. He rose to his feet, keeping his arm at an awkward angle to prevent it from brushing against his damp shirt.

He tried to step around her, but at the same moment she turned the same way, causing them to collide. He steadied her, lightly grasping her shoulders. "Sorry," he murmured.

"Oh, Logan," she whispered, before wrapping her arms around his waist and hugging him. "I'm so glad you're all right."

"Hey, now, what's this?" he asked, alarmed by the uncharacteristic display of emotion. "Don't cry, Kate. He didn't even get close to hitting me."

"I keep seeing his gun," she muttered against his chest. "If I hadn't caught a glimpse of his watch…"

"Shh, it's all right." He tightened the embrace, ignoring the fact that he was getting his dry bandage damp again from her clothing. “You were awesome back there, Kate. You truly saved my life.”

“I was so scared,” she admitted. “How am I going to be a cop if I’m afraid?”

It was on the tip of his tongue to tell her to drop the whole idea of being a police officer, but he held back. Because in that moment back in the park, when she’d thrown the rock at the homeless guy with dead-center accuracy, shouting a warning at him, he had realized she’d be a great cop. She had uncanny instincts and hadn’t hesitated to act.

“What makes you think cops aren’t afraid?” he asked instead. “Being fearless would make a cop reckless. All police officers are afraid at some point. But they rely on their skills and training. You haven’t even attended the police academy yet, and you already have great instincts.” He rubbed a hand down her back. “Instincts that you probably inherited from your dad.”

She lifted her head and leaned back to look up at him. “Do you really think so?” she asked, her gaze full of hope.

“Yes, Kate. I do.” And because she was so brave, and so incredibly beautiful, and because he couldn’t stop himself, he leaned down and kissed her.

Kate soaked in the warmth of Logan’s mouth against hers, locking her knees to keep them from buckling.

Her heart swelled with hope and longing. For the first time since they’d met over six months ago, Logan seemed to understand exactly who she was. He wasn’t trying to make her into something else. He’d told her she had great instincts. Cop instincts.

Just like her father.

She kissed him back, trying to put her feelings into words. He groaned low in his throat, deepened the kiss, making her toes curl. But then he pulled away, gasping for breath.

"You're dangerous, woman," Logan said in a low voice. "But I have to call Butler, before it gets too late."

Of course he did. They were still running for their lives, unable to figure out who they could trust.

But she wanted to linger in his arms, drawing in his heat and his strength.

"Kate?" he asked, tipping up her chin so that she met his gaze. "Are you all right?"

She forced herself to step away, flashing him a wry smile. "I'm okay. Didn't mean to cling like a vine. You'd better call your detective friend. Actually, I'm anxious to hear what he has to say."

He held her gaze for a long moment before turning away. "I hope he still has the same cell number."

She hoped so, too. While Logan made his call, she quickly cleaned up the small table, dumping out the warm, soapy water and rinsing the blood from the washcloth and towel before hanging them up to dry.

When she emerged from the bathroom, Logan was already off the phone. "He didn't answer?"

"I left a message." He shrugged and tossed the phone on the bedside table. "It's probably better that we get some sleep anyway—we'll have plenty of time to talk to Nick tomorrow."

"All right." She understood that was her cue to return to her own room. "Good night, Logan. Let me know if you hear from Detective Butler."

"I will. Good night, Kate."

She slipped through the connecting doorways, closing her side before she shimmied out of her wet clothes and draped them over the heater to dry, as Logan had suggested. She wrapped up in the blanket from the bed and closed her eyes, willing herself to relax.

But graphic images from the park kept replaying over and over in her mind, like a horror movie.

So she turned to prayer, reciting the Lord's Prayer over and over until she finally drifted off to sleep.

The next morning she was thrilled to see that her clothes were dry, if rather wrinkly. She hung them in the bathroom, hoping the steam would help make them look better. After a quick shower, she dressed and dried her hair before going over to knock on the connecting door. "Logan? Are you awake?"

He opened the door, and she quickly realized he wasn't alone. Behind him stood a tall, broad-shouldered man with sandy-brown hair and piercing blue eyes. "Kate, this is Detective Nick Butler. Nick, this is Kate Townsend."

"Pleased to meet you," Nick said, stepping forward to shake her hand. "Any relation to Burke Townsend?"

"Yes, he was my father." She knew her smile had dimmed, but thanks to yesterday's church sermon, she didn't feel like bursting into tears.

"I'm very sorry for your loss," Nick said somberly. "He was a great cop."

"Thank you." Her stomach rumbled and she caught sight of a bag of giant muffins on the table. "You brought breakfast?"

"On the Feeb's orders," Nick teased, waving a hand toward them. "Please, help yourself."

She knew from her dad and her brothers that *Feeb* was slang for federal agent, and she couldn't help smile. "Feeb, huh? Haven't heard that term recently."

"He's just jealous because he couldn't get into Quantico," Logan drawled, his Southern accent seemingly more pronounced. "He knows that's where the best of the best end up, right, Butler?"

"Yeah, right," Butler agreed sarcastically.

She stepped closer to the table and helped herself to a chocolate-chip muffin. "Delicious," she murmured after the first bite.

"I called all the hospitals in a hundred-mile radius," Nick said, getting back to the conversation she'd interrupted. "No suspicious reports of gunshot wounds."

"I can't believe there haven't been any gunshot wounds," she argued with a frown. "That's just not possible."

"There were plenty of gunshot wounds, just none brought in without being accompanied by law enforcement."

So no leads on the guy who'd followed them from church. "I called 9-1-1 on the fake homeless guy," she said, turning to Logan. "He would have been brought in with law enforcement, right?"

"Right." Logan glanced at Nick. "Which hospital would a victim go to after being shot in Maplesville Park?"

"Northwestern University," Nick said as he reached for his phone. "I'll check to see if they brought anyone in after seven last night."

She finished her muffin and washed it down with a large glass of water. What she wouldn't give for a tall glass of freshly squeezed orange juice.

After several long minutes, Nick finally got off the phone. "Those privacy laws are a hassle, but I did find out that they brought a guy in last night, about seven-thirty. He went straight to surgery and his condition is listed as critical."

Critical. The muffin she'd eaten suddenly felt like a rock, expanding in her stomach. "Do you think he'll survive?"

"No way to know, not without visiting, which would be impossible considering we don't know his name. We can't just show up at the hospital, asking to see the guy who was shot in the park."

"No, I guess not." She glanced at Logan, not surprised by his grim expression. He'd shot in self-defense, but she wasn't sure that would make him feel any better.

"I think I need to contact Salvatore directly," Logan announced.

Her jaw dropped at his abrupt declaration. "What? Have you lost your mind?"

Logan's tawny eyes locked on hers. "It's time to end this, Kate. And if that means offering myself up as bait, then so be it. As long as we bring down Salvatore."

But she cared! No. No way. She wasn't going to allow Logan to be bait.

Not when she knew she was losing her heart to him.

TWELVE

"Logan, don't do this," she begged, hoping to carve through the emotion he must be feeling to find cool, clear logic. "We'll find another way, won't we, Nick?"

"Absolutely," the detective agreed.

But a fiercely stubborn expression had settled over Logan's features. "I know Salvatore, better than either of you. He'll draw out this cat-and-mouse game for months if not years. He has a lot of important people under his control. You need to listen to my plan before you reject it outright."

Kate didn't want to listen to his plan. She couldn't bear to have Logan exposed for Salvatore to come after. But she could see the acceptance in Nick Butler's eyes, and knew she didn't stand a chance if he agreed with Logan.

"All right, I'll consider your plan. What are you thinking?" Butler asked.

"I'll call Salvatore and offer to sell him the high-tech bug," Logan said firmly.

"And what makes you think Salvatore will agree to buy it? Or believe that it even exists?" she challenged.

Logan glanced at her, and she caught a flash of pure

agony in his gaze, before it disappeared. "For one thing, I'll be able to prove it existed, as I used it to eavesdrop on Salvatore's conversations with Russo. And second, he may not care if it truly exists, as long as he gets the opportunity to find me and kill me."

"And what is the point of that?" she demanded harshly. "Suicide by Salvatore?"

He narrowed his gaze, and she realized she may have gone a little too far. But what he was proposing did resemble a suicide mission, and she wasn't going to sit there while he offered himself up to Salvatore on a platter. "No, despite what you're obviously thinking, I'm not trying to get myself killed. I'm trying to trap Salvatore, so that we can nail him once and for all, before he kills anyone else."

His declaration made her feel a little better, but she still didn't like it. She especially didn't like the way Logan seemed intent on distancing himself from her.

Because he didn't trust her? He'd thanked her for saving his life, but that previous gratitude seemed to have evaporated. Now he was in full agent mode. Making it clear she didn't belong.

Giving her the impression that he might just walk away again, the same way he had six months ago.

"Maybe if we time this right, we can make it work," Nick agreed. "Say the evening of the grand opening of the Berkshire Racetrack?"

A small smile played along the edges of Logan's mouth. "Yeah, that's exactly what I was thinking. We'll listen in on the bug I planted and see if we can get anything useful. I'll contact Salvatore early that Friday to arrange for the sale of the device to take place after the race is finished."

"How are you planning on getting it out of the conference room?" she asked.

Logan shrugged. "I may not have to. If we can get enough on him, we'll be able to arrest him."

She stared at him incredulously. He was making it sound far too easy. "And if we don't?"

Logan avoided her gaze. "Then we'll have to wait until he tries to kill me."

Logan tried to hide a wince, as disapproval radiated off Kate in nearly tangible waves. He resisted the urge to cross over, take her into his arms to offer comfort and reassurance.

"Fine, if you're so determined to do this, you'll need body armor," she said in a clipped, irritated tone. "And even then, it's a stretch to think we can make this work, with only me and Nick backing you up."

He let out a soundless sigh. "Kate, you can't. You're not a cop."

The hurt that shadowed her gaze made him want to take back the words. "What happened to those cop instincts you claimed I had?" she asked.

"It's not that you aren't capable," he hastened to reassure her. "But you're not a cop, which means you can't legally carry a gun."

"Actually, I do have a permit to carry," she said. "My father often took me to the shooting range."

He couldn't hide his surprise. "Okay, maybe you do have a permit to carry a weapon, but don't you understand that you could be charged with a crime if you end up shooting Salvatore or one of his men?"

"I'm fairly certain I can shoot in self-defense, or in defending someone else," she replied calmly. "And who says I have to shoot anyone? Just the threat of having a gun might be enough to tip the balance in our favor."

"No way. I'm sorry, Kate, but I'm not going to allow you to do that." The very idea made his blood congeal.

"Hold on, Logan," Nick said, interrupting them. "Back up a minute. Why can't Kate be included? We're going to need all the help we can get. Salvatore isn't going to show up alone, if he shows up at all."

He gnashed his teeth together in frustration. The last thing he wanted was for Kate to be put in the position of having to shoot anyone, even in self-defense. She'd followed through at the park, throwing the rock at the fake homeless guy, but shooting a person was far different.

That moment Jennifer had stood frozen still haunted him. In the split second she had had to make a life-and-death decision…

She'd died, because she couldn't do it.

In his mind, he could easily see Kate struggling the exact same way. Kate had faith, which meant she wouldn't be able to take a life easily. Not even in self-defense or to defend him.

And he didn't want her to have to make that choice. Especially not if she died, too, like Jennifer had.

"Do you have a floor plan of the building?" Nick asked, drawing Logan's attention from his dark thoughts.

"Yeah, on my laptop." He took a couple steps and brought the sleeping machine to life with the click of a button.

"We need to figure out where to have the transaction take place," Nick murmured as he peered at the blueprint.

"I planted the bug here," he said, lightly tapping the

computer screen. "I thought that if Salvatore was going to talk anywhere it might be in this conference room."

"How much of the racetrack does Salvatore own?" Nick asked.

"Not quite half, with the money I gave him as part of my Tex Ryan cover," he admitted grimly. "I was supposed to make another deposit to get him to the 51 percent mark."

Nick raised a brow. "So you were a silent partner?"

He nodded. "With a chance to double my investment, and to have a place to race my prize Thoroughbred, Running Free."

Nick whistled under his breath. "Do you really have a racehorse?" When Logan nodded, the detective looked impressed. "Okay, what happens now? Where does Salvatore come up with the rest of the money?"

"That's exactly what I'm hoping to find out." He glanced at his watch. "We need to get within range of the track to listen in."

Kate straightened in her seat. "I'm coming with you," she announced.

He didn't see a way around it, so he reluctantly agreed. "All right, let's go."

He hoped and prayed that they would get something useful from their midnight breaking-and-entering caper to plant the bug.

Otherwise they'd be flying blind the day of the grand opening. Which wasn't at all reassuring, considering how the notorious crime boss already had the deck stacked against them.

Seated inside Nick Butler's car behind darkly tinted windows while parked a few blocks from Berkshire

Racetrack, Logan fit the earpiece to his ear and turned up the receiver. Instantly, he could hear people talking from inside the main building. But it was difficult to figure out which voice belonged to which person. And from the jumble of voices, it sounded as if they were picking up conversations from outside the conference room.

Both Kate and Nick had earpieces, too, so that hopefully, between the three of them, they wouldn't miss anything important. Sitting around and doing nothing more than listening was tediously frustrating, but necessary if their plan was to succeed. He concentrated on trying to pick out either Salvatore's voice or Russo's from the crowd.

They all had notebooks so they could jot down anything they overheard that might be significant. From the corner of his eye, he noticed Kate was writing almost nonstop, which made him wonder if he was missing something.

At least Butler wasn't taking any notes yet, either, so Logan figured he must not be too much of a slacker. Or was Kate determined to write down everything in an attempt to put together the puzzle pieces later? He had to admire her dedication.

The hours passed slowly. Until a deep, raspy voice with a heavy Sicilian accent caught his attention.

"Is the place clean?" There was another noise that sounded like a door closing, before there was an answer from another man with a similar accent.

"Yes, it's clean."

He smiled with grim satisfaction that Salvatore was actually using the conference room as he'd predicted, and that Salvatore's bug sweep hadn't found their high-tech device.

"Good. Do we have him yet?"

"No. Unfortunately, he escaped, doing far more damage than expected."

Logan's breath froze in his lungs as he recognized both Russo's and Salvatore's voices. He wrote down exactly what was said, figuring they had to be talking about the park incident with the fake homeless guy. Although without proof, it was his word against theirs. Especially when the two mafia men were masters at not giving anything away that could be used against them.

"Does our source have a new location for him yet?"

"He claims he's working on it."

Who? Logan wanted to shout. *Who's the source?* He didn't want to believe it was anyone within the FBI task force, but the way it sounded, that was a distinct possibility. Obviously he and Kate had been followed at least once.

"If he doesn't produce results soon, we may have to replace him with someone better connected." The familiar edge to the tone convinced Logan the voice belonged to Salvatore. *"This has already gone on too long. We should have had him seventy-two hours ago. We can't afford any loose ends."*

"I agree. We need to get him and the woman before the opening. Which reminds me, did you get a commitment for the additional funding?"

Logan tensed at the reference to Kate. He'd hoped they were only after him, but apparently Kate was also a target. *Give me a name*, he silently begged. Something they could use as a potential starting point.

"Yes, the congressman came through. We have what we need and a little extra."

A little extra? He couldn't help but smile. Good to know. With money to spare, he was more convinced than ever that Salvatore would bite on buying the high-tech listening device. Especially since Salvatore wouldn't be able to resist the chance to get close to Logan.

"Call me if you hear from our source."

"Of course."

Moments later, there was the sound of a door opening, and more voices in the background filtered through, making his head hurt with the effort of trying to sort out anything. With a wry grimace, he tugged the device out of his ear and tossed it down.

"They didn't give us much," he muttered in disgust.

"Did you really think they would?" Nick asked mildly. "They haven't stayed in the organized crime business for this long without knowing how to keep their mouths shut. Even if they don't think that anyone can overhear them."

"I know," he said with a sigh. He glanced at Kate, who was still listening intently and taking notes. He wanted to tell her not to bother, but knew she wouldn't take any criticism from him very well. Since what she was doing was harmless, he turned back to Nick. "Which congressman do you think is dirty?"

"Very good question," Nick murmured. "I think we should head back to the motel to search for possible candidates."

He glanced at Kate, who'd finally taken out her earpiece. "Do you still think it's a good idea to contact Salvatore?" she asked. "He's obviously looking for you.

That whole bit about you escaping and causing damage had to be related to the incident near the statue."

"Yeah, but did they say enough for us to prove it? Not even close."

"No, but isn't it enough that he threatened you?"

He stared at her for a long moment, wishing things could be different. But he wasn't ready to risk his heart again. And even if he were, the last thing he wanted was a relationship with another cop, whether she was one now or later.

A teacher, a nurse, a doctor, even a lawyer would be preferable to someone within the field of law enforcement. No matter how much he cared for Kate, he just didn't think he could go through that again.

Not after losing Jennifer.

Since she was still staring at him, with a mixture of hope and despair shining from her Irish-mud eyes, he forced himself to answer. "Don't worry, I'll be careful."

She set her jaw and hunched her shoulders as she turned away. He wanted to reach out and put his arm around her, to reassure her that everything would work out fine, but he stayed where he was.

Because he couldn't offer false promises.

And because it was better to distance himself from her now, before the attraction shimmering between them interfered with getting the job done.

For the next twenty-four hours, Kate's anger and frustration simmered beneath the surface. Logan and Nick spent hours either listening to what was going on inside the racetrack or searching out various Illinois congressmen, in an attempt to figure out the identity of Salvatore's newest financial partner.

The two men probably thought she was crazy to take so many notes, but there was a conversation in the background that had caught her attention. She wasn't able to get everything down, especially once the two Sicilians shut the door, but that didn't stop her from poring over her notes, trying to make sense of the snatches of words she'd captured on paper.

But time was running out. They had less than twenty-four hours before the grand opening and she knew Logan fully intended to contact Salvatore after the race.

He must have sensed her thoughts because he tapped on the connecting door between their rooms. "Butler is heading out to pick up supplies—do you want to come along?"

She glanced up from her notebook, searching his gaze. In the few days since Butler had joined their team, Logan had drifted further and further away. At times like this, she couldn't imagine he'd ever held her in his arms or kissed her. And she was surprised at how badly she wanted to turn back the clock, to recapture those stolen moments. "What kind of supplies?"

"Body armor, for one thing. Clothes to help us blend in during the grand opening."

She wrinkled her nose, knowing she probably needed a dress. Although there was a discount store across the street that she'd thought would work well enough. As much as she wanted to be a part of the team, there was no point in tagging along. "No, I'll stay here for now. But do you mind if I borrow your computer while you're gone?"

His eyebrows shot up in surprise, but he shook his head. "Of course not. Help yourself."

"All right." She forced a smile, although she wanted very badly to ask Logan what she'd done to make him pull away from her. "I'll see you guys later, then."

"Sure." Logan turned, hesitated, as if he wanted to say something more, but instead he left the connecting door open, and walked away.

Her heart squeezed painfully, and she waited for several minutes after she heard the door shut behind them before she went over to boot up Logan's laptop.

Glancing at her notes again, she did a search on a few of the phrases she'd written down. She managed to get a hit on the third one.

She stared at the computer screen in shocked surprise. Chicago's Best was actually the name of a racehorse. A filly sired by the recent winner at the Churchill Downs Racetrack. When she glanced back at her notes, the seemingly nonsensical sentences suddenly became crystal clear.

THIRTEEN

Kate continued searching the internet for information.

She could hardly wait to show Logan the connection she'd discovered. They were starting to put together the puzzle pieces, but time was running out. They needed to be able to draw Salvatore away from his thugs, another long shot at best, in order to put the mobster behind bars once and for all.

While rubbing the fatigue from her eyes, a loud noise startled her so badly she fell off her chair, managing to catch herself just before she hit the floor.

"Are you all right?" Logan asked, rushing over to her side. He steadied her with his arm, and she felt the warmth of his touch all the way down to her toes.

She was hyperaware of his closeness and wished she wasn't, as her cheeks burned with embarrassment. "I'm fine. I guess I wasn't expecting you to be back so soon."

"Didn't take long to get what we needed," he murmured, glancing at her quizzically, as if trying to gauge her mood.

"Great." She tried to inject cheerfulness into her tone. "Look what I discovered while you were gone." She tapped the computer screen. "I took notes from the bits and pieces of a conversation I could hear going on behind Salvatore and Russo. See here? Chicago's Best is actually the name of a racehorse. And guess who owns her? Congressman George Stayman."

"Congressman Stayman," Logan echoed, leaning over her shoulder to read the article she'd found on the computer. "He must be Salvatore's silent partner."

"That's what I think, too," she agreed. "Plus his district includes the racetrack. And from what I gathered, it almost seems like the race is being fixed. According to this article, Chicago's Best is the least likely to win, at twenty-six-to-one odds. Yet what I overheard was that Chicago's Best was a sure thing based on an inside tip."

"Why am I not surprised?" Nick asked with a hint of sarcasm. "If that's true, I can see why the congressman put up the rest of the money for the track. He'll get his return on his investment almost immediately, along with the opportunity to win lots more."

"A perfect partnership, as this also gives Salvatore a way to launder his dirty money," Logan added grimly. He stared at the article for a long moment. "Too bad we can't prove it."

"Maybe we should go to the press?" she said, causing both men to turn to stare at her in surprise. "Why do you look so shocked? Any investigative reporter would love to dig into this allegation."

"Not a good idea. We can't afford to let Salvatore know before the race," Logan said. "Although maybe later, if our plan doesn't work, we could reconsider that option."

She wanted to remind him that using himself as bait was hardly a plan, but she held back with an effort. "A good investigative reporter wouldn't tip off Salvatore, and maybe having someone else watching the guy on race day would work in our favor."

"She has a point, Logan," Nick pointed out calmly.

She wanted to hug Nick for sticking up for her. "An investigative reporter would be more interested in the story than double-crossing us."

But Logan was shaking his head. "No way. We're not dragging anyone else into this mess. We'll only do that as a last resort."

Kate wanted to argue, but the stubborn set of his jaw told her that she'd only be wasting her breath. Logan might be strong, smart and caring, but when he decided something, he could be more stubborn than a mule.

And she was very much afraid that his stubbornness would be his downfall, if he insisted on contacting Salvatore and putting his life on the line in an attempt to set up the guy.

Logan could tell Kate was upset with him, but he refused to back down. Didn't she understand that he could handle just about anything except for losing her? He needed for her to stay safe more than he needed to breathe.

"What in the world did you buy?" she asked when Nick dumped out their bags on the table.

"A disguise for you to wear tomorrow," Nick teased. "Big floppy hat, bottle of hair dye and a long sundress."

"Hair dye?" she echoed with a grimace. "Yuck."

"It's temporary dye," Nick reassured her.

"Or you can stay here at the hotel where you'll be safe, and then you wouldn't need the hair dye," Logan couldn't help interjecting. "No reason for you to put your life on the line."

"Reddish-blond, huh?" she said, ignoring him. The smile she flashed at Nick was dazzling. "Great! I've always wanted to be a redhead."

Logan scowled, trying to rein in his temper. He didn't want Kate to be a redhead. He didn't want her to be at the racetrack, backing him up. He especially didn't want her anywhere near when he met with Salvatore, but Nick overrode every single one of his objections, telling him that they needed all the help they could get.

Which was probably true. But he didn't care. It was only because he wanted Nick to be safe, too, that he went along with the detective's plan.

"Do you both have disguises?" she asked, dragging his attention away from his dark thoughts.

"Yeah, although nothing dramatic," Nick said. "Dark glasses, baggy clothes—that type of thing."

"I need Salvatore to recognize me when we're ready to make our move," Logan spoke up.

He could tell her lips tightened, but she didn't say anything more. She picked up the hair dye and the clothes and headed toward the connecting doors between the rooms.

She shut the door and then locked it, making him wince. "She's not happy," he murmured.

"Look, buddy, far be it for me to pry into your business, but I think you're a little too anxious for this showdown with Salvatore. I'm getting the impression you don't care if he kills you, as long as you take him down with you."

Logan couldn't deny the thought had occurred to him. The world would be a far better place without the likes of Bernardo Salvatore. "I'm fine," he said tersely.

"I don't have a death wish. I just want to put Salvatore behind bars before he kills anyone else."

Nick lifted up his hands. "Hey, I know. I feel the same way. But you have a personal vendetta against the guy, and I'm concerned that you're allowing your emotions to overrule your brain."

He let out a sigh and rubbed the back of his neck. Since Nick was going along with his plan, he couldn't hold back the truth. "Okay, yeah, I can't deny having a personal vendetta against the guy. He's into everything illegal—drugs, prostitution, gambling—you name it and he's behind it."

"Drugs?" Nick's eyebrows levered up. "I didn't know about that."

"I started my law enforcement career in the DEA, and during a sting operation, me and my partner were planning to raid a known drug house. Based on our intel, the place was supposed to be empty, but when we arrived, a couple kids were doing a buy right in front of the place." Even without closing his eyes, he could see the scene playing out in front of him. "I went after the guy with the money and the druggie ran straight toward Jen. She had her weapon trained on him, but she didn't move. Didn't shoot. The kid actually looked stunned for a moment, but then he didn't hesitate to fire at her. I ran over but too late. She died in my arms."

Nick's dark eyes were full of compassion. "I'm sorry, Logan. I can't imagine what you went through."

"And you know the worst of it? The house was rigged to blow, because Salvatore knew we were going to bust in and he didn't care how many people he killed as long as he continued making a profit. Going back to Jen saved my life. Several good DEA agents were killed that night, along with Jen. And Salvatore got off scot-free to open up a new drug shop someplace else."

"Don't worry, we'll get him," Nick said grimly.

"I know." Logan wasn't worried. Because he'd been working for the past two years on nailing Salvatore, and nothing was going to stop him now.

Nothing.

Kate sat in stunned shock, her back pressed against the connecting doors between their rooms. She'd had no idea that Salvatore had been directly responsible for the death of Logan's fiancée.

But now that she'd overheard Logan's story, his actions and decisions made perfect sense. This was the reason he'd volunteered to go undercover as Tex Ryan. This was the reason he'd made the switch from being in the DEA to working on the FBI task force against organized crime.

And this was the reason he'd never allow himself to fall in love.

She knew she shouldn't take it personally, but there was so much to admire about Logan that it was difficult to ignore her feelings. She'd been so happy that he seemed to be renewing his faith. She'd assumed he'd accepted her for who she was. And thought for sure he was ready to move forward with his life.

Obviously, she was wrong. On all three counts.

Granted, he'd warned her about his past and had made his feelings about her chosen profession clear. But she hadn't listened.

She closed her eyes and rested her head back against the door. *Please, Lord, keep Logan safe. Give him strength and help him to understand revenge isn't justice. Amen.*

Several hours later, Kate ran her hands through her newly dyed hair, trying not to wince at the result. So much for reddish-blond. The strands were bright red.

Don't be vain, she reminded herself. What she looked like on the outside didn't matter. As long as she could assist with keeping Nick and Logan safe, she didn't care.

Her stomach rumbled painfully. Glancing at her watch, she realized the hour was well past dinnertime. Resolutely, she marched across the room, unlocked and opened her door.

Nick Butler glanced up from the computer. "Wow, is your hair red!"

"Yeah, I noticed." She frowned. "Where's Logan?"

"He just called to let me know he's on his way back, but was stopping to pick up a bucket of chicken."

Just the thought of fried chicken made her mouth water. "Where was he?"

"Listening to the bug. Picking up more info if possible." Nick's teeth flashed in a broad smile. "You impressed him when you figured out about the congressman's racehorse."

She shouldn't have been happy to have gained Logan's approval, but deep down, she was. "He went there alone?"

Nick shrugged. "I've been working another angle, and since we're running out of time, we split up. I discovered that Salvatore donated funds to Congressman Stayman's election fund two years ago. I'm getting the distinct feeling that the two of them have been in cahoots for a while."

She dropped into the chair next to him. "First a state

senator, and now a congressman? No wonder the public doesn't trust politicians."

"All it takes are a few bad apples," Nick agreed. When the distinct sound of the SUV pulled up, he stood and crossed over to the door.

Moments later, Logan strode in carrying a bucket of fried chicken, a tub of mashed potatoes and several bottles of water. He was also wearing a black cowboy hat and cowboy boots.

That was his disguise?

"Did you get anything?" Nick asked as he helped to unpack the food.

"Unfortunately not," Logan said, handing out paper plates and napkins. He swept his cowboy hat off his head and ran his fingers over his close-cropped hair. "The place was quiet, which surprised me. I figured the night before the opening day would be busy."

"Tomorrow morning might be busy," Nick mused, moving the computer and pulling up a third chair.

"We can only hope so." Logan sat next to Kate and then paused, looking over at her expectantly.

Despite her annoyance with him, her lips twitched. "Are you waiting for something?"

He looked startled. "Aren't you going to pray?"

"I think it's your turn." She put her hands together and bowed her head. She could feel Nick staring at them, as if trying to figure out if they were serious or not.

Logan hesitated a moment and then began. "Dear Lord, thank You for this food we are about to eat. Please keep us all safe from harm tomorrow. Amen."

"Amen," she echoed, pleased that he'd prayed out loud. "Thank you, Logan, for doing the honors."

"I'm just glad you included yourself in the part where you asked God to keep us safe from harm," Nick teased. He picked up a drumstick and took a huge bite. "Mmm, this hits the spot."

She took a thigh and silently agreed. Maybe Logan's faith would help him to realize that he had a lot to live for.

Even if he chose to leave her once they'd arrested Salvatore.

Kate slept better than she'd expected, and the next morning, she found herself anxious to get going. They packed up the SUV and checked out of the motel right at eleven o'clock.

She'd be thrilled if she never had to stay in a dive motel again.

Wearing the long gauzy dress and the wide-brimmed floppy hat felt weird, and she'd been forced to run over to the outlet store right before they left, to get a pair of flat shoes to wear with the dress, as the typical men hadn't thought about her footwear.

The dress was a bit impractical if she had to run, but at least the pockets were deep enough for her to hide a gun. Logan hadn't wanted her to carry one, but Nick had insisted that she be able to defend herself.

The weapon felt heavy, and for a moment she considered giving it back. She could shoot. Her father and her brothers had often taken her to the shooting range, but she wasn't a cop yet and despite having a permit to carry, she'd never walked around with a concealed weapon.

Yet the thought of being helpless if she needed to

back up Logan was too much to bear. She'd rather step out of her comfort zone than risk losing him.

Logan pulled over to the side of the road, about a half mile from the Berkshire Racetrack. "We need to split up."

"I'll walk in from here," Nick volunteered. "You and Kate can go in together, and then from there you can spread out. The first race isn't scheduled until two o'clock this afternoon."

"All right." Logan waited until Nick jumped out of the SUV before glancing at her. "Are you ready?"

"Of course. Let's go."

They drove the rest of the way in and parked. The lot was full, with tons of people milling around, and she realized that the disguises were likely overkill. Who was going to be able to find and recognize them amid this mass of people?

They strolled inside holding hands as if they were any other couple here to enjoy the day. Although in her mind, Logan was far more noticeable wearing his cowboy hat and cowboy boots, yet to be truthful he wasn't the only one. The clank and whirl of slot machines could be heard the instant the doors closed behind them, and she wrinkled her nose at the cloying scents of perfume mixed with aftershave. The building was broken into two main sections: to the left was a small casino area with slot machines and only about a half-dozen blackjack tables, whereas the area to the right was indoor seating and wide windows overlooking the racetrack. Straight ahead was a snack bar area, and right next to that were the lines for people to place their bets on the horses.

They meandered over to the snack bar, where there

were hot dogs and hamburgers for sale. Logan ordered a quick lunch, paying an outrageous amount of money for the basic fare.

Kate swept her gaze over the crowd and caught her breath when she thought she saw a familiar face.

Garrett? Was that really her brother she'd seen ducking into the casino area?

"I'll be right back," she said, leaving her half-finished chicken sandwich and cutting through the crowd. She stood in the doorway and scanned the people playing slots and blackjack, but didn't find him.

As she made her way back to Logan, she tried to tell herself that maybe she had let her imagination get away from her. Garrett wouldn't be here at the racetrack or the casino.

Unless he thought he could help by keeping tabs on Salvatore?

When she reached Logan's side, he clamped his hand around her wrist. He leaned close, putting his mouth right by her ear. "Glance over to your right," he said tersely.

Moving slowly, she did as he asked. For a moment she didn't know who he was talking about, and then she saw him.

Congressman George Stayman. Looking older and at least twenty pounds heavier than his photograph she'd seen online. "I see him," she whispered.

"Keep your eyes sharp," Logan said softly. "I'm sure Salvatore will be here soon."

She nodded, trying not to stare at the congressman, who was surrounded by a mini-entourage of people. When a woman with particularly heavy perfume came up beside her, she sneezed several times in a row. For whatever reason, she hadn't expected the place to be so crowded.

"I'm going to follow him for a bit," Logan murmured. "Are you going to be okay?"

She nodded, not afraid of something bad happening within the crowd surrounding her. Before Logan could move, the doors opened and her heart squeezed in her chest.

Salvatore and Russo! She gripped the back of Logan's shirt to stop him from leaving. He stiffened as he caught sight of them, too. The two men were unmistakable and just happened to be surrounded by several other men who were no doubt thugs paid to protect them.

Salvatore crossed the room, jovially greeting the congressman. From the other side of the room she caught sight of Nick Butler, and it took her a moment to realize he was subtly taking a picture of the two men shaking hands. They spoke for a moment before turning away, heading through a set of doors to the private office area.

The conference room! Logan must have had the same thought, because he moved swiftly through the crowd, intent on getting back outside to the SUV and the equipment they'd stored there.

She stayed where she was, sipping her water as if she didn't have a care in the world. She saw Nick Butler again, but didn't make eye contact. She continued to scan the crowd, hoping to catch a glimpse of the man who resembled her brother.

If Garrett was here out of some misguided idea of helping her, she needed to warn him to stay away. The last thing she wanted was for her brother to get hurt in the midst of taking down Salvatore.

So where was he?

* * *

Logan lengthened his stride to get to the SUV as quickly as possible. He wanted to hear the conversation going on in that room.

He reached the car, and yanked open the door. He fit the earpiece inside his ear and immediately heard voices.

"It's clean?"

"Yes, this place is secure. My men swept for bugs."

Logan smiled grimly.

"Is everything all set?"

"Yes. Did you doubt my ability?"

"No, of course not." Logan identified the speaker as the congressman, and when he laughed, Logan sensed a hint of nervousness. *"You know I'm grateful for our alliance."*

"And our mutually beneficial alliance will continue, as long as you hold up your end of the bargain."

Logan was glad to have this conversation recorded. The first step of proving the congressman and Salvatore were in business together.

"Here you go, five hundred Gs. I always pay my debts."

"Debts?" Salvatore let out a humorless laugh. "My dear congressman, this is only the beginning."

There was a long pause, leaving Logan to imagine the scene in the conference room. Clearly, Salvatore was planning to use his connections with the congressman in the future, and he wasn't sure the congressman was thrilled with the idea. Something he should have considered before creating an alliance with a snake like Salvatore.

"The beginning of this racino making us both rich."

"I certainly hope so. Now, there's less than an hour before the start of the race. If you want to place your bets, better do so before the windows close."

"I plan on it. And I'll see you in the winner's circle."

Logan ripped out the earpiece and shut off the recorder. For the first time in a week, he felt they were getting close. There was no mistaking the intent during this conversation, and while he was somewhat surprised that the congressman and Salvatore had gotten together on race day, he knew they were both arrogant enough to believe they could get away with anything.

Even murder.

FOURTEEN

Logan headed back inside the building, settling the cowboy hat firmly on his head as adrenaline surged in his veins. They had the first part of the plan nailed. They had proof that Salvatore and Congressman Stayman were in cahoots together.

It was almost time to put the second part of the plan in motion. The part where he made contact with Salvatore and convinced the mobster that he was in trouble with the FBI and wanted to sell off the high-tech listening device.

But first, they had to watch the race, which was obviously fixed so that Chicago's Best would win.

He found Kate chatting with an elderly couple, and tried not to wince at her attempt to talk with a Southern accent. "Why, here's my husband now. Tex, I'd like you to meet Sharon and Clive Erringer. They've come all the way up here from Kentucky!"

"Do y'all have a horse in the race?" Logan asked, as he slipped an arm around Kate's waist. He gave her a warning squeeze, not at all happy that she'd referred to him as Tex Ryan. And that she was playing the role of his wife. What in the world was she thinking? The

Tex Ryan cover was blown. Although he'd only used it when dealing with Salvatore and his men.

"Why, yes, as a matter of fact we do," the elder gentleman said with a broad smile. "We have a two-year-old colt in the race, Jacob's Pride."

He searched his memory; his brother and his father, who ran the Lazy Q ranch, often talked about various racehorses. They'd trained several Thoroughbreds. "Wasn't Jacob's Run his sire?"

Clive Erringer let out a loud bellow of a laugh. "Yes, indeed he was. Great horse, won several major races back six or seven years ago. We have high hopes for his colt. He's favored to place in the top three, if you're interested in placing a bet."

"I'm not a betting man, but I still like the excitement of a good race." It bothered Logan that this nice couple was about to be a victim of Salvatore's scam, but there was nothing he could do right now to salvage the race. Although now that he thought about it, he wasn't sure exactly how the congressman and Salvatore would sabotage the other horses that would be running their hearts out, like Jacob's Pride. Did they have someone working inside the stables? Would they slip the horses some sort of drug that might slow them down? Didn't vets take blood samples of the horses? Probably not in a lower race like this one. It wasn't as if Berkshire Racetrack was on the same level as the big three, the Preakness, the Derby and the Belmont.

Either way, he figured it wouldn't be easy to fix a race, since most owners were pretty protective of their racehorses, to the point of serving all food and water themselves from only trusted sources. But those details were something to figure out later.

Tonight, all he could do was to follow their plan, as loose as it was, to make sure that Salvatore paid for his crimes.

Kate followed the Erringers outside, putting a hand up to prevent the floppy hat from flying off her head in the wind. The excitement in the air was tangible, hundreds of people anxious to partake in the first race of the newest racetrack.

Although she noticed that several stayed in the casino portion of the building where televisions had been mounted in strategic locations for casino players to keep an eye on the race. Obviously they weren't about to give up their spot at the blackjack table or at a hot slot machine to watch the two-and-a-half-minute race.

The crowded casino helped her understand why the congressman had worked so hard to make sure that the racino bill went through. The racetrack itself wasn't where he and Salvatore would make the bulk of their money.

Not only would the casino bring in cash, but it was a good place to launder dirty money. She shook her head at the casino players' foolishness. Gambling was a waste of time and money.

She stood next to Logan, watching as the race handlers helped line up the horses and their respective jockeys in the gate. One horse balked at going in, fighting its rider by rearing his head back and prancing sideways. After a few minutes the jockey managed to control the horse long enough to get him into the gate.

"Jacob's Pride is number seven," Sharon confided. "Lucky number seven and our colors are red and gold."

Kate smiled and nodded, even though she was feeling sorry for the horses. Injuries were not uncommon, and no matter how often Clive and Sharon tried to say that the colt loved to run, Kate felt for the endangered horses. Soon, the last gate was filled and there was just a brief moment before the bell sounded and the gates flew open to start the race. She caught her breath at the sight of the racehorses flying out across the track. Kate found herself gripping the railing tightly as the horses crowded together along the turn.

Clive and Sharon were yelling at the top of their lungs, screaming for Jacob's Pride. There were immediately several front-runners, including Jacob's Pride and Chicago's Best. She reverently hoped that Salvatore hadn't figured out a way to fix the race, as Chicago's Best lagged behind in fourth place.

But as the horses rounded the last turn and headed down the home stretch, she could see Chicago's Best inching up the middle between Jacob's Pride and Freedom Rings. Her fingers tightened on the railing as Chicago's Best gave one last surge, winning the race by a nose, followed by Jacob's Pride in second place and Freedom Rings in third.

For a moment she could only stare in shock, as the winning horse pranced around the track. If she hadn't overheard the comments about the race being fixed, she never would have suspected anything was amiss.

Certainly Clive and Sharon didn't suspect anything; they were cheering at the fact that Jacob's Pride had come in second place. "Did y'all see that?" Clive asked, thumping Logan on the back. "I told y'all that Jacob's Pride would place in the top three."

And probably would have won, if not for whatever Salvatore and Congressman Stayman had done to fix the race. If they really had. She couldn't help feeling some doubt. "Congratulations," Kate said warmly. "I'm so happy for you."

"That horse has a lot of heart, just like his daddy," Sharon murmured, giving her husband a hug. "And the way he ran today, he's going to do great."

"That he is," Clive agreed. "Nice meeting you both, but we're going to head down to check on the colt. Want to make sure he's all right."

"I understand. It was nice meeting y'all." Logan tipped his hat and moved over to the side, giving the older couple room to maneuver around them.

"What do you think?" she asked Logan in a low voice as soon as the older couple vanished through the crowd. "Was that race really fixed? And if so, how? I have to say from here it certainly looked real."

"Hard to know for sure, especially since it's not going to be easy to confirm how it was done. On the other hand, considering the horse had twenty-six-to-one odds, everyone who bet on him made a nice bundle of cash, so it's a bit suspect." His gaze swept over the crowd, searching for Salvatore, she was certain.

"He'll be watching the congressman accept his win," she guessed, gesturing down to where a crowd had gathered around the winner's circle. She could see the heavyset congressman smiling and shaking hands, accepting his congratulations with grace.

Regardless of the fact that he might not have earned it fairly.

"Maybe," he acknowledged. "But it's time for us to split up for a bit."

She didn't want to split up. She'd rather stay glued to Logan's side. But now that the race was over, she knew he planned to make contact with Salvatore to make the offer of selling the listening device.

"Logan," she called as he moved away. He paused and turned back toward her. "Please be careful. Remember that you have a lot to live for. I'll pray for you, asking God to keep you safe."

He stared at her for a long moment, his gaze enigmatic. "I appreciate that," he finally murmured. "And I'll pray for you and Butler, too. We're going to get him, Kate. By the end of the night, this will be all over."

As he turned to weave his way through the crowd, she tried to be comforted by the fact that Logan didn't act like a man who was willing to recklessly endanger his life in the process of getting close to Salvatore. Determined, yes, but not reckless.

Full of hope, she did as she'd promised, sending up a quick, silent prayer to keep him safe.

Logan waited for what seemed like forever for the hubbub of the race to settle down before he decided to draw out Salvatore's attention. As the group around the winner's circle began to disperse, he made his move.

"Congressman Stayman!" he called. "Congrats on your win today."

"Thank you very much," he said, although his gaze narrowed as he stared at him, seemingly trying to figure out who he was. "Have we met?"

"We have a mutual friend, Bernardo Salvatore."

The congressman looked appalled for a fraction of a second before his expression cleared. "Mr. Salvatore has assisted with my campaign, but I don't know him well enough to call him a friend. Excuse me, but I have to check on my horse."

"Of course." Logan stepped back, thinking the congressman should have taken care to check on his horse much sooner. But he stayed where he was, scanning the crowd until he found Salvatore standing roughly fifty feet away near the top of the stands.

Their gazes clashed and held, and Logan couldn't help tipping his hat toward the mobster. Then he picked up his phone and dialed Salvatore's private number.

"You're a dead man, Tex Ryan," Salvatore growled into his ear. "I don't care who you work for, you're a dead man."

"Maybe. But before you try to kill me, you should know I have a high-tech bug that I think you'd be interested in owning for yourself."

There was a pause before Salvatore spoke. "I don't trust you and I don't believe you. A rather pathetic attempt on your part to set me up, don't you think?"

"Look, since your guy Russo busted me, my boss cut me loose. I'm hanging in the wind without backup. The only thing I have is a device that can't be picked up through a regular sweep. And I'd be happy to sell it to you, for a nice price."

"You're bluffing."

Logan began to move, weaving his way through the thinning crowd, since he wouldn't put it past Salvatore to kill him on sight. But he stayed on the phone. "No, I'm not. I heard every word of your conversation with the congressman. He paid you five hundred thousand dollars for his portion of the racetrack, and maybe a little more to cover the way you fixed the race. And I believe you said something about how this was the beginning of a mutually beneficial alliance."

"How do I know you haven't already gone to the Feds with this information?" Salvatore asked.

"I told you, they cut me loose. I need the money from this bug to leave the country. Why else would I be calling you with this offer?"

He expected Salvatore, or maybe Russo, to head straight for the conference room to look for the bug. Although by now, Nick Butler had already removed it. The detective had texted him a while ago and they'd agreed to bump into each other, to make the handoff with the device, since Logan needed it in order to convince Salvatore he was serious about selling it.

"All right, you have my attention," Salvatore finally said. "Name your price."

"One hundred thousand," he said. "After all, you received more than you needed from the congressman, didn't you?"

Salvatore muttered a string of phrases in his native tongue, something less than complimentary, he was sure. "Fine. But I will control the timing of the transaction."

Logan didn't have any illusions about Salvatore's intent. If there was a way for the mobster to kill him and get the listening device, he'd do it. "I'm not a fool, Salvatore. I can always find someone else to sell the device to. Meanwhile, the Feds will still have the technology, and I'm sure my former team won't hesitate to look for a way to use it against you."

Another stream of Sicilian curses burned his ear, and he was glad he didn't know exactly what was being said. Still, he waited for Salvatore to calm down. "What do you suggest?" Salvatore finally asked.

Logan smiled grimly. "I'll call you back in a couple

of hours." Before Salvatore could protest, he disconnected from the call.

Next, he contacted Butler. "Salvatore is interested. Have you found a location for the transaction?"

"Yeah, I think so," Butler said. "There's a small building toward the end of the barns, used to store tack and other supplies. It's far enough out of the way that, once the last race is over, we should be able to use it without being disturbed."

Logan could see only a corner of the building from where he was standing. He kept moving, trying to stay far away from Salvatore. "I think I see it. We'll have to make sure that it's empty. I don't want any innocent bystanders to get in the way."

"I hear you. The place will clear out pretty fast as the races end, although the casino portion of the building will be open until three in the morning. Let me take a look around, and I'll call you back."

Three in the morning. He didn't like it, but surely the die-hard gamblers wouldn't bother to wander down to the stables where the owners kept the horses. He knew from his father and brother that the owners liked to have the racehorses on site for up to a week before the race to help keep the animals calm. But he couldn't be sure how many of them would clear out as soon as the race was over.

Hopefully most, if not all.

Because he couldn't afford to fail in the third portion of the plan. The most dangerous part of all.

He moved into the casino area, where it was easier to get lost in the crowd, and tried to think of another place to use for the transaction. There might be something close by, but they didn't exactly have time to set up an elaborate plan. They were winging this on a hope and a prayer.

He'd have to trust Butler's judgment. And find a way to keep Kate well out of the way.

His phone rang again, about ten minutes later. It wasn't easy to hear over the din of the slot machines. "I had a conversation with a stable hand, and most of the horses are getting packed up right after the last race," Butler informed him. "I'd say we'll have most of the area around the stables to ourselves by early evening."

"All right. Is there cover nearby?"

"Not as much as I'd like," Butler said frankly. "We can probably place Kate in the empty horse stall next to the tack room, but she won't have a clear shot at covering you."

As long as Kate was safe, he didn't much care if she had a clear shot at covering him. He didn't want her anywhere near him once he confronted Salvatore. "All right, let's do it. But I don't want to give Salvatore time to set up a trap. We have to be ready to roll when I make the call."

"I hear you." Butler paused, and then asked, "Have you told Kate the plan?"

"Not yet." He was a little surprised he hadn't seen Kate since they parted ways. "Do you know where she is?"

There was a tense pause. "No. I thought she was with you."

Logan pinched the bridge of his nose and tried to breathe normally. There was no reason to panic. Kate had told him on more than one occasion that she could take care of herself.

He'd thought it would be safer for her to stay away

from him while he made contact with Salvatore. Now he doubted the wisdom of his logic. He worked to keep his tone even. "We just split up about forty-five minutes ago. She can't be too far."

"We need to find her before Salvatore or Russo figure out who she is," Butler said in a tone full of grim determination.

A chill rippled down his spine, spreading cold fear through his entire body. What if Salvatore already had her? What if he wanted to make a trade for Kate's life?

Dear Lord, please keep Kate safe. Don't let Salvatore get his hands on her. Please?

He strove to remain calm. "I'll find her," he said. "You figure out the logistics of my meeting with Salvatore."

"All right, call me back as soon as you have Kate."

Logan ended the call and carefully looked around the casino portion of the racetrack. They hadn't replaced Kate's cell phone, so he couldn't simply call her. But surely she was here somewhere. As far as he could tell, every single blackjack table was full, as were most of the slot machines. He didn't see her brightly colored dress, her red hair or her floppy hat. He moved back toward the main area of the racetrack, but she wasn't there, either.

Was it possible she'd gone back to the SUV to get a change of clothes? They'd packed all their things from the hotel, and the jeans and sweatshirt would be more functional than the long dress.

But even so, she certainly didn't have time to dye her hair back to its normal color. So he concentrated on searching out the redheads.

But to no avail. Kate wasn't anywhere in the building, so he went back outside, first to the stands overlooking the racetrack, and then back through the building to head to the main entrance from the parking area.

He went as far into the parking lot as he dared. He didn't want to draw Salvatore's attention. Frustration mounting, he went inside.

He stood once again, in the back corner of the casino, racking his brain as he continued to scan the patrons.

Where on earth could Kate be?

FIFTEEN

Logan fought the rising sense of panic, even though he knew there was an entire area outside the racetrack building where Kate could be hiding. He was about to call Nick to ask him to search the stables when he noticed a redhead who wasn't Kate get up from her seat at the blackjack table and walk over to the ladies' room.

The one place where Kate could go without being followed by a man.

He inwardly rolled his eyes at his own foolishness for not thinking of that possibility earlier, but couldn't relax completely, not until he knew for sure that Kate was fine. He couldn't bear the thought of her being in danger from Salvatore.

He wandered closer to the door of the ladies' room, avoiding eye contact with the redheaded woman who wasn't Kate when she came out. He wanted to duck inside, but hesitated for fear of being seen and tossed out.

A short, rather heavyset woman with gray hair approached the restroom. He stopped her, flashing his most charming smile. "Ma'am, my friend Kate is in the ladies' room and hasn't come out for a long time.

I'm getting worried about her. Would you please check for me?"

"Of course, dear," the woman assured him. "What does your lady friend look like?"

"She's not very tall, about five feet four inches, slender with red hair." He avoided describing how Kate was dressed, in case she'd changed.

"I'll check on her," the older woman assured him, patting his arm as if he were her son. She disappeared inside and he waited tensely, hoping he wasn't wasting his time here if Kate needed him elsewhere.

Several long minutes later, Kate emerged from the ladies' room, dressed in the black jeans and black boots from their midnight breaking-and-entering run. A black baseball hat covered a good portion of her dyed red hair. He wanted to collapse against the wall with relief, even though she was scowling at him.

"What were you thinking, sending that lady in there to find me?" she asked in a low voice. "Talk about being obvious!"

"I needed to know you were safe," he murmured, unwilling to apologize for what he'd done. Because given the same set of circumstances, he knew he'd do it again. "Come on, let's get out of here."

"Did he take the bait?" she asked in a low voice as they edged through the casino. He kept Kate close to the wall, hiding her as much as possible from the people at the tables and slot machines. Once they reached the main area of the building, they ducked outside and walked around to the side of the building. The races were over and the crowd was thinning out.

There was a chill in the air as the sun had started to set, although not quickly enough to suit him. He'd prefer if it was pitch-black when they made the high-tech disk swap.

"Yeah. He's waiting for me to make the call," he informed her. He took out his phone, intending to call Butler, but she grabbed his arm.

"Wait! Let's talk this through first!" She looked horrified. "We need a solid plan."

He quickly realized Kate was afraid he was going to call Salvatore right now. "Relax, I'm just letting Nick know that I found you. We've both been a little worried."

"Oh." She dropped her hand and flushed as if embarrassed. "Go ahead then."

"Thanks," he said drily. He pushed the button to call Nick, and the detective answered almost immediately. "I found her."

"That's a relief. I brought the equipment from the SUV down to the tack room. A few horses are still being housed in the stable, but none close to the tack room."

The setup wasn't perfect, but it would have to do. From where they stood against the north side of the building, he had a clear view of the stables. "All right, we'll head down there before I call Salvatore."

"Okay, see you soon."

He disconnected the call and turned to Kate. "We're going to arrange the sale of the device down in the tack room at the end of the stable. There's an empty stall on the other side of the wall. I'm going to ask you to stay there."

Kate narrowed her gaze. "How am I going to back you up from there?"

He hesitated, knowing this was the tricky part. "I need you to listen in on the transaction. I'm going to get Salvatore to talk and I need you to record everything so that we can arrest him."

She stared at him as if he'd completely lost his mind. "That plan doesn't make any sense at all. Why would Salvatore talk to you? Especially when he knows you have the device? He isn't going to say anything when he knows we could be listening."

"I'm going to do my best," he said, knowing it wasn't exactly a reassuring answer. "I'm hoping to use the information I already know from the time I was undercover."

She slowly shook her head. "I don't like this, Logan. We don't have much leverage."

"We'll make it work," he assured her. But he refrained from adding that he'd do whatever possible to make that happen.

Including putting himself in God's hands to do as He willed.

Kate held back from unloading her frustration on Logan as they made their way to the stable. The grassy area between the main racetrack building and the stables was fairly open, with just a few strategically placed trees to provide some shade from the daytime sun.

But now, with dusk setting in, the trees helped to provide some coverage for the two of them, hopefully without being seen.

"Where do you think Salvatore is?" she asked as they reached the relative safety of the stable.

"I'm sure he's inside the conference room, plotting a way to get rid of us after we make the deal."

Great, and wasn't that a reassuring thought? Her scowl deepened as she tried to think of a way to improve on Logan's plan. There had to be some other way to spring this trap, one that didn't put Logan's life at risk.

"How do you know he doesn't have someone following us?" she asked.

He shrugged. "I don't know for sure. But I knew that he'd head back to the conference room to try to find the bug I'd originally planted there. Since he knows I have it now, the room is probably the most secure place for the moment."

"And you really think he'll come here to buy the device?"

"Yes, I do." Logan's clipped tone put an end to that line of conversation. He tapped on the door of a small building. "This is the tack room."

The door wasn't locked, and when they walked inside, there wasn't much light provided by the single bulb that hung down from the center of the ceiling. There were harnesses, stirrups and other gear lining the walls. On the one closest to the door there was a sawhorse with a saddle sitting on top of it.

Butler was standing behind the saddle, working on the wall with a small knife. "What do you think?" he asked, stepping aside. "Can you tell there's an opening here?"

"Not from back here," Logan drawled. "We'll have to make sure that Salvatore and his goons don't get too close."

"Let me see," she said, crossing over to where Butler stood. There was a natural knot in the wood that had a small hole in the center from where he'd drilled through with the knife.

"Is that going to be big enough?" she asked doubtfully.

"Has to be." Nick's expression was grim. "I made two openings, one for you to look through and another in case you need to use your weapon in self-defense. Go and see how they look from the other side."

"I'm calling Salvatore," Logan said, pulling out his cell phone.

Kate didn't waste another second, quickly leaving the tack room and going around to the empty horse stall, which unfortunately smelled too much like the wrong end of a horse. She wrinkled her nose and felt along the wall until she found the small opening. Thankfully, the hole was low enough for her to see through without crouching, and when she pressed her eye to the opening, gave her a surprisingly good view of the tack room.

Drawing back, she found the other small hole Nick had created, down and to the right, just large enough for her to shoot through if necessary. The angle probably wouldn't be enough to aim at a person, but she could cause a diversion. Down in the right-hand corner of the stall she saw the small receiver and tape recorder from the SUV, completely covered in hay. She could just barely make out the small green blinking light, and realized that Nick had somehow strung the wiring to tie into the light up in the ceiling.

Stepping back, she surveyed her surroundings. Not bad. If she hadn't been looking for it, she wouldn't have seen it. Although it wasn't a foolproof hiding spot, she felt a little better about the third phase of their plan.

She peered through the small opening, watching Logan's face as he made the call. "Do you still want the device or not?" She found herself holding her breath as he listened intently to whatever Salvatore was saying. "Meet me in the tack room at the end of the stables in fifteen minutes," he said. "Don't bring anyone else except Russo and make sure you bring the cash."

Salvatore must have agreed, because Logan hung up the phone and glanced at his watch. "We have five minutes at the most. I figure it will take at least that long for them to get down here."

She pulled out the small gun Nick had given her from the small of her back, but the palms of her hands went damp with nerves. She swiped them on the sides of her jeans, taking a slow deep breath to steady herself. She lined up the barrel of the gun against the small opening, and then pressed her eye against the part of the wall where the knot in the wood would be. "I'm okay on this side," she said in a low voice.

The two men glanced at the wall and nodded. "Make sure the recorder is on," Logan said.

"I'll be outside," Nick said, heading for the door. "Unless you've changed your mind? You know Salvatore will come down with more backup than just Russo."

A rueful grin tugged at the corner of Logan's mouth. "That's why I need you outside. I'm counting on you to help even the odds out there."

"Don't worry, I'm on it." Butler disappeared before she could blink.

Kate closed her eyes for a moment, the bitter taste of fear coating her mouth. What were they thinking? Three good guys against how many bad guys?

They should have called Logan's boss again. Or a few cops Nick trusted. Or her brothers. Anyone who could help even the odds that seemed to be stacked so steeply against them.

She remembered that night six months ago, when

she and Logan had helped Mallory Roth and Jonah Stewart to escape the Milwaukee police chief who'd trapped them in an old abandoned warehouse that had been rigged to explode. The odds hadn't been in their favor back then, either, and somehow they'd managed to escape.

She could only pray that they'd do the same this time.

Please, Lord. Please keep Nick and Logan safe. Provide us the strength and wisdom to stop Salvatore. Let Your will be done. Amen.

Within two minutes Kate could hear the sounds of footsteps outside the tack room door. Logan stood in the center of the room, waiting, looking as relaxed as she was tense. She jumped when the door burst open.

"You're a bit early, Salvatore," Logan greeted the mobster. Although she noted that Russo was the one who stepped inside first, putting his life on the line in order to protect his boss. Both men were armed, their guns trained directly on Logan.

Salvatore bared his teeth in what she assumed was his attempt at a smile. "Why would I give you more of an advantage than you already have?"

"I don't have the advantage," Logan protested, holding up his hands to show he wasn't armed. "You two have your guns pointed directly at me. All I have is the device. Thanks to your goon Russo, I lost everything."

From her vantage point, she could see Russo was walking the perimeter of the room, as if assuring that no one was hiding there. He didn't look close enough to see the holes Nick had made in the wall. And she hoped Russo wouldn't go so far as to come around to search the stall where she was hiding.

"I believe it was your own weakness in choosing to

save the woman that caused you to lose everything," Salvatore countered. "And for what? Where is she now?"

"I let her go. She's not a part of this. Isn't it enough that you have the congressman on your payroll? Makes me wonder why you bothered to try to get money from Tex Ryan in the first place."

"Obviously, I was hoping to get a piece of your oil wells," Salvatore admitted. "However, since you're not Tex Ryan, I'm assuming there are no oil wells, which doesn't make me happy. It's a good thing I always have a backup plan."

The tiny hairs on her neck tingled in warning, and she tightened her grip on the gun, trying to line up the angle of the hole in the wall with the two armed men standing in the room.

She recognized a veiled threat when she heard one. Were they going to kill Logan right in front of her eyes? If that was their intent, she would be helpless to stop them. Granted she could return fire, but the chance of her actually hitting either man was slim to none.

"I hate to admit, I admire your cunning," Logan drawled. "What did you and Russo want with the blonde anyway? I can't believe that slip of a girl posed a serious threat to your vast organization."

"She had information I wanted. However, we managed to work around it. As it turned out, you showed your true colors for nothing." Salvatore was obviously trying to get under Logan's skin.

"Maybe, but the way you blew up Burke Townsend's safe to destroy the evidence he'd gathered against you wasn't exactly subtle," Logan said calmly. "All you managed to do was to draw attention to yourselves."

"Aah, so you do know the identity of the woman you saved." Salvatore took a step forward, but Logan stayed where he was. "I can see the two of you were obviously working together. So where is she now?"

Fear caused her heart to pound so loud, she could barely hear Salvatore's low voice. So far, the mobster hadn't said anything terribly incriminating. Other than pointing their weapons at Logan with the intent to get the listening device.

Would that be enough to arrest him? To convict him? Even if they managed to get out of this alive?

She doubted it.

"I left her days ago," Logan said. "She doesn't deserve any part of the cash you're about to pay me."

"You really think I'm going to pay you?" Salvatore asked. "Why wouldn't I simply shoot you now?"

"Because the device is encrypted with a code." Logan held up the nickel-sized disk for both Russo and Salvatore to see. "Did you think I'd be so foolish as to meet you here without some sort of ace in the hole? Here's how this is going to work. You pay me, and I give you the disk. Once I'm safe, I'll call to give you the code."

Salvatore and Russo hesitated for a moment, glancing at each other as if to judge whether or not to believe him. That fraction of a second was all they needed.

Logan rushed Salvatore, who was the closest to him, at the exact same instant that Nick Butler kicked open the door, aiming his gun directly at Russo.

Instinctively, she squeezed the trigger of her own weapon aimed as close to Russo as she could get. She didn't hit him, but the sound of gunfire coming from the wall behind him was enough to distract his attention from Nick.

Nick shot Russo, while Salvatore and Logan wrestled on the floor for Salvatore's gun. Russo staggered backward, clutching his wounded right shoulder as blood streamed down his arm. But he didn't let go of his weapon, gripped in his right hand.

"Drop the gun!" Butler shouted.

Russo brought up his injured right arm, intending to shoot, but too late. Butler shot again, this time hitting Russo in the chest.

Kate wrenched herself away from the wall and ran into the tack room. By the time she arrived, Nick and Logan were tying up an unconscious Salvatore.

For a moment she could only stand there in shock. "Is there anyone else outside?" she asked, afraid to believe it was really over.

"Russo and Salvatore brought two other thugs with them, but me and my buddy took them out," Butler assured her. "Jake Andrews is one of the few cops I trusted implicitly, and he's already hustled the two of them out of here."

She dragged her gaze away from Logan, who was tightening the harness he'd used to tie up Salvatore, to look over at where Russo had fallen to the ground. She tucked her gun into the waistband of her jeans at the small of her back and walked forward. She was fairly certain the thug was dead, but she forced herself to make sure.

His skin was still warm, but there was no pulse. Russo was dead.

"I didn't have a choice," Nick said grimly, coming up beside her. "He didn't drop his weapon."

"I know." She didn't understand why she was so upset. This was the same man who'd held her at gunpoint, threatening to kill her if she didn't talk. She knew that Butler's first shot had been an attempt to disarm him, and the thug had the opportunity to toss down his weapon.

But no matter what she knew logically—that Nick Butler didn't have a choice but to kill him—she still felt sick.

"At least it's over," she murmured. "I only hope we have enough evidence to put away Salvatore for a long time."

"We will."

"Don't move," a deep voice said loudly, interrupting them.

She spun around to find her older brother Garrett standing next to Logan. For a moment, she didn't understand, because her brother had his arm locked around Logan's neck, holding the tip of his gun firmly against the side of Logan's temple.

"What are you doing?" she asked.

"Drop your weapons and stay right where you are," Garrett said harshly. "Don't make me kill him."

Kill him? She stared in shock, unable to wrap her mind around the scene unfolding in front of her. None of this made any sense. Why would Garrett hold Logan at gunpoint? Did he think she was still in some sort of danger? She heard a thud as Nick dropped his gun.

"Take one step slowly backward," her brother said to Logan. She met Logan's gaze as he obliged Garrett by doing so, bringing the two men closer to the door.

"Garrett, stop it," she pleaded. "Don't you understand? Logan works for the FBI!"

"Shut up!" Garrett shouted. "You weren't supposed to be here. Why didn't you listen to me, Katie? Why?"

His words slowly sank into her brain, and her stomach clenched painfully as she realized the truth.

Her brother Garrett was one of the dirty cops working for Salvatore. And he was acting like a desperate man with nothing to lose.

SIXTEEN

Waves of anger and despair battered her with the unrelenting force of a tsunami. How she stayed on her feet, she never knew. She desperately tried to pull herself together, as if her life as she knew it weren't disintegrating before her eyes. She sensed Nick stepping closer to her as if trying to offer support, but she ignored him.

She couldn't tear her eyes from her brother Garrett. His blond hair and Irish-mud eyes, both so similar to her own. She recalled his strength, especially the way he'd given her a shoulder to cry upon when she was younger.

The brother who'd sat beside her in church, week after week, along with the rest of the family.

A rising denial threatened to choke her. How had this happened? When? Why? So many questions without time for answers.

Dear God, help me! Save Logan! And save Garrett, too. Please, Lord, please don't abandon us now.

The prayer helped her to gather some semblance of control. "Don't do this, Garrett," she pleaded. "I'll help you. I promise I'll help you if you stop right now."

"You can't help me," Garrett said harshly, his face

grim. "Only Salvatore can. I want you and that cop friend of yours to stand back against the wall."

She gaped at him, her feet glued to the floor.

"Do it!" he shouted.

She forced herself to move, taking a tentative step backward, as did Nick. She couldn't bear to look at Logan, not wanting to see the censure in his eyes. She couldn't imagine how he felt right now, being held at gunpoint by her brother. *Her brother!* A situation that was all her fault.

Somehow she had to save them both. Because if either Logan or Garrett died tonight, she'd never recover.

"Garrett, please listen to me," she begged. "You can see we have Salvatore tied up, we'll turn him over to the FBI. He can't hurt you from prison." Or could he? Her stomach twisted painfully, and she tried not to consider the possibilities. "What is it you need? Money?" She remembered how she'd thought she'd seen Garrett ducking into the casino and the pieces of the puzzle dropped slowly into place. "You owe him money, don't you? From gambling?"

"Stop talking." Garrett pushed the gun harder into Logan's temple. "I will kill him if I have to. Katie, I need you to untie Salvatore."

She was already shaking her head. No way. She couldn't do it. She just couldn't do it! Salvatore, now coming to, was watching the scene unfold, a satisfied smirk etched in his face. She tried one last time. "I can't believe you're turning your back on me, Garrett. And what about Dad? Did you have something to do with Dad's death, too?"

Garrett's face twisted in agony, but he didn't relinquish his hold on Logan. "Dad wasn't supposed to pull over Ravden. And Dad never works nights. He shouldn't have been there, just like you shouldn't be here now. There was nothing I could do. I didn't know Dad was a target until it was too late."

So her brother had known all along that their father was murdered. She fought the rising nausea. Would this nightmare never end? How could she get through to him?

Nick came closer, brushing ever-so-slightly against her. And belatedly she realized she still had the weapon she'd tucked into the back of her waistband. She took a tentative step sideways, turning enough to give Nick easier access to the gun.

But even as she stared at her brother, she knew with a sick sense of certainty that it wasn't likely they would all make it out of this alive.

And she didn't know how to stop the ultimate destruction.

Logan couldn't stand watching Kate torment herself like this. He shouldn't have been so stupid as to get caught by Garrett in the first place. And he bitterly resented being used as a hostage.

He tried to catch Kate's gaze in an attempt to communicate what he wanted her to do, but she avoided looking at him. She was pale, her eyes wide with horror as she stared at her brother. He swallowed a helpless fury. The last thing he wanted was for her to untie Salvatore. Right now the odds were in their favor, three to one.

The situation would be better if Garrett wasn't holding a gun to his head, but he was deeply relieved that Kate wasn't the one he'd grabbed.

Please, Lord, keep Kate safe!

A movement caught his eye and he glanced at Nick, who was now standing directly behind Kate. For a moment he could only stare in shock. Anger radiated through him. What was Butler thinking to use Kate as a shield? He should be protecting her. Just because Garrett was her brother didn't mean she wasn't in grave danger.

He glared at Nick and saw his arm move, just a bit, as if he were reaching for something. What was he doing? Then he remembered—Kate had still had her gun before going over to make sure Russo was dead.

Nick was going to even up the odds, by getting Kate's weapon.

"Killing me isn't going to get you what you want," he said in an attempt to draw away Garrett's attention from Nick and Kate. "We can protect you through the witness protection program. Salvatore won't get his pound of flesh from you, unless you give it to him voluntarily."

"What good is witness protection?" Garrett asked harshly. "I'll lose everything, my family, my friends."

"And you think you won't lose them if you let Salvatore go?" he asked quietly. "Kate and your other brothers will become targets, just like your father was. Is that what you want? The only difference with you going into witness protection is that the rest of your family will be alive and safe from harm."

Was it his imagination or had Garrett loosened his hold? They couldn't afford to wait much longer—frankly he was surprised more of Salvatore's goons hadn't come looking for him yet.

Somehow, he needed Garrett to loosen his grip enough that he could get out of this.

"Don't listen to him," Salvatore growled, speaking up for the first time. "I'll find you no matter where you run and hide. And I'll find your family, too. I'm the only one who can keep you alive. If you try anything else, you and your family will die an ugly, slow, painful death."

There was a long pause as Salvatore's words sank deep, but surprisingly, Garrett's hold loosened even more and Logan glanced at Nick, knowing it was now or never. Nick flashed a barely perceptive nod and Logan abruptly twisted in Garrett's grasp, using both his hands to push Garrett's gun hand up and away from Logan's head. Garrett didn't go down easily, but struggled against him.

The sound of gunfire shattered the night.

Logan was suddenly free and he staggered back, trying to catch his balance. And then Garrett shocked him again, by turning and aiming his gun at Salvatore.

"No!" Kate cried at the same instant Garrett fired point-blank at Salvatore.

"Drop your weapon!" Nick shouted. Garrett didn't listen and Logan rushed him, hitting him in the center of his gut and pushing him backward.

Garrett's breath whooshed from his lungs, but he still held the gun, and it went off again before Logan could wrestle it away.

There was a cry of pain from behind Logan, but he didn't dare take his eyes off Garrett. He grabbed the guy's wrist and smacked it against the ground until he opened his fingers, letting go of the weapon. Logan snatched the gun and jumped to his feet, placing one squarely in the middle of Garrett's back, glancing behind him even as he pointed the weapon directly at Garrett. "Everyone okay?"

"Except for Salvatore. He's dead," Nick said, coming forward with another harness he'd taken from the wall of the tack room after he'd checked Salvatore's pulse and found none. He pulled together Garrett's hands behind his back and began tying him securely.

"Kate?" Logan tossed a worried glance in her direction, when she just stood there staring in horror at her brother. His heart twisted in his chest. She looked so forlorn. So shattered. He ached for her. "Hey, it's okay, Kate. We're safe. Everything is going to be fine." He didn't dare loosen his grip on the gun, not until he knew Nick had finished securing her brother.

"I have him," Nick said, tightening the harness around Garrett's wrists. "Call your boss because we're going to need help sorting all this out."

He wasn't quite ready to call Ken Simmons yet, not until he knew for sure who he could trust, but he took a deep breath and stepped back, lowering his gun. It was over. They didn't have the satisfaction of arresting Salvatore and Russo for their crimes, as both men were dead. But at least they were safe.

Kate was deathly pale and swaying on her feet. He frowned and crossed over to put his arm around her. "Kate? What's wrong? Are you all right?"

"I don't think so," she whispered right before her knees buckled, and she collapsed against him.

He held her close, preventing her from hitting the floor. Had the shock of her brother killing Salvatore been too much to handle?

Gently, he lowered her to the ground. It took him a

minute to see the blood seeping down her arm, and reality hit hard. Kate had been shot!

Cold. She was so cold. The pain in her shoulder was barely noticeable compared to the coldness seeping through her muscles. Spreading into her heart.

Reaching down to her soul.

"Kate? Don't you dare give up on me." Logan's terse voice penetrated the coldness. "The ambulance is on its way, so you need to hang on. Can you hear me, Kate? You need to hang on!"

She tried to shake her head, but it was too heavy. The coldness was everywhere now, making it impossible to move. Truthfully, she wasn't sure she wanted to fight against the sensation. Logan didn't understand, and she didn't have the energy to explain how the pain and the coldness was exactly what she deserved.

Forgive me, Lord. Forgive me for not seeing the truth about Garrett. And forgive me for not stopping him sooner.

"Here, put this over her."

"Are you crazy? That's a horse blanket. She'll get an infection."

"She's going into shock, Logan. You have to keep her warm."

Something heavy was draped over her, surrounding her with the smell of horses. Strange, it wasn't as unpleasant as it had been earlier.

Or maybe she was losing her sense of smell. *Dear Lord, I'm ready to come home. Let Thy will be done.*

"Kate, please don't leave me." Logan's voice in her ear was full of worry. "I love you, Kate. Do you hear me? You have to fight for us."

Fight? Love? No, that couldn't be right. Her last conscious thought was that she didn't deserve Logan's love.

Logan was never so glad to see the paramedics, followed closely by several squad cars. "Save her," he said frantically as they rushed over with their gurney and the bag of medical supplies. "Hurry! She's already lost too much blood."

He could feel Butler's hand on his shoulder urging him backward, and he obliged, moving enough to give the paramedics access to Kate. But he wasn't leaving. Not until he knew she was going to make it.

"Do you have IV access yet?" the first paramedic asked.

"Yeah, I'll start fluids wide-open."

"Better add some O-neg blood, too. Her pulse is weak and thready."

"Gotcha."

The moment the paramedics had Kate's condition stabilized they lifted her onto the gurney and strapped her in. In some part of his mind, he heard Nick talking to the officers who'd arrived at the scene, but he didn't care. All he cared about right now was Kate.

"Logan, the officers here need your statement," Nick said, grabbing his arm as he started to follow Kate into the ambulance.

"Not now." Rudely, he shook off Nick's hand. "I'm going to the hospital with Kate."

One of the officers sputtered with anger. "Oh, no, you don't. You can't leave, I've got two dead bodies here and I need to know what happened!"

"Logan, she's in good hands," Nick said in a low voice. "They're not going to let you into the trauma room anyway. I'll drive you to the hospital as soon as we're finished here. We need to make sure we take care of this mess first, okay?"

No! He didn't want her to leave without him. But logically he knew Nick was right. Sitting in the waiting room of the E.R. wasn't going to help. The paramedics lifted Kate inside the ambulance and then climbed in after her, shutting the door behind them.

He shoved a frustrated hand over his hair and spun away from the ambulance, glaring at Garrett Townsend, Kate's brother, who was responsible for shooting her. By accident, maybe, but the end result was the same. Kate's brother refused to meet his gaze, but simply sat there, with his shoulders slumped as if he didn't care what happened to him any longer.

"I need your statement about what happened here," the annoyed cop repeated, breaking into his thoughts.

"Why don't you just play the tape?" Logan asked wearily.

The cop's jaw dropped. "Tape? What tape?"

If Kate's life wasn't hanging by a thread in the ambulance that was right now rushing her to the closest hospital, he might have smiled. As it was, he could barely manage a tight grimace. "Here, I'll show you."

The cops followed him from the tack room and into the empty horse stall on the other side. Walking over to the corner, he hunkered down and brushed the pile of straw out of the way. "Right here. We recorded everything from the very beginning."

The cops exchanged an incredulous look. The annoyed cop wasn't going to give in that easily, though. "I still want your statement, and then we can compare everything to the taped version."

He sighed, irritated beyond belief at the cop's stubborn insistence. He didn't want to stand around here rehashing everything that had happened tonight. He wanted to get to the hospital to check on Kate.

"Logan, why not just call the head of your task force?" Nick asked in a low voice. "I'm sure your boss can pull rank over these guys and get you out of here."

"Not yet," he murmured. There wasn't time to tell Nick that he'd set up a meeting with his boss, only to be ambushed by a pretend homeless guy who'd tried to kill him.

Unfortunately he didn't know who to trust. And he didn't have time to figure it out now. Every instinct in his body wanted to get him to the hospital as soon as humanly possible. He desperately needed to know how Kate was doing.

The best way to get out of here was to cooperate, he realized abruptly. He turned and pinned the annoyed cop with a sharp gaze. "Fine, let's get this over with."

The cop headed to his squad car, leaving Logan to follow. As clearly and concisely as possible, he explained how he'd set up a trap for Salvatore to buy the listening device. He talked for almost fifteen minutes straight.

"You're a Feeb?" the cop asked with a smirk.

His jaw tightened with annoyance at the detested nickname. Local cops never appreciated the Feds taking over their turf. "Yes." He rattled off his badge number and then rose to his feet. "That's all I'm able to tell you for now. I need to get to the hospital and touch base with my boss. I'm sure we'll be able to fill you in on the rest later."

Apparently his story matched Nick's, because this

time, the annoyed cop didn't stop Logan as he strode determinedly toward his friend. "Let's go."

Nick nodded in agreement. But before they took more than two steps, he stopped abruptly when a trio of men emerged from the darkness, heading straight toward them.

Of course, he recognized them immediately. His boss, Ken Simmons, led the way, flanked by Jerry Kahler, the man who'd come to meet him at the park only to take off when the bullets started flying, and Steven Johnson, the second-in-command to Simmons.

A cold chill snaked down his back.

What were they doing here? He hadn't called them, and no one else here would have known to make the call, either.

He stood stiffly beside Nick Butler, staring at the three familiar faces, knowing his life depended on figuring out which one was the leak who'd set him up at the park in order to kill him.

SEVENTEEN

"What's going on here, Quail?" Ken Simmons snapped as they approached.

Logan tried to cover up the deep sense of foreboding as he faced his boss. "Actually, I was just about to call you. Since I haven't made the call yet, I'm wondering how you knew to come here."

Simmons scowled deeply at the challenging note in his voice. "When we heard about a gunshot wound here at the racetrack we decided to come and see for ourselves what was going on. Obviously you're not the one with a gunshot wound, so who is?"

We? Logan ignored his boss's question as he swept his gaze over both Jerry Kahler and Steven Johnson. He wanted to trust Simmons, but truthfully the leak could be any of the three. Or someone else entirely, although his instincts warned that one of the three men in front of him was the culprit.

"You were listening to a police scanner tuned in to this district?" he asked without bothering to hide his doubt. His boss wasn't one to interact with the locals.

Simmons turned to look at his second-in-command, Steven Johnson. After a brief pause the man responded.

"I happened to be on the phone with Lieutenant O'Sabin, and he mentioned the call. I immediately reported the information to Ken and here we are."

Logan nodded, even as he tried to remember where he'd heard the name O'Sabin. There was something, just vaguely out of reach. All his instincts went on alert. Where had he heard that name before?

Suddenly, the memory clicked into place. Lieutenant Daniel O'Sabin was Kate's father's boss, the one she had talked to regarding her suspicions that her father's death was murder. His mind raced. Burke Townsend had worked out of a precinct in Chicago, which meant O'Sabin didn't have any jurisdiction here, forty-five miles outside of Chicago.

And O'Sabin wouldn't have overheard any chatter on the scanner about what was going down here, unless Garrett or some other dirty cop had tipped him off.

"I see," Logan drawled, considering his options. "Well, then, you should probably hear the whole story, right, Nick?" Logan glanced at the detective, trying to send a wordless warning. He needed to stall, needed time to think this through. If Johnson knew that both Russo and Salvatore were dead, then he'd get off scot-free. Somehow they needed to prove Johnson was actually working with the mob, before announcing the leader and his right-hand thug were now dead.

Nick looked puzzled, but apparently decided to play along. He leaned to the right, as if favoring his left leg. "Yeah, okay. But can we sit somewhere? My leg is killing me."

"Your leg?" Simmons asked, glancing sharply at Butler's jean-clad legs. "Are you the one who was shot?"

With the lights from the police car behind them lighting up the area, it didn't pay to fake a gunshot wound. "No, I wasn't shot. Just took a kick to the kneecap."

"So who was shot?" Simmons demanded irritably.

Logan lifted a hand. "It's a long story and I'll explain everything," he promised. "Let's head up to the race-track. There's a private conference room inside that we can use without being disturbed."

"Fine." Simmons didn't look pleased, but he didn't argue. Logan gratefully swept past the three federal agents, leading the way to the main building housing the casino and racetrack. The farther he could take them from the crime scene, the better.

The backside of his neck tingled, and it took all his willpower not to turn and glance at the men following behind him. He imagined Steven Johnson was staring a hole through the center of his back. He seemed to be walking slow; was it possible he was injured? Maybe Johnson had either been the fake homeless guy or the man who'd followed them after church?

As they walked, he came up with a quick plan. He wanted to clue in Butler, so he bumped against him, knocking the detective off balance.

With an Oscar-winning performance, Butler groaned and sagged to the ground, as if his knee had given out on him. Logan quickly bent down to help him up. "Johnson's dirty," he whispered directly into his ear. Then louder, he said, "Sorry about that, are you all right?"

"Anyone ever tell you that you're clumsy?" Butler said with heavy sarcasm. He took Logan's arm to get back on his feet, but then shook it off. "I can walk."

"If you're sure," Logan said as they approached the building. He held open the door for Butler and the three federal agents. "This way," he said, leading the way through the building to the conference room.

It wasn't locked, and no one spoke until everyone was seated around the table. Everyone except Logan. He stood, positioning himself directly across from Johnson, who was seated right next to Nick Butler.

"As you already know, my cover was blown, but I still set up a sting operation to sell Bernardo Salvatore our surveillance technology," he said, starting from the beginning and hoping that Butler had his gun trained on Johnson. "I had been listening to Salvatore's private conversations with Congressman George Stayman, which helped Salvatore believe me about the technology."

"Congressman Stayman?" Simmons echoed with a feral gleam of anticipation in his eyes. "Did he say anything incriminating?"

He nodded, filling them in on the money and the fixed race. "But that's not all I overheard. Seems as if Salvatore has a federal agent on his payroll, as well."

"What are you talking about?" Simmons asked harshly, the look of shock seemed real enough. "That's impossible."

"Is it?" Logan glanced at Kahler, who was seated across from Simmons. Jerry Kahler shifted uncomfortably in his seat, as if remembering what happened at the park. "Russo is dead," Logan continued, "but we managed to get Salvatore alive. He told us about the leak from inside the task force. Didn't he, Butler?"

"Yes, he did." Butler smirked as he played along with Logan's story, and Logan could see from the position of his shooting arm that he had his gun trained directly on Johnson under the table.

"Not very smart of you, Johnson," Logan drawled.

"Salvatore gave you up, and even if he hadn't talked, I know that Lieutenant Daniel O'Sabin was Burke Townsend's boss. He's in Chicago's fifth district, without any jurisdiction here. Which means you couldn't have talked to him, unless one of his dirty cops clued him in. You sold me out that day I went to the park, didn't you?"

"Don't be ridiculous," Johnson snapped, although a hint of sheer panic shadowed his eyes. "You don't have a shred of proof."

"Oh, but we do," Logan said smoothly, hoping to wring a confession out of the man. "I told you we have Salvatore in custody. Why don't you tell us your side of the story? Otherwise we'll have no choice but to listen to his version."

By now, Simmons was glaring at Johnson, as if he was starting to believe Logan. "You told me O'Sabin was a lieutenant on the police force here."

"I made a mistake, so what?" Fear was beginning to ooze like sweat from Johnson's pores. "Whatever Salvatore told you is a lie. I wouldn't work for that scumbag."

"But you did," Logan countered. "It was you who told Salvatore about how Burke's daughter, Kate Townsend, was poking her nose into the circumstances around her father's death. It was you who instructed Salvatore and Russo to get rid of her. Wasn't it?"

Johnson shoved away from the table and leaped to his feet, but Butler was there, pointing his weapon at the center of his chest. "One move and you're a dead man," he said quietly.

There was a tense moment, before Johnson caved. "All right! Salvatore was blackmailing me," Johnson said, then suddenly dropped into his chair in defeat. "He threatened to kill my wife and my two daughters if I didn't feed him information. I only told him enough to make him think I was playing along. I didn't tell him hardly anything! And I didn't have a choice!"

For a moment, Logan couldn't believe he'd managed to get the confession. "You set me up to be killed, didn't you?" he asked again.

"Yes. I sent a dirty cop to follow you and to meet you at the park, but I also sent Kahler to help you," Johnson admitted. "You don't understand, he threatened to kill my whole family."

Logan took a deep breath and let it out slowly. They had him. This part of the nightmare was finally over. Salvatore and Russo were both dead. They had one dirty cop, Garrett, in custody. Now they had the leak in the FBI task force plugged. His work here was done.

"I need to get to the hospital," he said, looking at his boss. "The gunshot victim is Kate Townsend, and I need to know how she's doing."

Simmons nodded. Nick tossed a set of handcuffs at Kahler, who didn't hesitate to secure Johnson's wrists. The minute they were finished, Nick holstered his gun and turned to Logan. "Let's go."

He took off running for the SUV, urgency driving him to get to Kate as soon as possible. Nick was hot on his heels and slid into the driver's seat. As Nick drove to the hospital, Logan sat in the passenger seat and prayed that God would be merciful, sparing Kate's life.

The sharp scent of antiseptic pierced Kate's subconscious. Gradually, she became aware of her surroundings.

She could hear the murmur of voices, but couldn't understand what was being said. Her eyelids were too heavy to lift, although she could tell there were bright lights on overhead. The coldness that she remembered was gone, although now she could feel pain, mostly in her left shoulder.

With an effort, she tried to move her arms and her legs, even though that only made the pain worse.

"She's waking up," a deep voice said from beside her. "Kate? Open your eyes for me. Please?"

She tried to do as the voice asked, but the lights were too bright, forcing her to squeeze her eyelids tightly.

As if the person beside her bed had read her mind, the bright lights were abruptly turned off.

"Try again, Kate," the deep voice said again. "Open your eyes for me. I'm here for you."

She could feel a warm hand clutching hers and the memories clicked into place. Logan. Held at gunpoint by her brother Garrett. Logan's arms catching her as she fell. The way he told her that he loved her.

She should feel something in return, shouldn't she? But all she felt was emptiness.

"Everything's fine, Kate," Logan said softly. "You had surgery on your shoulder, but the damage wasn't too bad. You're safe now. Salvatore and Russo are both dead."

She knew that, remembered the events from the tack room with Technicolor clarity. She forced open her eyelids and immediately saw Logan's face hovering above hers, his tawny gaze full of worry. But then the corners of his eyes crinkled as he smiled. "There you are. I've been waiting for you to show me those Irish-mud eyes of yours," he whispered huskily.

Irish-mud eyes, just like her father's. And Garrett's. The thought of her brother filled her with sadness. "I'm sorry," she croaked, her throat dry and scratchy.

"You don't have anything to apologize for, Kate," he

murmured, staring down at her with relief mixed with wonder. "Do you want some water? They said you could have a couple sips when you woke up."

"Yes." Logan's face moved out of her line of vision as he reached to pick up a glass. He pushed the button on her bed, raising the upper half enough so that she wouldn't choke, before he held out the cup and straw.

"Slowly, now," he cautioned. She took a tentative sip and savored the coolness on her sore throat. After a few more sips, Logan gently took away the cup. "Easy, you don't want to be sick."

"No," she agreed. The water seemed to have infused strength as well, because she was able to glance around the room curiously.

"You're in a room on the surgical floor," he said, answering her unspoken question. "You had surgery last night, and now it's ten o'clock the following morning."

She'd managed to lose twelve hours, but figured it could have been worse. She was alive. Apparently God hadn't taken her after all. She knew that meant God had a plan for her, but she was too tired to try to figure out what that plan might be. It seemed as if her whole life had fallen apart, lying in tatters at her feet. Everything she'd once had seemed to be gone, forever.

"Garrett?" she asked, bracing herself for Logan's anger. Not that she could blame him. It was her fault that her brother had found them.

"He's in custody," Logan said gently. "And he's cooperating fully, telling the police and the FBI everything he knows about Salvatore's operation. He's confessed to every single one of his crimes. And apparently, he gave Angela Giordano money to disappear. So she's safe, not dead the way we feared."

"I'm glad," she said huskily, fighting tears. At least Garrett had tried to do that much. Part of her wanted to be with her brother, supporting him through this, yet there was another part of her that was disgusted with his choices. How could he have sold out to Salvatore? She wondered if his marriage had broken up because of his gambling. Guilt seared through her that she hadn't known about his problem. A problem that had led him so astray, he'd inadvertently caused their father's death. She knew she needed to find a way to forgive him, but it wasn't going to be easy.

Please, Lord, help me find a way to forgive Garrett.

Logan took her hand again, and she didn't have the strength to pull away. "Kate, it's over. Salvatore's operation is going down. We may not get everyone involved, but we've made a big enough hole in his organization that the ones who are left will scatter like roaches. There was a guy from inside the FBI task force working with Salvatore, but we got him, too."

"That's good," she murmured. Her eyelids were starting to feel heavy again, and she blinked, trying to pry them back open.

"Rest now," he crooned. "You need to build up your strength."

She gave in to the overwhelming exhaustion layered with pain medication, even though she knew there was something she needed to tell Logan.

Something important. But for the life of her, she couldn't remember what it was.

The next time Kate opened her eyes, there were two men in her room, and she almost wept with relief when she saw the familiar faces of Sloan and Ian, her middle brothers.

"Katie? How are you, sis?" Sloan was on the right side of her bed, while Ian hovered on the left.

"Okay," she whispered, even though she really wasn't. But she couldn't deny being happy to see them, and wondered if this was Logan's doing.

For a moment she considered how things might have gone down if she'd called either Ian or Sloan rather than Garrett the night Angie had called. Probably very differently. But it was useless to play the what-if game, so she thrust aside the thought.

"We heard about everything from your cowboy federal agent," Sloan said, his dark brown eyes full of concern and reproach. "You should have called us. We would have kept you safe."

She didn't have the energy to explain why she hadn't called them. At the time, keeping her family as far from Salvatore as possible had been her priority, but now she felt foolish. Easy to understand why her brothers were upset with her. "I'm sorry."

Ian and Sloan looked at each other, but she must have looked pathetic enough that they didn't pursue the issue. "Do you need something for pain?" Ian asked.

Her shoulder felt as if it was on fire, but she shook her head. She didn't like feeling fuzzy and incoherent. "Water," she croaked.

Awkwardly, Ian held up the cup of water so she could take a sip. Idly, she wondered where Logan was. It was nice of him to get her brothers to sit with her, when he'd obviously needed to go back to work. Hadn't he said something about a guy inside the task force being in league with Salvatore? Logan would be tied up for a long time. Days. Weeks. Maybe longer.

The thought of never seeing Logan again hurt worse than her shoulder.

Yet at the same time, she knew that pushing him away was the only option. She'd failed him. In so many ways. She still couldn't get over how her eldest brother had almost killed him. And worse, the moment Garrett had grabbed him, she'd frozen in place. No matter how much she cared about Logan, she didn't think she'd have been able to pull the trigger on her own brother.

She'd wanted Logan to treat her as a partner, but instead she'd been a liability. She had a degree in criminal justice, but with her injury, she couldn't try out for the academy. Even if she wanted to.

Which she didn't.

A tear slipped out from the corner of her eye, trailing down her cheek. She normally hated people who had their own pity party, but somehow she couldn't manage to pull it together. For so long, she wanted to be loved for who she was, yet she didn't know who she was anymore.

All she knew was that she didn't have anything to offer Logan. Nothing but a shell of the woman she'd once thought she was.

"Katie, don't cry," Ian begged. "We're here for you. You can stay with one of us when you're ready to bust out of here."

She wiped away the moisture with her hand of her uninjured arm and tried to smile. She had to reassure her brothers, or they'd camp out here and never leave her alone. "I'm fine. Just tired."

After all, there was no cure for a broken heart.

EIGHTEEN

By the next morning, Kate felt much more human. Her shoulder still hurt like crazy, especially when the physical therapist, better known as the torture specialist, made her move her injured arm, but all in all, she'd recovered from surgery without a problem.

Her brothers had finally left her alone, and while she missed them, she was also grateful to have some breathing room. She decided right then and there to go back to her old apartment once she was discharged, rather than live with one of them. She needed time and space to figure out who she was now that she knew she could no longer qualify as a cop.

She was sitting in the chair beside her bed, waiting for the pain meds to kick in once the therapist had left, when she heard a sharp knock on her door. "Come in," she called, expecting the doctor, since he'd talked about discharging her within a day or two.

But to her shocked surprise, it was Logan who walked in. "Hi," he said with a warm smile. "You look tons better than the last time I saw you."

"Yeah, I'm great." Well, not really great, but good

enough. She ignored the dark thoughts. "How is everything with the task force?"

He shrugged. "It'll be busy for a while yet, mostly because of Johnson." At her puzzled look, he added, "The second-in-command who was being blackmailed by Salvatore."

"I bet." She couldn't begin to imagine the mess Logan had left behind in order to come see her. She took a deep breath and let it out slowly. "I need to thank you, Logan, for saving my life."

He sat down on the edge of her empty hospital bed so he could face her. "I'm the one who should be thanking you," he corrected softly. "The way you kept your brother talking was brilliant."

She narrowed her gaze, trying to figure out if he was joking. "If it hadn't been for my brother, your life wouldn't have been in danger at all."

Logan grimaced. "I'm not proud of the way he managed to get the drop on me. It was my own stupidity that got me in trouble, Kate. You're the one who saved me."

He was just saying that to be nice. And suddenly she was overcome with a flash of anger. "Just stop it, Logan. You were right. I'm not cut out to be a cop. All my life I wanted to be like my brothers and my dad..." She blinked, willing away the tears that threatened. "But obviously, that career path is over." And she'd have to figure out what to do with the rest of her life.

Figure out who she was.

She hadn't felt this lost since her mother had died.

"Kate, you're the strongest, smartest and most courageous woman I've ever known," Logan said, his steady gaze capturing hers. "You can do anything you want to. When you were injured, I realized just how much I love you. And I want you to know, I will support you, no matter what career path you decide to choose."

The *L* word distracted her. She'd cared about him for so long, even though he was irritatingly protective. But that was when she had something to offer. Now she had nothing. She was still an empty, useless shell. "I don't know what to say," she whispered. "I'm sorry, Logan, but I can't love you the way you deserve to be loved."

For a moment, his eyes darkened with what almost looked like panic. "What are you talking about? I know you care about me."

She couldn't lie to him. "I do care about you, Logan. That hasn't changed. But I can't give you what you need. Not now."

And maybe not ever.

Logan couldn't believe that Kate had sent him away. He stood propped against the wall outside her hospital room, trying to figure out what had gone wrong. He'd told her that he loved her and he'd been fairly certain that she'd felt something for him, too. He hadn't imagined her response to his kiss, had he?

Frustrated and feeling helpless, he scrubbed the back of his neck beneath the brim of his cowboy hat. Just as he was about to push away and leave, he caught sight of her brothers walking toward him.

"What's the matter, cowboy?" Kate's brothers looked similar enough to be twins, but he'd already figured out that Ian was slightly taller and leaner than Sloan. "You look like you lost your best friend."

Because I did, he thought bleakly. "Kate will be happy to see you," he said instead.

The brothers exchanged a long look. "Nah, we tend to get on her nerves," Ian said.

"Yeah, and she's already talking about going back to her apartment, rather than bunking with one of us," Sloan spoke up. "She's so stubborn, I doubt we can talk her out of it."

He thought briefly about taking her home to Texas, although he doubted she'd agree. He, along with his parents and his brother, would love to have her.

But her medical team was here, so taking off halfway across the country probably wasn't the best option.

He curled his fingers into helpless fists. "Don't let her go home alone," he said tightly. "I'd take her back home to my folks in Texas, but she'll need ongoing care, so you'll just have to make her go home with one of you. Understand?"

The brothers exchanged another long look. "I'm getting the impression you care about our baby sister," Sloan said slowly as Ian nodded thoughtfully.

There was no use in denying it. "Yeah, I'm in love with her. But right now, she doesn't seem to want anything to do with me." And for the life of him, he didn't know why.

"I hope you're not going to give up that easily?" Ian asked, crossing his arms over his chest. "Because our sister is worth fighting for."

"I'm not giving up," he murmured. "I just need a new battle plan."

Ian grinned and Sloan slapped him on the shoulder. "Good for you," Sloan said. "And we'll help, right, Ian?"

"Right."

Logan lifted a brow, his gaze wary, since he wasn't

sure if they had the power to really help him or to just make things worse. And he suspected the latter.

"I'll take care of it myself," he said finally, pushing the brim of his hat farther back on his head. "Go in to see her. I'll wait here until you're finished."

Kate's brothers looked as if they wanted to argue, but Sloan shrugged and Ian went to knock on the door. "Your funeral," Sloan muttered.

When the brothers disappeared inside Kate's room, he stayed where he was, thinking over everything that had happened in the ten days since Kate had reentered his life.

And he formulated his battle plan.

"For the last time, *no!*" Kate's patience with her loud-mouthed, overbearing brothers was wearing very thin. Her shoulder was throbbing and she desperately wanted to crawl back into her bed. "I will not come home with either of you. End. Of. Discussion."

"Fine. Then you leave us no choice but to make other arrangements," Ian said, throwing her his best no-nonsense look.

She didn't have the energy to go round two with them. "I need to use the bathroom," she muttered, knowing it was the one place they couldn't follow.

Her brothers backed up comically. "Aah, sure. We'll get your nurse."

She stayed right where she was, closing her eyes as she rested her head against the pillow that was propped behind her back.

"Are you all right?"

She opened her eyes to find Logan standing there. And for the first time, she was extremely glad to see him, especially after the relentlessness of her brothers. "I'm fine. I'd be better if you'd kick out my brothers for me."

Logan's lips quirked in a lopsided smile. "I might do that, if you'll do something for me."

Instantly, her guard came back up. "What?"

"Come recuperate at my family's ranch, the Lazy Q. Allow my mother to fuss over you, treat you like the daughter she never had."

Her mouth dropped open. "Are you crazy?"

"Kate, I'm only crazy about you. I love you. And I understand you need time to recover from all this, but I know you care about me, too." He knelt in front of her so their eyes were level. "Please tell me you don't believe your career defines who you are?"

His question stabbed deep. Because he was exactly right. Her career had defined who she was. She'd wanted to be accepted for herself, for being the tough cop she'd wanted to be, but maybe she'd only been fooling herself. Logan's earlier words echoed through her mind. *You're the strongest, smartest and most courageous woman I've ever known. I will support you, no matter what career path you decide to choose.*

Stunned, she stared at him. "I don't know," she whispered. "But I think I have been doing just that."

"And I don't believe any career could define all of you. And you know why I know that? Because you have faith. And you helped show me the way back to my faith. God has given you special gifts, Kate, and He has a plan for you. Isn't that what you've told me?" Logan's smile was sad. "Think about it, Kate. I'm offering you a chance to recuperate at my family's ranch, which will provide plenty of time for you to think about and pray about God's plan. Time to consider what you really want out of life."

"I couldn't," she whispered, even as the possibility turned around in her mind. Could she? The idea was far more tempting than it should be. If she'd been following the wrong path, then she needed time to understand what path she was to take.

"Sure you can. I spoke to your doctor and he said he'd make arrangements for you to have follow-up care, including physical therapy, at a hospital in Texas. I have some time off coming, so I'd be there to drive you back and forth. And my folks will be there, so you wouldn't ever be alone." Logan looked nervous, as if he was afraid of her answer. "Think about it, Kate. Just promise me you'll at least think about it."

"She'll do more than think about it," Sloan piped up from the doorway. She glanced past Logan to where both her brothers were standing, obviously having listened to every word. "She'll choose, won't you, Katie? You'll choose between staying with me and Ian, or going to Logan's ranch."

She narrowed her gaze, annoyed with the way her brothers always wanted to bulldoze over her feelings. "There's a third option, you know," she pointed out with a scowl.

"No, there isn't." Logan's tone was gentle yet firm. "You can't do this alone, Kate. You're the one who taught me the value of partnership, remember? I'm offering that same partnership opportunity to you now. Come home with me. My family will love you and my mother will help take care of you."

She bit her lip, knowing he was right. She couldn't manage everything on her own; she needed help. But the thought of going with Logan to his ranch, to live temporarily with his parents, for goodness' sake, was intimidating. Yet staying here with her brothers wasn't exactly appealing, either.

Staring up into Logan's eyes, she realized that he was right. She had been using her career to define herself as a person. Maybe being around men for so long, especially after her mother died, had made her lose sight of the fact that she was so much more.

If she were honest with herself, she would admit that she wanted to be a detective, solving puzzles and crimes, more than she really wanted to be a cop. But you had to be a cop first, before you could sit for the detective exam.

Plenty of time to figure that out later. Right now, she needed to get healthy. "All right, Logan," she said quietly. "I'll go with you to your ranch, so I can recuperate. And pray for God to show me His way."

He blinked, and then a broad smile split his face. "Really?"

She couldn't help smiling back at him. "Yes, really." She reached out to take his hand. "I need you, Logan. I'm feeling a little lost at the moment, even though it helps to have you here with me."

"I need you, too, Kate. But I'm not feeling lost. I feel exhilarated. Like this is the beginning of something great."

Her heart swelled with emotion. And love. Suddenly, she didn't feel empty anymore. This was what God wanted her to understand. He'd brought Logan into her life to make her realize that she had so much more to offer. If she were strong enough to listen. And believe. She stared at Logan intently, unable to hold her feelings back any longer. “I love you, Logan. I’m sorry I didn’t tell you earlier.”

“There’s no rush, Kate,” he murmured, his fingers tightening around hers. “We have plenty of time. I want you to take as long as you need.”

That made her smile, especially when she could see the goofy grins on her brothers’ faces. “I don’t need time to let you know how I feel,” she said. “I love you and nothing is going to change that.”

Logan gently leaned forward to give her a sweet kiss. “I’m glad to hear it,” he whispered huskily.

“Well, I’m glad that’s settled,” Ian said, breaking the moment.

“Yeah, me, too,” Sloan agreed with a smirk. “She’s all yours, cowboy.”

“Just don’t hurt her, or we’ll have to come find you,” Ian added.

“And hurt you,” Sloan piped up.

“He won’t,” Kate said confidently, raising her hand to cradle his cheek. How did she get so lucky to have this wonderful man come into her life? “And you both know full well I can take care of myself.”

“That you can,” Logan murmured. He kissed her again, this time lingering over her mouth, until she was breathless.

And she couldn’t help being extremely glad when her brothers finally turned to go, leaving them alone.

So she could kiss Logan in private.

EPILOGUE

Two months later...

Kate was sitting in a lawn chair Logan had set up for her in a perfect spot to watch him and his younger brother, Austin, break in a new horse. She winced when Austin hit the dust for the second time in a row. He picked up his hat, swatted it against his thigh and put it on his head before heading determinedly back toward the horse.

Logan shook his head, and stood beside Austin, letting the horse trot off. Clearly, Logan thought the new colt had been through enough. Then he glanced over and headed toward her.

"Hey," she said, shading her eyes from the sun.

"Hey, yourself." Logan dropped his head to steal a kiss before he lowered himself onto the ground next to her. "My boss is due to arrive tomorrow," he said casually, as if he were discussing the weather.

She glanced at him in surprise, hiding a stab of disappointment. She knew Logan would have to go back to work eventually, but she'd been enjoying having him to herself. Well, along with the rest of his family. His mother had been nothing but wonderful. "Really? Vacation time over, huh?"

"Actually, it's not just me that he wants to see." Logan stretched out, propping himself up on his elbows. "He wants to talk to you, too. He's waiting for your answer."

She still hadn't quite comprehended that his boss wanted her to join the FBI. "What if I'm not sure yet?"

Logan tipped his head to the side and studied her from beneath his brim for several long moments. "Kate, I keep telling you that I'll support you in whatever you want to do. But before my boss gets here, I do have one question to ask."

"Oh, yeah? What's that?"

He rolled up so that he was kneeling beside her chair, holding out a small velvet ring box. "Will you marry me?"

"Marry you?" She couldn't help the surprised squeak in her tone. "Oh, Logan, are you sure?"

A smile played along the edge of his mouth. "I'm sure I love you. I'm sure I'll support whatever you want to do, whether it's stay home and have our babies, which is a top vote in my book, by the way, or whether you want to return to work for a while first. Your shoulder is almost healed, so it's really up to you."

She held out her hand so that he could slide the engagement ring on her finger. "Yes. I'll marry you. I'll have your children. And I'll love you for the rest of my life."

"Thank You, Lord," he muttered, before dragging her up out of the chair and into his arms. "I love you, Kate, so much."

"I love you, too." She kissed him, and then leaned

back so she could look into his eyes. "As much as I want to have your children, I would also like to do something important with my life. I want to make a difference." In some weird way, she wanted to make up for Garrett's mistakes, although he was serving a reduced term due to the way he'd cooperated with the authorities.

"I know," he murmured, reaching up to tuck a strand of her hair behind her ear. "If you decide to join the bureau, after you finish your training, we can work together. As partners."

The idea was tempting. Ken Simmons had told her that, with her four-year degree in criminal justice, she had a good shot of getting in. "Partners?"

"Yes. I think we'd make a great team."

She felt a sense of completion. She'd spent the past eight weeks falling more deeply in love with Logan, renewing her faith and getting stronger physically. Logan had been at her side the entire time.

And suddenly, she knew that being his partner—in every way—was exactly what she wanted. She leaned into his embrace. "I think you're absolutely right, Logan. Whether we're working together, or creating a family of our own, we make a great team."

"Career first, then babies," he murmured, before kissing her again.

And she kissed him back, agreeing with his timeline. Because she was willing to accept whatever God had in store for them.

* * * * *

Dear Reader,

I have the utmost respect for officers of the law, and once even considered trying out for the police academy. However I made do with my career in nursing, but my fascination with the men and women who uphold the law tends to spill over into my stories. You met Logan and Kate in *Twin Peril* and according to your emails, you've been patiently waiting for their story.

Kate comes from a long family of cops, and has made up her mind to join her father and her brothers by becoming a police officer. But her plans are interrupted when her father dies unexpectedly. Determined to prove his death was murder, she ends up being held at gunpoint by Salvatore's thug. Logan rushes to the rescue, even though it means blowing his cover.

Believing in God's plan is the theme of this book and I hope you enjoy reading Logan and Kate's story. I'm always thrilled and honored to hear from my readers and I can be reached through my website at laurascottbooks.com.

Yours in faith,
Laura Scott

SPECIAL EXCERPT FROM

Love Inspired®

Widowed single mom Rebecca Mast returns to her Amish community hoping to open a quilt shop. She accepts carpenter Daniel King's offer of assistance—but she isn't prepared for the bond he forms with her son. Will getting closer expose her secret—or reveal the love she has in her heart for her long-ago friend?

Read on for a sneak preview of
THE WEDDING QUILT BRIDE
by Marta Perry,
available May 2018 from Love Inspired!

"Do you want to make decisions about the rest of the house today, or just focus on the shop for now?"

"Just the shop today," Rebecca said quickly. "It's more important than getting moved in right away."

"If I know your *mamm* and *daad*, they'd be happy to have you stay with them in the *grossdaadi* house for always, ain't so?"

"That's what they say, but we shouldn't impose on them."

"Impose? Since when is it imposing to have you home again? Your folks have been so happy since they knew you were coming. You're not imposing," Daniel said.

Rebecca stiffened, seeming to put some distance between them. "It's better that I stand on my own feet. I'm not a girl any longer." She looked as if she might want to add that it wasn't his business.

No, it wasn't. And she certain sure wasn't the girl he remembered. Grief alone didn't seem enough to account for the changes in her. Had there been some other problem, something he didn't know about in her time away or in her marriage?

He'd best mind his tongue and keep his thoughts on business, he told himself. He was the last person to know anything about marriage, and that was the way he wanted it. Or if not wanted, he corrected honestly, at least the way it had to be.

"I guess we should get busy measuring for all these things, so I'll know what I'm buying when I go to the mill." Pulling out his steel measure, he focused on the boy. "Mind helping me by holding one end of this, Lige?"

The boy hesitated for a moment, studying him as if looking at the question from all angles. Then he nodded, taking a few steps toward Daniel, who couldn't help feeling a little spurt of triumph.

Daniel held out an end of the tape. "If you'll hold this end right here on the corner, I'll measure the whole wall. Then we can see how many racks we'll be able to put up."

Daniel measured, checking a second time before writing the figures down in his notebook. His gaze slid toward Lige again. It wondered him how the boy came to be so quiet and solemn. He certain sure wasn't like his *mammi* had been when she was young. Could be he was still having trouble adjusting to his *daadi*'s dying, he supposed.

Rebecca was home, but he sensed she had brought some troubles with her. As for him…well, he didn't have answers. He just had a lot of questions.